GW00492637

TIM'S PROGRESS

First published 2022

Copyright © Bill Carmen 2022

The right of Bill Carmen to be identified as the author of this work has been
asserted in accordance with the Copyright, Designs & Patents Act 1988.

All rights reserved. No part of this book may be reproduced, stored in a retrieval
system, or transmitted in any form or by any means, electronic, electrostatic,
magnetic tape, mechanical, photocopying, recording or otherwise, without the
written permission of the copyright holder.

Published under licence by Brown Dog Books and
The Self-Publishing Partnership Ltd, 10b Greenway Farm, Bath Rd,
Wick, nr. Bath BS30 5RL

www.selfpublishingpartnership.co.uk

ISBN printed book: 978-1-83952-527-8
ISBN e-book: 978-1-83952-528-5

Cover design by Kevin Rylands
Internal design by Andrew Easton

Printed and bound in the UK

This book is printed on FSC certified paper

Book two in the *Love in Store* saga

TIM'S PROGRESS

The middle years

BILL CARMEN

BROWN
DOG
BOOKS

REVIEWS

JULIA

Absolutely love this story, *Tim's Progress*, I like the way you keep introducing new characters and ideas. This made me think of dramas on TV, like *Upstairs, Downstairs*, where characters provide a patchwork of interesting, personal backgrounds to develop the story. Another great feature is that as I was reading the book I could not anticipate the ending-this is unusual for me as some are obvious from the first few chapters.

Whenever you mentioned the river I thought someone was going to drown.

You should be proud of this latest achievement. Well done.

Can you make it a trilogy?

DREW S

Thoroughly enjoyed Book One, *Love in Store*, from start to finish. Great characters whose lives I was interested in from start to finish. I can only hope that their story continues in a sequel.

YVONNE

Reading the continuing story of the barrow boy and the heiress in book two, *'TIM'S PROGRESS*, The Middle Years,' is like revisiting old friends from Book One *Love in Store* and now meeting new ones. Thoroughly enjoyable.

DEBBIE

In Book One, *Love in Store*, the characters became friends and I've missed them. I can't wait to read about the next events in their lives.

A big thank you to those readers who were kind enough to send me wonderful reviews for love in store. I am very moved and surprised that you would go to the trouble of doing so. It means a great deal to me, so thank you, thank you.

I must thank my wife Clare for her patience, reading and correcting passages from the book for me when she was doing other things and nowadays sorting my IT. It would not happen without your input my love.

To my daughters Sue and Sarah for their help and encouragement, my son-in-law Rob for driving the IT and the website. To my early readers Yvonne and Julia who do a very thorough job in correcting my errors. To Janey Hewitt and Carol Preston my creative writing class tutors. Finally thanks to the folk at SPP for doing an excellent job publishing my books.

Book Three is underway, it will be a while yet. The good news is that my characters are still sharing their lives, their hopes and fears, their loves and their laughter with me.

Thank you all for your continued support and your kind words

CHAPTER 1

LONDON 1975

Tim and Sophie were ensconced in a low-ceilinged, old, pub overlooking the River Thames called The Boat. A cheerful fire helped to drive back the damp chilly weather. A heavy, rough-sawn shelf ran its length at the back of the bar. Large beer barrels were sat on it in low wooden cradles; old-fashioned taps were provided to draw the various ales. It was the good-looking young couple's local. Chick Evans, the landlord, and his Irish wife, Molly, were family friends of long standing.

Tim loved this old pub, the grey stone walls, the heavy black beams supporting the ceiling. The effect of centuries of smoke had darkened the interior. The bay windows on the river side overhung the water.

Tim was transfixed momentarily by the traffic on the river. He had lived near it all his life. He had become beguiled by it when he was little more than a baby, there was always something happening, something absorbing to see. Today he was watching a pleasure boat motor past. It was all white paint and varnish.

The band were playing dance music. The dancers, mostly teenagers, were well-dressed he noticed, the young women in their bright dresses were being partnered by young men wearing blue blazers, and white trousers. The small dance floor was protected by a large once white awning overhead that kept the occasional drizzle off them. Their determination to enjoy themselves in spite of the weather was plain for all to see.

Tim could see elderly folk sitting in the cabin downstairs, the misted windows were a sure sign that it was much warmer below deck. Here and there the glass had been wiped, allowing him to see in. These men and women were not dancing but the conversations were in full flow.

Through one recently cleaned window an elderly gentleman with a close-trimmed beard and a mid-blue blazer with white stripes was slapping the table with the flat of his hand to drive his point home.

Tim's attention was torn away from the river as he and his wife were joined in the bar by Mr Seymore, a reporter from the local paper, a rotund, balding elderly man in a dark-grey, three-piece, suit, white shirt and a navy tie. The reason for his presence was that Tim and his team were proposing to open a third shop. Greetings were exchanged as the man sat, then leaned back into a comfortable armchair saying, 'Please call me, Robert' when they had addressed him as Mr Seymore.

'Tim,' asked Mr Seymore, 'will this shop be the same as the first two, a delicatessen?'

'Yes, I see no reason to change, it's what we know, despite all the naysayers with the first shop, it works. We will not buy just anywhere; it must have appeal. Nothing we have seen so far fits the bill.'

'Initially people were very rude about foreign food, weren't they Tim?'

'Yes, they were but apart from a few diehards most people I believe have some foreign foods in their diet, if it's only rice or pasta.' This is not going how I thought it would, he said to himself. 'Nowadays the TV has some wonderful foreign recipes on there. The range of cookbooks featuring foreign food is expanding all the time. We hope to publish our own in the not-too-distant future. Our confectioner, Sara Trentino, is also a first-class cook and has a range of Italian recipes we hand out to our customers. Her husband Harry is one of our Directors.'

Mr Seymore was thinking, It's obvious Sophia is the brains here, she is allowing him to take the credit, but I'm sure it's her hand on the tiller. Her family, the Vieri's are highly regarded locally in the business world and are very wealthy. She is highly educated, a good degree from Oxford, the Swedish finishing school, holding down a Finance Director's job elsewhere. On top of that she is incredibly attractive with her blond hair and perfect figure.

Tim is obviously poorly educated – I can tell by his voice; he really is no more than a labourer. It will be interesting to see over time whether she gets bored with him. It was important to Mr Seymore that people went to the right schools and came from the right family. If she were my daughter, I would have paid him to go away, he thought.

Little did he know that Tim had in the past refused a considerable sum of money from Mr Vieri, Sophie's father to do just that.

'So, who's in the team then, Tim?'

'Well, Sophie of course who is our Finance Director, and she holds the same post with Terry Wells company.'

'What made you decide to call the shops Sophie's, Tim?'

'I met this wonderful woman on a train, and I fell in love.'

Tim reached out placing his hand on her arm. The reporter made a note. Sophie went a little pink.

'Harry and his wife I have mentioned, there's Mr Woodman who still owns the first shop, he's a Director, the major shareholder and my godfather. My father Tom Cooper who was responsible for starting the delicatessen from a market stall, he is an employee by choice. It was he who travelled across Europe finding the suppliers we still use today. All three of the men I have mentioned are past retirement age but choose to keep working. The market still exists opposite the first shop, Number One, as everyone calls it.'

'That's the one by the river, isn't it?' asked the reporter.

Tim nodded. 'Then there's Number Two on Fish Hill.'

'Now that's a bit special, my wife and I have been in there. The glass-covered well in the flagstone's downstairs, the lighting down in the well makes it a real feature, and on sunny days that big window in the roof floods the place with sunlight. My wife tells me people go there just to see the well and the sunlight. The other thing that's clever Tim, is it smells right, the combination of strong cheese, garlic and smoked meat is completely Italian.'

Sophie watched Tim as he spoke to Robert Seymore. He had come such a long way since the day they had met on the train; they had got talking and she realised that he was the first man she had been attracted too. Hard work kept him slim, his dark curly hair and his ready smile were attractive, the blue chinos and the pale blue shirt and brown brogues suited him. She had watched other women take a second look.

They had overcome enormous resistance from her family; her mother always referring to him as that barrow boy which, thought Sophie, was what he had been. Now he was her husband and the chairman of a growing company. She suspected she had fallen in love with him because he reminded her of her father. Tim was not as irascible as her father nor was he Italian, but many of his characteristics were the same, his ability to focus on the objective, his determination to succeed. His belief that the answer to many problems was to work harder.

Tim was pleased to see that the reporter had become almost euphoric, well perhaps that was a slight exaggeration, but he was more enthusiastic than previously.

'I need to mention the rest of the team, please.'

'Don't worry, Tim, I think I have all the major players – we don't need to include the ordinary staff.'

'Mr Seymore,' said Tim, in a voice that contained a cold splinter of the steel he was made of, 'none of our staff are ordinary, they all give 110 per cent all day, every day. Jessica our PA works many hours beyond what we pay her, then there's Daisy who we have trained from scratch and is a real asset to the company. This is a remarkably special team, Mr Seymore.'

Tim's rebuke, which it clearly was, and the flash of anger under the calm exterior made the reporter question his original decision about Tim's competence.

He jotted down some more notes, then said, 'Sophia can we talk about you for a minute?'

She interrupted him; 'I prefer to be called Sophie, please.'

'That seems a shame, Sophia is a lovely name for a lovely lady.'

'It is simple, I prefer, Sophie.' What she didn't share with him was that when she was at her private girls' school, and later at her finishing school she was badly teased because of her name. Shortening her name at Oxford uni had overcome the problem.

'I understand,' continued the reporter, 'that initially there was a lot of resistance to Tim by your family?'

Tim was silent and Sophie was deep in thought. She realised that this question had to be handled extremely carefully; she knew that giving him the slightest hint of the horrors of the fire storm that had broken out when her family had discovered their relationship would be the main focus of the article. There could be no hint of the verbal abuse and rude behaviour that she and Tim had endured from her mother and father. She would always be sure that this young man sat beside her loved her unconditionally. The baptism of fire they had both withstood instead of separating them had welded them together into an unbreakable partnership.

'My father is extremely protective of me and always will be which I think is understandable given that I am an only child, but now I believe all that is behind us. I think my father sees Tim as the son he did not have,' said Sophie looking across at her husband.

'How would you describe your relationship with your father-in-law, Tim?' His tone of voice clearly indicating that he expected Tim's response was going to be quite different.

'It's first class. If I have a business or financial problem, I go straight to him. I will always seek his advice before I decide, I don't always take it but what he says always informs my decisions.'

Sophie was a little annoyed with Mr Seymore, men like him always patronised her, when questioning her he had worn a silly smile and sounded condescending when he spoke to her. They assumed that because she was an attractive blond, she was dumb. She had, on purpose, dressed in her business attire today. Her signature black skirt, cream blouse, black heels, and a single string of pearls, with a black leather handbag on a long strap hanging from her left shoulder. She watched Tim at work, selling his company and his dreams to this reporter. She was so proud of him, not that she would tell him that, his ego was big enough already. His start in life had been difficult, he had watched his mother die in a London hospital when he was thirteen, taken over his father's stall when he was fifteen and been made homeless by his father soon after. His absolute refusal to quit was one of the major reasons she loved him. Those people who knew him now recognised him as successful. Few of them knew what it had cost him.

'Tim, it's common knowledge that your aunt Mrs Longstaff, settled her not inconsiderable fortune on you, but there has not been any noticeable vast expenditure. Do you have any plans?' asked Robert.

'Yes, but it is too early to talk about it when I do you will be the first to know. The only thing I will say is that some of the money will be used to benefit young people.' With that the reporter shook their hands and left.

CHAPTER 2

'It's a girl, dear,' announced a tidily dressed, elderly lady wearing a navy two-piece suit who was just leaving the shop. 'Boys are carried in front. I should know I was a midwife for more years than I care to remember. Have you got a name yet?'

'No, not yet we cannot agree.'

'There's still lots of time love, good luck to you.'

Sophie thanked her and held the shop door open for her. She knew that this business of the name was going to become a problem. Her mother, Olivia Vieri, a stern elderly woman, kept offering archaic names from the last century. Tim would just shake his head, not even prepared to discuss them.

One thing they did like for a middle name, if it was a girl, was Angela, Sophie's aunt, an ebullient, happy, attractive widow in her middle years, Sophie's mother's sister. Angela had avoided most of the rigours of her mother's child-rearing that had been strict to say the least. Angela's upbringing had been supplied by a kind, gentle nanny. The polar opposite to the hard, cold parenting her sister Olivia had endured. Choosing Angela's name, however, and not her mother's was inconceivable.

Talking to Tim about the problem that evening she said, 'Why cannot everything be simple?'

'It's the nature of the beast,' he replied.

'Are you talking about my mother?' she queried, frowning as she spoke.

'Of course not.'

Sophie could not really chastise him, there had been a running battle between Tim and her mother since the moment they met. Things had perhaps quietened down a little of late, although her father Victor Vieri, reported to her that on occasion he would correct his wife when she would refer to Tim, as that "barrow boy". Tim was never going to agree to his child being named Olivia.

She decided to put the naming problem out of her mind for now. What she was enjoying was converting the small second cabin on the houseboat, Sea Maiden, now their home, into a nursery. They were moored in a Boatyard across the river from Kingston on the River Thames.

*

'Tim?' she asked one evening, the pair had just made love gently so as not to hurt the baby. 'I would like to paper the nursery with giant yellow sunflowers on a white background, then everything else white gloss. The window is too small to use dark colours, what do you think?'

'It's a porthole, not a window,' he responded, correcting her, knowing his beautiful wife would always think of the houseboat as a floating flat.

'You are a pedant,' she replied, tutting as she spoke. 'Seriously though, would you be OK with that?'

Tim, starting to doze, agreed enthusiastically, 'I think that would look perfect.'

Sophie, surprised, lifted herself onto one elbow so she could see his face. Was he just agreeing for the sake of it, or did he mean it?

He was nodding and smiling with his eyes shut. 'I think it would look great, and it's appropriate for a girl or a boy.'

Rupert, the boat's owner, now in America with a star role in a new film in production had said they could repaint it any colour as long as it was white. 'I don't suppose he will mind,' Tim decided.

Sophie settled back, she loved her husband to distraction, but she would never completely understand him. A cast iron moral code that brooked no relaxation. Once a course had been decided on it was difficult if not impossible to achieve any deviation. His temper when released was a little bit scary. She could forgive him that, her own temper was thoroughly Italian.

He constantly surprised her; maybe, she mused, that was a good thing. One thing she was sure of was that the love they shared, one for the other was absolute, without any censure or qualification.

In the small hours of the morning, Sophie was lying with her right leg thrown across him, an arm across his chest and her head resting on his shoulder, her breath gentle on his neck. They were jerked from their slumber when the baby kicked them both awake.

'Was that you?' mumbled Tim, still climbing up through layers of sleep.

'No, it was our baby,' replied Sophie, now sounding emotional and in awe of what was happening in her body.

Tim sat up, his face displaying his amazement. He placed his hand gently on her tummy. They both slept naked.

'Has this happened before?' he asked.

'No, not as strong as that, up to now it was just the baby shifting around, I think I may have been squashing her lying against you.'

'You have never mentioned it. Why did you say she?'

'A customer in the shop told me it was going to be a girl and I suppose it just feels right.' I did not mean to exclude you, I just wanted to keep it to myself for a while. I hope you are not upset?' she queried, looking into his eyes.

He shook his head. 'Can I listen?'

'Of course.'

Tim placed his cheek very carefully on her tummy.

'I do not think you need to be too worried, babies are pretty tough,' Sophie informed him, smiling. Tim, now listening hard, thought, the baby that we lost was not so tough. He remembered the searing pain of the miscarriage. He put it aside. This was now, a new life. Tim felt, heard, the baby change position slightly, lifting his head he gave Sophie the biggest smile, his eyes wide. His face contained a whole gamut of emotions. First amongst these was joy and wonder.

*

Before sleep reclaimed her, she realised that at this moment in time she was truly consciously happy. Her husband loved her, her baby was doing well and now they had a good lifestyle. Smiling still, she slept on.

The following day Tim awoke, thoroughly energised. Now he had a reason to chase the tiger, to follow his dream, to build an empire strong enough and large enough to ensure that those he loved would never have to worry or feel threatened by the fear of poverty.

He kissed Sophie's ear, that was all he could see under the avalanche of bedclothes. Waking she rolled onto her back and saw how excited he was.

'Are you all right?' she asked looking puzzled, he was never this active first thing in the morning.

'Can I kiss the baby, please?'

'You can, but you have to kiss me first otherwise I shall get jealous.' She smiled at how carefully he kissed her bare tummy, seconds before he had been bouncing around the cabin like a child's clockwork toy. Clear proof that the child in her womb had thrown a switch in him. If he is going to be like this all the time it might take some getting used to, she thought to herself. He rushed around getting breakfast, placed hers on the bedside table, wolfed his down, kissed her, and made for the door.

'Are you going already, it is only just gone seven?'

Reaching the door, but then turning back he kissed her again and as he left, he was doing a silly crouching walk, arms bent at the elbow, pistoning backwards and forwards in time with his stride, whispering, 'Places to go, people to see, places to go, people to see. Bye,' he called shutting the door behind him and locking her in.

'Goodness me baby, what have we done?' she asked, addressing her tummy.

Later that morning on the train, the baby was kicking her hard.

A mum with twins in a pushchair asked, 'Is that the baby? I saw you wincing with your hand on your tummy, I used to think my two were fighting. It might be that you need some maternity wear rather than your business suit,' suggested the woman, noting her dark suit and heels.

✳

Later that week Sophie contacted the Westminster Nanny Services to alert them to her condition. The lady who answered the phone was very well spoken, though rather cold initially.

'I was brought up by a Westminster nanny,' Sophie disclosed. The temperature of the conversation improved dramatically.

'So, you are one of ours my dear,' enthused the woman. Sophie could hear the smile in her voice. 'What was your maiden name?' Sophie, with a grin on her face, noted it was assumed she was married.

'Vieri, Sophia Vieri,' she told her.

'Right, give me a moment my dear we shall soon track you down.' After a short silence, the woman said, 'Ah, I rather think I may have found you, Olivia and Victor, London?' she asked, a query in her voice.

Sophie confirmed the details.

'Married name my dear?'

Now amused, she wondered how long the conversation would continue had she been single. 'Cooper,' she replied, 'Sophia Cooper.'

'Is that one of the Surrey Cooper's, the Cooper-Thorn's perhaps?'

'No, I do not think so,' she replied, trying not to giggle.

'Can I have your address, please?'

Sophie explained they lived on a boat called the Sea Maiden and that it was moored in a Boatyard at Kingston on Thames.

'How delightfully bohemian,' was the response. The rest of the questions were very straight forward, and soon answered.

Mother will be pleased, she thought.

'You will be contacted my dear, by one of our ladies who will come to visit you. Is that satisfactory, Mrs Cooper?'

She agreed that it was. Later she discovered her assumption was correct about her mother's reaction, which was, 'How eminently sensible my dear.'

CHAPTER 3

'What are you doing today?' asked Sophie, still in her dressing gown as Tim placed bacon and eggs in front of her. Following that up with his breakfast and a pile of toast. Sophie poured them both a glass of orange juice.

'I'm meeting with your father. The idea of having a Sophie's on the third floor of your father's department store is finally up for discussion.'

Mr Vieri, Sophie's father, was of medium height, ram-rod straight, jet black hair with a little steel around his ears; he was dictatorial, abrupt and completely Italian.

Mr Vieri's store was huge, three floors with offices above. A broad, pale, marble staircase connected the floors with a lift in the corner. The walls were clad in matching stone. The staff were dressed in white shirts and black suits.

'You must be renting, I thought you said you would never do that. You said it just makes rich people richer.'

'It's what my father always says,' confirmed Tim.

'I still do not see what the appeal is to have a shop there?' said Sophie shaking her head.

'It's a very prestigious place to have a shop, it's us moving up. People will recognise we are not just a corner shop. Sophie, from a strictly business point of view anyone who wants to go to the café in the store has to walk past our shop, well through it almost. I did some research, I sat in there reading my paper, drinking coffee, and watching. The footfall is incredible, more people will pass by our new shop in a day than all of the others in a week. Also, the rental we have agreed, although quite stiff is below the interest we would pay on a bank loan on a similar property. Victor is very keen.'

'He will be, he can obviously see a good profit. Tim, I do not want to speak ill of my father but if it does not work out to his satisfaction, he will throw you out without a second thought.'

Your father did point out to me that you will inherit it all anyway.'

'What do the rest of the team say?' asked Sophie, sounding unsure. 'I have a nasty feeling this could go horribly wrong.'

'My father is unhappy that we are renting but has conceded that in this case, long term, it may work out, but he insists we keep a close eye on the turnover and the outgoings. He also pointed out that Mr Vieri will set the working hours. That means no late-night shopping. He reminded me that the income from that has saved our bacon sometimes.'

'Hmm,' she responded.

'It was your father's idea,' Tim reminded her.

'Yes, that is the fact that worries me most,' she rejoined. 'Let me go through the final figures. I have to tell you Tim, I would not do business with my father. What did Mr Woodman and Harry say?'

Tim took a long breath in, then huffed it out, frowning as he did so. 'Harry raised a good point, he is concerned, he cannot see how Sara will be able to produce enough confectionary for all three shops if the turnover is as high as we are predicting.'

'And Mr Woodman?' she queried.

'He's not happy to sign anything until he has sight of the final agreement. I don't think he is against the idea. He wants to be careful, that's all.'

'And?' said Sophie, sensing Tim was keeping something back.

'He is not really comfortable with losing full control of a portion of our business. He did add that as long as there were no nasties in the final agreement, he would go along with it.'

'Tim, I know what I am talking about. When we get the final offer from father, I want to take it to work and get Terry Wells' company solicitor to go through the fine detail.'

Two weeks later all the staff of Sophie's were gathered in shop Number One. It was old with heavy oak beams on the ceiling. These had been given a thin coat of white wash and the plaster in between was now bright white, the walls were white, the floor mid-blue-and-white tiles. There was carefully arranged lighting to ensure that the modern glass and wood-trimmed counters sparkled. The shop had a wonderful aroma of Italian cured meats, strong cheese and garlic.

It was still owned by Mr Woodman who was now a Director of Sophie's. He was dressed in his usual multi-pocketed blue coat and dark trousers. The other members of the board were also there. Harry, an elderly Italian, an ex-stall holder with a big white beard and a twinkle in his eyes. Sophie, and Tim as Chairman, including Jessica, Tim's and Sophie's PA, who was as smart as a new pin as usual; she was an attractive dark-haired young mum in a dark-grey skirt and matching jacket, pen and pad at the ready. She and Sophie had met at uni and were firm friends.

Whenever major decisions regarding the business were being made everyone was involved. Daisy, a shop assistant at Number Two, was dressed similarly to Sophie in a navy pencil skirt and cream blouse, and Sara, Harry's wife, the company's world-class confectioner, sat in the group. This included Tim's father Tom Cooper who had started the delicatessen when it was a market stall. All had a say.

After everyone was seated and had a cup of tea and a biscuit, Tim called them to order. He reiterated the reason they were there: it was to decide whether to accept Mr Vieri's offer of a shop in his vast department store. He explained everybody would get a vote.

Tim started by saying, 'I'm going to ask Sophie to start the ball rolling. She has had the offer reviewed by a solicitor and this is his explanation of the things we need to discuss this evening. I haven't seen it myself yet.'

'Can you all hear me?' asked Sophie. There was nodding and a soft affirmation. 'The first item is one that Tom raised' – looking at him as she started – 'we will not be able to offer our late-night opening.'

Tim's father went to speak but Tim held his hand out and said, 'Can you hold that thought please, Dad, until we have been through all the points? Sorry, I should have said.'

His father nodded.

After a pause Sophie continued, 'I have to say that a lot of what we have uncovered was cloaked in legal mumbo jumbo. The next point concerns staff clothing. We would have to buy and wear the same clothing as Mr Vieri's own staff. There would be little or no Sophie branding, it would all be VV, Victor Vieri.' Now those present were frowning at each other and muttering was breaking out.

Tim jumped in and said, 'Come on folks let's hear what Sophie has to say.'

She continued, 'Mr Vieri wants a 30 per cent reduction in the retail prices.'

Tim's father scraped his chair back and went to stand.

'Please Dad, can we do this properly? Let's hear it all then it will be your turn first I promise.'

Tom Cooper paused for a moment then sat back down, obviously angry.

Sophie turned to Tim and with his encouraging nod she continued, 'It says there would be a week's notice of termination of lease.'

Jumping up from his chair, Tom said, 'I have heard enough. In my opinion he is trying to take over our business. The years I have stood out there in the rain and snow so we could build what we have today. I will be outside where I belong.' He underlined his anger by putting on the jacket of his brown suit before kicking his chair down the shop and walking out.

There was complete silence for quite some time, then Harry said, 'I'm not surprised Tim at Tom's reaction, as your father said he and I have stood out there in all weathers shoulder to shoulder building the basis of this business. Now apparently, we are going to be working for someone whose only concern is the bottom line. We are selling a quality product. Sorry Sophie, but your father wants to stack it high and sell it cheap.' Now his Italian accent was so strong you could cut it with a knife. This a clear emotional indicator of how angry he was. 'Tim, I will resign in the event of this going through!!' Even his white beard appeared to be bristling

'WE will resign,' said Sara jumping from her chair to stand beside her husband, her face the same pink as her dress.

'And I give you fair warning Tim,' continued Harry, 'Tom, Sara and I will open up across the road. See how you get on then.' These his final words as he and Sara made to leave.

Sophie could see their business flying apart in front of her eyes. Racing the couple to the shop doorway and stepping through first she seized Tom's arm who was standing outside and said, 'I am going back in there and voting against this damn silly idea, who will come and vote with me?'

They all looked at each other and then Harry said, 'I will. I have worked too bloody hard to lose it all like this.' Striding back into the shop Harry, now extremely angry and red in the face said, 'Right, let's put an end to this bloody nonsense – we want a vote.'

'We should hear the rest of—'

'No, Mr chairman,' growled Harry loudly. 'We have heard more than enough. Call a vote or this business goes down the toilet right here and now.'

Tim was extremely upset; he could read the look of betrayal on his father's face, and on Jessica's a display of such deep disappointment in him. Tim was aware she was one of his staunches supporters. Their disapproval hurt him for a long time when he remembered the incident in the future.

Tim thought for a moment and realised that he had no choice. 'Those for the proposal?' Nobody moved. 'Those against?' Everybody raised a hand, including his wife.

'I declare the proposal defeated.'

The meeting broke up. Everybody but Tim and Sophie were in a huddle venting their anger.

Sophie pulled Tim aside and said in a voice that brooked no argument, 'You need to sort this now, if you let them go home in this state the repercussions will damage the company for years to come. You have to make a full and frank apology and most importantly admit you were wrong. Do it now.'

Taking a deep breath Tim said, 'Ladies and gentlemen, can I say a few words?'

'There's nothing left to say is there, lad?' his father shouted, obviously still angry.

'There is Dad, I want to apologise to all of you. I recognise I was completely wrong, and if you want me to stand down as chairman, I will do that now. Tonight. You have displayed the belief and the loyalty you have in this organisation, and I am very humbled by that. I hope you can forgive me. In closing I can tell you Sophie and I will go straight from here to tell Mr Vieri of our decision. I promise in future that if I am still in my current position, we will always discuss any idea between us before we do anything. Now do you want me to step down?'

The group formed a huddle again and a couple of minutes later Mr Woodman, who obviously had been elected spokesman said, 'We would like you to stay on with the proviso that this never happens again. Almost certainly this would have been kicked into touch straight away if we had all been informed.'

Before leaving Tim took Jessica to one side and said, 'Jessica we don't need all the blood and tears in the minutes, nice and straightforward, please. Just report that the proposal was defeated.' Tim noticed Jessica's raised eyebrows indicating her surprise.

Tim, his voice a lot harder than she had heard before said, 'We don't need to wash our dirty linen in public. Is that clear?'

To her surprise Jessica found herself saying, 'Yes Mr Chairman.'

Tim said, 'Good,' and turned away.

Jessica, walking home, was mulling the brief conversation over. It was clear that there was more in Tim's makeup than she had realised. Though when she thought about what Sophie had shared with her about his upbringing, it was really no surprise. The loss of his mother as a child, being thrown out of his home by his father, the feuds with the Vieri's. Perhaps tonight's glimpse of steel should not be a surprise.

*

Later at Mr Vieri's after the pleasantries and when they all had a cup of tea in hand, Tim said, 'I'm sorry, but your proposal has been refused.'

'Oh really. That is understandable, there are some areas we can tinker with. I assume though that the general idea was acceptable, that they could see the benefits to all involved?'

'No, it was not seen as of any benefit to Sophie's.'

'I thought you said your partners were good businessmen. Clearly they are still stallholders, too dumb to see the bigger picture, I am casting pearls before swine.' It was obvious that Mr Vieri was now becoming extremely angry. 'Tim, could you not explain the benefits in simple terms so that they understood?'

'No, in the end I was fighting to save the business. I had the threat of a mass resignation on my hands, they believed your proposal was a poorly disguised attempt at a takeover.' It was now apparent that Mr Vieri was not the only one who was angry.

Mr Vieri said, 'Once a stallholder always a stallholder. I should have realised that you would not have the intelligence to see a good deal when you are offered one.'

Sophie, now on her feet and facing her father said, 'I was the one who called for the no vote, so put that in your pipe and smoke it.'

Mr Vieri started shouting at the young couple in Italian.

To everyone's surprise Mrs Vieri intervened, screaming at her husband saying, 'Shut up you horrid rude man, how dare you shout at Timothy like that. Now apologise.'

Mr Vieri did not apologise. He marched out of the room instead, slamming the door behind him.

Mrs Vieri said, 'I am sorry Timothy, I apologise on his behalf.'

'Please don't worry,' he replied.

The young couple said their goodbyes.

Sophie was leading the way down the long hallway to the front door. It was decorated the same as the rest of the house, with pale varnished doors inset with eight small square panes of bevelled glass and matching honey-coloured parquet flooring with cream walls. Glancing over her shoulder, stern-faced, she whispered, 'You have done this walk before.' To her surprise she could see her husband trying to hide a smile. She found out why seconds later as he slammed the door shut behind him with all the force he could muster.

'I realised what the smile was for just before you slammed the door – you laid down a challenge didn't you. Now you have me, the baby on the way and the business, the power has shifted?'

'I haven't given it that much thought, but I guess you're right.'

'What really surprised me was my mother defending you.'

'Mmm,' replied Tim, not knowing what to make of any of it. Up to now Mrs Vieri had never a good word to say about him. He found himself wondering if there would come a time when he could visit this house without the fear of a war breaking out. The white-hot anger that had roared around them when Sophie's and his relationship had been discovered was still a painful memory.

CHAPTER 4

On a Saturday morning two weeks later, a quiet 40-year-old smartly dressed woman wearing a dark-green suit, stood tapping on the door of the Sea Maiden

Sophie, who was expecting her, welcomed her in. The woman introduced herself as Bridget.

Sophie guessed she was Irish, her wonderful complexion and dark shiny hair along with the lilt in her speech gave away some clues. An hour and a half passed while the two women got to know each other and discussed what was possible, the woman confirmed that she loved children but regrettably had never had any.

'I look after my sister's children most days – she and her husband are both working. I have been caring for them for twelve years. They are about to move away; her husband's firm is relocating up north. He has worked for them for a long time, and they have offered him a very lucrative contract to move with them. I don't know the amount but Beatrice, my sister, has said they will be able to buy a house with enough bedrooms so the children can have one each, and that's the reason I am here. I would go mad without a job, staring at the same square of wallpaper every day, I would go doolally. I will miss the little ones though.'

Bridget disclosed she was a widow and had a flat of her own, just a short bus ride away. 'My husband was a soldier, but he was killed in Vietnam,' she explained

Sophie leaned forward and squeezed her hand, saying, 'I am so sorry.'

'It was a long time ago now,' said Bridget, wishing to change the subject.

She thought to herself some days his loss feels like yesterday. Occasionally on waking, she still reached across the bed for him. The pain of her loss though still flowed through her when she realised he was not there and never would be.

Sophie had noticed the woman's short absence from the conversation but did not say anything.

'How flexible can you be?' asked Sophie. 'My husband and I work long irregular hours.'

'That's not a problem, but in that case, I would like to be paid an hourly rate please. I think that is fairest on both parties.'

Sophie thought for a moment then said, 'I would rather I paid you a fixed amount each week, a normal week, then we will pay any extra hours on top. Otherwise, you might find yourself on little money some weeks. What do you think?'

'That's very generous Mrs Cooper, thank you.'

'Please call me, Sophie. I expect we will be using you a lot because of our hectic lives.'

'That's fine, I would rather be working.'

Shortly afterwards Sophie asked her if there was anything else she wanted to know, Bridget shook her head.

'Welcome aboard, Bridget,' said Sophie, both women laughed at the intended pun.

Walking away, Bridget was looking forward to getting back into harness. Wait till I tell the women at church that I am going to be working on a boat, she thought to herself.

Sophie was content with her choice. Bridget was warm and confident; the baby would love her.

Thus started a relationship that would last for years.

CHAPTER 5

'Tim, we have to do something about my father. Since the row he is almost monosyllabic, when I phoned him two days ago the conversation lasted about two minutes. Angela has told me he is upset. Will you write to him and apologise? Please.'

His long breath in and the furrowed brow were clear indicators of how that had been received.

'I know it is always us who end up mending the fences, but I can see no other way of solving the problem.'

She had put her hand on his arm and looked up into his face. He could see how much this argument was hurting her. He knew she loved her father very much. She was closer to him than her mother who was often cold and distant.

'Can I have a day or two to think about it? At the moment I haven't a clue what to say.'

'Yes,' Sophie replied, clearly worried by the whole affair.

Tim mulled it over for another week then realised they could not continue this disagreement; however, he was damn sure he was not going to get down on his knees and apologise.

Dear Victor,

I am writing in the hope that we can put an end to this nasty misunderstanding. Sophia and I miss your advice and company. The fact that it did not work this time is something I hope we can put behind us. I would point out that every member of my team has historically ploughed their own furrow prior to forming our company. The whole team is fiercely defensive of the organisation and will always react if they feel it is under threat. They are totally committed to the business and what we are all trying to achieve. Every member of staff performs over and above the call of duty So, can we restore our previously amicable relationship with you that Sophia and I have enjoyed?
Yours sincerely, Tim and Sophia.

Some ten days later the postman pushed a letter through the door. This was now unusual since Tim's deceased aunt's house had been registered as the company address. The previous deluge of mail to arrive at the boat had slowed to a trickle. The letter was brief, it was from Mr Vieri, it said:

Dear Tim and Sophia
I am unaware of any nasty misunderstanding. I prefer to think of it as a business discussion that will not now come to fruition
We would like you to come to dinner on Saturday evening in a fortnights time if you are free. Let's make it formal then we can all dress up. Long dresses for the ladies, tuxedos for us men. Shall we say eight? Sally and Angela will come.

Having read the letter Sophie was almost spitting with indignation. 'The arrogant old b------' She was struggling not to swear. They had made a pact in anticipation of the baby's arrival, no swearing under any circumstances. 'He is absolutely incorrigible. He is getting worse. I am tempted to go in my old jeans and a T-shirt.'

Sophie was currently wearing a white cotton maternity dress with a large red rose print that her mother had bought her. She was sure Angela had a hand in it, her mother preferred her in heavy wool two-pieces.

Tim was shaking his head, 'No, no ... We will do the opposite – how do you fancy a new dress? No, a whole new outfit – handbag, shoes, hairdo and jewellery?'

Sophie was shaking her head. 'No, Tim. That will be a lot of money, and it will have to be a maternity dress. I may never use it again.'

'What else will you wear? I doubt anything in your wardrobe will fit you now.'

'I am tired Tim, carrying madam about all day. I do not want to drag her about from one shop to another.'

'You don't have to. Mr Graham will drive you in the Bentley and it might be a boy.'

Tim had inherited the driver and gardener, Mr Graham, and his wife, Mrs Graham, who cleaned and baked cakes, with the estate that Mrs Longstaff, Tim's aunt, had bequeathed him.

'You are keen on this are you not? It will be incredibly expensive, Tim.'

Tim knew that Sophie was wealthy in her own right but financially she always lived carefully.

'I can afford it. I've hardly touched the vast sum my aunt left me. Please let me spoil you?' he pleaded.

She thought for a moment, it was clear that he wanted to do this for her. Her simple nod was enough for Tim.

'Right, there is to be no scrimping, nothing but the best. You have ten days. I will sort the jewellery and pay for everything else.'

Angela was roped in to help. On more than one occasion when he returned from work in the evening there was a note on the table and what his mother would have called a cold collation in the fridge.

Tim was busy himself in his lunch hours searching for some jewellery for her. He wanted a necklace, a bracelet and perhaps an eternity ring. Because she was so blonde, it was suggested that he bought her diamonds set in white gold. The first few shops produced nothing he liked, then he found them. They were everything he was looking for including earrings. The necklace was beautiful, a white gold chain with tiny white gold hearts clipped on to it, all encrusted with diamonds. The whole thing sparkled, a thousand tiny surfaces giving off light. The eternity ring was a beautiful multifaceted diamond nestled in a clasp of white gold leaves. The bracelet mimicked the necklace with the same tiny white gold hearts encrusted with shimmering diamonds. The earrings although tiny were perfect works of art, a white gold rose with a diamond set in the heart of it.

The shop owner, a large man in a dark suit, was a little haughty with him. 'How do you intend to pay for this sir?'

'Cash,' he replied. 'If you tell me how much it is, I will walk round the corner and draw the money out.' By chance he was only a few hundred yards from his own bank.

The amount was disclosed. Tim asked him to write it down. As he left the shop, he heard the owner mutter to his co-worker, 'I bet you he won't be back.'

Tim considered going elsewhere but the jewellery was perfect for Sophie.

Reaching the bank, he slid the slip with the amount on it across to the teller who studied the amount and said, 'Can you excuse me please sir, I won't be a moment.'

Two minutes later Mr Murdoch, Tim's bank manager opened his office door and beckoned him in.

Mr Murdoch, a Scotsman from Edinburgh, was always immaculately dressed in a dark three-piecesuit and tie complete with a pocket watch strung across his stomach. The first time Tim had explained his ideas for the business the Scotsman had been so sceptical of Tim's ability to succeed with his ideas he had laughed at him. Now they had a first-class-working relationship. Tim noted he still had a picture of the Queen on the deep oak wall behind his large desk.

'Hallo, Tim. I would guess this is a present for Sophia. I see it is a jeweller. Have you asked for a discount?' Tim shook his head.

'The money is being sorted as we speak.' As he finished there was a tap on the door and the young man from the counter entered holding an envelope. There was a brief exchange of words and then Tim was on his way.

Mr Murdoch standing at the bank's front door called after him saying, 'Tell them I said you should have a discount.'

Entering the shop again the shop owner was clearly surprised. 'Do you have the money?' he asked.

'I do. Mr Murdoch my bank manager tells me I should ask for a discount.' The man smiled and reached for the money. Tim drew the money away, also smiling.

'What should we say,' asked Tim, '10 per cent?'

This time the man laughed.

Tim had been drawing the money from the envelope but now he pushed it back inside. 'It's a shame we can't come to an agreement, this is a present for my wife, I am sure she mentioned to me she had been here for some of our wedding jewellery. Her maiden name is Vieri, Sophia Vieri.' Tim saw the man's face change.

'Yes, I do recall the name, sir, a wonderful family. I have had the pleasure of doing business with them in the past.'

Tim had never seen such a rapid change in a man, he was now almost servile. 'I am sorry I cannot offer you 10 per cent, how about 5 per cent and I will throw in the polished wood, red velvet lined display box that is normally extra?' Indicating the box that lay open on a shelf in the glass counter. The diamonds sparkling as they lay there. 'Would you like to take a seat sir? I will have it wrapped for you.'

Tim nodded and took the seat offered.

A little while later the jewellery reappeared, now enclosed in a red velvet bag with a tiny company logo embroidered on it. Tim pulled the drawstring open a little and peeked inside. The box was wrapped in black satin. He was stunned. Thanking the man, Tim walked back to where Mr Graham sat with the car. He found himself quite excited. He recognised how lucky he was to be able to buy something as beautiful as this for such a beautiful woman.

CHAPTER 6

Sophie came out of the back cabin, their bedroom, in her new maternity dress. A full-length, navy-blue gown with a sweetheart-neckline top, short sleeves with a matching lace trim.

'Give us a twirl.'

Sophie obliged revealing that from behind, apart from the short sleeves she appeared virtually naked from the shoulders down to the curve of her hips.

Tim took a swift pace forward, but Sophie fended him off saying, 'If you mess up my hair or makeup, we will be an hour late,' she said with her hand in the middle of his chest.

Looking down he saw that her new court shoes peeping out under the hem were a perfect colour match for the dress.

Tim was aware that she had taken him at his word. The only jewellery she was wearing was her wedding ring.

'One moment madam, I may have something for you.' This said as he opened his desk drawer and withdrew the box of jewellery.

Sophie looked surprised, 'I thought you were buying me a necklace.'

'I have, open it and see.'

Sophie moved to an armchair and sat down placing the box on her knees, releasing the drawstring, and removing the black satin. She was by now shaking her head, pulling the lacquered wooden box from its satin covering increasing her surprise. The little catch on the side of the box took her a few seconds to release, then she opened it.

Sophie, with a quick intake of breath, looked up at Tim saying, 'What have you done? I do not believe it, Tim, this … it is too, too everything. Can you give me a hanky, please? If I cry, I will ruin my makeup.' Never in her whole life had anyone given her a gift as special as this.

He did as he was asked.

Holding his hanky to her eyes and shaking her head she said, 'I cannot wear it Tim.'

'That's ok,' he responded, 'I'll take it back, I may lose a little but that's all right.' He was reaching for the box as he spoke.

'No,' she said emphatically, slapping his hand away. 'I cannot give it back either. However much did it all cost?'

'That's not what you should be saying, you haven't said whether you like it or not yet. It's a small token of how much I love you. It's beautiful diamonds for a beautiful woman.'

She stood, placed the box on her chair, wrapped her arms around his neck and kissed him gently, running her hands through his hair as she did so. A little later he put both hands on her bottom and pulled her into a full body embrace. Her biting his chin brought him back to the here and now, breaking the kiss he said, 'If we keep this up, we will never leave the boat this evening.'

Sophie, murmuring something he couldn't hear was trying to return to the kissing.

Taking her gently by her upper arms he held her away from him. 'Come on, let me put the jewellery on for you.'

'This is the second time I have offered myself to you and you have refused me. How the hell do you do it?' There was both hurt and surprise in her voice.

They remembered the time on the boat before their marriage when they had both become naked and Tim fighting to overcome his roaring desire had observed the promise he had given to her mother that he would not make love to her before they were married. As an old boy scout, he had no choice but to honour his promise. After a delay of about half an hour, Sophie had joined him on the bow of the boat moping her tears and said, 'I hate the bloody boy scouts.' He did remember it was a damn close-run thing.

Sophie handed him the necklace and turned to allow him to place it around her neck. Next was the bracelet then the eternity ring, and finally the earrings. She moved to the full-length mirror and stood looking at her image. Reaching towards Tim with her fingers splayed she linked their fingers, pulled him beside her and wrapped his arm around her.

In a small voice she said, 'We are so lucky.'

At that moment there was a knock on the cabin door, and Mr Graham poked his head around saying, 'Hallo, it's only me.'

'Come in,' said Tim. His chauffer was dressed in his normal pale-grey suit, he had never worn a hat.

Sophie was making her way to their bedroom. 'We will not be long, Mr Graham. Tim, can you give me a hand, please?' Shutting the cabin door, they descended into helpless giggles.

Tim said, 'I don't know what we could have said had he found us rutting on the carpet.'

'Tim, please do not be so rude, although thinking about it that is what could have happened. Hold still while I remove the lipstick, you are wearing more than I am.'

Sophie threw a black, wool cloak around herself as she left the boat with still the occasional stifled giggle.

The journey to the Vieri's was quickly accomplished. Mr Graham jumped from the car to open Sophie's door for her.

Sophie said, 'Thank you, Mr Graham.'

'You're welcome, Mrs Cooper,' was his response.

'You can call me Sophie, Mr Graham.'

'Thank you, Mrs Cooper.'

'We can get a taxi home to save you turning out again,' said Tim.

'That's kind of you but I will worry all night if I don't drive you. Just ring when you are ready, Tim.'

'OK, thank you,' said Tim as he turned to the front door.

'Why will he not call me by my first name?' asked Sophie.

'Because you are a Vieri,' he responded. 'He never called my great-aunt anything other than Mrs Longstaff when he worked for her. Around here you Vieri's are like royalty.'

'I am Mrs Cooper now, and my darling I am proud of it.'

*

Angela, smiling, opened the door, then she saw the pair of them in the hall light. Tim in his tuxedo, Sophie in her dress and diamonds. Putting her hand to her mouth she said in a wobbly voice, 'You look like film stars.'

Sophie looking down at herself said in a worried voice. 'Is it too much?'

'Oh no my darling it is fabulous, you are fabulous – take your cloak off and turn around.'

Sophie did as she asked.

'Did you choose the jewellery Sophia darling?'

'No, it was Tim.'

'What remarkably good taste you have Mr Cooper.'

'That's obvious, I married Sophia, didn't I?'

The rest of the family were in raptures.

Mrs Vieri said how pretty she looked. Mr Vieri said, 'Sound investment, Tim.'

Considering the recent row and its ferocity, to Tim's complete surprise the evening was all blue skies and sunshine. Mr Vieri was jovial; Mrs Vieri was polite all evening. The young couple swapped surprised looks occasionally. Later Sophie was helping Angela with the desert in the kitchen. Speaking quietly she asked, 'Whatever is going on Angela? Are my family high on something?'

'Yes, they are, it is you and the baby, you have blown a breath of fresh air through this family. You know what Italians are like, the family is everything, you keep on producing little ones it will be smiles all the time.'

'Oh, thank you, if you think I am going to be permanently pregnant just to keep my parents happy you can all think again,' she said, only half joking.

'Are you still working?' asked Angela.

'I am at the moment, part-time. I am being thoroughly spoiled. When it's for the company, Tim insists Mr Graham comes and gets me. When it's for my day job, as Tim calls it, Mr Wells asks me when I can come in and always arranges the taxi.'

'What do you mean the day job, I am sorry I do not understand?'

'The position I hold with Terry Wells, the owner of the big store in the high street. The job I won when my father and I had that huge row about my seeing Tim, and I resigned from the job with my father.'

'I did not know you were still doing that, remind me what it is you are doing there.'

'I am the financial director. I love the job. Terry tells me what he wants and leaves me to get on with it. I have far more independence working there than I have with Tim and the rest of the team, and it is a proper job that I can point at that I gained as a result of my own abilities, it was not because I am a family member.'

'I had completely forgotten about that Sophie; I must be getting old. How much longer will you work before the birth?'

'As long as I can. I cannot lie around all day; I would go mad.'

Angela said, 'I understand your need to be busy, I would go potty if I did not have my little job in the bookshop and my garden to fill up my days. Shall we join the rest?'

Later travelling home Tim said, 'I still have problems believing your mother and Angela are full blood sisters, they are polar opposites, your mother is … your mother.' Sophie frowned at him. 'Angela is all sunshine and laughter. I know you have explained in the past that Mrs Vieri was brought up by her hard strict mother, whereas Angela had a loving nanny …'

CHAPTER 7

Three months later Sophie woke Tim at four am in the morning. Calling from the bathroom she said, 'My waters have broken, and I am having contractions, can you help, please?'

'Should it be happening now?' he asked.

She read the concern in his voice. 'Yes, it is only a week early.' She was aware of his fear of a repetition of the miscarriage. 'This is entirely normal Tim. Will you ring the hospital please and tell them we are coming in, and we need a taxi?'

The taxi driver was extremely young and nervous. He kept asking, 'Are you all right back there missus?'

The problem for Tim was that the driver was constantly turning round.

The next time the driver did it, Tim, in a firm voice said, 'We are fine back here, will you concentrate on your driving. If you crash, we're really in trouble.'

'Yeah, sorry guv, it's a bit worrying like.' He behaved better for the rest of the journey, only stealing quick looks in his rear-view mirror occasionally.

A nurse was waiting for them in reception. She checked Sophie's name and then turning to Tim said, 'If you take a seat, we will make your wife comfortable.'

Sophie now sat in a wheelchair was disappearing through a set of double doors. Her hand waving goodbye over her shoulder, as she disappeared.

Time passed and Tim started to become concerned. He asked a nurse, 'Is my wife all right?'

'Yes,' she replied, 'there are lots of tests to do, it takes a while, someone will come and see you soon.'

Eventually a young Doctor stopped to talk to him, 'Mr Cooper?' he asked. Tim nodded. 'Your wife is fine, everything is as it should be, we have settled her down. You can go home – nothing will happen for some time.'

An attractive senior nurse who had come to stand beside the Doctor, said laughing, 'You have done your bit, go and get some sleep. We will ring you when you are required.'

Tim walked away unsure of what the nurse had implied.

*

Reaching the boat, it was still early, but he decided to ring Angela anyway. He now used her as the bridge to Mrs Vieri.

Angela, sounding befuddled by sleep asked nervously, 'Is there a problem, Tim?'

'The baby is on its way Angela, and everything is ok.' She could hear the excitement in his voice. 'They sent me home. Apparently, it will be some while before anything happens.'

'Oh! Tim I am quite overcome. I said to Sophia, this is exactly what this family needs. A baby will breathe new life into it. Do you want me to tell Olivia?'

'Yes, if you don't mind.'

'I will ring them later, it is still early, bye Tim.'

Later that morning Tim had just stepped ashore on his way to the hospital when he became aware of the phone ringing. He bounced back on board and struggled to unlock the door. 'Come on, come on,' The panic in his voice was audible, he was so scared the caller would ring off. Finally, the key turned, and the door opened, he snatched the phone from the cradle: 'Hallo.'

'Can I speak to Mr Timothy Cooper, please?'

'Yes, speaking.'

'Congratulations Mr Cooper you have a bonny baby girl, and your wife is fine. She said I had to tell you to hurry up. Will we see you soon?'

He had trouble speaking, his emotions were making coherent speech difficult. 'Yes,' he said in a funny high-pitched squeak. 'I'm on my way.'

Wiping the tears from his eyes with the palm of his hand he locked the door, then he broke into a run. Passing the boats tied up along the mooring then turning the corner and taking the gentle uphill path towards the exit he saw Tabby, the boatyard owner standing in the porch of his attractive stone built house on the right hand side opposite a high laurel hedge on the left. He was a kind and gentle man with a large white beard, a pair of sharp blue eyes peered out over the top of this remarkable edifice. Tim drawing level with him and as he passed jogged backwards so he could still see him. He called, 'It's a girl, Tabby, it's a girl and Sophie's fine.'

The two men were shouting to make themselves heard as the distance between them increased.

'Give her my congratulations,' shouted Tabby.

'Will do,' replied Tim as he rounded a corner and turned left into the road.

When he reached the ward that the receptionist had named, a nurse met him. 'You must be Mr Cooper, your wife described you very accurately,' she said with a half-hidden smile on her face. 'We are tidying the mums up ready for visiting, you are a little early, but that's not a problem. I can show you your baby if you like?'

'Yes please,' he responded.

The nurse led him down a corridor and stopped outside a large room with a full-length glass wall, enabling a good view from where Tim and the nurse could see rows of oblong, clear plastic fish tanks with babies in them. Some were sleeping, others moving, one was lying on its tummy, arms pushing its body up to enable it to see over the edge of the tank.

'Can you recognise your baby?'

He shook his head.

'It's the one doing press-ups, I've never seen that before,' she informed him. 'It's not supposed to be possible for babies to turn themselves over at this age, let alone do press-ups. Make yourself comfortable in the waiting area and when all the ladies are decent, we will bring the babies through, then you can come in.'

'Thank you,' he said making his way to the only armchair. He felt completely out of his depth, this was a world he knew nothing about, being an only child.

He was in the middle of a magazine article on fly fishing for trout and salmon. One day when he was not so busy, he might try it, he thought. His reading was disturbed sporadically as more men made their way to the chairs. Shortly after, they were all called through on to the ward.

Sophie was in a bed at the far end. He thought she would be exhausted and perhaps sleepy, but this could not be further from the truth, she was a vision in pink holding a baby, their baby, his baby, his daughter. He was totally overcome.

A nurse pulled the curtain round to give them some privacy. Leaning it to kiss her she could see how emotional he was. Her free hand strayed into his hair to hold and prolong the kiss.

When they parted, she whispered, 'Thank you for my baby.'

'It should be me thanking you.'

He sensed the step into motherhood had changed her. Her eyes indicated there was a new depth, a new purpose. Her eyes reflected a knowing maturity that had not been there before, a women's wisdom.

'You look lovely but different.'

'I feel different,' she agreed. 'Would you like to hold her?'

'Erm, yes, er what do I have to do?'

'She will not break Tim – hold her the same as I am.'

Nestling in the crook of his left arm the baby opened her deep blue eyes and smiled at him, his heart was stolen away. He knew his life, their lives, had changed forever. He could see she was going to be blond and beautiful like her mother.

Sophie did not tell him that the smile was almost certainly wind.

'Tim, you do not have to say yes, but the nurse who was with me all through the birth is called Charlotte, Charley for short. I think it is a lovely name, even the abbreviation is charming – what do you think?'

He immediately thought of Charlie the cheerful cockney who did all their building work but decided not say anything.

'That's good,' he agreed. 'It will suit her in the future, she is going to be a beauty like her mother.'

Sophie reached over and squeezed his hand and smiled at him.

'I'm sorry, but I need to go to work, we are really busy. I will come and see you this evening.' Saying this as he handed Charley back to her mother. The baby awoke having fallen asleep in Tim's arms.

Kissing mother and child he walked from the ward; turning in the doorway and looking back he saw Sophie holding their baby and talking to her. He felt his heart move in his chest. He recognised a new deep obligation to those two people he was watching, mother and child. He was experiencing an incredible emotional tsunami; it was changing him and his thinking irrevocably. He would not be able to explain it to anyone, but he was a different man from the one who had walked into the hospital earlier tonight.

Mr and Mrs Vieri were arriving as he was leaving. Victor increased his stride towards Tim, reaching him he grabbed Tim's hand and pounded his shoulder with the other.

'Bravo, bravo.' His use of Italian indicated how moved he was. 'How is she?' he asked.

'Mother and baby are doing well,' responded Tim. 'Good morning, Mrs Vieri,' he said with a lot more warmth than he had used when addressing her in the past.

Her reply was frosty: 'Good morning.' Tim was completely confused. In the row with Mr Vieri over the shop in his father-in-law's store, she had defended him and attacked her husband for his lack of manners. Deciding he never would understand her he said, 'Sorry Victor, I have to go to work. I will see you soon – Goodbye, Mrs Vieri.' He didn't wait for her reply.

Arriving at shop Number One, he discovered it was full and somehow most knew about the birth. His father was the first to shake his hand. 'Is it a boy or a girl, lad?' he asked.

'A girl, eight pounds four ounces, mother and baby doing well.' His back was pounded, and his hand shaken until he was sore. Eventually everything settled down and he got back to work.

CHAPTER 8

Three days later Sophie and the baby came home to the houseboat, her presence onboard underlined how much he missed her when she was not there to go home to. She brought a warmth that was difficult to define, perhaps it was her womanhood. Tim was certain that a home needed a woman in it.

Later that evening, Tim had the baby in his arms while Sophie showered. Afterwards, unobserved, she watched her husband with their child. It was clear he was completely ensnared, he was speaking very quietly and gently to her, the baby staring up into his eyes. Sophie's heart flipped; this was an indelible image that would stay in her heart forever.

Later, having settled the baby down, Sophie joined him in bed wearing her nighty, he pulled her into an embrace and started to remove it.

'Tim, sorry, but it may be a few days before we can do this,' she explained. 'I am still a little sore.'

'No, you misunderstand, I just need to hold you. I was so scared something may have gone wrong.'

Slipping her nighty off she pulled him to her and held him close, her proximity comforting him.

'I have never loved anyone the way I love you and baby,' he whispered into her hair, kissing the top of her head.

Lifting her eyes to his she saw how moved he was. How important she and their baby were to him was writ large on his face. They kissed gently, then she snuggled into him, and they slept, still in a loving embrace.

Tim awoke early, the bed was empty … had he dreamed about Sophie's homecoming yesterday? Sleep still befuddled him. Then he heard her in the nursery whispering to Charley, throwing a warm beige dressing gown on, and in bare feet he tiptoed quietly to watch mother and baby together.

He stayed very still, not wanting to draw attention to himself. Sophie was holding the baby to her breast. It was one of the most moving things he had seen. He was aware that this was an act that was as old as the presence of mankind on the earth. He recognised that the fact of giving birth and now the provision of sustenance in such an intimate way must make the mother's connection to the baby something that no man could ever experience.

However, one thing he was certain of was that this tiny morsel, so perfect in every detail, had captured his heart and soul, and now ranked highly alongside his wife in his love and affection for her.

Sophie having sensed his presence turned her face towards him and smiled, saying, 'She is feeding well. I think she must be done. Will you hold her while I get a nappy? Pat her back gently while I get sorted out.'

A minute later, Tim groaned, 'You mucky pup, Charley Cooper.' He heard and felt his daughter throw up down his back.

Sophie returned; fighting to hold back the laughter and failing, she managed to utter, 'That is your initiation into fatherhood, Tim.'

With a wry look on his face, he went to change. 'Tea?' he called.

'Yes please,' was the response.

✳

Tim found great pleasure in reading to his daughter. On one occasion Sophie found him reading Darwin's *Descent of Man*.

'Why are you reading that?' she queried. 'It should be a nursery rhyme.'

'I am certain that Charley cannot understand a word we say yet, it is obviously simply the soothing voice and this way I get something from it as well.'

'If she grows up weird it will be your fault.'

'Sophie love, I think she'll be fine, and anyway I'm showing her the pictures.'

She left them to it, shaking her head as she went.

CHAPTER 9

Tim, Sophie and the baby had moved into the company office that was once his great aunt's home. Charlie and Tommy, The man and his son that they employed to do the work around the shops were busy painting the exterior of the Sea Maiden. The houseboat had been hauled out of the water and was now sitting up on blocks so that her hull could be scrapped clean of weed and given a coat of black paint to slow down the growth of future weed and stop the hull from rusting.

In the small hours of the morning, Tim went from sound asleep to wide awake in a heartbeat. The florescent face of his bedside clock told him it was three am. He had heard an unusual noise. Scrolling through his memory he recognised it was the small ornamental brass bell that sat on the windowsill of the upstairs toilet across the hallway from their bedroom door. Leaving the bed very quietly and not stopping to don a dressing gown, he tiptoed to the toilet door; opening it slowly and carefully he saw in the light from a nearby streetlamp, two hands grasping the window surround. His heart began banging against his ribs.

Someone was threatening his wife and family. He was transfixed for a moment not knowing what to do. His mind skipped back to a recent local burglary. The elderly couple had been beaten to make them reveal where their savings were hidden. Tim stood there frozen, unable to believe what his eyes were telling him. The heavy toilet window was large and glazed with an intricate pattern in the glass, with hinges at the top. There was a long brass prop holding it open sitting in a bracket on the windowsill. A hand shifted and took a better grip on the frame, then a distorted image of a man's face appeared beyond the frosted glass.

Tim was now a primitive man facing a rabid wolf at the entrance to his family's cave. This burglar was threatening all that he held dear. A savage blind, primeval rage fuelled by fear overtook him. Without conscious thought his hand swept forward and slapped the prop from its catch. The heavy window slammed down on the two hands; the face and fingers disappeared.

After a short pause he opened the window an inch to listen. About 20 seconds later he heard a concerned voice whispering, 'Tel, are you all right Tel?' Then there was silence. Securing the window, he went back to bed.

Sophie still half asleep mumbled, 'Is everything OK?'

'Yes, everything's fine, the wind blew the bell over.' He pulled the covers up around his neck and fell asleep. He never did tell Sophie.

On future occasions when he recalled the incident, he experienced no regrets about his actions, how could he gauge how serious the threat was? Once inside, the burglar's first move would have been to let his accomplice in. Tim knew he could not have fought both of them. The papers often related the details of the most horrific acts perpetrated on the innocent by intruders. Since the attempted break in, an elderly widow living on the far side of the town had been beaten unconscious because she would not disclose where she kept her money. No, he had no qualms about his reaction to the attempted break in. He knew in his heart he would do whatever it took to protect his family. He was prepared to use whatever level of force it required.

CHAPTER 10

1976

Three weeks later the Sea Maiden was being released back into the water. She was resplendent with her gleaming white paint on her upper works and the fresh blacking to her lower hull. The newly varnished window surrounds and hand rails shone in the sunlight. Charlie and Tommy, helped by one of the Boatyard workers who had advised them on the task were undertaking the relaunch. Much to Tim's surprise, there was a small crowd watching her slide back into her natural element, there was a ripple of unexpected clapping as she re-entered the water. Looking at Sophie as she stood watching, holding Charley, he noticed the tears in his wife's eyes. Putting his arm around her hugged her gently.

Wiping her tears way, she said, 'It is like watching her come alive again, like when you let a wild animal go free, it feels the same.'

He bent down and kissed her hair.

Charley pointed at the Sea Maiden and burbled something unintelligible, then she faced her mother.

Sophie, still moved, kissed her daughter and with her lips in the baby's hair agreed with her, saying, 'You are right Charley, darling.'

Tim, with a quizzical frown asked, 'What did she say? I only heard a meaningless mumble.'

'Do not listen to your silly Daddy,' responded Sophie covering Charley's ears, 'I know what you said, and you are right she is beautiful.'

Tim was unsure about the Sea Maiden's beauty. The boat was a converted second-world-war troop-landing craft, designed to put soldiers ashore on enemy beaches. She was a steel open-topped box with a drop-down ramp at the front to let the infantry off. At the end of the hostilities a cabin was constructed on the flat deck to turn her into a houseboat. Perhaps not beautiful but certainly very practical and extremely comfortable and warm.

The first six months since his daughter's birth had sped by. He lay in bed one Sunday morning listening to his wife talking to their daughter. Sophie had laughed at him when he declared that Charley was going to be stunningly attractive like her mother.

'There is no way you can know that you silly man,' she chided him, secretly delighted that her husband was so enamoured with their baby.

Sophie returned to the bedroom after feeding Charlotte. Throwing off her dressing gown, and now naked, rejoined him in bed. Lying on his back, his hands behind his head, he was staring at the ceiling.

'What are you thinking about?' she asked, sliding a leg across his lower body.

'I was counting my blessings, how lucky I am, we are. In the past, I believed this happiness was beyond me.'

Propping herself up on an elbow so she could see his face, she sensed their relationship had changed since Charley's birth, it was somehow gentler, but bigger.

Tim's hand, released from behind his head slid slowly from her shoulder down the length of her back, finally gently cupping her buttock.

She leaned in to kiss him, pressing her bare breasts to his chest.

Their tongues touched; her free hand journeyed down his body.

He rolled her on to her back, beginning to growl.

Sophie, a giggle starting, was saying, 'Shhh, do not wake her.' Laughing as she spread herself for him and guided him in. The growling got louder. There was no sound from the nursery as they were carried away sharing their love for each other. Sophie was no longer aware of time or place; Tim's possession of her body took her to a land she had named 'elsewhere'. Finding her rhythm, emotional bombs were going off in her head. As they climaxed Sophie shouted out his name, all of the sensations overwhelming her, this did wake the baby.

'Tim, can you let me up, please? I must go to her.' Struggling to get free, he, laughing while holding her in place. Growing cross she shoved him aside and left the bed, he watched her naked bottom walk away before she was hidden in a large, pink, fluffy dressing gown.

'Sophie' he called, stopping her in her tracks.

'Yes,' she said looking over her shoulder at him. Her annoyance with him still showing on her face.

'You have a beautiful bottom, well actually you have a beautiful everything.'

'Tim!' she complained, frowning at him, 'that's rude!' Sophie did not realise as she turned away that he could see her secret woman's smile reflected in the mirror on the far wall.

CHAPTER 11

Tim and his partners were discussing Daisy, a full-time worker at the second Sophie's shop, now referred to as Number Two.

Mr Woodman, a partner, and the owner of the first shop had suggested that they make her manager.

'In some ways she is ahead of us in customer relations, she knows all the customers' names and their preferences for the food they buy. I think we should get her to work in Number One, the first shop, for a while so we can see how she does it? That achieves two things, we can assess her as a manager and watch her undoubted skills with the customers. In two instances when I have been working with her, customers have asked to wait until Daisy is free.'

'Her diction has improved,' observed Tim.

'She asked me not to say anything but as long as it goes no further,' confided Sara, 'Daisy is taking elocution lessons. I mention it because it shows her commitment. She often stays at the shop after closing, she calls it putting the shop to bed.'

*

Sophie stopped off at the second shop the following day as Daisy was closing. She noticed Daisy's look of concern when she saw her.

'Daisy, please do not be alarmed, this is good news.' Flipping the door sign to closed, Sophie held Daisy's arm. 'Come and sit down.' When the two of them were seated Sophie said, 'We would like to offer you the manager's job here in shop Number Two.'

Daisy was already shaking her head saying, 'Oh no, no, no, I ain't good enough. Sorry I mean, I'm not good enough, I'd mess it up,' now shaking her head even more vigorously.

'Daisy, now stop this,' said Sophie firmly, trying to stem the girl's growing panic. 'Take a deep breath while I explain what we propose.

'The truth is that you are already doing most of the jobs a manager would do. We know you balance the till every night, no one has asked you to do that.'

Daisy started to apologise.

'Daisy it is not a criticism,' Sophie said with a half laugh. 'It shows your level of commitment.' Now with a gentle smile on her face Sophie asked, 'Will you just let me explain what we have in mind, without interrupting?'

Daisy nodded.

'We have been watching you work for some time – you are exceptionally good at what you do. Your rapport with our customers is excellent, you know their names, their preferences, their likes and dislikes, their family details. In fact, what we want you to do is to come and work at Number One for a while so we can evaluate your work practices, and you can show us how you manage to acquire all this information. You will be on a three-month probation period. This works both ways, if you really do not want the job you can tell us, and we will advertise the position in the paper. Finally, can I say if you do take the job, we really hope you do, there will always be help if you need it. Oh, and there will be a significant rise in pay.'

'So iffen, sorry, if I doesn't, if I don't take the job,' said Daisy correcting herself for the third time, 'you will put annover person in charge of my, er, this shop?'

Sophie nodded.

'Can I ask how much I'd get paid?'

Sophie told her.

'Cor, blimey, me and Mum working togever never earnt that … can I still works here some of the week in that three months? I'll miss me customers.'

'Of course, you can, so will you give it a try?'

Daisy thought for a moment then said, 'Yes, please.'

'Good, we will let you know when we have sorted out when and where. I am pleased you have agreed to do it. You will be great at it, now I must go, Tim will want his dinner.'

Daisy was extremely cross with herself, why did she allow the timid frightened mouse inside her to take over when she had to face even the smallest challenge. Well no more, she thought vehemently, you are gunna get slapped right back to where you came from and that's a promise.

*

Daisy lay awake a long time that night struggling to believe how much her life had changed since her childhood. She remembered the ghastly housing. The frequent midnight flits to worse and worse slums just ahead of the bailiffs. The last was unfit for a dog let alone a family. The stench from the broken sewer, the peeling wallpaper, the mould. The reason for their poverty was that her father would drink the rent money. He insisted that her mother handed over the money she earned under a threat of another beating if she refused. Thinking of her father, unsure now whether he was alive or dead. He was a gross, drunken wreck of a man. She remembered vividly the night he had tried to rape her; she was fourteen, he was almost too drunk to stand. The groping hand under the thin blanket, her kicking her legs like mad and shouting stop it, stop it, at the top of her voice. She could still smell the vile combination of urine, stale beer, the sharp repulsive stink of his filthy body, his bristles scratching her face as he tried to kiss her.

Suddenly his upper body had fallen across her. He was so heavy. She recalled struggling to breath. His body slid off her, then she had seen her mother standing in the doorway holding the fire iron she had hit him with. He never tried it again. From that night on the fire iron stood in plain sight downstairs, her mum threatening that if he hit her again or attacked Daisy, she would finish him for good. Her mum had held her for hours that night while she cried.

Her mind came back to the present, almost unable to believe that she had been offered the manager's job. Her mum had forced her to attend the interview for the shop assistant's position. The fact that she had been given the job still amazed her, and then today's promotion on top.

She remembered too, when she had been with the company for some time she was trusted to run the shop on her own for a while, while the person in charge went for lunch. Then her father had appeared stealing money from the till and knocking her around when she tried to stop him. His theft was discovered, and a trap was laid for him. He punched Daisy in the face and knocked her out when once more she tried to stop him before the trap was sprung. Lying on the floor and while unable to see she could hear that her father had taken a beating from Mr Woodman. He was of the old school and always placed women on pedestals. Hitting a woman was unforgiveable in his eyes.

Everybody had decided that it was too dangerous for her to go home. Sara and Harry had taken her in. Shortly afterwards Sara had taken her to one side and said in her gentle Italian accent, 'As far as we are concerned, you're the daughter we never had and if you want to you can live with us for the rest of your life.'

Sara held her while she cried, both women were sniffing and wiping their eyes when eventually they regained control.

Daisy had been on tenterhooks for the first few weeks, afraid she would spoil something or break a valuable ornament; Harry had some decanters and glasses that were Waterford crystal. One day she had spilled gravy on the beautiful corn-coloured carpet and got terribly upset thinking she had ruined it.

Sara, cuddling her, had said, 'It will clean up. It doesn't matter if you burn the place down, we still won't throw you out.'

She had often woken in the night and switched her bedside lamp on just to make sure it wasn't a dream.

There had been one small blip: Harry had refused to let her pay her way. Sara had realised that Daisy was not happy about that and had persuaded Harry to take a nominal sum from her each week. With this new job she would be able to give them more money and pay for her elocution lessons herself.

CHAPTER 12

One evening Sophie said, 'Tim we will need to think about the christening soon otherwise Charley will be too old. The church prefers that they are still young.'

'As you know I am not deeply religious myself, but I do believe that we should have her christened so that she can make up her own mind in the future, what do you think?' he asked.

'I do have a faith, although it is not something I want to trumpet aloud. I suppose it is more about how I live my life, do unto others as you would be done too, or something like that,' said Sophie. 'I would like our children to have a faith. As I have just said if nothing else it is a good guide.'

'Do you want to make a big splash of the christening or something smaller?' he asked.

'Smaller I think, I do not know why but I do feel that in some ways it is a private affair, family and close friends.'

'Do you want to include the staff and their partners, those people who we now know well, Charlie and co, Mr and Mrs Murdoch? We could extend it to some of our suppliers, it would help to keep them sweet.'

'Tim, you have helped me make up my mind, not everything is about business. I want this to be a small private affair, we can extend it to staff and partners but that is it.'

Sophie had a problem, she wanted one of the family to be a godparent but because she was an only child with no siblings she could not think of anyone suitable. Mr Vieri, Sophies father had solved the problem by inviting the Italians, one of whom was a young distant relative, Joe Mancini.

Sophie had met him before. He was a churchgoer and seemed a nice guy. She had chosen Jessica, her oldest friend as the other godparent.

*

On the day, they were blessed with bright, warm sunshine. The women in their colourful pretty summer frocks and hats and the men booted and spurred in freshly pressed suits, crisply ironed shirts, their best or perhaps their only tie, shoes polished to a mirror finish.

A small group standing slightly apart was a hub of laughter and boisterous discussion. Tim with his daughter in his arms and Sophie by his side went to greet the Italians, the three of them were soon enveloped by warm greetings. Charley was passed around the women and made a great fuss of. They all admired her white dress trimmed with matching lace and ribbons.

Seated in a pew waiting for the service to start Tim, as usual, was looking up into the roof of the church at all the clever woodwork. He did not know for sure, but it always reminded him of a drawing of the interior of a Viking longship.

The church service was conducted by a gentle, bearded, elderly priest who it would appear Charley had taken a liking too. Tim, who had never been to a catholic christening was very moved when the four of them, he, Sophie and the two godparents were standing around the font holding a candle each while the priest carried out the baptism. When the water was placed on his daughter's forehead she cried.

As the ceremony ended, Tim was surprised by how quickly the time had sped by. He and Sophie both thanked the priest for how special they both felt the short service had been. Tim ensured that the priest knew where the local hotel was where some food and drink was available.

The hotel had provided a wonderful array of finger food both savoury and sweet. Bottles of red and white wine were placed on the tables along with glass jugs of spring water. On every place setting there was one example of Sara's amazing confectionary nestling in an attractively folded tissue with a discrete 'Sophies' written in one corner.

Tim's wife rolled her eyes and shook her head, she recognised that her husband was always at work and considered everyone a customer. When any bottle was emptied Tim had made it clear that it had to be replaced. There were arrangements of white orchids on every table. There was no music arranged. Sophie had decided people would rather talk, especially as there were foreign family members present who rarely saw each other. Charley was sitting on Nanny's lap on another table in amongst the Italians who were making a great fuss of both of them.

When the guests had eaten their fill and sitting back with a glass in their hands, Charley's new godparent Joe Mancini, stood and made his way to the grand piano and sat down. Tim frowned and was just going to get up when Victor who was sitting on his left, the other side of Sophie, reached round and put his hand on Tim's arm to restrain him and whispered, 'Don't worry.' The young man sat down and after a while began to play, quiet, beautiful classical music. Tim didn't know the music, but it was very moving. It was a perfect match for the occasion. When he stopped there was a small ripple of applause. After a short rest, the young man began to play something else.

A tall, elegant woman in a long, backless, dark-red dress eased her chair away from the table and walked towards the piano, her shining black hair hung to her waist. She was beginning to sing in Italian as she moved across the room.

Tim shivered as he always did when the music touched his soul. It was so sad, he had no idea what the words meant but knew the music was speaking of terrible pain, grievous loss and sorrow. Tim was moist-eyed, he became aware that the hotel staff had come out to listen. There was a long silence after the piece finished, then as the pianist and the singer walked back to their places one person at the back of the room began to clap… slowly at first, then as others were woken from the reverie that the music had induced, the applause blossomed and grew in volume. Gazing around Tim could see many in the gathering had been, like him, visibly moved by the performance. Sara sitting on his right was dabbing her eyes with Harry's handkerchief.

Then the mood changed, and the chatter resumed. The hotel manager came to remind Tim that the staff needed to clear up for an evening event.

Tim stood and thanked everyone for coming especially the musicians and the Italian contingent.

Gerald, Jessica's husband was the only person who hadn't risen to his feet. He saw the man had a newly opened full bottle in front of him. Jessica who had just been talking to her husband came to Tim and began to apologise for Gerald's behaviour.

'Please don't apologise, he's had an awful lot to drink. I'll sort it out.' Tim walked across to Gerald, leaning down he said quietly, 'Sorry Gerald it's time to leave, you can take the bottle with you.'

The drunkard began to berate him. 'I don't work for you Mr High and Bloody mighty. I'll go when I'm ready, you fancy bloody—' He said no more because Tim jerked the chair out from under him. Gerald nearly fell to the floor, he struggled back onto the seat and turned around to say something and found he was face to face with Tim, their noses only inches apart.

Tim whispered, 'You can go quietly now, or I will get the staff to throw you out in front of everybody.' Tim's anger was evident in every word. 'Shall we put this down to the drink talking. Goodbye Gerald.'

The cowed man wobbled his way to the front door that was held open for him and disappeared into the crowd, still grasping the bottle of wine.

Sophie approached Sara who was holding Polly, Jessica's daughter. 'Have you seen Jessica?' she asked.

'Yes, she has gone to the toilet,' explained Sara, nodding in the direction Jessica had taken.

Sophie found the ladies toilet at the far end of the corridor. There was only one cubicle in use.

'Are you in there Jessica?' asked Sophie.

At first there was no reply, the second time she called, the reply was, 'Yes I will be out in a minute, you carry on, I will find you.'

Sophie could hear the choked back tears. 'I can hear how upset you are Jessica love, come out – we can talk about it.'

'I am ok.'

'I am going to remain here until you do come out,' replied Sophie. 'Please Jessica.'

There was a short delay then the toilet flushed and moments later the door opened and Jessica, crying hard, stepped into Sophie's open arms. They hugged each other until the worst of the tears were over then Sophie handed her a hanky.

'What happened? Why did he behave like that?' asked Sophie.

'He began drinking some time back' – there was a pause – 'it started, I realise, shortly after I began working for you. Until then he had me at his beck and call, now I ask him to do some things because I am working in the evenings, he has until lately just grumbled but then he has done it. Now he refuses and says he has had a hard day and goes into the lounge and switches on the football and drinks. He will not allow me to watch anything else. If there is no football on the tv, he goes down the pub and comes home rolling drunk, rude and abusive. Looking back, I realise that after Polly had gone to bed, I was so bored. He and I have nothing in common now. I think he is jealous of my job. I have I think been over enthusiastic about it, made it sound more interesting and important than his. Sophie what am I going to do? I love my job. I will go crazy if I have to go back to how things were. I will die of boredom.'

Sophie had let her friend spill it all out without interruption. She could not think of much to suggest.

'I have to be active. I am never happier than when I am doing research or arranging things.'

Sophie remembered that when they were at university together it was always Jessica who volunteered to arrange their activities. Even today she or Tim would hand Jessica a sheet of paper with the merest amount of detail on it saying as they did so, 'Can you sort that out please?'

Jessica would fall on the task like a dog with a juicy new bone and immediately become completely absorbed by it, unaware of nearby conversations or questions addressed to her.

The two women made their way back to the function room. Sophie was so upset by her friend's unhappiness but could think of no solution to her problem. She had to admit to herself that she did not like Gerald; derision of others seemed to be part of his make-up. She did not think he was very bright, certainly he was not as bright as his wife, he lacked any conversational skills, and she could usually smell alcohol on his breath. He was always ready to tell you how important he was at work.

Sophie did not like the way he looked at her either, this made her skin crawl.

*

Later, Tim was sitting on the rear deck of the Sea Maiden in the twilight. A stage in the day's surrender to the night that was romantic, the world became softer, less distinct. As always, he was fascinated by the reflections of multi-coloured lights that slid and changed and slid again on the surface of the water, never duplicating the same shapes or juxtaposition of shades, tints or tones.

Sophie joined him carrying a bottle and two wine glasses, she showed him the bottle of Merlot, he nodded, she poured the wine. The young couple sat in companionable silence for a while.

Finally, Sophie said, 'Do you want to talk about what we are both thinking about but not discussing.'

'Hmm,' mused Tim. 'I was angry initially.'

'Oh, really, I did not notice. I was worried it may have become a brawl with both of you rolling about on the floor throwing punches,' she responded cynically.

'Now,' he continued emphatically, 'I'm left feeling extremely sorry for Jessica, she is far cleverer than her dope of a husband. He is clearly jealous of her growing success. He could demand she stayed home and waited on him and Polly. Putting the business first—' said Tim.

Sophie interrupted him, saying, 'I have never known you do that.'

Rolling his eyes and taking a deep breath in he said, 'What I was going to say is that if she did leave, we would be in the soup and it would condemn her to a half-life of mind-numbing boredom, poor woman. Can you have a chat with her and make sure she knows how important she is to the company, and how crucial her role is.'

Sophie frowned and said, 'I am not sure I am comfortable doing that, it feels as though we are manipulating her. What I will do is to discuss it with her and see what we can do to help. Now I am going below I need my bed.'

Sophie was so sorry for her friend, as she considered the relationship she had with Tim. 'We are incredibly lucky to have found each other, Tim.'

'I won't argue with that my love,' he replied.

'Are you staying out here?' she asked.

'No, I'll turn in as well.'

In a short while they were both sound asleep.

✳

Sophie did discuss the situation with Jessica the following afternoon, but the two women did not come up with any useful suggestions; the only thing that had Jessica decided was not talk about her work with Gerald.

CHAPTER 13

Tim, Sophie and Jessica were sitting in the company office discussing a new venture. Tim's great aunt had died a while back and had bequeathed him a large sum of money including this spacious house that they were now sitting in. Tim was still struggling with her loss; she had cared for him after his mother had died and his father had thrown him out. He wanted to do something with the money to remember her by because she was renowned for her philanthropy, both at home and abroad.

Tim was going over his ideas and the reasons behind them. 'I know I have roughed this out previously, but I just wanted to recap, to make this a starting point as it were.'

'Do you remember I said that while my education had been cut short, I left school when I was fifteen in 1960. I knew that some of my friends who had continued up into the sixth form were very clever. Only one of them went to university and I believe I know the reason why working-class youngsters don't go to university.'

Jessica broke in and asked, 'But surely their education is free at university so that is not a drain on the family purse, is it?'

'Your right, but the families expect their sons to go to work to ease their financial situation.'

'Or their daughters,' corrected Sophie.

Tim nodded agreement and then continued saying, 'Many families today have three, four, five children. It costs more and more money to clothe and feed them as they grow. Any extra money coming in is going to make a big difference.'

Obviously confused, Jessica said, 'Tim, I am sorry, I had to take in so much information on my first day I am not really clear about how it will work.'

'Sophie,' said Tim, handing the task of explaining to his wife.

'The first thing you need to know is that we are making this up as we go along, everything may change. Our present thinking is that we will find one school, one headmaster, one group of interested parents to act as guinea pigs,' said Sophie. 'However, I believe this will only grow extremely slowly so I do not anticipate there will be an avalanche of students wanting to take up our offer.'

'Will we have to approach ILEA, the Inner London Education Authority?' queried Jessica.

'That can be your first task please, Jessica. Find out who we have to talk to and if possible, fix an appointment. This is going to be a lot of work, especially for you' said Tim.

'I have given that some thought, Tim. He goes to football nearly every week with his pals, he is often not in until late. I will work then.'

'You must keep a record of your hours.'

'I can do that Tim, but first can you map out what we are offering, please?'

'This may change but here goes with my current thinking. By the way, I expect we will have to employ a qualified person from the field of education. OK, the first step is to contact ILEA, next a school, headmaster, or headmistress, design an exam, and an interview protocol for the young person.' He could see both women scribbling away.

'I also thought we could call it the Victoria Longstaff fund.'

'That's nice, yes, I like that,' replied Jessica. 'Also, it may trigger a response from those people who currently support her other charities.'

Sophie was nodding her agreement.

'Some early rules, the payment will be a fixed amount, it will start when the youngster opts for higher education. It will stop if they leave unless the problem is illness – then it will be up to us to decide if the payments stop or continue.'

'Who should be on the committee that is going to run this?' asked Sophie.

'One thing I am adamant about, my decision will be final, no member will have executive powers. I am not having this stolen away from us by some smart-arse who wants to take over.'

Sophie said, 'I am not sure you can do that Tim.'

'It's that or nothing. One thing we will get you to do, please, Sophie love, is to make sure the money is ring-fenced, only you and I to have access to it. I am not averse to having working capital held separately but that is all.'

'We may have to take advice as to how we do that as well,' offered Sophie.

'Are there any more questions?' asked Tim.

Jessica shook her head thinking, golly I had not anticipated anything at this level. Her thoughts must have been displayed on her face because Sophie said, 'Jessica, I told you this was going to be fun.'

They all exchanged goodbyes and went their separate ways.

CHAPTER 14

Serving Tim his dinner one evening, Sophie relayed the details of hers and Charley's visit to the post-natal clinic.

'The Doctor was talking about the whooping cough vaccine for Charley.'

He could hear the query in her voice. 'Isn't that the one there's been all the furore about in the newspapers?' he responded.

'Yes, there have been reports of some worrying side effects, like brain damage. I do not know what to do for the best.'

'How about we make a separate appointment to see the Doctor and ask for more detail. I think this needs to be a joint decision so I would like to come as well please, if you don't mind.'

Sophie still obviously concerned confirmed she had no problem with him attending.

Two days later, Tim, Sophie and the baby were sitting with the Doctor, a young dark-haired woman, listening as she explained the benefits of the whooping cough vaccine. When the Doctor had finished speaking there was a thoughtful silence.

Sophie asked, 'Is there any truth in the newspaper articles.?'

'I am not sure,' replied the GP. Another silence ensued.

Tim sat with his chin in his hand, staring at the apple-green surgery wall, a sure sign he was thinking hard; finally removing his hand and leaning forward, elbows on his knees with his hands clasped, now looking at the Doctor, he asked, 'Do you have children?'

'Yes,' she replied, 'two boys.'

'Will you have them immunised?' he asked.

The silence stretched on while the Doctor stared out of the window. Finally, she straightened up, took a deep breath in and held it. Locking her eyes with Tim's she emitted a long sigh, and replied, 'No!'

✻

The two of them spent hours during the following days going over and over the same fragments of information available to them. Tim noticed his wife was often lost in thought.

One evening the three of them were sitting on the small rear deck of the boat watching the sun go down across the water when Sophie said, 'Tim, I am this child's mother, she is flesh of my flesh. I have to make this decision; I am the only one who can. Charley is so bright, to have her maimed by brain damage would destroy me. I recognise the terrible risk of losing her, but I will not have her immunised.'

Tim understood he had no choice but to agree, they were forced to decide and there must appear to be mutual agreement in case their decision was the wrong one.

Later that evening the couple were sitting in front of the television watching the remembrance day service. He was always deeply moved by the pageantry knowing the tens of thousands of men and women who had given their lives so that Briton could be free. Tim was aware that his wife had not spoken for a while. He realised she was still struggling with her decision regarding the vaccination.

CHAPTER 15

They had been going out for six weeks and had just enjoyed a wonderful evening. He was an accomplished dancer. Daisy loved his appearance and he smelt so nice; now they were talking and laughing as he walked her home holding her hand. She was wearing a pretty multi-coloured dress with petticoats. Reaching the lamp post at the end of her street she stopped in the pool of light. She was not comfortable going any nearer her home, well, Harry and Sara's house.

He drew her towards him and slowly so as not to surprise her he kissed her on the lips so gently, the same way her mum kissed her when she was a tiny little girl. It was nice. He had gently kissed her goodnight for the last few evenings but now the kisses were growing firmer. At the same time, he pulled her closer to him and wrapped his arms around her. The kisses were now continuous. She began to feel uncomfortable. A few minutes later she sensed his arm moving and then his hand moved across her ribs, his palm slid up and over her breast. Daisy jumped as though she had received an electric shock, pushing him away so hard that he was struggling to keep his balance. Now in a blind panic, she was transported back down the years to her childhood, reliving her father's attempted rape. She could smell the stench of him, the sour sweat and urine, all mixed together with vomit and stale beer.

She broke into a run, hampered somewhat by her high heels. She could hear her date shouting, 'Daisy I'm so sorry. Daisy, please don't run away.'

His shouting added further impetus to her flight, terrified he was coming after her. Reaching the front door in her panic she stood hammering on it, unable do anything else. Sara opened the door extremely concerned; Harry was hurrying down the stairs.

'He, he …' she blurted out, unable to say any more, there was not enough breath left in her body. The mad dash to safety and her fear had robbed her of speech.

Sara could tell Harry was worried, he pushed past the two women and peered down the street. There was no one in sight. Coming back indoors he closed the front door saying as he did so, 'Did someone attack you love?'

'Harry, will you make a strong cup of tea, please? I will take Daisy into the front room.'

Seated on the couch Sara had her arm around the child, this was all she was at this moment in time, an adult-sized child. Harry brought in the tea and went out again following his wife's silent instruction.

Eventually, Daisy had recovered enough to talk about the dancing, then the happy walk home; when talking about the kissing she became more sombre …

After a long pause she said, 'Then he put his hand here' – mimicking him placing his hand on her breast. She was in tears again. 'I don't want no one else to know, apart from you, Sara. I'm so ashamed of my life before I came here, it were awful.' There was a long pause as she gathered herself. 'Just now I thought I was gunna get attacked again.'

Sara was unsure of what to say, hugging the girl to her, she said, 'Daisy what he did was obviously too soon for you but that is what people do who love each other. It's called fondling, it is supposed to be pleasant, for both parties.'

She felt the girl shudder, then vehemently she said, 'Well, it ain't for me. I think it's disgustin'.'

Sara held her for a long time until the crying stopped. She recognised the damage her father had done to her. She doubted whether Daisy would ever be able to have a normal relationship with a man. What a terrible loss she thought.

CHAPTER 16

A whooping cough outbreak occurred; Sophie did everything she could to prevent her daughter catching the disease. She knew it could be fatal. She spent days watching her child like a hawk but, almost inevitably, the baby's breathing became laboured. A visit to the GP was inconclusive. He agreed Charlotte's breathing was difficult, but he was unable to confirm whooping cough. There was no whooping.

Bridget, their nanny, had taken a week's holiday and gone home to Ireland. Sophie took leave from work to care for her child.

Charley's condition slowly worsened; her breathing became ever more difficult. The long period of coughing which was debilitating for the baby was also tearing at Sophie, now worn down by lack of sleep and fear for her child. She was grey with fatigue. One evening when Tim came home, he saw her in the back cabin kneeling by their bed silently praying.

Tim slipped back out of the door and sat on a fold-up chair they had placed there. A long time later he heard the whistle of the kettle. Re-entering the boat, he found his wife crying her eyes out. Holding Charley in her arms near the stove. The walls of the galley were running with water.

He went to turn the kettle off, but Sophie stopped him. 'The nurse said the steam would help.' Turning towards him, sobbing uncontrollably, she said, 'I don't think I can save her, Tim.' Her words a clear indicator of her terrible fear and torment.

Seeing her face in the galley lamp he saw how old she appeared, her eyes red, her cheeks sunken, she had clearly lost weight.

'When did you last eat?' he asked.

The only reply was a shake of the head.

Tim realised he had not paid enough attention. On more than one occasion on his return from work he had been told that Sophie had eaten earlier. He now realised this was not true. 'Right, we are going to get some food into you, how about a tin of mushroom soup, you like that?'

'I cannot eat anything.'

'You have to try, if not for you for Charley.'

'She will not feed – she chokes on it.'

'I will heat up a tin of soup and you try one mouthful.' Tim was really worried, not just for his child but also for his wife. There was no milk, so Tim went outside on to the front deck and opened the cold storage, removing a bottle of milk; he threw his head up at the dark sky and shouted: 'IF THERE IS ANYONE UP THERE, WE NEED HELP NOW, PLEASE.' All this roared in a mixture of fear and anger. He had not been this scared since he had sat beside his mother all those years ago when she was dying of flu in a London hospital.

Sophie must have heard but said nothing when he went back inside.

She ate most of the soup but that was all and then agreed to try and sleep. Ten minutes later she was sleeping soundly. Tim cuddled his child into dawn's first light. Cold and stiff he rose and walked around the cabin.

Sophie appeared, he apologised for waking her, she took Charley off him saying nothing.

'Tea, madam?' he asked.

'Yes please, why did you let me sleep so long? You will be out on your feet at work.'

'I will call and tell them I'll be late in.'

He washed, shaved, and climbed into the still warm bed; he fell asleep almost immediately.

It felt as though he had been asleep only a few minutes when he was woken by Sophie's terror-filled voice. 'Tim, wake up, wake up, she is not breathing. I think she is dying.'

Tim went from sound asleep to wide awake in a heartbeat. Taking his daughter from Sophie he marched out into the galley and turned on the bright ceiling light, holding her over his arm he patted her back. Nothing happened, she was still not breathing, when he turned her face up, he could see her colour fading. Opening her mouth, he spotted a ball of grey-green mucus blocking her throat. Now with her in the crook of his left arm he used his little finger to probe the ghastly lump. Some of it started to come away. Finally, he had it all. Then he noticed the child's greying face. Putting his daughter over his arm again he patted her back, nothing. Transferring his grip to her ankles he held her upside down and began a firm repetitive slap on her back.

He heard Sophie's cries becoming desperate, 'Tim she is … she is dying. Oh, please God help her. I cannot bear it.' Sophie tried to take the child from him, he held her off. He recognised she was in a blind panic; he could see the terrible pain she was in.

He cudgelled his memory to remember what he'd been taught at scouts. How many times do I press down? I can't remember.' He was fighting back his own panic. He placed Charley down on the rug. Gently he used what he could remember from all those years ago.

His mouth covered hers, one gentle breath into her, still nothing, then more gentle presses on her chest another breath into her, the same result. Now he was shouting at the top of his lungs: 'Breathe child breathe!!' – commanding his daughter to respond. His voice carried all the power in his body. Again, his mouth covered hers and he breathed into her more firmly, his life-giving warm breath filled her lungs. His baby spasmed, pulled a long, long breath in, then cried louder than either of them had heard from her before. Both adults were laughing and crying at the same time while holding each other and their baby who was still crying extremely loudly.

Later the two of them sat quietly, saying little, alternately holding their sleeping child while watching the sun come up.

*

Tim, thinking back a week later, with Charley showing real improvement, he recognised that the terrible night when she almost died was her turning point.

CHAPTER 17

Tim, on a whim one morning, stepped on the scales before getting dressed, 'What!' he exclaimed before rapidly stepping off again. Bending down he picked up the scales to correct the obvious discrepancy, he knew they needed adjusting. He was horrified to discover they were accurate. Placing them back down on the floor he stepped on them again. He was half a stone heavier than when Sophie became pregnant. She was now attending keep-fit classes to lose the weight which she had gained while she was carrying Charley.

Talking to himself, he grumbled, 'I'm not going running.' He had hated it ever since secondary school, there it was compulsory. He had thrown up every twenty paces or so for the full two miles, and he was made to do it anyway.

✳

Tim was still racking his brain trying to think of something that would make him fitter. Then he thought of the rowing eights. The rowing skiff crewed by the women was a common sight on the river, the men's Eight appeared less often. What appealed to him was the precision, the control of strength, ensuring that every ounce of energy was used to drive the craft forward. Perhaps he would wander down to the club house next Sunday. He would check with Sophie first.

When he broached the subject at breakfast later that morning he was surprised when Sophie disclosed that she had rowed at university and then added, 'I would like to take it up again.'

Hang on, he thought, this was supposed to be my idea. From what she is saying, it sounds as though she had been good at it. I am going to appear to be a right wally.

Sophie read his body language, 'Sorry I did not mean to take over. You go and do it, we cannot both do it anyway because of madam.'

'No, no, no. Are you saying that because you think my ego is so fragile, I could not stand you being so much better than me?'

'Nooo ...' Sophie responded. Her face giving away the truth. The half-hidden smile was another clue.

'Right, we will both do it and you can help me train. We will get Nanny in to care for Charley and we will row on Sunday mornings, both of us.'

Sophie said nothing, Tim's response sounded like an ultimatum, then she realised she was looking forward to it. The time spent on the river in the past had always been one of the highlights of her week. The peace and quiet, the regularity of the stroke had been somehow cathartic. She always felt refreshed and relaxed when she came off the water, tired but pleasantly so.

'I will ask Nanny if she can help on a Sunday morning?'

'Don't ask her, tell her, we pay her a lot of money to be here when we need her.'

'You are starting to sound like my father you arrogant ... thing, and before you say anything, I know you will consider that a compliment. Well, it is not.' Sophie could see the barely controlled laughter dancing in his eyes as he turned away.

Tim had huge admiration for Sophie's father. Yes, he was arrogant, autocratic, and demanding and expected people to jump when he said jump. But if you worked hard and were respectful and diligent, he was extremely supportive and willing to help.

Thinking of her father, Sophie had noticed how he always seemed pleased to see Tim when they were together. Most of their discussions were business-based but given the similarity of their companies that was not surprising. Often their conversation moved on to politics and world affairs, subjects that both Tim and her father held strong although differing views, but, to Sophie's surprise, the two men were able to discuss it even if at the end they had to agree to disagree.

✳

The following day Sophie's first meeting was a lunch appointment with her boss Terry Wells and a large supplier. Business lunches were now the norm, this was one of the reasons she was putting on weight. Rowing would help.

When she broached the idea of working Sunday mornings to Nanny over a cup of coffee her response was unexpected.

'I would love to do that if Charley and I can come and watch.'

'You go to the eight am mass on a Sunday, do you not?'

'I do, it's simple, I'll go to the evening service.' Noting Sophie's hesitation, she said, 'I'll not let her anywhere near the water I promise – it sounds such fun. Me and my brothers were always in the water at home. I was a good swimmer in those days. We had a large lake on our land, my father taught all of us to swim.'

'Where was home?' asked Sophie.

'We lived in County Kerry on my father's farm near a little village called Dooks, its bigger today. There's a golf course and the sea. It's very pretty. I never appreciated it as a girl, I wanted excitement, bright lights and rock and roll.'

'You do not sound very Irish, more American sometimes.'

'Like many Irish folk, I went to America – I was eighteen. Do you remember, I told you? I married a serviceman, but he was killed in Vietnam in 1971.'

'Oh, I am so sorry Nanny. It must still be raw for you.'

'I'm OK most of the time, now and then it hurts. I am happiest when I'm working with Charley.'

*

The following Sunday morning found Tim, Sophie, Charley and Nanny at the local rowing club. A tall fair-haired man in shorts, an Aran cricket jumper and a life jacket was standing by the door to the wooden clubhouse.

'Can I help?' he asked. Tim explained they were hoping there may be some vacancies.

The man said, 'Yes there are, will you all be wanting to join?'

'No, just me and my daughter,' said Tim.

The man thought for a moment, then laughed. Sophie just tutted.

'Perhaps we should introduce ourselves, I am Gordon, the club's skipper, and you are?'

'I'm Tim – my wife Sophia.'

'Sophie,' she said, correcting Tim, then introduced Nanny Bridget, who said, 'Everyone calls me, Nanny.'

A large, dark-blue Jaguar pulled into the club car park. Out of the corner of her eye, Sophie saw a young redheaded man in shorts and a blue T-shirt spring from the vehicle. He seemed familiar but she could not place him. He walked past her but then stopped and turned to face her.

'Sophie, Sophia Vieri, goodness it has been ages, how are you?' Then seeing Tim and the baby he said, 'You are obviously very married.'

Sophie said, 'This is Tim, my husband and this is Charlotte, known as Charley.'

The redhead introduced himself as Quentin, then Sophie explained they had been at uni together.

'So, what are you doing here?' he asked.

'They are hoping to join the club, Quentin,' responded Gordon.

Sliding his eyes up and down her body and mentally undressing her as he did so, he said, 'You will cheer the place up, Sophie.' Tim didn't laugh, he gave Quentin a quick hard stare – drawing a line. Sophie, he noticed was a little pink. Tim had marked his card; he would be watching him.

'Come in and have a cuppa,' suggested the skipper. 'We can give you some info.'

Minutes later they were sitting on wooden benches at a long deal table sipping hot tea from white, blue-banded mugs. The building was an extensive pale timber structure with exceptionally long narrow boats suspended off the floor in racks. Tim fell in love with one. It was all varnished wood and it shone as it lay there. It was the same colour as a new conker.

Pointing at it, Tim asked Gordon, 'Is that called a skiff?'

'Yes, it's mine. I don't use it very often. I would hate to damage it, if I did it would cost a lot to mend it.'

'It is beautiful,' agreed Tim.

Sophie saw the almost imperceptible nodding as Tim looked at it. 'I think Daddy might be buying a wooden boat if he is any good at this rowing malarkey,' whispered Sophie into Charlotte's ear.

Tim looked at her sideways, having half heard her, one eyebrow raised in a query. Sophie smiled at him.

'Have either of you rowed before?' asked Gordon.

Tim sat shaking his head, Sophie said nothing. Tim poked her in the arm. The skipper appeared perplexed, wondering what was going on.

'I rowed at university,' offered Sophie.

'At what level?'

'The women's eight,' said Sophie quietly.

'At what university?'

'Oxford.'

Tim sat bolt upright in his chair totally surprised saying, 'So you have raced in the Oxford and Cambridge boat race?'

Sophie just nodded.

'Did you win?' asked Gordon.

'No, we finished second,' there was a pause and then Gordon and Tim laughed. Suddenly their table was surrounded by men and women all asking questions at once. Sophie answered their question as best she could through the hubbub.

'Steady folks,' said Gordon. 'I think you should back off now. Sophie and Tim have not agreed to join yet, let's not frighten them off.'

The crowd moved away after congratulating her, talking nineteen to the dozen as they left.

'How come you've never mentioned it?' asked a surprised Tim. Sophie shrugged her shoulders.

Gordon said, 'Do you know what's funny? I have been sitting here wondering what the best way is to start your training. I think you will be training us, Sophie.'

She was shaking her head in denial. 'All I want to do it for is to get fit and enjoy it.'

'Would you like to have a try today? You could use the practice boat.'

She looked at Tim who could see the shine in her eyes, he knew she wanted to do it.

'I've got Charley,' said Nanny. 'You carry on.'

A kind-looking young, blonde woman wearing jeans and a pale cricket jumper approached with a bundle of clothing, saying, 'This is my kit, all freshly washed and ironed. You are very welcome to use it, then I can brag that it has been worn by you.'

'This is Sam, Samantha, my wife,' Gordon informed them.

'Thank you Sam, that is kind of you. I will take you up on your offer.'

'If you follow me, I will show you the women's changing room,' said Sam.

'You must be extremely proud of her,' said Gordon, as the two women walked away.

'To tell you the truth I never knew, until today. Her mother does not like people making a show of themselves, as she puts it.'

'While we are alone, I would like to point out how important it would be to the club if your wife joined, and you of course,' said Gordon.

Tim laughed out loud. 'Let's be honest, it won't make a scrap of difference if I am a member or not,' he said, still laughing.

'Oh, I don't know, there is always the extra membership fee,' said Gordon, also laughing, 'and by the way we would not expect your wife to pay.'

'She will insist on paying,' said Tim.

Shortly afterwards the two women rejoined them. 'Oh wow,' said Tim, you look fantastic in that gear.'

'I have to say,' said Sam, 'I don't look like that in those clothes.'

At Sophie's insistence, Gordon gave her a briefing about the skiff just to reacquaint her with the specifics. There was a worrying wobble as she got into the craft.

'Oops nearly,' she called out.

Once seated Sophie gathered the oars together and eased the skiff away from the pontoon until she could put the bankside oar onto the water, then she began the strokes. Slowly and with care she rowed away from them down river and around a bend. Stopping, Sophie placed both blades flat on the water's surface making the craft stable. Wiggling her bottom around she settled into a better position. Turning the craft, she rowed back towards the clubhouse. Rounding the bend in the opposite direction she began to feel the nervousness fade, then the rhythm came back. The long pull, the seat sliding, feathering the blades so they skimmed back across the surface, cheating the wind. The hundreds of hours she had put in at Oxford on the water made themselves felt, muscle memory took over, her brain remembered. Now it all happened with a fluid purposeful symmetry, boat and body now one. Sliding past the clubhouse the years flew away, she was twenty again, the posture, the timing, the accuracy returned, it was once again effortless. Her heart swelled in her chest. She was ecstatic.

Clapping broke out, above it all she heard Gordon shout out. 'That! Ladies and gentlemen, is how you do it.'

Gordon came and plonked himself down next to Tim. 'What about you Tim? Would you like to give it a try?'

'Gordon, I think it is blindingly obvious to everybody I will never achieve my wife's level of competence.'

A few people helped her put the skiff to bed. They had not seen Nanny for some time, she appeared from a group of women who had been talking babies.

Sophie got changed and they drove away, Tim having paid for both of them. She was quiet, surprised by how much she had enjoyed it. Next week could not come fast enough.

Later that night Sophie was preparing Charlotte for bed and as usual Tim could hear them whispering. He tiptoed over to the partially open nursery door and listened.

'Mummy was awfully nervous at first, it has been a long time since I sat in a skiff, I nearly fell in. Towards the end it was as though I had never been away, the pull, the glide, the feather. Would you like Mummy to teach you when you get older?'

Charley nodded.

'OK then that is a deal.'

Tim tiptoed away from the door; he already understood just how much his wife had enjoyed it. Her work schedule was punishing. This may encourage her to take some time out he thought.

CHAPTER 18

Tim had recognised that for the last few days Mr Woodman had not been himself, withdrawn and uncommunicative. Twice during the day, he had found him staring into space and had appeared startled when Tim said something.

'Are you ok?'

Answering the older man pulled a wry face saying, 'No not really Tim, today would have been my 50th wedding anniversary. I don't know why it has affected me like this. I have always observed the date but this time ...' He ceased talking leaving the sentence hanging. He shrugged then raised his eyes at Tim, sighed and went back to work.

Later that afternoon, Tim rang Sophie and explained how upset his godfather was and why.

'I think it would be nice if we took Charley and fish and chips around this evening,' suggested Sophie.

'You make it sound as though she is part of the meal,' laughed Tim.

Sophie told him off for saying such a terrible thing and then continued, 'I will ring him now, if I tell him the baby is coming, he will agree. He loves her almost as much as we do.'

✳

Tim and Sophie were sitting in Mr Woodman's flat above shop Number One. The place he had lived in ever since he'd left the merchant navy.

Tim felt that his godfather had always been a very private man; very efficient, self-reliant, he could not remember when he had not achieved whatever he had set out to do. He'd always been Tim's role model. To see the elderly man so unmanned surprised him. He recognised that without him noticing, time had taken its toll on Mr Woodman. He made a mental note to be more supportive and involve him more in the life of his family.

The arrival of Sophie and Charley had wrought a real change in the man. It was the first time Tim had seen him smile in days. Tucking into fish and chips, he had Charley sitting on his lap, a supporting arm around the child and he, eating one handed.

'Shall I take her Mr Woodman, so you can eat properly?'

'No, we are fine thanking you Sophie, aren't we little one?' The question was addressed to the child on his lap who was stuffing her face with a cooled chip.

Watching him smiling down at her daughter, Sophie recognised that this was the first time in a long while that she had seen him so happy.

'Did you want children, Mr Woodman?' enquired Sophie.

'We wanted a large family, but she died while I was away.' Sophie was aware that there was more that was not said.

'What did she die of Mr Woodman?' asked Tim gently.

'Her mother always said that she died of a broken heart. She had received a telegram saying I was missing, presumed dead. Apparently, she just gave up, she sat in a chair and faded away.'

'Oh, poor you,' said Sophie leaning across and squeezing his arm.

'Poor lady,' said Tim.

Charley, sensing the emotion in the room started to cry.

Sophie half rose from her chair saying, 'Let me have her, Mr Woodman.'

'No, you're ok, I've got her.' With that he stood up and walked the baby around the room humming quietly deep in his throat

The young couple exchanged glances.

Charley quickly fell asleep and was then placed in a deep armchair with her cover.

Tim said, 'Can I ask what had happened to you that triggered the telegram?'

'Tim you cannot ask that, it is none of our business, you are raking up the past. It must be painful for Mr Woodman,' chided Sophie.

'I don't mind, the first time I was torpedoed we got the Lifeboat away and were soon picked up by a nearby destroyer. The next time was a completely different kettle of fish. It happened in the early evening. I saw the tracks of the two torpedoes coming towards us and I ran to the side of the ship to watch them – a really stupid thing to do. I was immediately above them when they hit. The explosion blew me up in the air, a long way up. Then I hit a derrick, a type of crane, that knocked me to one side. It dislocated my shoulder, but it also saved my life. If I had fallen back on the deck from that height I may not have survived. I remember seeing how high I was. I don't remember much after that. I think hitting the water knocked me out. I came to, shivering with cold in a Lifeboat with some other men. I had lost most of my clothing. I had a pair of shorts to keep me decent, that was about it. There was some machine-gun fire, so the fitter men rowed us away into the dark in case the U-boat was shooting survivors. When dawn came, we were totally alone, the sea was virtually still so if there had been other Lifeboats, we would definitely have seen them. I drifted in and out of consciousness, I did not realise how badly I had been injured. The Doctors later told me a lot of things I didn't understand but apparently, I had severe concussion and various other internal injuries. The worst thing was I had no memory, I didn't know my name, my address, nothing. There was a medic in the Lifeboat. He almost certainly saved my life.'

'Oh, my goodness,' said Sophie, clearly on the edge of tears.

'Don't fret lass, I was a lucky one, eight of us got into that Lifeboat two weeks later three of us got out. Most of them died of their injuries, the rest of us endured. We were always short of water – rain was a blessing. To this day I never complain if it rains.'

'What happened to you?' Tim asked.

'I was six weeks in a military hospital on Crete. I still had little or no memory. Eventually they shipped me home to England. Our journey home was all fits and starts, calling at different places. Sometimes we stayed in port because of enemy activity. We were homeward bound for what felt like forever. Then I was in Plymouth hospital for quite a while, until one morning I woke up and knew who I was. They shipped me home, that was when I discovered she'd died.' Mr Woodman's head dropped to his chest his eyes screwed shut. His voice broke, he asked, 'Can you pour me a large whisky lad please – have whatever you two want.'

When his drink arrived, he accepted it, wiped his eyes with the back of his hand, lifted the glass to his lips and swallowed half of it.

Sophie walked across to his chair and threw her arms around him. Moments later he straightened, Sophie stepped away.

'Sorry about that you two, I must be getting old.'

'God help us,' said Tim, 'please don't apologise, I think you are amazing.'

'You certainly are,' added Sophie. 'What did you do then?'

'Not a lot really,' he replied. 'My injuries were slow to mend, I was extremely weak for months, but slowly I grew stronger. My mother made sure that I ate properly to help me regain my strength. I think both my parents lived frugally to make sure my diet was good. Eventually I felt well enough to do a few hours here in the shop every day. I will always remember the date my Doctor finally signed me off as fit for work – VE Day, 8 May 1945.'

On the way home that night in the Bentley the young couple sat close together holding hands, silently reliving in their minds' eyes the terrible things that Mr Woodman had talked about, that he had never talked about before. After this, Sophie arranged for Mr Woodman and Tom Cooper, Tim's father, to have supper on Sea Maiden on a regular basis.

CHAPTER 19

Tom Cooper awoke early one morning to the sound of strange, barely audible noises from the kitchen. Tiptoeing downstairs he discovered a small boy half in and half out of his kitchen window. The lad was trapped, his blue, padded coat had become snagged on the window catch and he could not reach behind himself to free it. There was a loud ripping noise as the child's struggles became evermore frantic.

Tom Cooper seized his arm saying, 'I'm not gunner hurt you, lad. You can't go out that way you're thoroughly stuck. Come back in, I'll make you tea and a biscuit. You are gunna tear your coat to pieces if you carry on like this.' He made a mental note not to leave the kitchen window open in future. Reluctantly the youngster obeyed him. As the boy reached the floor Tom saw his bloody knee.

'How did you do that?' he asked.

'I fell getting over your fence, Mr.'

Applying a dilute solution of Dettol to the wound with a twist of lint, he became aware of how terribly thin he was. The boy's dark hair was trimmed very short into what in Tom's youth would have been considered a crew cut. He could not explain why he felt the way he did but to him the boy looked feral. He had something of the wild about him. His clothing wasn't shabby, but it was creased and dirty.

'When did you last eat, lad?'

'Err, I dunno.' He could see the boy working out when it was.

'About four days ago, I pinched a pie out 'uv a shop.'

'How about a hot cup of char and a sandwich?'

'Nah, I'm gunna go I am.'

'Ok, I'm having some breakfast. If you do go, I suggests you go out the front door, you won't hurt yourself that way. Now let me see, cheese sandwich, cuppa tea. Pickle?' he asked the lad.

'No, I'm off ta.'

'Oh well, please yourself son,' he said peering into the fridge. 'You know what, I think I'll have a bit a bacon, I love a bit a bacon. There's a couple of eggs in here as well, they'll do.'

The smell of the bacon cooking filled the kitchen and wafted out into the hall where the boy was standing holding the front door open. There was no sound from the hallway as the kettle began to boil. Tom ignored the child. He knew the boy would either run or he wouldn't. He certainly wasn't going to hold him here by force. He began humming to himself as he assembled the meal on two plates. As he placed them on the table he heard the click of the door lock and the footsteps returning. Half an hour later, having eaten every scrap plus two slices of buttered toast and two cups of tea, the lad was struggling to stay awake.

'Why don't you go and have a nap on the couch. I won't lock the front door – you can go if you want. I'll get you a blanket.'

It was mid-afternoon before the boy came too. Tom had rung the shop and explained he would not be in.

The boy had woken with a start. 'Where am I?' he asked, clearly frightened.

'You're in the same house as you were in this morning and the front door is still open if you want to go. I found your bag under the hedge outside. I assume it's yours,' he said as he passed it to him. Nodding the boy searched through it and seemed happy there was nothing missing.

'Now if I may say so lad, you need a bath. I'll find some pyjamas for you. They will be too big but better than nothing. They were my sons. Does that sound like a good idea?'

One hour later Tom heard the boy coming downstairs. 'How was your bath, lad?'

'I fell asleep, Mr. I ain't never been in a proper bath before.'

Tom noticed the pyjamas hung off the boy. He found it difficult to judge the child's age, the lad was so small and thin.

'Cup of tea or a mug of cocoa?'

'Tea please, Mr. I ain't never 'ad cocoa. I don't know what it is.'

'How about you try a mug an' if you don't like it, I'll make you tea.'

'Thanks, Mr.'

Halfway through preparing the drinks Tom stuck his head around the kitchen door and discovered the boy had fallen asleep again. Tom stayed in the kitchen while his tea brewed, allowing the boy to sleep. He realised this could have been Tim. His son could have run away when he threw him out. Shaking his head, he was so ashamed of how badly he had treated his boy after his wife died, selling the house out from under him, leaving him on his own to run the market stall, blaming the lad for his wife's death. He had apologised on more than one occasion, but he still didn't feel right about it. He would, he realised, have given anything if he could have undone it, wound the clock back.

Shaking his head, he walked the tray into the lounge, the rattle of the cups and saucers as he placed the tray on the coffee table roused the child.

A little later as the boy was slurping the hot cocoa and obviously enjoying it, Tom asked, 'What do people call you, lad?'

'Sammy.'

'I reckon you've travelled a long way – where have you come from?'

The boy was clearly alarmed and said, 'I ain't telling, I've got to go, I 'ave. Where's me cloves?'

Tom recognised if he tried to keep the child here the boy would definitely run at the first opportunity.

'They are all ready for you – I've washed them.' Walking into the kitchen he gathered the clothes. Returning he said, 'Pop up stairs and put 'em on.'

The lad returned downstairs fully clothed a few minutes later. Tom said, 'Now listen lad I'm not gunna stop you going but if you ever want somewhere safe to stay come back. Have you got any money?' Knowing full well the child would have nothing.

'I'm all right thanks, Mr. I gets by.'

'OK son, I tell you what, there is a brick on the front step that I leave the milk money under, I will put a pound under it when I remember. You can't have the milk money though. Do you understand?'

'Thanks, Mr. I don't think I'll need it.'

He stood and watched as the boy made his way down the street. The lad turned the corner without a backward glance. Shutting the front door and walking into the lounge he said to himself, 'Sorry, Tim lad, I recognise that could have been you. I would never have been able to forgive myself.' He lay awake a long time that night.

The following morning in the shop he shared the details of the boy's visit with Tim, Mr Woodman and Harry.

They all agreed there was little or nothing they could do. Tom checked under the brick every morning; the money was always still there. The weeks passed; he could not get the lad out of his head. He knew it was guilt over how he had treated his son after the death of his wife.

It had been years before he recognised the injustice he had visited on his son and the foolishness of blaming the death of his wife on his boy. He had apologised but knew his behaviour had been inexcusable.

CHAPTER 20

Tim seized the left side of his chest with his right hand, the box he was carrying fell to the floor, breaking open and spilling its contents across the tiles. With his eyesight greying out he felt his knees buckling and the pain in his chest was all consuming. He was unaware but he was emitting a loud growling noise. The sound and the grimace on his face, a clear indicator of the agony he was experiencing. Now he was following the trajectory of the wooden box downwards. He flung out an arm to grasp the nearby counter edge but miscalculated the distance, his fingernails scrapped across the shiny rounded edge but found no purchase. His last thought was that this was a silly way to die. Before he reached the broken timbers that were going to give him some nasty cuts he passed out. His head banged down hard and bounced twice as he hit the floor.

*

When he came too sometime later, he could not work out where he was. He had a mask on his face and there were various wires that connected him to a large monitor. A nurse was sitting beside his bed.

Sitting forward she asked, 'How are you feeling? Do you know where you are?'

He was not sure where he was, everywhere was bright. Bright white, bright light. There was a strong smell of something, he couldn't place it. He knew he had smelt it before.

The nurse asked him again, 'Mr Cooper, do you know where you are?'

Tim shook his head, that was a mistake. The pain in his head was so severe he thought he was going to pass out. A grimace distorted his face.

'Please try and lie still. I will contact the Doctor.' She pressed a button by his bed.

Minutes later a Doctor with a shock of red hair was standing by his bed taking his pulse. While this was happening, Tim became aware of something on his cheek, reaching up he felt a dressing of some kind and began to fiddle with it. The Doctor reached down and stopped him pulling at it. He explained, 'A large splinter of wood from the box punctured your cheek, you have some stitches in there. You can tell the girls it's a duelling scar. You need to leave it alone for a few days to let it heal.'

'Why am I so tired, Doctor?' asked Tim, in a slurred voice. He could feel sleep stealing over him again.

'We have given you something to keep you quiet,' was the response.

Much later he could hear Sophie talking quietly to someone at his bedside. Fighting the desire to return to sleep he forced one eye open and saw Sophie holding Charley on her knee talking to the Doctor. He realised she had dressed with him in mind and was wearing the delphinium blue dress he loved that floated around her knees as she walked. The child spotted his eyes were open and slithered off her mother's lap and began an assault on the bed side determined to be with her Daddy. Watching her climb he was struck again by how she was the perfect likeness to her mother with her good looks, blue eyes and blonde hair.

Sophie reached out to stop her, but the Doctor intervened and said, 'That's fine as long as she is quiet. We will talk again tomorrow when we have done some tests.'

Sophie moved the chair closer as Charley made herself comfortable under the blue blanket in Tim's arms. She asked, 'Are you all right now Daddy?'

'Yes, Charley, thank you.'

Sophie held his hand; he could see moisture in the corner of her eyes. 'Are you in any pain? The Doctor said you have a mild concussion. I did not hear my phone over the noise. I am so sorry Tim. We were in a factory viewing a new line Terry Wells wants to stock. Do you remember what happened?'

'It was like a band tightening around my chest. It was getting tighter all the time. I must have passed out. As I fell, I do remember thinking this was a silly way to die.'

Now the tears were very evident, sliding down Sophie's face. 'You must get better. How the hell will I cope on my own?' Her fear was driving her anger. 'You will get better or else, do you hear me?'

A nurse walking by raised an eyebrow.

Sophie noticed and mouthed an apology, 'I am sorry, but I am so scared Tim. What would I do without you?' Now she was even more emphatic.

Speaking slowly and quietly, he said, 'Firstly, you would manage perfectly well. Secondly, I am not going anywhere. I have not achieved half what I want to do yet.'

Charley, now aware of the tension in the air and her mother's fear began to cry.

Sophie, wiping away the tears with a pretty pink hankey, stood up and attempted to lift her daughter from the bed who was now beginning to cry harder still and at the same time locking her arms around Tim.

'Don't worry I've got her,' he said using his fingers to dry the child's tears. In a deep, calm voice and smiling at his daughter he said, 'Don't worry little one, Mummy is all right now and Daddy's fine.'

Leaning in she rubbed her face against his chest to dry it.

'How long has she been doing this?' he asked. Tim's frown indicating his disapproval brought laughter from Sophie, changing her mood, and dismissing the fear for now. Her amusement deepened his visible displeasure. 'I suggest you make her aware it is not acceptable.' This delivered in a stern voice a little above whisper.

'Why me? That should be we, you and me. She is your daughter as well, you arrogant so and so.'

Matron appeared. 'You need to rest, Mr Cooper.' This was clearly a command not a request. 'Mrs Cooper, I suggest you return at the normal visiting hours. Shall we see you later?'

Sophie nodded.

Matron marched away down the ward.

Sophie, pulling a face said, 'I am sorry, I did not think.'

'My fault for getting cross. The Doctors and nurses are terrified of her.'

'So am I,' admitted Sophie as she leaned in to kiss him goodbye.

Tim could see the fear return to her eyes.

Charley, now riding on Sophie's left hip, was big eyed, unsure what to make of all the different emotions she was sensing.

'Please don't worry, I am feeling much better, and I am in the right place. Can you make it later?'

'Yes, I will get Nanny to see to madam.'

Sophie kissed him again.

'I am really sorry, I've frightened you. I am sure the Doctors will sort me out.'

With their foreheads touching Tim could feel the torrent of her tears.

'Tim, what will I do if I lose you? Without you nothing makes sense. I have never loved anyone the way I love you.'

Charley reached out and tried to wipe away her mother's tears. The child's actions served to break the mood. Both of her parents smiled through the tears. Tim spotted matron returning and said, 'You had better go.' He nodded towards the advancing woman.

Sophie gathered her coat and bag, placed Charley on her right hip, kissed him quickly and walked away down the ward. As usual most of the male patients' eyes followed her. Tim was unsure how he felt about it. He realised it must happen to her all the time. One thing he was sure of, he would never take her beauty for granted.

*

On her return that evening Sophie was more relaxed than she had been earlier. 'I have had a long chat with the Doctor, and he has assured me that you will be fine as long as you take notice of this warning. When you get home, we will discuss your lifestyle.' Tim went to interrupt. 'This is not up for discussion, Tim, you have responsibilities now, there will be changes.'

*

The following morning, Tim was returned from the Xray department to his bed in the ward. A tall young Doctor came and introduced himself as Dr Goddard, lowering himself on to the beside chair as he did so.

'Hallo Mr Cooper, I am sure you will be pleased to know we have found no visible damage. There is an anomaly however – you are fairly unique.' The Doctor paused, smiling.

With a furrowed brow Tim said, 'I'm sorry, I don't know what you mean.'

'You have an extra rib. It's remarkably rare. Apart from that everything seems OK. You will be with us for a few days while we do some more tests.' – rising from the chair the Doctor patted him on the arm – 'Bye for now.'

*

Later that evening Sophie arrived with Charley on her hip, still wearing her working clothes, black suit and white blouse, she appeared a little less flustered.

'Are you ok?' he asked.

'Yes, it has been one of those days and I had forgotten Nanny was having a night off. Never mind we are here now.'

Sophie made herself comfortable in the chair beside the bed. Charley climbed up and wiggled herself into the position she had adopted before, snuggled into the bed, legs tucked under his blue blanket. Tim explained what the Doctor had said, and it helped put Sophie's mind at rest.

*

The following morning, Jessica came to see him. She was looking very smart in her pale-grey, wool, skirt and jacket and carrying a brand-new briefcase. 'May I say Jessica you are a welcome sight.'

'Thank you Mr Cooper,' she responded, straight faced. Jessica now had the measure of her boss.

His reply was proceeded by a burst of laughter. Eventually having gathered himself, he said, 'That's slapped me back in my place.'

Jessica just sat.

'I like the briefcase,' he said.

'I treated myself,' she announced, stroking the soft pale leather.

'Give Sophie the receipt, we'll pay for it.'

'I do not want to do that Tim, thank you. I need it to be mine.' She did not explain that for her it was a symbol of her first proper job since leaving uni. Working for her father, who was a Doctor, she had carried a lot of responsibility, but the money was less than half what she was earning now. Also in this job, she had gained on her own abilities not because she was family' but through hard work and showing Tim and Sophie how capable she was.

'You obviously have some stuff for me?'

Jessica quickly had the bed strewn with papers and had started relaying the information. Suddenly a loud stentorian voice boomed out across the ward.

'WHAT DO YOU THINK YOU ARE DOING?' Reaching the bed, matron wrenched the briefcase from Jessica and began stuffing paperwork into it any old how. 'This is the reason you are in here you stupid man, you are supposed to be resting.' With that she slapped the now full case back into Jessica's arms, saying, 'I would like you to leave now, please.'

Jessica scuttled from the ward.

Tim looked around the ward, there were a lot of scared faces.

*

Mr Woodman and his father visited the ward that evening. After the normal questions Tom said to Mr Woodman, 'You know this is all put on don't you, anything to get out of having to do an honest day's work.'

'I'm sure your right, Tom. The stunts some people pull.'

Tim had to admit to himself that he felt better for the jokes and the banter.

*

Two days later, Tim was pushed by a porter in a wheelchair down to a large room with various exercise machinery around the walls. He was met by an attractive, middle-aged Doctor who introduced herself as Linda. A large Afro Caribbean male nurse stood nearby.

'This is Robert,' said Linda. The two men exchanged a greeting.

'Have you used a treadmill before, Mr Cooper?' asked the Doctor.

Tim, shaking his head, was surprised to find himself a little nervous.

'If you feel any pain or dizziness, you must tell us and we will stop,' the Doctor assured him.

Various wires were attached to his chest and abdomen which led from a large box of dials, switches and lights. It occasionally emitted various beeps and other noises.

As Tim stepped up on to the treadmill, Robert noticing Tim's concern, said quietly, 'I won't let you fall, Mr Cooper.'

'Thank you, Robert. If I pass out, I'll try and fall your way.' Both men laughed.

The Doctor noticed but said nothing.

The treadmill was started, slowly at first gaining speed as time passed. Tim decided they were trying to kill him; very quickly he began to gasp for breath.

'We are going to slow the machine down now, are you ready?'

Tim gasped, 'Yes.' Suddenly he felt unsteady and wobbled.

'Take my hand,' commanded Robert.

Tim reached over and grabbed his arm. As the machine stopped Robert led him to a wheelchair.

Tim feeling foolish said, 'Thank you, Robert. I went all wobbly.'

'That's why I'm here.'

The Doctor said, 'OK, I need to ask you some questions, we can go in the other room.'

After all the wires were disconnected, Tim was wheeled next door.

*

'Right,' said the Doctor, 'I want to get an idea of your lifestyle. Do you smoke?'

'No,' said Tim, dismissing the occasional cigar at Christmas.

'I have your weight – you are a little heavy. You could lose a few pounds. Have you put on weight lately?'

'Yes, I have. My job is now office-based before I was on the go all day.'

'What is an ordinary working day like?'

'Erm, I'm in the office reasonably early, I—'

'I need the detail. What time do you get up in the morning?'

'About six am. Breakfast's finished by seven, on my way shortly after.'

'Do you walk, bus, train or do you drive?'

Tim was becoming embarrassed. He found talking about his lifestyle – the considerable fortune, the Bentley, his chauffeur, the six houses, the two shops – difficult.

His mother, now long dead, was a woman with a firm opinion on braggarts and people boasting about how well they are doing.

'I don't drive, I get driven.'

'Taxi, you mean?'

'No. I own a car.'

'So, who drives that – your wife?'

'No,' said Tim, clearly becoming more uncomfortable by the moment. Huffing he said, 'My chauffeur drives it.'

The Doctor, surprised, sat back in her chair. She realised her error in deciding that this was an ordinary young man, drinking too much with a poor diet. The strong London accent had helped her pigeonhole him, incorrectly she realised.

'What is your job now?'

'I'm the chairman of a small retail company, a delicatessen chain. Although I'm rarely in the shops these days.'

'Were you promoted into your position?'

'Not really, after my mother died my father became too ill to work. When I was fifteen I began running my father's market stall full-time, since then we have opened two shops, hopefully another one soon. There are four of us on the board, one is my wife.'

'What do you do for lunch?'

Tim was quiet for some time.

The Doctor, tired of waiting for his response said in a stern voice, 'Let me put this another way, how many times a week do you miss lunch?' He could hear that she was not amused by his vague answers which were wasting her time.

He realised there was no point in him lying. 'It all depends …' Taking a deep breath he confessed that most days he worked through.

'When do you stop work?'

'Erm, about eight.'

'Then do you go straight home?'

'No, Mr Graham drives me to The Boat, that's my local, and I have a few drinks before I go back. I buy him a half of pale-ale – he will only have the one because he is driving.'

'What do you drink?'

'Whisky and dry ginger.'

'How many?'

'Two or three.'

'Doubles?' asked the Doctor.

Tim nodded. What he didn't mention was that Chick Evans, the landlord of The Boat, a long-time friend of Tim's father, kept his usual seat free for him each evening. A large whisky was sitting on the bar as he walked through the door.

'What time of night do you eat?'

Tim, wagging his head said, 'About 9.30 pm.'

'Wine with the meal?'

'Only one,' said Tim firmly.

'How many days a week do you work?'

'Six.'

'Sundays?'

'No, that I spend with my wife and child.'

'So, you work about, what, seventy hours per week, with fourteen hours between meals, too much alcohol, no exercise, and not enough sleep? Have you set out to kill yourself, Mr Cooper?'

Tim said nothing.

'I will make out a prescription for you. I want you to take it easy for a week or so. Lots of rest.'

Later while he was getting dressed, he could not believe how weak and giddy he felt, twice he had to grab hold of the bed to prevent himself falling.

The Doctor watched Tim being driven away in a large black Bentley.

CHAPTER 21

Sophie, unaware that he had been released from hospital, came home later that evening to find Tim asleep in his favourite shabby, chestnut-brown, cloth-covered armchair, now worn threadbare in places from constant use. She would have thrown it out ages ago if he would have let her.

His need for the toilet roused him from the chair and he swayed unsteadily as he became upright.

Sophie, now frightened, dumped Charley on the sofa and grabbed hold of him. 'Why have they let you out? You are obviously not well.'

Tim explained that the Doctors had warned him he may be unsteady because he had been lying down for six days, it would pass.

'I am going to put Charley to bed and then we will talk about this,' warned Sophie.

Half an hour later his wife handed him a cup of tea and said, 'You must tell me everything.'

He started to make light of what the Doctor had told him saying, 'I have been reassured that it was nothing to worry about.' Sophie, clearly extremely worried was becoming angry because of his prevarication.

'Tim, I am terrified that I am going to lose you and now you are obviously lying to me. How will Charley and I cope without you? Tell me the truth for God's sake. What did the Doctor say?'

Sophie did not disclose that she had cried herself to sleep most nights since his attack. She had at one stage thought that she should make some contingency plans in case the worst happened, then she had banished the idea, concerned that doing it might trigger some dreadful response. She gave herself a good talking to for even having such silly superstitious thoughts – she did not make any plans.

He realised she was not going to be fobbed off. 'I have had a mild coronary. The Doctors tell me that the medication I have been prescribed will protect me in the future.'

'Is that all?'

'No, I have to take more exercise and change my lifestyle.'

He recognised that the Doctor's question – "Have you set out to kill yourself?" – had brought him up short and made him realise things had to change.

'So, what specifically?' she enquired, determined to get a clearer picture of what needed to be done.

'As I have said, exercise, sensible hours, proper mealtimes, more sleep, more time off. The problem for me is that I enjoy the work, and most of it requires my day-to-day oversight.'

'I understand that Tim darling, we are both work obsessed, but there must be changes. We have to reduce our hours.'

He interrupted saying, 'But I have to make the decisions for most of what goes on.'

Sophie flapped her hand at him indicating he needed to move his legs so that she could sit on his lap. Now her tone was gentle and concerned as she placed her arm around him.

He sank his face into her neck and drew in a long breath then kissed her. 'If we could bottle your aroma, we would make a fortune.'

Sophie frowned at him then saying, 'Yes you do have to make the decisions, but have you seen the way my father uses Sally, his PA?' Seeing

Tim's knowing smile she admonished him. Both of them knew the couple were lovers.

'What I meant was my father reads the paperwork and then instructs Sally to complete the tasks. You do the whole thing yourself – you do not need to. With respect Tim, she would eat the workload, freeing you up for other things and shortening your hours.' Sophie also thought with her first-class education Jessica would make everything appear more professional.

Tim sat nodding while he thought about it. 'I expect she would make a better job of it.'

Sophie was searching for a response that would not be unkind. 'I am not sure about that, but it would make sense to use her skills. We are paying her enough.' Jessica had just received a pay rise.

Tim recognised Sophie was being kind to him. He kissed her on the ear.

'I hate it when you do that,' she complained.

'Thank you for being gentle with me,' he whispered.

Sophie struggling to escape said, 'I do not know what you mean.'

Tim let her go. 'You are a bully, Mr Cooper,' said Sophie as he unlocked his arms, then kissing him quickly as she stood up. 'I shall pack you a lunch, and then you can come home for dinner, and in future only one whisky at the pub with Chick and Molly Evans.'

Tim went to say something, but Sophie put her finger on his lips and said, 'I have interrogated Mr Graham and finally he told me that it had crept up to three or four doubles Tim – this is going to stop.'

He raised his eyebrows and just nodded. He knew she was right, and he had to admit the trip to hospital had frightened him – perhaps he was not as immortal as he once thought.

He soon settled into the new regime; all the team now closely monitored his daily activities so much that it began to be irritating. One morning when he started to lift a heavy box, Mr Woodman stopped him saying, 'Leave that Tim, let me do it.'

Checking there were no customers in he said, obviously irritated, 'Can everybody stop treating me like an invalid, the Doctors have told me to live normally, I'm taking medication every morning that will protect me for years to come, so please just give me some space. I'm grateful for your concern but let me assure you I'm not going anywhere. Thank you.'

There were some raised eyebrows, but no one said anything.

CHAPTER 22

It was early one sunny Sunday morning; Tom Cooper was sitting staring out his front window lost in thought. He had realised recently that he was lonely. He enjoyed his work at Sophie's but once he got home there was nothing. The television bored him; he loved the documentaries, but the rest was not his cup of tea.

He watched Mrs Russell who lived in the house opposite as she stepped into the street, her small white poodle proceeding her, bouncing around in its excitement. He was unable to remember its name for a moment, was it Bobby. Mrs Russell, a widow, a short, sixty something, had become a little overfriendly after his wife died. There was a steady delivery of cakes and soup. There was a deeply embarrassing moment when he was forced to gently explain that he was grateful for the food, but he was not ready for anything more. Now the interaction between them was a formal 'hallo', when they met and nothing more.

He was concerned he may sink back into that terrible malaise that had held him prisoner for years. It was only working at Sophie's for his son that had allowed him to climb out of his pit of despair. The days were OK when he was at the shop, but the rest of the time dragged. Perhaps a dog was the answer, he didn't want a puppy he decided but a rescue dog might fit the bill. There was a dog's rehoming centre not that far away.

He could remember his wife getting cross with him when he procrastinated; seize the day she would tell him, seize the day, all delivered with a Shakespearian flourish of her arms. He found himself smiling as he recalled her theatrics.

Two hours later he was standing in reception at the centre completing some paperwork. They did not believe in allowing the would-be owners to parade through the cages, it wound all the inmates up and it was hours before they were calm again.

'We select a dog that we think might be suitable and you meet them out in the yard, then you can see how you get on,' said the receptionist. She handed him a lead and showed him through a door out into a paved area.

His first impression was not good. It was readily apparent the dog was not well; she was severely underweight, had a nasty skin condition and there were marks on her back that indicated she had been thrashed. One positive, she was attractive with black-and-white markings. She sported a white nose, a black back with white socks and a white plumed tail.

As Tom Cooper started to put the lead on the dog, she slid her teeth down his hand. Grasping her collar he pulled the dog in so that they were cheek to cheek and then said in a deep, calm, but powerful voice, 'If you ever do that again I'll beat the living daylights out of you.' Later he could not understand why he had adopted that particular behaviour, but unknown to him the dog and he had bonded at that moment. After a short walk, he returned to the office agreeing to take the dog. The woman asked a lot of questions, one of which stuck in his mind afterwards was, where would the dog sleep? 'On the end of my bed of course.' His answer obviously surprised her.

'Her name is Beth – she is five years old and is a pure-bred Welsh collie. The price for her is £60 but if you want the thoroughbred papers, it's £120.'

'The £60 will do fine thank you.'

Again, his response surprised her. Most people in her experience wanted to brag about the quality of the animal.

'Well, thank you Mr Cooper, if you would like to call back in ...' She perused the list on her desk. '... in four days' time we will have her ready for you. In the meantime there will be a home check.'

'No, that's not what's going to happen, this dog is unwell, she's seriously underweight.' Pointing at her back he continued, 'There's a nasty skin infection, and you can see where she's been beaten, this dog is coming home with me today, our first stop will be the vets. I'll pay the bill. I'm staggered that you've not sorted out all these problems before you've tried to rehome her. All I need you to do is to complete whatever paperwork you need, and she'll come home with me now.'

Twenty minutes later Tom and Beth walked out of the rescue centre. Tom had to help her up into his little, old green van. Stroking her head he said, 'You'll be all right now old thing.' She licked his hand.

∗

The vet was surprised at Beth's poor condition and asked, 'Do you mind if I follow this up? Not all of these places operate as they should do. Although I have not heard anything bad about this one – leave it with me. Feed her cold, boiled rice for a couple of days, use the powder on her back. Don't let her eat too much at a time, say a cupful. She may also have a digestive problem, but these things can be managed. I would like to see her again in two weeks – I think she has taken to you.'

Tom settled the bill on the way out. Again, he had to lift her into the van.

Now at home and having wolfed down the bowl of cold rice and drunk a lot of water she settled herself down beside his armchair and fell asleep. Lunchtime came and went, he tried not to make too much noise. It didn't seem to make any difference. By mid-afternoon he was becoming concerned, she had barely stirred.

He sat on the floor next to her and began to talk to her in a soft gentle voice, the very end of her tail flicked once. Very gently he stroked the top of her head. Not her back, that was still sore. After a while she lifted her head and placed it on his knee.

'It's a damn good job, I don't know who did this to you, girl – I'd end up in prison.' Again, the tail flicked. Tom was concerned that his new-found friend was going to die. He was surprised that an animal that had been mistreated so badly could still trust someone else. Another hour slipped by; the dog was asleep again. His back and arms were aching now, speaking quietly he said, 'I've got to get up, girl.' He lifted her head off his knee. Standing now, he stretched out the knots that had formed in his joints.

Beth looked up at him and struggled to her feet. Visibly unsteady, she went and stood by the front door.

'Do you need to go out, girl? We'll go out the back, it's safer.' As he walked through the kitchen the dog followed at his heels.

He fed himself, while Beth had another bowl of cold rice. Later that evening the dog was already dozing when Tom found Tim's sleeping bag that he had left behind, pulled some cushions off the couch, and made up a bed on the floor. It was not long before he fell asleep as well.

In the night, as the temperature dropped, Tom was aware of Beth moving to lie against his back. He smiled and went back to sleep.

The following morning, he had just finished breakfast when his phone rang.

'Good morning,' said the voice on the other end, 'are you, Mr Thomas Cooper?'

'I am,' he replied, thinking, this all sounds extremely official.

'I understand you re-homed a dog yesterday?'

'Yes,' he said, now becoming defensive; he was worried it may be because he had bullied the woman into giving him the dog there and then. I don't care what he says he is not getting her back, he thought.

'I have been asked to come and inspect your home's suitability. I am from the RSPCA.'

'When do you want to do that?'

'Now please, I am standing at your front door.'

Tom let the man in; he was a pleasant-looking man with a ready smile. He offered him the armchair while he sat on the couch. Much to Tom's surprise, Beth jumped up forcing herself between Tom and the arm of the couch and started barking at the visitor. Tom bent down and said, 'Quiet' – the dog ignored him. Leaning closer still this time with a growl in his voice he repeated, 'Quiet.' Beth's head went down and there was silence.

'Have you owned a dog before?' the visitor asked, his tone of voice indicating he expected the answer to be yes.

Tom nodding said, 'We always had dogs when I was young, my wife was frightened of them, something in her past I think. This is the first one for many years. I was worried you were here to take her away.'

'I don't think I could if I wanted to. I have never seen an animal bond so fast. Strong-minded dogs like collies are looking for someone who will be the pack leader, who they can respect. I understand she was in a bad way when you collected her yesterday?'

'Yes, I was extremely worried last night so we went to the vets. She seems a little better this morning.'

'I will have a word about them allowing a dog out in that condition. Thank you for letting me see her. She will obviously be a lot happier in the future. Goodbye Mr Cooper.'

*

Tom and Beth established a relationship based on mutual understanding. It was the connection that had existed between man and dog since the dawn of history.

CHAPTER 23

There had been arguments of late, mostly over trivial things, the big one was about another child.

'Tim,' said Sophie, 'I do not understand why you are so reluctant to have another baby. You often say how much you regretted being an only child. Money is not an issue, what is your objection?'

'I don't know really. I am so damned tired – I can't take anything more on.'

They were both working horrendous hours, early starts and late finishes.

Sophie, now worried about him and his recent stay in hospital said, 'Shall we have this coming Sunday off? No work, no phone calls, no child. Angela will have her.'

The next Sunday morning found the young couple at Tim's deceased great-aunt's house, now the company office.

They were lying in the bath, she with her back to him her head resting in the angle between his shoulder and face. They both enjoyed bathing together, regrettably the bath on the boat was so small Tim had to sit cross legged in it, there was no room for two.

Tim was slowly sliding his hands across her upper body making patterns in the soap on her skin, caressing her breasts then moving on. Eventually she whispered, 'Kiss me.' Turning her head their lips met, as they did so she touched the tip of his tongue with hers. This was the start of what they called a bedroom kiss. She could feel his growing arousal against her back. Suddenly she sat bolt upright and climbed from the bath, water cascaded from her body, she grabbed a towel as she landed. Scrubbing the majority of the water off, she said, 'Come on, Tim.'

'No, come back in, the water's still warm. I was enjoying that.'

Leaning down towards him allowing him a wonderful view of her bath-warmed breasts, she whispered in his ear, 'I am offering you something you may enjoy more.'

Tim stared into her eyes to check if he had understood her proposal then stood upright and stepped out.

Sophie burst out laughing, it was very obvious she had Tim's full attention; still laughing she linked their fingers together and guided him to the bedroom.

∗

Angela, Sophie's aunt, had agreed the day before to have Charley overnight; the young couple were to dine there later that evening and collect their daughter.

Sophie had a secret that she had kept from Tim, she had stopped taking the pill some time back. She remembered with the first pregnancy her body had signalled a change when she had fallen for Charley, but nothing had changed yet. Of late their lovemaking had become occasional and brief. Mostly because they were both so tired.

One thing she did know was they were going to have to make some changes. The two of them had slept the afternoon away lying under a large umbrella on loungers in the warm sun on the back lawn. A bottle of good white wine cooling in the ice bucket.

Sophie refused to discuss their unsustainable workload today but, it would have to be aired at the next director's meeting.

*

The evening was to be pleasantly rounded off with dinner at Angela's, she had invited Jessica and her husband Gerald, Tom Cooper, Harry and Sara, Mr Woodman. Daisy had initially refused but had been encouraged to change her mind. Tim suspected her original refusal had been because Mr and Mrs Vieri would have been there, but they were already committed to another engagement.

It was clear Gerald was an avid football fan from the fact that it was his sole topic of conversation.

Later that evening Jessica said to her husband, 'Gerry, not everyone is as big a football fan as you are.'

He did not say another word, but Sophie noticed him direct an extremely unpleasant scowl at his wife.

The dress code had been smart casual, no jeans or trainers. Daisy, when she did arrive, looked extremely attractive. In the past she had made every effort to hide her femininity. Tim watched surprise appear on a number of faces. She was wearing a little black dress with a modest heart-shaped neckline and a flared skirt that played around her knees as she walked. A pair of black patent stilettos and a small silver brooch completed her outfit. Tim then noticed her hair had also undergone a transformation. His mind was drawing comparisons with beautiful butterflies emerging from the drab pupae. He knew Sophie's good taste had influenced the choice of clothing.

Daisy, still standing in the doorway of the lounge was receiving so much attention she had gone a little pink in the face.

Angela said, 'Will you men leave the poor girl alone before she gets so embarrassed, she decides to leave.'

Mr Woodman rose and offered Daisy his seat on the sofa. Initially shaking her head, she said, 'I'm fine on here.' She lowered herself on to a hard kitchen chair.

'Daisy, sorry,' he said as he crossed the room to her side, 'I am an old-fashioned male from another age. If my mother were alive, God bless her, she would insist we swapped seats – will you oblige me and sit on the couch, otherwise I will have to stand up all evening.'

Now even more embarrassed she decided the easiest way out was to just agree and so she crossed the room and sat where Mr Woodman had moved from.

As she sat down, he mouthed a thank you.

Daisy was entranced by the cut-glass ornaments around the lounge windows. They were all giving off light, the suspended ones were slowly turning, throwing reflections on to the ceiling, the furniture and the people in the room. Daisy's expression was childlike, in awe of the beauty of all the different glass shapes and patterns. On some of the static pieces, as she moved her head, the reflections changed colour. She stood transfixed unable to believe anything could be this beautiful. Now she was looking down at herself as the myriad colours moved across her clothing and her arms.

Angela seeing her fascination beckoned her up to the window. 'Would you like to know more about some of it?' she asked.

Tim watching Daisy was reminded of his daughter's face at Christmas time. Wide-eyed, and open mouthed, Daisy was entranced. She had never seen anything this beautiful. Her memory was dragged back to the horrors of her childhood. The last place they had stayed the Bitter green mould climbed the filthy wall. A gale howled through the ill-fitting window. The wind carried the stench of a nearby broken sewer into the room. The terrible smell did on occasion make her gag.

Returning to the here and now the wonderful light show in front of her was such a contrast. Whilst she recognised that her parents could not afford anything to compare with this she did know that had her drunken sot of a father not drank his wages every week things could have been a damn sight better.

'I started collecting it as a girl,' Angela informed her. 'Do you collect anything ?'

Angela spotted the beginnings of tears. 'Daisy and I are going to sort out some food, there is no room for all of us around the table, so it is a buffet. We will not be long.'

Reaching the kitchen, Angela pulled her into an embrace and hugged her, saying as she did so, 'I am so sorry, I did not mean to upset you.'

'It weren't you, it's all that beauty. I ain't never seen nuffin' that perfeck …' Her expensive elocution lessons had been set aside again because of the depth of her emotions.

'You could start a collection yourself now you are working full-time,' said Angela.

'I can't afford nuffin' like that.' She sniffed.

Looking at the soft, white lawn handkerchief she had besmudged with makeup, she said. 'I'm so sorry, Angela, I've ruined yer 'anky.'

'No, you have not you silly goose, a gentle wash in warm soapy water will soon put it right. I have an idea,' Angela continued, 'would you like to start a collection yourself?'

Daisy laughed. 'No ta, I could never afford it.'

Angela noticed Daisy's diction was improving as she gathered herself together. 'You would be surprised,' she said. 'There are lots of little stalls open on Sundays along the riverbank, you can find some beautiful things if you know what you are searching for, and before you say anything, I was thinking we could go together, and I will teach you – how's that for an idea?'

Daisy's whole demeanour changed; she was clearly thrilled with the idea.

'… and' said Angela, 'you keep the hanky then I do not have to wash it and it is now the first item in your collection.' Watching the girl start to refuse she added, 'If you are going to argue with me there will be no trips out. I am not bragging but I get given lots of hankies, what else do you give an older woman who has everything?'

Daisy said, 'You're so kind, thank you so much.' Her wide smile displaying the depth of her appreciation.

The two women bustled about transporting the food into the other room, Daisy obviously now more comfortable in this environment.

CHAPTER 24

The following morning, Tim, Sophie, Harry and Mr Woodman, directors of the company, met at 9.30 am in the office for the monthly board meeting; Jessica was there to make notes. Tim welcomed everyone and set the ball rolling. Moving swiftly through the items to be discussed, the rest of the team had learnt that he would not put up with talking for the sake of it. They already knew everything but the fine detail anyway. Everybody was pleased, they were appreciably in front of the month's target.

After a short interval while Jessica poured the tea, Tim moved the meeting on, tapping the table to ensure their attention.

'The next issue as you can see under any other business, is the workload,' said Tim. 'It has become unsustainable. Sophie and I have found we are working in the evenings as well as all day. We have asked Jessica to list her commitments and see if there is any more she could take on. I would also point out that once the Longstaff fund is up and running the work will increase again.'

Jessica said, 'I have given my current workload close scrutiny and yes there is some slack but not enough time to do what is proposed. A lot of my time is taken up with typing, a competent girl could do that, or most of it.'

'What we have in mind everybody,' explained Sophie, 'is for Jessica to work here most of the day with Tim. He makes the decisions and Jessica drafts the letters etcetera.'

'The only thing I would point out is that everything is growing like topsy, the amount of paperwork seems to escalate almost daily,' revealed Jessica.

'Shall we see how the new system that we have decided on goes then visit this again in the near future,' said Tim, concerned about the escalating wage bill.

Jessica was shaking her head. Sophie asked, 'Jessica what do you think? You will be the one with the extra workload.'

'I will struggle. Gerry is already taking Polly into school and complaining about it. I cannot ask him to do any more, and if he stops helping I will be up a gum tree.'

'It is very obvious, Mr Chairman,' said Mr Woodman, 'that if it all gets too much for Jessica and we lose her, there will be a much bigger problem than a hike in the wage bill.' Knowing full well what Tim was thinking, he continued, 'We need an office girl.'

'We can start to think about that,' agreed Tim. 'Now, can I—'

Sophie and Jessica jumped in interrupting him, initially talking over each other, they both apologised.

Jessica with a nod of the head demurred to Sophie who said, 'Tim is going to be cross with me, but I would like to remind everyone that Tim was advised by the Doctors that he must take more time off. We are now both working Sundays again.'

Tim's frown said it all. 'Jessica what were you going to say,' he asked.

'Should Gerry get really cross, he will insist I leave straight away, without any notice – remember I have no contract of employment.'

There was a long silence, then Mr Woodman said, 'You have no contract of employment?' His surprise was self-evident. His voice had risen an octave.

'Nobody does,' revealed Sophie. 'Everything has been done on trust so far.'

'So, you have no guarantee of holiday or sick pay?' asked Mr Woodman, in disbelief.

'No.'

A general discussion began that Mr Woodman quickly overrode, saying, 'We need a girl Friday who can type, who will work for Jessica.' All this said in a commanding manner that he rarely used.

Tim was surprised; Mr Woodman was the major shareholder in the company, he had never exercised his authority before. His suggestions were usually polite and to the point. His decades of experience in the retail trade always ensured profound respect from the other board members. Now he was demanding to be heard. It was apparent that he felt extremely strongly about this issue.

'Mr Woodman,' said Tim forcefully. The babble died out.

'Thank you, Mr Chairman,' said Mr Woodman ensuring that what he was going to say would be added to the minutes. 'We are lucky Jessica's workload has come to our notice now, her giving her notice in effective immediately would have been disastrous. It has to be addressed now, today. I suggest we put an advert for a typist in the paper this week.'

'Who is going to take the interviews?' asked Sophie. 'There is no way I can do it for at least a month with the pressure of my day job.' She knew her boss, Mr Wells, would give her the time off, but it would feel wrong to ask. 'Jessica, will you run the interviews, please?'

'I will but I have two things to say. One, the advert will need to say shorthand typist, and we will need to assess them, and secondly I do not want to do it on my own.'

Tim and Sophie sat shaking their heads knowing they had no time.

'Sara might do it,' suggested Harry. 'She can type, and she is a good judge of character – just don't tell her that I suggested it.'

They all laughed. Knowing that Sara appeared timid until she lost her thoroughly Italian temper, then her rebukes could be quite scathing.

'That is a clever idea, Harry,' said Sophie. 'Thank you, I will ask her. Jessica, can you and I get together afterwards please for a few minutes?'

Jessica nodded.

'I would like to offer my services to help pull something together regarding the staff contracts,' said Mr Woodman. 'I sit and twiddle my thumbs most evenings. I may as well be doing the research to see what we need. I am quite happy to work with Jessica rather than you. You have no spare time anyway, Mr chairman.'

'I am sorry to say this, but the staff contracts will have to wait a little while until the new post is filled. There is no way I can do it at the moment,' said Jessica

'Understood,' said Mr Woodman. 'I can be pulling something together in the meantime, ready for you when you can.'

'It will have to be board approved anyway,' said Tim.

Tim called for a vote, Mr Woodman's suggestions were carried unanimously.

'Any other business?' asked Tim.

'Yes, you mentioned the Longstaff fund, we have heard nothing about it. Can you tell us what's happening please?' asked Harry.

Tim turned to Jessica and said, 'Over to you.'

'Well, I have to admit Mr Chairman, I have had to do this in the evenings, other things have on occasion taken priority.'

'Motherhood and marriage?' suggested Sophie.

Nodding in agreement, Jessica said, 'To be honest I have done a lot of work without much to show for it. Most of it is the guidelines that must be obeyed when children are involved. Also, the financial side is complex, I will need to involve you Sophie in the near future, and the solicitor to make sure everyone is safe, us and the children.' Flipping open a heavy file, she said, 'I can give you more detail if you want.'

They all declined her offer.

'We need to agree an overtime rate with you,' said Mr Woodman.

'I can sort that,' said Sophie checking with Tim who nodded. The meeting finished soon afterwards.

CHAPTER 25

A month later Jessica and Sara were sitting in the office watching the sunlight filtering through the leaves on the trees in the front garden. They had interviewed five girls for the post of shorthand typist, one had been ok, but the rest were regretfully not what they required. Jessica had received a phone call from another girl yesterday to say that she would be about half an hour late.

'Could I still be interviewed please?' She had explained it was a hospital appointment she could not postpone.

Punctual to the minute the doorbell rang, Jessica answered the door to a young, pretty, curly-haired, out of breath brunette, wearing a white blouse, brown slacks and a huge smile that lit up her face.

'Hallo, I made it.' She checked her watch. 'I am Bonny, Bonny Atkins. I am here for the post of shorthand typist.'

Jessica shook her hand and received a firm grip in reply. Good sign, she thought – a limp wrist always gave her the heebie-jeebies. Following the girl in she noticed that she limped slightly, then she spotted her brown shoes, the left one a boot.

Guiding the girl to her chair she was surprised when instead of sitting down she said, 'Can we get something out of the way, please?'

Jessica nodded, not sure what was happening. The girl walked around the desk to their side and then standing facing them pulled up her slacks a few inches revealing the difference in her footwear. Still wearing a big smile, she said, 'I had polio as a child, so I ended up with one leg shorter than the other. It doesn't hinder me at all. I taught my two younger brothers to climb cliffs.' She walked back around the desk and sat down, saying, 'I prefer to get it out in the open.'

Half an hour later Bonny had sailed through the shorthand and typing tests. Jessica sat checking her work. Putting the papers to one side she asked, 'Are you working now?'

'No,' was the reply. 'I did have a job in a shop, but it closed down, the owner died. I have been to a few interviews but never been lucky.'

'I do not understand why,' said Jessica.' Your speeds are excellent, and you are extremely accurate.'

'I can't prove it, but I think it's my boot, polio is still a scary word. I saw a woman shudder when I showed her my boot.'

'You are obviously very mobile,' said Sara.

'I decided it was not going to limit my life. Mum is a great help – she's never told me I couldn't do something. She was tough at the beginning when I was learning to walk again, she insisted that when I fell, I got up on my own. She pointed out that she wouldn't always be there to pick me back up. It was me who decided to throw my stick away.'

'That must have been hard for you at times,' said Sara, obviously deeply moved by the girl's determination.

'I don't know if I should say this but getting angry helps sometimes.'

'I have also found that to be the case,' said Jessica.

'Sara?' enquired Jessica. The question was a prearranged coded message asking if she thought the applicant was satisfactory.

'Oh yes,' enthused Sara, her Italian accent growing stronger.

Bonny, unsure of what was happening, was glancing between the two women.

'We would like to offer you the job if you want it,' said Jessica.

Bonny for all her tough façade found she was quite overcome.

Sara, aware as always of people's emotions stepped around the table and hugged the girl saying, 'Welcome aboard, Bonny.'

Jessica smiling at the girl thought, I have not been hugged in months, that includes by my husband.

The girl stood to shake Jessica's hand who said, 'I am sure we are going to get along very well.'

They were to discover that she was Bonny by name and bonny by nature, she seemed to wear a permanent smile.

'I must return to work,' said Sara as shook Bonny's hand and said goodbye.

'The hospital appointment, Bonny, is that something I need to know about?' enquired Jessica, realising it was a question she should have asked before offering her the job.

'No, it is my annual check-up on my leg, they are extremely pleased with me.'

'Jolly good. Are you ok to work today?'

'Yes, but can I ring my mum first, please?'

'Of course, follow me. This is Tim's office; you will have some privacy in here.'

'Tim?' enquired Bonny.

'He is the boss, the chairman. I will give you a brief rundown of who's who and where things are when you finish your phone call.'

When Bonny returned to the front office, Jessica asked, 'Is everything ok?'

'Yes, my mum, who is usually a real tough nut, got quite emotional.'

'She is obviously pleased for you. Now if you will grab your notebook. It's on the top of your desk over there,' said Jessica pointing. 'I will give you some detail. I have told you about Tim, the chairman. He is married to Sophia, née Vieri, our Finance Director, she prefers Sophie. She has a similar post with another company run by a Mr Wells.'

Bonny knew that Mr Vieri owned the big department store in the high street.

'Harry, a lovely man, is a company Director married to Sara who you have just met. Sara is a world-class confectioner who receives offers of vast sums of money from major companies for her recipes, but she always refuses. Mr Woodman is the owner of shop Number One as it is called. He is also a director.

'Tom Cooper is Tim's dad – he started the delicatessen on a market stall years ago opposite shop Number One. He is by choice a shopworker with a vast knowledge of the produce and who and where to buy from. He has travelled right across Europe sourcing the food.

'Daisy has worked her way up from the bottom, her words not mine and is now an excellent shop manager.

'I am PA to Tim and Sophie. This is the reason you are here now, because the three of us cannot handle the workload. I think that covers most of it, oh, there are two shops. I know Tim wants a third. Do you need me to recap on anything?'

'No thank you, I have all that.'

'Well done, if you want to spend a few minutes sorting your desk then we can get to work.'

*

At home, that evening Bonny was telling her mum all about her day. She finished by saying, 'And I have my own desk and everything.' Her mum, moist-eyed, hugged her hard. She was so proud of her little fighter.

*

Later that evening, Sophie phoned Jessica, 'How did it go?' she asked.

'Really well in the end, the first five girls were not what we were looking for but the last one – I told you she asked if we could wait for her because she had a hospital appointment she could not cancel.'

'Uh huh,' responded Sophie. 'What was the hospital appointment for?'

'Her annual check-up, she had polio as a child. It has left her with one leg a little shorter than the other.'

'Is she going to need extra help?'

'You can ask her if you like, I am not going to. She is a lovely person – it has been a delight working with her today, she grasps new things at the speed of light. Her typing speed and accuracy are outstanding. She is faster than me.'

'Wow!!' said Sophie. She had admitted to herself years ago that Jessica was always going to be quicker than her. 'This new girl must be like lightning.'

'She really is the fastest I have met.'

'Jessica, I will pop in and have a word with her about her leg, see what we can do to help.'

'I do not think that is a clever idea, she showed us her boot before she sat down. She really is a lovely girl, rightly christened Bonny, but by golly she is tough. Apparently when she was learning to walk again her mother refused to help her daughter when she fell down, she insisted Bonny had to be self-reliant. Once Bonny had achieved that the girl threw her stick away. She does not need help from anyone.'

'Thanks for the warning Jessica, I would not like to get off on the wrong foot, pardon the pun. She sounds as though she is exactly what we require, well done you. So, is everything OK at your end, now?'

'Yes, thank you.' The women exchanged goodbyes and hung up.

CHAPTER 26

Tim had arrived at shop Number Two early one Saturday morning. An occasional day working in the shop was a treat he gave himself when he had spent days sat in a chair moving paperwork around. It was the part of the business he loved: the wheeling and dealing, the banter with the customers. Working alongside Harry when they had the stalls across the road, side by side had taught him the chat. He was quite sure that he would not get away with the risqué stuff Harry came out with, but Tim was comfortable with the give and take that made the customers laugh; he was surprised sometimes with what the women said. It was as his mother would say, a little close to the knuckle. He had just flipped the door sign to open and was now holding the door to allow a regular customer to enter when the phone rang.

'I'm in no rush if you want to get that, Tim.'

'Thank you,' he replied. 'Hi, Tim Cooper here.'

'Tim, George Wainwright here, have you found your third shop yet?'

'No, other things have taken precedence. Why? I assume you have found one, George?'

'Correct, it may be too big, I don't know. I think it's worth a visit.'

'Where is it?'

'Clapham.'

'Clapham, George, that's a bit rough out there, isn't it?'

'It used to be Tim, but here in the late seventies it has been gentrified, the posh people are calling it Clahm – sounds a bit like farm with an L. I have had a quick poke around, it's sound but scruffy. It's been used as storage. The owners have moved their business away so don't require it anymore. I think they just want to offload it, Tim. It does need some work though.'

'Sounds as though it's worth a visit. Just one thing though, I assume it's you we will be working with?'

'Yes Tim, I fired my idiot son.'

'Oh dear, sorry.'

'Not your fault Tim, I couldn't afford to keep him on anyway. I had spent a lot of time and money teaching him about estate agency, I was wasting my time.'

'OK George, like last time please, can we arrange to view the property on Sunday morning so as many of our people can come as possible?'

'Only for you Tim, only for you. Speak soon, bye for now.'

'Bye George.'

✳

A week later all the staff were gathered outside the large building in Clapham. Tim had arrived early for a walk around the area with his dad. The building itself was on the left-hand side of a small square set back from the high-street pavement. The side facing the road had a low knee-high private hedge divided in the middle by three steps up from the pavement into the square. This was paved except for a central circular raised stone-walled flower bed that was now a riot of annuals of all colours. A ring of dark wood benches faced out from the flower bed; a small green-leaved Acer stood in the middle of the flowers. There were more smartly trimmed hedges growing against the walls of buildings up to window sill height, this included the one they were there to look at. The buildings on the other two sides appeared to be offices. There was little movement of people in the square, except for a small pathway between the buildings on the opposite side of the square that had a few people coming and going.

'We might be short on footfall, Dad.'

'It's Sunday, Tim. We can ask some of the locals before we leave.'

'Ok, but I would still want to see for myself in the week, if we are interested. Here's George and the rest of the team. Good morning, George, thanks for coming out on a Sunday. I have to say it's an impressive building.'

'I'm glad you think so. I love the tall windows.'

'The brick work is attractive as well,' Tim continued, 'with the radiused corners on the window surrounds and the buttresses between the windows.'

There was a flurry of greetings as the team came together and walked towards the front door.

Following the estate agent inside through the heavy wooden doors, the sight that met their eyes was so impressive there was a chorus of, 'Oh wows.' This included Tim.

The empty space was cavernous. Tim guessed it was about eighteen-feet high, the upper floor was supported by a double row of ornate steel columns that marched down the middle of the room, they were topped by intricate supportive scroll work where they met the ceiling. The windows stretched from waist high at ground level to a half circle at their highest point just short of the top of the white walls. A wide staircase climbed the far wall to the floor above. As they walked around Tim was becoming increasingly excited. This was the most energised he had been since the birth of his daughter.

His father could sense his son's enthusiasm, but he didn't know what had generated it. 'Go on then Tim, what has got you so pumped up?'

'Dad, pretend we are not inside and that there is no roof and that we are in a market square in Puglia.'

Tim was now looking up, his hands raised above his head. 'Look Dad, the sun is beating down, there is a blue sky with white clouds sliding by.

'I can see how it could be, Dad. The theme is back to our roots – imagine this, blue and white costermonger's stalls with the big wheels, maybe not the long handles, but all gaily painted with striped canvas tops to keep the imaginary sun off, one for each product. There will be one row each side of the line of columns.

'There will be ordinary market stalls around the outside, the same as our old market stall with canvas covers, the same blue and white. These would be the ones needing chilling for the meat etcetera.' Throughout Tim was waving his arms about and pointing at imaginary objects.

'It will cost a fortune lad and a sizeable increase in staff numbers – I don't know.'

'Dad, most of the time shopping is boring, this will be an experience, and we can afford it.'

Mr Wainwright lead them upstairs; the ceilings were lower, and it was clear it all needed work, paint mostly.

'I have just had another idea. We will have buildings in the square.' Tim by now was clearly extremely excited.

'The café for instance, it will be downstairs. We will build it as though we were building it for outdoors. It will be placed on the far wall opposite the entrance. When you enter the café it will look and feel exactly the same as though you had entered a café in Italy with the counter and coffee machine, everything exactly the same. You will be able to eat inside the café, or you will be able to choose to sit at the tables in front of the café if you wanted.'

Harry said, 'I think it's a brilliant idea, Tim. Italian food in an Italian environment. Sara will love it.' She had not attended as usual, Sundays were set aside for mass and making the chocolate confectionary.

'The lights around the outer edge will also be streetlamps,' confirmed Tim. 'The old-fashioned gas ones with the scrolled post, the cross bar at the top for the lamplighter's ladder and the four-sided tapered glass lantern with the peaked top.'

'It will be incredible at night,' enthused George Wainwright. 'Goodness knows what it will cost to carry out though Tim.'

'I think it will allow me to achieve what I wanted to do with Victor. Have a store that is a monument to all our hard work. Talking of money George, have you got some numbers for us?'

'Yes I have, the present owners are I think a bit stretched financially so I don't believe they are going to come down a lot. I am also sure they do not want to spend weeks getting the place ready for sale, the repaint alone is a big job as you can see.' He handed Sophie a sheet of paper that had the figures on.

Tim called them all together then said, 'Right, is anybody dead against it?'

There was a lot of shaking of heads, then he asked, 'Anyone for it?'

Now there was nodding, Mr Woodman and Tom Cooper started talking at the same time. 'Go on,' said Tom.

'Thanks Tom,' said Mr Woodman. 'I would not be happy to talk money until we have had the following ...' Now the fingers of his left hand were spread wide, his index finger of his right hand extended ready to tick off the points he wanted to make. 'We need a survey' – tapping his thumb – 'then we need to find out if Charlie can handle a job this big' – he tapped the next finger – 'we need a source to produce the barrows, then the need for a lift' – more tapping – 'the lighting, the painting – the list continues.'

Sophie jumped in next saying, 'I have just been working out the price quoted against the square footage. This price is low, it is clear they need the money. As your accountant, I would advise that we check there are no gremlins anywhere, smarten the place up and sell it for the right price. Not as interesting as your idea Tim but less risky.'

'Right, I will buy it myself, that way there is no risk to the company, and I should make a big fat profit.'

His father walked away shaking his head. Mr Woodman fixed him with a hard stare, other members of the team were perplexed, unsure of what was happening they stood staring at each other.

Tim waited until his father turned round and then before he could speak, Tim asked, 'But where's the fun in that?' Then burst out laughing.

'Tim you …' Sophie didn't say what she was going to call him but then she said, 'I may call all of you as witnesses when I divorce the ugly beggar.'

Tim was unable to quench the small outbreaks of laughter that kept erupting from him.

'Dad,' called Tim as the staff were starting to leave.

His father stopped and turned towards him. 'Yes lad, what can I do for you?'

'How do you know I want you to do something?'

'It's the tone of voice, lad.'

'What was the name of your carpenter mate, the one with the workshop?'

'Gerry.'

The same name as Jessica's husband thought Tim. 'Can you have a word with him about the stalls and the barrows please, see if he could make them?'

'You are asking me to take charge of the building of the barrows and the stalls?'

'Erm, yes I suppose I am, Dad,' said Tim scratching his neck and pulling a face. 'What do you think?'

'I think he will need to find a wheelwright, that's going to be expensive.'

'It's all going to be expensive Dad. Will you do it, please? You are the one with the technical skills. The wheels can be simple, no fancy trimmings, plain spokes, canvas tops, legs at the front and some way of steering them so we can move them around.'

Tom thought for a moment; he wouldn't tell Tim but he quite fancied having a crack at it. Could be an interesting job. 'Aye, I'll have a go at it and see what we can do, lad. Leave it with me.'

✳

In bed that night, Sophie said, 'You are keen on this are you not?'

'I am,' Tim admitted. 'It's a really exciting project, I think it will be superb.'

'Can I give you something else to be excited about? I am fairly sure I am pregnant again.'

Tim was pleased the lights were out, it gave him a chance to gather his thoughts. 'What did you say?' he asked.

'I think I am pregnant again.'

'Oh wow,' he said; what he thought was entirely different. There could not be a worse time for her to be pregnant. They were just about to take on the biggest project yet and now one of the most prominent members of the team is going to be, at best, part-time.

'You are quiet, are you all right with this?'

'Yes, sorry, it's come as a huge surprise. We hadn't talked about it or anything. Is it an accident?'

Sophie was tempted to lie but she would not do that. 'I want another baby, Tim. I hated being an only child. A lot of the time there was no one to play with and mother would not allow me to play in the street with the other children. I spent a large part of my childhood with Nanny as my only companion, the two of us shut in the nursery out of the way. Please do not be angry with me. The best of times for me were in the summer when Nanny, mother and I would go to her villa in Puglia. I ran wild in the fields all summer long, playing with the local children.'

Tim wrapped her in his arms and speaking into her hair said, 'I'm not angry with you, I'm just stunned. So, I am going to have a son, that's great, someone to carry the name forward, and I decree he shall be named Martyn. If it's not a boy, it will be sent back.'

Sophie was giggling now. 'Do I not get a say in the name?'

'No, you've done your bit by getting pregnant, from here on in it is all down to me.'

'Two things my lord and master, you are as guilty as I am regarding this pregnancy, you were there. Secondly, suppose I do not like the name?'

Tim lifted the sheet and called down towards her tummy, 'Don't listen, Martyn. Mummy is just in a pout because on this one occasion she can't have her own way, she will love you any way. Sorry if I was a bit offhand just now, I was just surprised. I have dreamed of having a proper family. You know how poor my childhood was after Mum died, and now you are going to provide one, thank you. I suppose we need not stop at two, we can have as many as we like. A big Italian family what do you think? I would love that.'

Now it was Sophie's turn to be shocked. 'Do you mean that?'

'Yes, I do,' he replied thoughtfully. He had surprised himself when he understood that while he had said it in jest, he meant it. 'I do mean it,' he repeated.

Moments later, now excited, he said, 'I want a house full of children's laughter. I never want to be lonely again. We can start a dynasty – we will need a bigger house, a large garden, dogs – we will need dogs. The girls will have horses. Their friends will visit and play in the pool – we will semi-retire.'

'Do you mean all of this?' asked his stunned wife.

'I do, I really do.'

'Well, that's fine husband as long as you give birth to at least half of them.' They both laughed.

'Now can I change the subject, just for a minute?' asked Tim. 'I need your advice, I was excited about the new venture, but now some common sense has kicked in. We are not just setting something up; we are going to be climbing a mountain. There are some massive changes going to take place – firstly the number of new staff we will need, both out front and behind the scenes. What's your best guess?'

Sophie thought for a moment and then said, 'Shop staff, café workers. Let's ignore the restaurant for now that can be one of our far star projects. We may need some more admin staff and we need someone to run the human resources side of things now, before we start.

'Tim let's go and put the kettle on and start making some notes, it is clear we are not going to get much sleep tonight. I want to say first though if it is the money that is the issue, I would like to substantially increase my stake in the company. I think your vision for this new project will be bigger than either of us realise, it will be the signature store for Sophie's. It puts us alongside my father. That will be a hell of an achievement. Things will go wrong, we may make mistakes, but we know a lot more now than you did when you started. I believe in you my darling, let's do it.'

Tim kissed her, said – 'Thank you' – and went and put the kettle on.

It was three am when they finally agreed they were both too tired to do any more. There were pages of notes and jottings, but both now had a clearer idea of the way forward. Sophie was going to sort out the architect and inform the solicitor. Tim was to talk to George Wainwright, Charlie their builder, Larry the electrician and ring one of the executive staff agencies for a human resources manager.

✳

Monday morning, Tim, Charlie and his son Tommy were standing in the middle of the vast space that was the ground floor of the building. Charlie was looking around shaking his head.

'Well, Tim … this is summat else again, you've really jumped off the cliff with this one mate.' Tim had spent the last fifteen minutes explaining what he had in mind.

'Do you think we are making a mistake, Charlie?'

Tim waited while Charlie turned through a full circle. 'Let's 'ave a walk around, Tim, and then I'll let yur know what I think.'

The men spent the next hour working their way through the building.

Tommy, who had wandered off shouted, 'Dad I've found the lift, it's over 'ere.' It was around the corner from the front door set back in an alcove.

'That'll make it easier to organise late-night diners in the restaurant upstairs when you get that far. You can run a rope cordon from the door to the lift when the store itself is closed,' said Charlie.

Finally, standing upstairs Charlie was looking around. 'There's loads of room for storage, Tim. Where'll you put the restaurant?'

'Charlie, I haven't a clue. I am not even going to think about it now. It might not be for some time. I want this to become profitable first.'

'Well, it's up to you, Tim. I reckon one might be dependent on the other if yur knows what I mean.'

As they made their way back downstairs, Tim was thinking on what Charlie had said. He realised there may be more than a grain of truth in it. 'Charlie, what if we get the shop open first and then sort the restaurant out?'

'That's a better idea, yur can use the shop opening to advertise the future opening of the restaurant. As regards the building Tim, I uses me nose as much as my eyes. The good news is that I can't smell no rot or gas and no sewage. You still needs a surveyor, but I think it's all right.'

'That's a good start Charlie, thanks for coming. Can you start putting some numbers together for what we have discussed?'

'No problem, Tim, you realise it will not be cheap. I'm gunna have to bring in some outside help, two maybe three more painters. Is it all right if Larry does the electrics again?'

'Yes. As I said earlier, ignore upstairs, we'll give that a good clean so we can keep stock up there. In the meantime, I'll start gathering the info for the restaurant.'

Tommy had rejoined them.

As Tim and Charlie reached the front door there was a loud knocking.

Opening the door much to Tim's surprise Victor Vieri was standing there. Tim holding out his hand to be shaken said, 'This is a pleasant surprise, Victor.'

'Sophia told me you would be here. I thought I would come and have a walk round if that's all right.'

'Yes, that's fine. This is Charlie – he did all the work on one and two.'

'We met Mr Vieri when I was doing Number Two.'

Mr Vieri appeared confused.

'We'll speak soon, Charlie. Thanks for coming, bye Tommy.'

'Yeah, bye now Tim.' Charlie nodded at Mr Vieri as he left.

'Right Tim, let's see what you've got.'

The two men spent the next twenty minutes retracing Tim's earlier walk-through with the builder.

Tim's father-in-law was mostly silent with a few incisive questions. When they arrived once more at the front door Victor said, 'Are you excited, Tim? You should be this scheme deserves to be successful. It is a great idea.'

'Victor, I don't know if what I'm feeling is excitement or fear.'

Mr Vieri, now with his hand on Tim's shoulder said, 'Both are good Tim, the excitement will keep you going forward, the fear will make you check everything twice. If this is as good as your vision it will be brilliant, well done. If you want another opinion ever, just ring. Bye for now.'

Tim locked the building and spotted some people strolling through the square. He approached a small group and said, 'Hallo, I wonder if you can help me. I am thinking of opening a shop here in this building behind me. Does it get busy around here?'

'What sort of a shop?' asked one of the women. She was dressed in a pink cotton dress with dark shoulder-length hair. In some ways she reminded him of Sophie, apart from the colour of her hair. 'A delicatessen, a café and later an Italian restaurant.'

One of the young men said, 'I knew I recognised you – Tim Cooper, Sophie's on Fish Hill. My wife knows your wife. They both went to the same baby clinic. We shop in your store. To answer your question it gets reasonably busy, more so I expect once you open, especially with the restaurant.' The group walked away with the gentleman explaining the food on offer in Tim's shop.

*

Later that day, Tim was on the phone to the estate agent.

'Hallo George, it's Tim. We are going ahead with the purchase at the price they are asking. Sophie says it is the right price, it is dependent though on us not finding any nightmares with the survey.'

'Understood Tim, I will let them know. Sorry I cannot chat; I have a client here. Bye for now.'

'Goodbye George,' said Tim into a dead phone. Man in a hurry he thought to himself.

The estate agent rang Tim back later and apologised for his brevity. 'I can't tell you the detail but occasionally I come face to face with some extremely unpleasant people, this was one of those occasions.'

'I have contacted the company selling the property and they are happy to go ahead. I am quite sure they are a little strapped for cash as we discussed. I did underline this was a cash deal. I have had a phone call from Mr Vieri notifying me that you will be using his solicitor, apparently he has discussed it with Sophie who agreed to it.'

'Ok, thanks George we will talk soon.' Once upon a time Tim would have been very cross thinking Victor was trying to control things. Now he knew that his father-in-law was doing what he could to help.

The following morning, Tim rang an executive staff agency about a human resources manager.

CHAPTER 27

Early one dark morning, Tom Cooper opened the front door to fetch the milk in. There was a bundle of rags on the step. An empty milk bottle stood beside them. He turned to put the porch light on, as he did so the pile of filthy rags moved. A grubby, bruised face appeared, a face he recognised; it was young Sammy, his lip was split, he had a black eye. The hand that had pulled the rags from his head was bloody.

'Oh, you poor lad,' said Tom. 'Whatever's happened to you? Come inside where we can sort you out.'

Sammy was unable to stand, obviously in great pain and still holding the filthy, ragged clothing to him.

'Hold tight lad, I reckon I can carry you. I'll try not to hurt you.' There was a long moan as he lifted the boy from the floor. Now upright, Tom realised the boy weighed nothing at all.

'You're a poor little scrap of humanity, aren't you?'

Gently placing the boy on the couch and sliding a pillow under his head, he asked, 'Would you like a drink?' All he got was a small shake of the head as the child's eyes closed. Moments later the boy was sound asleep. Tom bent down with his head on his side listening to the rhythm of the lad's breathing. It was clear he was knocked about but there did not seem to be anything life-threatening; there was no serious blood loss or broken bones as far as he could tell, lots of bruises that were going to be sore for some while. One eye was nearly shut because of the bruising that was slowly darkening his cheek what he could see of the eye appeared normal. His split lip would need a smear of something to stop any infection.

Tom noticed his dog Beth had lain down beside the boy as though to protect him, seeing Tom watching her she gave her signature single flip of her tail.

Tom working quietly brought the big old tin bath in from the shed and placed it in front of the fire he had started. The elderly man knew he would not be able to carry the child upstairs. That journey was a challenge for him nowadays. He was concerned that he may cause the boy unnecessary pain. He made some sandwiches quietly in the kitchen interspersed with numerous short journeys to the lounge door to check on the boy.

How on earth had the boy made the journey from the docks to here, wondered Tom. He must have been in so much pain. What sort of an animal was the person who had done this to him?

Three hours later a soft bark had him peering into the lounge again to find Beth licking Sammy's hand, and a big smile on the boy's face.

Tom noticed the boy's elbows and knees were rubbed raw. 'What happened, lad?' he asked.

'A drunken docker grabbed me an' told me to give 'im me money or it would be the worse for me. I pulled meself free and dived under a big trolley to get away from 'im.'

'Then what?'

'He reached under it and dragged me out, I braced me elbows and knees on the floor, but he was too strong, it scraped me skin off and I think I've cut me back. Then he gave me a right kicking and pinched all me money.'

'How are you feeling, lad?'

'I hurts a bit – it's me ribs.'

'I reckon a hot bath might help, what do you think? I've got the old tin bath out so when you are ready you can have it in front of the fire. You'll be nice and warm. I'll make myself scarce in the kitchen, so it'll be private for you.'

A short while later Sammy was immersed up to his neck in warm water, carefully washing off the dirt, there were few places that didn't hurt. Beth watched him as he did so.

Tom sat, in the kitchen, mulling over the boy's future. It pleased him that the boy had come to him in his *extremis*. He realised that here was the only choice.

Tom jumped, his musings interrupted as the lad appeared at his elbow, unheard, wrapped up in an oversized dressing gown.

Sammy wolfed down the sandwiches and a large chunk of currant cake, all washed down with two mugs of tea.

'That was a funny old breakfast, lad, but I guess it filled a hole. Now I must go to work. Are you going to be all right here on your own? I will call in at lunch time to make sure you are OK.'

'You don't need to do that Mr. I'm used to looking after meself I am.'

'I can see you are, but I think we can do a bit better than having you roaming the streets. Now, will you be happy to stay here for a while?'

'Yes, Mr.'

'Can I suggest, Sammy, that you stay here till we sort your clothes out and your lumps and bumps mend. What do you think?'

'Sounds good, Mr. I won't touch nuffin'.'

'Let me show you where everything is in the kitchen.'

'Don't bovver I've sussed that out already, when I was living wiv me mother on the boat she was of'en gone for days at a time. Lord knows what she was doin'.'

Tom shook his head and making for the front door said, 'See you at lunch time.' On his way to work

he informed the dock's foreman about the beating Sammy had taken and the theft of his money. The dockers had taken a shine to the boy and paid him a few coppers to run small errands for him.

At work that morning, Tom Cooper spoke to an elderly nurse who called in most mornings for the ingredients for her evening meal. It always made Tom smile. His mother had always gone shopping every day except Mondays, washing day. Then the evening meal was whatever had been left over from the Sunday dinner. He remembered how much he loved cold rabbit with a pile of mashed potato in a dark-brown pool of Mum's gravy. His mouth was watering as he remembered it, then he was awash with the pain of his mother's and his wife's loss. Pull yourself together you silly old fool was his reaction. It was then he noticed the nurse was leaving, he hurried across the shop and followed her outside.

'Nurse Mildred, can I have a word, please?' he asked.

'Hallo Tom how are you?' she said casting a professional eye over him. 'You're looking a lot better than last time I saw you. You're not so grey faced.'

'I am better thank you, I am working for Tim, my son, here in the shops. I wonder if I could ask a favour of you. I have a youngster staying with me who's been beaten up and won't go to the Doctor.'

'Tom, I cannot talk now, I will be late for surgery. I'll call round tonight after dinner, about seven?'

'Yes, thank you.'

Later that evening, Nurse Mildred arrived at Tom's house. On seeing her enter the lounge Sammy struggled up from the couch saying, 'You aren't a nun are yer come to take me away again? Yer won't 'old me this time, I'll be gorn I will. No one ain't never gunna shut Sammy M ...' The boy slammed his mouth shut; he had almost given away his surname. 'Not never agin,' he added.

'I am a nurse Sammy. Tom asked me to come and check your injuries, he is worried about you.'

Sammy, more reassured, settled back on the couch.

'Tom, can you give us some privacy, please?'

'Oh yes, sorry,' said Tom backing away into the kitchen.

The last thing he heard was Nurse Mildred asking, 'Where does it hurt the most, lad?' He closed the door and put the kettle on.

*

Fifteen minutes later there was a tap on the kitchen door. When he opened it Nurse Mildred walked in and closed the door behind her saying, 'He has had a serious kicking. He tells me he is not passing blood, but we need to impress on him that he must tell you if he begins to have problems. I would normally get the Doctor to put a stitch in his lip to close the split but when I suggested it, he was adamant he wasn't going to a Doctor.'

The three of them sat sipping their tea. Sammy grimacing as the tea stung his lip.

'We need to put a stitch in your lip, Sammy,' said Tom seeing the lad's pain.

The boy started to shake his head. 'What if I told you I could get the Doctor to come here in the morning to put a stitch in it?'

'No, I ain't doing that, where's mi clothes. I'm off I am.' He was struggling to stand up and throw his blankets off. Tim could see the fear on the boy's face and hear it in his voice.

'Sammy, do you trust me?' Tom was now kneeling on the floor holding the boy's arms and looking into his eyes. 'Well, do you lad?'

There was a long silence, the two of them – the man and the boy's eyes were locked together.

Eventually the boy gave the tiniest of nods.

Beth got up and licked the boy's hand.

'One thing I will say Sammy, if your lip becomes septic or you start to have other problems we will go to the Doctor, do you understand?'

'Yes, Mr.'

'Can we try, Tom?'

'Yes, Mr.'

Shaking his head, the man said, 'Yes, Tom.'

'Yes, Tom,' repeated the boy. Tom smiled.

Tom gave the nurse a good-sized bag of vegetables on the way out as payment for her time. This sort of thing was common currency locally.

Two days later an article in the local paper reported that a docker had sustained serious injuries in an attack by person or persons unknown. There were no witnesses to the assault. It was expected he would be in hospital for some time. The article ended in the usual fashion, anyone with information etc, etc. Tom knew there would be no response. The man had gotten what was coming to him.

Tom was given a small envelope by the foreman, who said, 'I'm sure the b----r stole more'n that off the lad. Some of the men was for topping the thieving blighter. He was lucky he didn't end up face down in the river. Tell Sammy if he wants his job back when he's better to come and see me.'

'Thanks Bert,' said Tom as he walked away.

Two days later the nurse called to check on the boy. Sammy was asleep when she tapped quietly on the back door. Tom opened the door with his finger at his lip indicating she should be quiet.

Nurse Mildred thrust a bag at him. It was full of the boy's clean clothes. 'That's kind of you,' he whispered. 'I'm going to shove them away at the back of the cupboard for a while.'

'I won't wake him, Tom,' she said. 'How is he doing?'

'He is on the mend, Mildred. Thanks for all your help.'

Two weeks later the lad was up on his feet ready to get back to his job. Good food, plenty of sleep and a warm bed had made a big difference to the child.

CHAPTER 28

'Tim, can we get together today? I have something interesting to discuss.' He could tell Jessica was quite excited, it was not her normal polite telephone voice.

'What's it about?' he asked.

'I do not want to tell you over the phone, can we meet this afternoon. You are free after three thirty?'

This was his early morning telephone briefing.

'Jessica, I was hoping to have a few hours off this afternoon. Can we do it tomorrow?'

'You are busy all day tomorrow – this is really good news, Tim.'

'OK, I will meet you at the office. You can buy the cakes to compensate me for losing my time off.'

'There is no need to buy cakes, Mrs Graham keeps the tins in the kitchen stocked with cakes and biscuits.'

'You never told me that.'

'I am sure I did, Tim.' Her laugh gave the game away

'Of course, you did, silly me. I'm always forgetting about cakes and the like.'

'Shall I see you later?'

'Yes, and make sure the tins are full.'

*

Tim had stumbled across problem after problem all day. What he really wanted to do was to go back to the houseboat and put his feet up. He nearly rang Jessica to tell her that was what he was going to do. Then he remembered how excited she had sounded that morning. I can keep it short, he thought. He rang Jessica to warn her he would be a little late. Bonny answered the phone.

'Hallo, it's Tim here. Can you tell Jessica, I will be a little late? I am just leaving Number Two, the Fish Hill shop now.'

'I'll do that, Mr Cooper.'

'Tim, Bonny – it's Tim.'

'Yes sir,' she replied as she hung up the phone. 'Goodbye, sir.'

Sophie always chided him when he said how embarrassing it was when the staff called him anything but Tim.

'You fibber, you love it,' she said.

He had thought about it a lot. He could hear his mother's voice before her life had been cut so tragically short. 'We are all born equal. Tim. We should not kowtow to anybody.' His mother had been a fierce advocate of female emancipation and the rights of the common man. No Sophie, he thought, your wrong.

He almost dozed off on the tube, coming to with a jerk as he heard the station tannoy announce the name of the station Three big strides and he was on the platform with the doors sliding shut behind him, brushing the back of his jacket as they did so.

As Tim let himself into the office he was met by the smell of coffee. 'Hallo,' he called from the hall, 'I'm here.' Walking into the head office Jessica was making room amongst the piles of paperwork to allow Bonny to put the tray full of coffee cups down. Both the women said hallo as Tim reached for a cup. Taking a long swig, he uttered a sigh saying, 'Phew, that's better.'

'It sounds as though it has been a long day, Tim.'

Nodding and settling back into his chair, he replied, 'You could say that. So, what have you got for me?'

The two women shared a conspiratorial smile as Jessica started speaking. 'It is about the Longstaff fund, Tim – we have finally found a school and a headmaster who is keen to talk to us.'

Tim lent forward; his hands clasped together on the table in front of him. He could sense the feeling of accomplishment being given off by the two women.

'We have two possibles – a girl and a boy. The girl's family are from Barbados. Her name is Tiana Marshall – the headmaster assures me she is a remarkable mathematician. The boy is a fine artist – the headmaster walked us down the main corridor, four of the charcoal drawings on the walls were his and I am assured they are a photographic likeness. His work I would describe as minimalist.'

Tim had an enquiring look on his face obviously unsure what was meant.

'Art, my other choice at university,' she explained. 'He is described as moody – this may be the result of what is believed to be a difficult home life. His father is a toolmaker and apparently unpleasant.'

'What's his name?' asked Tim.

'John Jones,' said Bonny after Jessica had paused with her brow furrowed. 'Known to his friends as JJ.'

'I thought artists all lived in garrets and slowly starved to death,' said Tim.

'Not true – a friend of mine now works for a major advertising company earning a small fortune,' volunteered Jessica.

'So, what's the next step?' he asked.

'We have done step one – the headmaster and the teachers are on board. Step two is to talk to the parents. The headmaster is sending out a letter to both families explaining in broad terms what we are offering and asking for their permission to talk to the children. The only thing is, Tim, Bonny and I are worried we may have jumped the gun, we have started this ball rolling without your agreement. Is that ok?'

'No problem, you have done wonders.'

'Thank you, shall I make more coffee while Bonny talks you through the info she has put together?'

Bonny showed Tim the minutes of the meeting with the headmaster and the teachers. Letters to and from the Inner London Education Authority.

Bonny continued, 'I don't know if you have realised boss, this will only concern us once a year when the students have taken their mocks and have decided to continue into the sixth form.'

'I have to admit to you both,' said Tim as Jessica returned with the coffee, 'I have had so much to do I have put this to the back of my mind and let you two work it out, and I must say you have both done an excellent job of it.'

'We can increase the advertising in the year before,' said Bonny.

'During that time, we can ask for expressions of interest from the school and the pupils so that we have a better idea of the numbers for the following year,' offered Jessica.

'Good idea, it will spread the workload,' said Tim. 'Thank you both, well done.'

CHAPTER 29

Tim and Sophie were sitting waiting in the office to interview a possible human recourses manager. At five minutes to the agreed time, the doorbell rang, Tim jumped up to answer it as Sophie moved to get up. She had noticed Tim was extremely protective of her since she had revealed her pregnancy. A good-looking, dark-haired young man preceded Tim into the room.

Stepping towards Sophie he offered his hand and said, 'Hallo my name is Oliver Adams.'

Tim said, 'Please sit, this is Sophia Cooper, my wife and the company Finance Director.'

'I am pleased to meet you Oliver and I prefer to be called Sophie.'

'I'm Tim Cooper. I'm the company chairman and general dog's body. Can you tell us a bit about yourself and why you came here this morning?'

'I went to Harrow School and then to Eton. I have been working for the same company since I left university and frankly I need a change. I am very attracted to all the new stuff you are starting. Should I get the job, I believe with my experience I will be able to make a real contribution to the development of the company, by finding the right people for the right jobs and handling any staffing issues that arise. That will mean one less job for you guys and I think for me it will be extremely exciting.'

The usual list of questions was asked and answered.

'Sophie has some info for you,' said Tim

'Oliver, if you are successful, you will, for now, be working from here. Tim and I have not discussed this yet, but I think we will outgrow these premises soon.'

Tim was nodding.

'We are blessed with our current staff – they all work their socks off and are extremely defensive of the company. To be blunt, initially the hours will be long and the pay poor but as the new venture comes into profit, we will be able to step up your salary – the hours though are always long around here. The starting remuneration will be as advertised. We expect to be able to increase this as the food hall and the Italian restaurant take off. I should warn you if the new venture fails, we will all starve.'

It was a good sign, thought Tim, that Oliver laughed.

Sophie glanced at Tim and said, 'Yes. So, what do you think Oliver, would you like to join us and have crack at building something new from the floor up?' asked Sophie.

'Well, you have been brutally honest in your attempt to put me off the job,' said Oliver smiling. 'But it sounds as though I may, for a change, look forward to coming to work in the morning, so yes please, I will take the job.' He didn't mention how astronomic the drop in salary was below his present pay scale.

'OK, I must go to the day job,' said Sophie. 'Tim will introduce you to the girls next door.'

'Sophie holds down the same job for Mr Wells in his store,' added Tim.

Tim kissed his wife goodbye before walking Oliver into the other office. Both women perked up as the handsome young man followed Tim into the other room. It was, Tim suspected, something Oliver was used to.

*

The work on the food hall was proceeding well. Charlie had gathered a team of painters and decorators that he had worked with before on large projects. He admitted to Tim this was the biggest yet.

'Thank God you only wanted one colour for the walls Tim – that makes it a bit easier, like. You knows this warm white changes colour wiv the time of day? We put up a similar colour some time ago, it's amazin', it changes from a pale grey in daylight to a soft pink at night. I reckon it'll be right smart. It will brighten the place up a treat.'

'I see you have brought in some wheeled scaffolding for the walls and ceiling – it certainly beats the terrifying tall wobbly ladders you used at the last shop.'

'You won't believe this Tim, these great big 'airy tough guys refused to use 'em.'

'I'm not surprised,' was Tim's reply.

'This bit of kit will save a lot a time. Mind you it's costing you a bloomin' fortune,' laughed Charlie.

'Thanks Charlie,' said Tim meaning anything but. As he gazed around it was clear the job was well under way.

CHAPTER 30

Two weeks after the previous meeting at the office, Tim, Jessica, Oliver, and Bonny were seated around the table discussing the Longstaff fund. Tim had asked Jessica to make sure that Oliver was involved in all the staff meetings so now there was an extra body at the table. He was quiet during the meeting, but he was making lots of notes.

Jessica began, 'We have visited Tiana's home – her family are lovely people, her father is a nurse, her mother works in the evenings in a home for the elderly. There was an older woman there who was introduced to us as Nan. Lots of children. We were offered tea and cake and made very welcome. It's a cheerful home.'

'Tiana is lovely. She is clever and quick,' added Bonny enthusiastically.

'They are excited about what we are offering,' continued Jessica. 'Tiana had refused to consider going to uni because she believed it was time for her to give something back to her family.'

'I am so pleased I am part of it. I have to admit Tim that a short while ago I was getting rather down. The job was all overtime and hard work. Bonny has been an immense help, but I would not tell her that, but visiting Tiana and her folks, I am so pleased I am part of this.'

Bonny was laughing.

'How are you finding it, Oliver?' asked Tim.

Oliver thought for a moment before replying then said, 'I am very surprised Tim. I have to admit that when I first arrived I thought people were putting on an act with regard to their attitude to the work because of the position I hold. I now realise it's how things are done.'

'I think it's because we all feel involved,' said Bonny. 'I have been here only a short while, but I know everybody feels committed to what we are all trying to do, and just as importantly I think we all sense the boss here and all the rest of the management are approachable.'

Tim's simple response was, 'Thank you Bonny, that means a lot. Now I must get on.'

*

Tim became aware over time that the office was really getting up to speed, the two women's skills meshed perfectly. Jessica would say, 'Can you do so and so,' only to discover Bonny had anticipated her requirements and was holding a file out to her.

'I am working with a telepath Tim,' remarked Jessica on one occasion.

'I am extremely impressed by how well you two work together. Well done, ladies,' said Tim as he gathered another pile of paper that needed his attention and made his way to his office at the rear of the building. Scan reading the page on the top of the pile he called, 'Bonny.'

When Bonny walked in, she was smiling.

'What's so funny?' he asked.

'We each made an educated guess at how long it would be before you called for one of us.'

'Who won today?'

'Me, boss.' She was unable to stifle a giggle.

'Go on then, how long was it?'

'Twenty-seven seconds.'

'Hmph, right – let's get on.'

The couple worked hard for the next hour.

*

In contrast to the reception they had received from the Marshall family, the talks with JJ's father and mother were not going well. The father at first was very loath to talk to them at all. When the idea of financial support was put to him by Jessica he had growled, 'He won't be doing any of this arty farty stuff, it's a waste of time, he's gunna get a job.'

Tim was sitting in the Jones's front room. He had arrived unannounced. He was initially tempted to move on and forget JJ. Then he remembered the amazing artistic skill the boy possessed. Time for a frontal attack he decided. Let's see if I can sell this, he said to himself.

'Why do you think it's a waste of time, Mr Jones?' asked Tim.

'Well, he ain't gunna earn any money doing that is he?'

'Can I ask what sort of money John will earn in the factory as an apprentice?' Tim suggested some numbers.

Mrs Jones laughed cynically saying, 'If only.'

'Can I show you some figures from the local paper. John wants to become a graphic artist, the jobs advertised are for graduates straight out of university. This is not pie in the sky. Your John is exceptionally skilled. This is the salary they are offering.'

He handed each of them a page, Mrs Jones studied the paper for a moment then said, 'Ted this is more …'

'Shut up woman, we don't want to tell everyone our business.'

'Do you understand how this payment works, Mr Jones?'

'Yeah, you gives him extra cash so as he can go to university.'

'No, sorry that's not right, we give you extra cash to make up for the money he would be earning as an apprentice at the factory.'

'Yeah right, why would you do that? Sounds like a scam to me, mate.'

'Mr Jones, I started working part-time long before I should have left school, I was fourteen years old, thirteen when my mum died, my father became ill, I was the sole provider. I worked from can see to can't see in all weathers outside, come rain or shine. Through hard work and good fortune, I have become very wealthy – I want to use my money to help young people like your son to develop this gift he has. He is extraordinary. Anybody who knows what they are talking about in the art world is excited about his skill at such a young age. Manufacturers, advertisers, book publishers are crying out for young people with your son's skills. If you put him in the factory, you will be harnessing a thoroughbred racehorse to a coal cart. I am going to leave you to think about it – your wife has the details. Goodnight.'

'I will see you out, Mr Cooper,' said his wife opening the door for him. She followed him down the path, reaching the gate she asked, 'Is John really that good?'

'Yes, he is.'

'Why are you doing it? What do you get out of it?'

'I went to school with a lot of gifted people from ordinary working-class backgrounds, they are all in ordinary jobs. They were capable of so much more. I'm only trying to spread a little of my good luck to help young gifted people out.'

She held his gaze for quite a while, then said, 'I'll do my best to persuade him.'

Mr Graham had parked a little way down the street, and as he reached the Bentley, he heard a wrought-iron gate clang shut behind him and the sound of running feet approaching him, as he turned JJ stopped by his side.

'Mr Cooper I was listening. Can I ask you somethin'? Did mean what yur said in there, about me being really good?'

'I did and I do, you are an exceptionally talented young man, I can understand why you find life hard, but you have been given a gift that will lift you out of this. Don't waste it, take up my offer. Whatever your father says stay in touch with me.'

Throughout this conversation JJ was staring at the floor his shoulders slumped. 'Stand up straight lad and look at me.' The boy did as commanded. 'Your new life can start here if you change your attitude and work extremely hard.' There was steel in Tim's voice now. 'Take my card and ring me, ok? Only a damn fool would pass this up, JJ. Do you hear me, lad? If you can't get me, ask to speak to Jessica, ok?'

'Yes sir,' was the response.

'It's Tim lad, call me, Tim.'

As the boy started back down the road Tim had an idea. 'JJ, here a minute.' Beckoning him to return. As the boy joined him, Tim asked, 'Have you a portfolio of your work?'

JJ nodded.

'If I fix an appointment with a professional gallery owner, will you be prepared to bring it along and talk about your work?'

'Yes, it'll have to be out of school though.'

'I think we can sort that out. Do we have your phone number?'

'Yes, I gave it to that lady, erm, Jessica.'

*

Back on the boat that evening, Tim was cuddling Charley when Sophie asked about the youngsters.

'I haven't met the girl or her parents, but Jessica and Bonny think they are lovely, they both agreed Tiana is extremely clever. It's not her I am worried about, it's JJ's dad – his mum's nice, but the father.' Tim was now shaking his head and sighing as he did so. 'I know you don't like me swearing but the nicest thing I can say about him is he is an oaf. I have given JJ my card and told him to keep in touch.'

'Tim, I think we should have anticipated this.'

'Anticipated what?' he asked in a rather brusque voice, sensing criticism.

'Please do not get cross with me, Tim, all I am saying is that you are a problem-solver, and you cannot help stepping in.'

Tim bit his tongue while he thought about it, he recognised there was truth in what she said. 'Can I explain, in this case, it's more than just his father. This boy has a gift. I saw a drawing of his mother in the hallway done in charcoal, it was just a few lines, but it captured his mother to a T.'

'How do you know it was his work?'

'I couldn't miss it; in the bottom right-hand corner he had written JJ in large capital letters. Are you ok?' he asked, noticing by her tone of voice that she was obviously exhausted.

'Yes, it is the baby, I get tired in the evenings.' She paused to draw breath. 'It was the same with madame,' said Sophie pointing at Charley.

'You need to back off a little. Let's see what we can transfer to Jessica and Bonny.'

Sophie nodded. 'I think that is a good idea.'

'And' said Tim, 'we'll get Nanny in more often so you can put your feet up, and someone to clean and do the washing.'

Sophie nodded and said, 'Thank you, Tim.'

Her response worried him; she was normally resistant to being told to slow down. He made a mental note to talk to Jessica and her assistant first thing in the morning and get them to find some staff to help with the household chores.

*

The following day Tim had his feet up on his desk savouring his first coffee of the day. Bonny walked in and said, 'You will have to put up with me for this morning's meeting, boss. Jessica is knee deep in the work you gave her yesterday.'

Tim was unsure whether he liked the title she used for him; he knew it was because Bonny was uncomfortable calling him by his Christian name, he realised she was young and obviously felt the age difference more than he did. 'Can you ask Jessica to come in for five minutes, please?'

Bonny leaned out of the doorway and shouted down the hall, 'Jessica can you come in, please?'

'Bonny, I could have shouted for her.'

'Whoops, sorry boss.'

'Did somebody shout?' asked the older woman as she entered the room.

'Sorry all,' said Bonny ruefully.

'The heading is new staff,' advised Tim. 'Jessica, why do you need another body in here?'

'Filing,' said Jessica. 'We are producing more paper. The truth is it gets put aside when we are busy and then it's a pain to sort the pile out later. We are extremely busy most of the time nowadays, and to be honest it needs rearranging as well.'

'Thank you,' said Tim. 'Bonny?'

'I agree with Jessica. It's a matter of the priorities with the workload – to be honest the filing usually comes last. Also the need to do research is an increasing part of the job, and that can be time-consuming when we can't find a file.'

'So, who do we want?' he asked?'

'A clever child,' said Bonny.

'We already have one,' observed Tim.

Jessica laughed out loud then said, 'Bonny is about right – a clever young girl that we can train would be ideal.'

'Why a girl?' he queried.

'It feels right,' said Jessica.

'And women are apparently better at the detail,' added Bonny.

Tim was going to mention that it could keep the wage bill down, but he decided it was too early in the morning to start that argument. 'Bonny, can you talk to Oliver? Where is he by the way?'

'He has taken all the employee information home and is going to sort it out and put it on his computer, then he will print off hard copies for our files. He has left his home number so I can ring him, boss, if you want me to.'

'No, tomorrow will do.'

'Tim, do you need me anymore? I really am up to my ears?'

'No, you carry on Jessica, Bonny can do the next bit.'

Tim leaning forward to talk to Bonny said, 'Sophie is finding this pregnancy extremely hard work and tiring. She has at last agreed she needs help. So, the idea is that we find a woman that does. Have you met the Vieri's housekeeper, Martha?'

'No, I haven't,' the girl responded.

'We need a version of her. We don't need someone to live in – it's cooking, cleaning, washing and ironing basically. Nanny is there for Charley – we need someone nice what does. You had better mention the houseboat. You could talk to Sally, Mr Vieri's PA, she will have the detail. Also, can you research the pay rate, please?'

✳

Tim was a little late arriving at the office the following morning. The two women were hard at work but stopped when he arrived. He was hardly in the door when they asked, 'Can we talk, Tim?'

Surprised Tim said, 'Yes, what's it about?'

Jessica said, 'Bonny will explain, it is her idea.'

'Boss I was lying in bed last night thinking about the filing problem. If we had a proper system rather than what we have now it would be easy to keep it up to date.'

'This is my fault, Tim,' admitted Jessica. 'When I started working for you there was little in the way of filing compared to now, there was not much of a system, there did not need to be. I knew where everything was. Nowadays that system is broken. Bonny will explain.'

'Boss,' continued the younger woman, 'I think if we buy in a modern system, this will save us a lot of time and then arrange for a temp to come in and implement it and clear the backlog, this means we will not need another full-time worker just yet. Jessica and I are working together more efficiently. With good systems in place, the two of us can handle this. I wondered if Sophie would have any ideas as regards the financial side?'

'What do you think, Tim?' asked Jessica.

'I think it is a great idea. I will talk to Sophie. Well done both of you.'

CHAPTER 31

The following Saturday, Sophie was sitting on the boat interviewing a part-time cook and housekeeper. The woman, a Mrs Brenda Grayson said, 'I prefer Mrs Grayson, my dear,' when asked what the family should call her. She was grey-haired and middle-aged, a little chubby. There was nothing notable about her. Sophie sensed that she may be a little severe, but she was so tired and nobody else had answered the ad in the paper and she agreed to take the woman on for a trial period.

'I hope this all works out,' said Sophie as Mrs Grayson was leaving.

The woman looked round and said, 'It won't take me long to sort all this, I can assure you.' Sophie was left pondering what it was that needed sorting.

✳

Sophie returned towards the end of Mrs Grayson's first day.

'Where have the cushions gone and the throw that was on the couch, and why are some of the saucepans outside by the bin,' she asked.

'I am decluttering for you my dear, three or four more days should see me done.'

Nanny emerged from the back cabin carrying a crying Charley.

'Why is my child crying?'

'I had to discipline your daughter, she kept trying to bring the saucepans back in.'

Nanny was in floods of tears saying, 'If this woman is going to work here, I will have to leave.'

'You did what to my daughter?'

'I slapped her, the merest reprimand, she disobeyed me. If I am to take over this household, she must learn that I mean what I say.'

Sophie exploded. 'You are not taking over this household and you have never had any authority over my daughter.'

'Mrs Cooper it is obvious that you have no idea about parenting, goodness knows how this child will grow up.'

Sophie now beyond reason, picked up the woman's bag and cardigan, marched to the front door and hurled everything as far as she could. As the bag hit the ground the contents flew everywhere. Tim had just arrived and had been forced to duck and take a few steps back. He stood watching the woman run from the boat and then begin scrabbling about on the ground retrieving her belongings.

Sophie stepped ashore and marched towards the woman, shouting, 'If I ever set eyes on you again, I will not be responsible for my actions.' She was so cross she was barely coherent. The terrified woman scuttled away.

Back on board, Tim gave both women a hug and went and put the kettle on.

At bedtime he was cuddling his daughter who was still unsettled. She said, 'Mummy was ever so cross, Daddy. I have never seen her like that.'

'You may never see her like it again, sweetheart. Let me explain.' Tim was aware Sophie could hear everything he was saying. 'You know Mummy is Italian, like Grandpa Victor.'

'Grandpa Victor gets cross sometimes, Daddy.'

'That's because they have both got dragons living in their tummies. Italian dragons are asleep nearly all the time unless someone threatens someone they love, then they wake up.' His voice was growing louder and more growly. 'Then the person who is threatening you or me, has to run away before Mummy's dragon eats them.'

'Will Mummy's dragon always look after us, Daddy?'

'Yes.'

As they got into bed later that night Sophie gave him a long, slow kiss and then said, 'I love you.'

Tim pulled her close and said, 'I love you too, thank you for my baby.' Minutes later they were both sound asleep.

The following morning Nanny was at the Sea Maiden early, the family were only just up, still in their pyjamas. 'Good mornings' were shared out then Sophie asked with a smile on her face, 'Could you not sleep, Nanny?'

'No, I couldn't, that woman scared me. I wouldn't work with someone like her, the thought of having to leave you all was very upsetting. I kept trying to think of who I knew that might want the job. I lay awake for hours, then I knew who to ask.'

'Who is that Nanny?' asked Sophie.

'Me!' she replied gleefully using both thumbs to point at herself, her face wearing a huge smile. 'I sit about waiting for you to ring – at least this way I will be busy. If you want, I can take little one to school every day? I can clean, cook, shop, basically keep house for you. The only difference between me and *that woman*' – these two words were spat out – 'is I will do it your way – you tell me how you want it done and that is how it will be.'

Now Charley was dancing about clapping her hands, singing, 'Oh yes, oh yes, oh yes.'

Nanny continued saying, 'And, I'm happy to work for the same money.' Her Irish, American accent was now very audible. Her heart fell when she saw Tim shaking his head.

'No,' he said, 'that's not going to happen.'

'Tim,' said Sophie, extremely surprised; thinking, it is perfect. 'I think it is a great idea, we will not have a stranger on here, and we will have someone we know and trust and are fond of.'

'Can I finish,' said Tim huffing. 'All I am talking about is sorting the money out so that Nanny gets a proper full-time rate. You can let us know what time you want off Nanny, for mass or seeing friends, and Mr Graham will ferry you around to school, home, etcetera. As someone once said, "It's an elegant solution".'

The enormous smile on Charley's face said it all.

Thus began an arrangement that was to last for years.

CHAPTER 32

A fortnight later, Tim was standing outside the art gallery waiting for JJ and his mum. Sophie had suggested that a parent should be with the boy. Tim had arrived earlier to introduce himself to the owner of the gallery, Mr Palmer, who gave off an air of quiet competence in his fawn suit and tie. Tim spotted JJ and his mother crossing the road towards him. There had been no resistance from the school when he had explained the reason for the time out.

Stepping inside the door they found Mr Palmer hovering close by. He introduced himself to Mrs Jones then turned to JJ and said, 'So this is the budding artist?' He shook JJ's hand. JJ was in his school uniform and appeared very young.

A middle-aged lady in a black suit standing beside the gallery owner stepped forward as Mr Palmer said, 'This is my man Friday, she does all the work really.'

'Hallo,' she said shaking their hands, 'my name is Linda. I will see you later.'

The gallery owner lead them into his office, cleared some paperwork off his desk and said, 'Over to you JJ, let's see what you've got.'

The boy spread six charcoal drawings across the desk, including the framed portrait of his mother. The room went silent, the only sound was the

occasional 'hmm,' from Mr Palmer. Finally, he said, 'I won't be a moment.'
He walked back into the gallery, soon to return with Linda.

There was another long silence while she perused JJ's work, then she
said, 'Wow.' Turning to her boss who said, 'Wow indeed.' Taking the boy's
hand in both of his he said, 'JJ, I apologise for calling you a budding artist,
I am sure your work will change overtime as you explore your gift. But,
make no mistake lad, it's a gift you have been given, this work is particularly
good.'

Linda said, 'It's extraordinary to find this confidence and control in one
so young – can I hug you?'

JJ just shrugged his shoulders, Linda hugged him anyway.

'May we hold on to all of them for a while?'

Tim was about to say something when Mr Palmer said, 'Yes Tim, we will
issue a receipt.'

Mrs Jones, sounding quite concerned and asked, 'Can we keep the one
of me please, Mr Palmer?'

'Of course,' he replied, handing the picture to her. 'Will you be handling
any business we may want to talk about Mrs Jones?'

'Oh no,' was her response. Shaking her head in denial.

JJ taking the initiative asked, 'Will you do it Mr Cooper? I didn't believe
you when you said I was good. I trusts you now.'

Tim thought for a moment. This was exactly what Sophie had warned
him about, getting over involved. For now, there did not seem to be much
of an alternative: his father would drink it, his mum has just said no, and JJ
is too young. 'My wife is going to give me so much stick over this so it's only
until we find a viable alternative, OK?'

Both Mum and son said, 'Thank you, Mr Cooper.'

Linda handed Tim a receipt.

Hands were shaken and goodbyes said.

'Now, how about I give you a lift home? I can help explain what's happening to your father, although to be honest I am not sure of the normal procedure. We will learn together. One thing I can help with is the business side. Now where is the car? Oh, here we go.' Tim had spotted the Bentley pulling out of a side turning.

Drawing to a halt in front of them, Mrs Jones was still searching up and down the street as Mr Graham opened the back door for her.

'Here we are Mum,' said JJ trying to ease his mother into the car. Refusing to move she turned to Tim and asked, 'Is this yours?'

'Yes Mrs Jones, jump in.' JJ and Tim followed her in. Tim watched her out of the corner of his eye. He saw her running her fingers over the heavy leather tan seats, then she was staring between her feet at the matching carpeted floor, she ran her hand along the varnished rail under the windows.

'I ain't never travelled in nothing like this before. It's lovely, 'ave you had it a long time, Mr Cooper?'

'It's been in my family since I was a child, maybe longer than that – it's beautiful though, isn't it? Mr Graham our chauffeur looks after it well.'

'Thank you, Tim,' said Mr Graham from the front seat.

'Mr Cooper, am I right in thinking they may try to sell some of my JJ's work?'

'I think he may, but I want to sort out one thing, please call me Tim.'

'Alright Tim, you can call me Aida. Can we talk about the money?'

'There is no guarantee of money, Aida, I am sorry to say. It all depends on people liking JJ's work, but Mr Palmer's interest is a good start. It can take years for an artist's work to become well-known.'

'I knows all that Tim, I'm more concerned if there is money, it'll need protecting from you know who.'

'I understand, I am sure we can set a bank account up, so it requires more than one signature. I must stress there is no certainty about all this. You might not sell a thing.'

The car pulled up near the boy's house.

'Would you like me to come in and explain to your dad, JJ? I'm not going to talk about money unless he brings it up.'

'He will,' grumbled JJ.

'I'll put the kettle on,' said Mrs Jones walking towards the kitchen.

'He's in here,' said JJ going into the lounge.

'Well go on then … I bet they laughed at yur didn't they?' sneered Mr Jones. Then he noticed JJ was not carrying his portfolio of drawings.

'What have yur done with all yur scribbling?'

'They are lookin' at 'em Dad.'

'You what, they've conned you already mate, you won't see a bloody penny?' Turning to Tim he said, 'Why are you helping? I bet there's summat in it fer yur ain't there? You flash beggars always finds a way of coming up smelling of roses.' Rounding on JJ he said, 'What have I told you about trusting the likes of him.' He nodded at Tim.

'Do I understand you to mean that you don't want the trust money while JJ is continuing his education?'

'What yur saying? Are you gunna pay me?'

'Yes, we are going to pay you, I've told you this once already.' More than a hint of Tim's anger could be heard in his voice.

Suddenly, thought Tim, this odious oaf is interested. Looking at his watch he said, 'I'm late, I will explain it one more time, it will help if you don't interrupt please.' Tim had his right hand raised, his palm facing Mr Jones. We discover how much JJ would be earning as an apprentice at your works and we will pay you that for the period of time that your son is in further education. If he leaves for any reason the money stops. Is that clear?' asked Tim rising to his feet and walking towards the door. 'Goodnight all.' He called out as he left the room. Mrs Jones scurried after him to see him out and apologise yet again for her husband's behaviour.

'Please don't worry Mrs Jones, goodnight to you.'

CHAPTER 33

Tim arrived early at shop Number One, expecting it to be open, instead he found his father standing outside the shop stamping his feet and flapping his arms trying to keep warm; it had been bitterly cold overnight, the pavements still sparkled with their mantle of frost.

'Tim I can't get any response,' said his dad. 'I'm very worried he is always up by the time I get here.'

'You've got your own key though?' queried Tim, unlocking the door and entering the shop, his father following him in.

'Yes, lad. I've a bad feeling about this,' said his father quietly. 'I thought I'd wait for you.'

As Tim unlocked the door and pushed it open he was aware of a cold silence, a stillness he had never experienced before, not in this shop or anywhere else.

'I'm sure it's nothing to worry about. I expect he's overslept,' said Tim as he bounded up the stairs.

Reaching the top, he could see the back of the armchair and Mr Woodman's jacket clad elbow resting on the arm. Tim silenced the hallo that he was going to call out realising his godfather had been there all night. Walking around the chair to the front he saw the old man's chin was resting on his chest, his knees were together, the book he had been reading placed neatly on his lap with the bookmark protruding. Tim touched Mr Woodman's hand, it was stone cold, he could feel no pulse at his neck.

His father had reached the top of the stairs. He saw his son's face and needed no further confirmation.

'He's gone lad, hasn't he?'

Tim, fighting to control his emotions, took a deep breath nodded his head and said, 'I think so, Dad.'

His father put his arm around his son, saying nothing.

'Why do the people I love keep bloody dying on me, asked Tim?'

'That's the way it is son, I'm afraid.'

'Well, it's bloody unfair.' The young man was struggling to control himself.

Tim looked at his godfather dressed as always in his blue jacket and matching trousers, his feet and knees together, his linked hands resting on the book in his lap.

'He died as neatly and efficiently as he lived, Dad.'

'I reckon he was getting ready for bed son, his cover for his legs is neatly folded down here on the floor,' he said pointing down at a red throw on the other side of the armchair.

Tim looked around the flat, everything was as it had always been. The square of dark-blue carpet that the dark wood table and two chairs sat on, all polished to a high shine down the years. The picture of his wife now long dead sat on the matching dark wood sideboard along with a cut-glass decanter and four glasses.

'I need to ring the Doctor,' said Tim.

'I can do that,' said his father.

'No, I'll do it.'

As Tim reached the ground floor a lady walked into the shop.

Tim stepped into her path saying as he did so, 'I am so sorry, we won't be opening today. Mr Woodman has died in the night; it may be a while before we reopen.'

'Oh dear,' said the woman. 'He was such a lovely man.' She plucked a hanky from the sleeve of her pink cardigan and started dabbing her nose as she left.

Tim rang the surgery and had to hold for a few minutes, the receptionist, who sounded extremely young and rather unsure said, 'Can I help you?'

'I have to report a death.'

'Oh, em, can you hold please caller?'

Tim waited; he could hear voices in the background, but he could not hear what was being said. The next voice was female deeper and more authoritative. She sounded older. She asked, 'May I take your name please and the name and address of the deceased?' Tim supplied both. Are you a relative?' she enquired.'

'I'm his godson. I'm all the family he has.'

'Thank you, can I have your name, please?'

'Timothy Cooper.'

'You own Sophie's?'

'Me and my fellow directors, yes. So, what happens now?' he asked, unsure why the woman had mentioned the shop.

'You need to ring 999 and tell the police about the death. The Doctor will call and tell you what will happen. He is out now on a call. I will tell him as soon as he comes back.'

Minutes later Harry and Sara were tapping at the door. Tom let them in. Tim was on the phone to the police. They noted his details and then the officer said, 'You must not move anything until we arrive sir.'

'Whatever has happened?' asked Sara.

Tom reached for a chair. 'Sit down love and I'll tell you.'

Once she was seated, he said, 'Mr Woodman has died.'

'Oh no, no, no. Please don't say that there must be some mistake. He wasn't ill, he was still a strong man.' The tears were flooding down her face.

Harry knelt beside Sara, put both arms round his wife and held her while she cried.

Tim went upstairs and put the kettle on. He walked across to where Mr Woodman sat and said, 'Thank you for everything you have done for me down the years and thank you for your generosity.' Then leaning down, he kissed the stone-cold forehead as the kettle began to whistle. Moving across the room he made the tea and took it downstairs.

The Doctor called later that afternoon and said, 'I have not seen Mr Woodman for ages and therefore there will almost certainly be an autopsy. I cannot sign a death certificate until the coroner releases the body. You are his godson I understand.'

Tim nodded.

'Are there any other family?'

'No,' said Tim shaking his head.

'That's fine,' confirmed the Doctor. 'There will be a van along later to collect the body.'

*

The black van had just called for Mr Woodman'. For a moment, Tim experienced a strange compulsion to stop the two undertakers from taking his godfather away; it was all too final, too soon. He was not ready to say goodbye yet. He experienced a strange desire for he knew not what. Taking his godfather away in the back of a black van felt wrong, he wanted some form of short service, not this well practiced collection of the body. It was wrong, it reminded him of moving house, unemotional, every day, just another errand. There was no recognition of the task signifying the end of an important human life. Moving across the room very slowly he carefully lowered himself into Mr Woodman's armchair. He experienced a comforting warmth as he sat there.

*

As Tim closed the curtains upstairs, he saw a woman in the street look up and cross herself. He was always amazed how fast news of a death spread through the community.

Sophie arrived on her own. 'How are you doing?' she asked him. 'Silly question I know but you seem to be coping well.'

Tim knew what she meant; he had not fallen apart like he had when his aunt died. 'I'm managing,' he replied. 'I assume Nanny has stepped in.' Sophie nodded.

The following day he asked everybody if they should shut the shop for a few days. Sara said, 'No.' Harry said, 'Yes.' Tom wouldn't answer.

Sophie asked, 'What would Mr Woodman say?'

'He'd stay open,' said Tim's father.

Tim realised that in future, 'What would Mr Woodman say?' may well become a mantra.

Later that evening Tim and Sophie were sitting on the stern of Sea Maiden sipping from glasses of Jura, Tim's favourite single-malt whisky; Sophie's a small one because of the baby. They both drank it neat. Since Tim had known Sophie, he had been surprised by her choice of alcohol, everything from a pint of lager to, as today, a glass of the hard stuff. He had assumed quite wrongly that her choice would have been expensive champagne or a glass of good white wine. He believed from previous observation that she had a harder head than him.

When asked about her capacity for drink she would explain it was another ability gained at university that had nothing to do with the curriculum.

'Can you hear Charley?' she asked, the roof vent above the child's bed was just ajar.

Tim with his head on one side listened hard but could hear nothing. 'No' he replied.

'I heard her turn over.'

'You have good ears, pretty too,' said Tim.

Sophie frowned at him; she always had a problem with compliments. He felt sure it was because of her mother was a hard cold woman who did not believe in praise.

They had both been quiet for some time. Tim finally ended the silence by asking, 'Where am I going to go for advice now?'

'Tim, I am sure that if you ask the question and listen hard you will hear the answer.'

'What from beyond the grave, you mean?'

'No, you duffer. I know with all the advice Mr Woodman gave you down the years that you will know the answer yourself.'

'I do hope so.'

'I am sure so.'

He tightened his arm around her and pulled her closer. 'Thank God, I have you,' he whispered into her hair.

Turning her head, she kissed his cheek saying, 'Likewise.'

Tim, quiet for a while, eventually said, 'I don't know if it's just me, but the world seems to be getting lonelier, fewer people that I'm really close to. Those that I have known for a long time. Do you feel like that?'

'No not really,' she replied thoughtfully. 'Everyone is still here except my nanny. I realise yours has been a tougher life than mine with your mother dying, then your great aunt, now your godfather, Mr Woodman.'

'I don't know if other people feel the same but for me the world is a colder place after I've lost someone. It's as though a chill wind is blowing all the time.'

'Come on, let us go inside, we can light the fire and make some toast.'

A little later the couple were sitting in front of the stove with the front down toasting both themselves and the bread. Sophie had noticed Tim was deep in thought again; rising from her chair she took his fork from him and moved sideways to the work surface.

'The usual?' she enquired.

Tim nodded. Sophie spread both slices thickly with their present addiction, peanut butter. Balancing the plates of food in one hand she began to arrange his limbs so that she could sit on his lap.

'How is Nanny doing with her new responsibilities?' queried Tim.

'I asked her today, how she was managing.'

'What did she say?'

'Nanny was laughing when she replied, she said, I am happier than I have been in years. I love looking after you all.'

With the last mouthful eaten he gathered his sleepy wife up in his arms and carried her to bed.

CHAPTER 34

Tim was informed that the coroner had ordered a post-mortem and that nothing would happen until that had been completed, then the death certificate could be issued.

Tim answered the shop phone, recognising the voice on the other end he said, 'Hallo, Victor.'

'I am so sorry to hear your news Tim, I was not aware he was unwell.'

'I don't think he was, it's a complete surprise. I hadn't heard him complain of anything.'

'I thought he would go on forever,' said Victor. 'Every time I saw him, he was always busy, never still.'

'You're right, "always busy" could have been his nickname. He's still now though.'

'I rang you for two reasons Tim, firstly to give our condolences, Mrs Vieri and I, but also to say that I am offering the use of the company solicitor if that would help. Because of the shop, the will, there will be inheritance tax to pay. Mrs Simmons can ensure you do not have to pay any more than you must. If you think I am poking my nose in, please say so.'

'No, you are more than kind, it would be an immense help. By the way, who is Mrs Simmons? The last time I used your solicitor it was a man.'

'Hmm, I am really cross, the silly beggar decided to retire. I am having to explain things to her every time something new comes up, and she is a bit prickly. I have to be a bit careful how I talk to her, she seems to take offence easily, although I have to say she seems particularly good at her job. Should you need a second opinion please call, I am more than happy to help.'

'Thanks Victor, I can see that it might get complicated.'

He also had some sympathy for the retiring solicitor, working for Victor Vieri all those years. Tim knew to his cost that Victor when angry could be extremely rude and aggressive.

*

Talking with Sophie, Harry, Sara, and his father Tom, it was decided that because Mr Woodman was a down-to-earth, practical person, it would not be appropriate to have a funeral like Tim's aunt with the horse-drawn hearse all in black, the mourners that were able walking behind.

Tom, on his day off, found Mrs Woodman's grave. It was arranged that Mr Woodman and his wife would share the grave, another stone to be made to include them both.

There was a lot of discussion amongst the friends and family as to what the new stone should say.

In the end it was decided that it would simply have their names and underneath would say, *reunited at last.*

Tim could not believe how many people were involved in arranging a funeral. The Doctor, the funeral director, cars, the church and the minister, a florist, a caterer, the venue for the wake, an old-fashioned term that he found people still used. The list seemed endless.

His meeting with Mrs Simmons the solicitor was very pleasant, a Scottish lady in her middle years who was well informed and pleasant.

'Are you settling in OK at Victor's?' he asked her.

'Weeell, we had some lively discussions at the beginning, but I think we have come to an understanding now.' All this said in a wonderful highland brogue.

Tim snorted with laughter, he wished he could have been a fly on the wall during those discussions. 'It appears that Mr Vieri has finally met his match,' said Tim.

Mrs Simmons's face didn't move.

*

Tim and his father were upstairs in Mr Woodman's flat above shop Number One clearing his few possessions one Sunday evening.

'This will not take long son,' said his father. 'He was a very tidy man, everything in its place.'

'I've found a bible,' said Tim holding a small black leather-bound book up in the air to show his father, who then joined him. Looking in the front and the back of the book his father said, 'There's nothing written in it. It's obviously old. I don't think he was particularly religious, although he did say there were no non-believers cast adrift in that open boat. I saw that article in the local paper that said he had been torpedoed twice. He seemed to be all right about it.'

'He wasn't Dad. One evening I'll tell you all about it. Would people mind if I have it as a keepsake?'

'I don't think it's anyone else's business son, you're his only next of kin.'

'Thanks Dad,' said Tim, slipping it into his coat pocket. Two hours later the few belongings that were important were packed into two medium-sized boxes, this included three files of papers, his medals and a will.

Checking that they had done everything before they left his father asked, 'Have you had any thoughts about what you might do with this place? You could let it out.'

'I honestly don't know Dad. It would have to be someone we trust, family I guess.'

'You could use it for storage, Tim.'

'No, I wouldn't be comfortable with that. Something will come up.'

'Right lad, I think we've finished here. I'm off home, are you coming?'

'I may stay awhile Dad if that's ok?'

'Once the will's proved lad it will be yours anyway, you can stay as long as you like.'

Tim sat at the top of the stairs staring down into the shop. It had changed so much since he was a boy, then it was an ironmongers. It was different then, the beams and the paintwork darkened by age. There had been various sizes of varnished drawers and cupboards that climbed the walls from floor to ceiling. Now they had all gone. White paint and limewash had transformed the shop's appearance, the light reflected off all the formerly dowdy surfaces.

When he was young Mr Woodman would sometimes show him the contents of some of the drawers and the cupboards that covered the walls. He would say, 'There is two of everything in this shop lad and I know where every one of them is.'

Tim knew he was going to miss the man terribly, he had always been there for him, especially when his own father had been rendered incapable by Tim's mother dying.

Taking a deep breath and scrubbing his eyes with the palm of his hands he set off homeward, whispering, 'Goodnight.' He closed and locked the shop door.

✳

Tim was up early on the day of the funeral, the weather was bright, a gentle warm wind was blowing. He had started taking his early morning coffee on to the small rear deck of the Sea Maiden when the weather was pleasant, watching the life on the river slowly gather pace. The tugs were already towing their long tails of barges behind them. Some of the barges had high rusty sides indicating they were empty, others so low in the water it looked as though one good wave would swamp them. This would never happen, the bargees were so experienced, many of them descended from families that had depended on the river for their livelihoods for generations. This was the place Tim felt really at home, the movements of the Sea Maiden as the small waves from the tug's passage gently rocked the deck under his feet. The wavelets made the Sea Maiden feel alive. He envisioned a horse tied to a hitching rail shifting its feet.

Growing up beside this river with its ceaseless activity, the water, the sights, and the sounds, had always held him in its thrall. His reverie was disturbed by Sophie knocking on the glass and pointing at her watch. Reminding him of the time. Walking around the narrow gangway on the side of the boat, his left hand trailing along the handrail fixed to the top of the cabin just in case he slipped. He reached the bow just in time to welcome Nanny Bridget. Tim and Sophie had discussed whether they should take their daughter to the funeral and had decided against it. It was going to be extremely emotional, and they had learnt that Charley quickly noticed other people's distress, and it disturbed her.

Following Nanny who had just stepped in through the front door he saw Sophie dressed in a very formal black outfit, he said, 'You look …' – for once he was lost for words. It was as if his heart had stopped in his chest. Eventually he said, '… stunning.'

'I am not supposed to look stunning – I am supposed to appear respectful.'

'Sophie darling you'd look good in a black plastic sack.'

'Good morning, Sophie,' said Nanny Bridget, 'and if I may say so Tim is right, you would look stunning in a black plastic sack.'

'Please do not encourage him, Nanny.'

There was a small double toot on a car horn. 'That's Mr Graham,' said Tim checking he was right by glancing out of the galley window.

'Are you OK Nanny? I have left some washing if you would not mind,' queried Sophie.

'That's fine, you get along,' she responded. Charley was propped on her left hip. The two of them stood in the doorway waving as the Bentley drove away.

When they arrived at the church, they were both taken aback by how many people there were.

'I suppose I am not surprised really,' said Tim. 'If I remember rightly, he told me his family, father and grandfather had owned the shop since before the First World War.'

He recognised quite a few of Mr Woodman's customers and some of the local traders. There were a lot of people he didn't know, some of whom came up and introduced themselves. A reporter from the local paper asked a few questions.

'Had he been ill?' Tim confirmed that he hadn't.

Then the reporter said, 'I still have the article I wrote about his war. That will help make the piece. I understand he had lived here all his life?'

'Apart from the war years, yes,' Tim confirmed, 'and his father and grandfather before him. He was always a little sad that he had outlived most of his friends. Then he would perk up and add that he had outlived most of his enemies as well,' said Tim with a wry smile.

A middle-aged woman came up and placed her hand gently on Tim's arm. She was wearing a black jacket and matching skirt.

'Tim, Tim Cooper?' she asked enquiringly.

'Yes,' he said, 'I'm sorry I don't know you.'

'I'm Edith Fry. I was a good friend of your mother's before she passed away. I tried to stay in touch but there was never any response from your father.'

'I'm sorry about that. To be honest it was a long time before he got over her loss, he is here today somewhere.'

'I shan't bother him. It's been nice to see you Tim, anyway.'

'Before you go can I introduce my wife, Sophie Cooper?'

'You were Sophia Vieri weren't you, before marrying Tim?'

'I was,' said Sophie. 'You are well informed.'

'I am still in touch with some people locally, they keep me up to date. I see they are calling us in, I had better re-join my friend. I am so pleased I got to meet you both. Bye, bye.'

Entering the church Tim was, as always, struck by the vivid colours that the sun splashed across the pews and the marble flooring as it shone through the ornate stained glass in the church windows. He remembered his time as a choir boy in this church singing descant before his voice broke. He missed the opportunity to make the church ring with his high notes.

The service flew by for Tim, he could hear Mr Woodman's voice throughout, snatches of conversation he found himself smiling at. A couple of times he noticed Sophie looking at him quizzically, not understanding why he was smiling. He remembered all the years of sound advice. It was always Mr Woodman he went to when he had a problem. His father's malaise as a result of the loss of Tim's mother had made him withdraw within himself. 'I just want everybody to leave me alone, and that includes you, just go away and stay away.' These few words of his Father had cut Tim so deeply, the scar still hurt when his memory scratched at it.

They had made their peace since, but his father had admitted to Tim he would carry the guilt for banishing Tim from the family home forever.

At the grave side later, as the coffin was lowered in, Tim found himself fighting back the tears, head down staring at his shoes. Sophie, sensing his distress squeezed his fingers hard; he saw the side of her face under the big black hat was wet with her own tears. When the Vicar and the rest of the congregation moved away, there was still a group around the grave. All the team were there.

Without any forethought, Tim reached down to the pile of earth and sprinkled it in, he felt for some reason throwing it in might disturb Mr Woodman and it would have been disrespectful, a silly thought but it was how he felt.

They were all starting to move away, all except Daisy who was stood with both arms wrapped around herself, her chin against her chest, her eyes shut tight, silent sobs shaking her thin frame. Tim started to move towards her, but Sophie, with her hand on his arm said, 'I will go Tim, you carry on.'

*

The wake was in a local hotel, there were rows of long tables covered with large, white, damask tablecloths. Bottles of red and white wine were placed in rows down the middle. The table settings were smart, and everything was beautifully arranged. Tom Cooper had suggested that there could be a continental flavour to the meal, not just because of the company that Mr Woodman had worked so hard for but also because of all his own travels during the "disagreement" in Europe as he had called it.

Tim had made it clear to the hotel that his godfather was highly thought of by the local community.

The conversation slowly got louder, the contents of the bottles and full glasses easing the sorrow a little. Tim had chosen the meal: cream of mushroom soup for starters, the main course was a choice between roast beef or lamb, with a range of vegetables including new potatoes served in butter, or an Italian dish, fettuccine pasta with strips of chicken in a dry white wine cream and dolcelatte cheese sauce. Tim could hear the growing conversations; everybody had a Mr Woodman story. Most of them amusing, some sad; those people who remembered the passing of his young wife in the war. Tim knew even his godfather believed she had died of a broken heart.

Tim had asked him once why he had never remarried?

'You'd be lucky to find the *one* a second time, Tim.'

*

After the meal Tim was making his way around the tables thanking everyone for coming when he noticed his father beckoning him from the far side of the room. Making his way over to him he asked, 'Is there a problem?'

'No lad, I want to have a word while you're here. Can we step outside where I can hear you?' The congregation's conversation and occasional laughter was gathering strength.

Now seated in the foyer Tom Cooper said, 'Mr Woodman's death is causing some real problems. As you know, we are struggling to cope quite often. Sara is coming in to help, she is running her delicatessen counter, and is doing long hours' he continued, 'but, not that she would admit it, she gets tired faster these days. Harry had a word with me this week – he does not want her to do as much. I think we tend to forget that she is making her confectionary in the evenings as well as Sundays after mass. By the way, she let it slip that now Daisy lives with them she is teaching her the sweet-making secrets.'

'One thing I do want to say Dad, is we need to put all this working at home on a proper footing. I know Sara says she doesn't want any more than the token financial amount we have agreed with her but that's not good enough now she works in the evenings as well.'

'We need to advertise Tim. We need at least one new shop assistant, preferably someone with experience.'

'Dad, I will get the ball rolling in the morning. Oliver, our new human resources man can put an advert in the local paper.'

'I met him the other day Tim, he seems nice enough.'

'Yes, he is. Now I had better join our guests, but thanks for letting me know. Now that I am office bound most of the time, I am not as well in touch as I once was. Perhaps we could meet occasionally for a beer, and you can bring me up to date with all the latest gossip.'

'There's always plenty of that,' replied his father, laughing. The two men went back to their guests.

Tim arranged for Mr Woodman's armchair to be moved to his office replacing the one he normally used.

CHAPTER 35

Tim pushed his chair away from the table running his fingers through his hair and sighing as he did so. Jessica was sitting opposite him in the company offices.

'Why didn't you stop me Jessica, when I said I was going to open a food hall? You were there, you could have said it's a stupid idea, it will be colossal amount of work and terribly expensive. Why didn't you do that?'

She considered her response for a few moments, then said, 'Firstly boss, you never listen to me anyway, and secondly I think it is a superb idea. I will be able to brag and say, I work for Sophie's the company that owns the food hall and Italian restaurant in Clapham. To be serious Tim, we have, I believe, broken the back of the work. All we have to do now is keep on keeping on.'

'I think it is the complexity of it that I struggle with, keeping so many balls in the air – the shops were simple by comparison,' replied Tim.

Bonny walked in from the kitchen. 'I overheard the discussion. We ought to allocate areas of responsibility, divide the work up more. Not all of it needs to go across your desk, Tim. If you write the brief, then whoever is responsible should be able to go away and do it.'

'You are right, Bonny,' said Jessica. 'Except, you do not write the brief Tim, you dictate it to me or Bonny and tell us who should do the work. I know Mr Cooper is busy with the stalls and the barrows, but Harry is not involved with anything now.'

The phone started ringing in Tim's office, striding away Bonny called over her shoulder, 'I'll get it.' They heard her say, 'Hallo Tim Cooper's office. Hold on I will get him for you. It's your dad, boss.'

Tim was already walking towards Bonny to take the call. 'Hallo Dad.' Tim listened, nodding occasionally. 'Ok, we will be with you shortly. Right girls is there anything you can't leave?' he asked as he returned to them.

The two women looking at each other both said, 'No.'

'Right get your coats we are going on a jolly.'

'Mr Graham?' asked Bonny. Tim nodded.

She disappeared out the front door.

Minutes later the front door opened, and Bonny called, 'Mr Graham is ready.'

The journey was slow through the traffic. Tim had started using the Bentley and Mr Graham more often. It gave Tim a short period away from the pressure. He loved his role in the company but occasionally he needed a little peace and quiet; the slow stately progress of the Bentley was restful. When Tim expressed concern Mr Graham had been adamant he didn't mind, 'I like to be busy,' he'd said, 'and anyway it's part of my job.' More than once, he had asked Mr Graham to drive out to Hampstead Heath and park up. Sometimes Tim walked amongst the trees, on other occasions it gave him the opportunity to sit in comfort in the back of the car and order his thoughts without interruption. It had never been more than an hour. Mr Graham knew not to speak unless spoken to. Tim just needed a break now and then.

Arriving in the car park near the food hall, Tim invited Mr Graham to come in with them.

Shaking his head, the response was, 'No thanks, Tim. I like to keep an eye on the old girl. I bet she is worth more now than when she was new, if you know what I mean.'

It was a short walk from the car park behind the square to the food hall entrance, the tall wooden doors were both open. Given the volume of noise emanating from the building it was obvious there was a hive of industry inside. In the middle of the space Tom Cooper and Gerry the carpenter were working around the body of a costermonger's barrow, fitting the four wheels, two large at the rear, two small at the front. There were halloes all round, then Tim said, 'I thought we were only going to have the two large wheels at the back and legs at the front?'

'We discovered that when it was loaded and fitted with legs instead of wheels a female staff member would struggle to manoeuvre it. Now it's easy,' said his father.

'You did get a revised estimate Tim,' said Gerry in a concerned voice.

Tim remembered he had only seen Gerry's name at the top of the document and the price and had agreed it, he had read no more than that. That has got to stop he told himself.

'How do you steer it?' asked Tim.

'Ah now that's quite clever, let's get the wheels on and we'll show you,' said his father. Minutes later the barrow was on all four wheels. 'Gerry designed this bit so he can demonstrate it.'

The carpenter went round the front by the small wheels, reached under the body and drew out a long lever that you used to steer and pull with.

Tom said, 'Here you are Jessica give it a wheel around.'

Away she went, moving in a large circle. 'It is extremely easy to pull, and it steers well,' she reported. 'Bonny, you have a go.'

Bonny decided to push it. She struggled for a moment but then got the knack and steered it back to the middle saying, 'My mum would love a small version of this for the garden.' Jessica watched the idea register with Tim.

Gerry was now sliding four upright posts into slots in the corners of the body, minutes later the vehicle had a blue-and-white-striped canvas cover set above it to keep the imaginary rain off the produce and the staff.

'I like the glass top on the display shelf. How do you access that?' asked Tim.

'There are doors around the back, they allow access to the display and to the storage underneath,' replied Gerry.

Bonny stepped to the other side of the barrow and sang out, 'Here we are ladies and gentlemen, oysters fresh off the boats this morning.'

Tim laughing said, 'You are in the wrong job, Bonny. What do we think of the colours people?' asked Tim. It was then he noticed the audience had grown, most of the workmen had joined them.

'Yer can't miss it,' said one.

'I reckon it's right smart,' said another.

'I love the alternate blue and white spokes,' said Bonny.

'The thin, blue, trim line around the white body is nice, it reminds me of the paintwork on the other shops,' observed Jessica.

'Does it carry the brand forward?' Tom asked his son.

'Yes, Dad, it's terrific – well done.'

'We are building six,' said Gerry, the tone of his voice seeking reassurance, his confidence a little shaken by Tim's apparent ignorance of the extra wheels.

'That's fine Gerry and the stalls around the sides?'

'They are under way.'

'How long then, team?' asked Tim.

'We have the painting to finish, the café to build and fit out. Do you want upstairs painted before you open?' asked Charlie.

'I wasn't going to, but Sophie pointed out we wouldn't want the smell of the paint competing with the cheese and the garlic. It's also one less job when we start the restaurant.'

Shaking his head, Charlie said, 'I ain't able to tell yur how long Tim, all I know is we're working as 'ard as we can.'

'That's fair enough Charlie, there's no point in rushing it. I will see you soon.' Tim raised a hand and called out, 'Thank you everybody, well done.' He ushered the two women out of the building.

*

Later back at the office he said to Bonny, 'Your idea about assigning tasks to people – I think it's a good one. I'm going to ask Harry to design the café – what do you think?'

Bonny nodded saying, 'Yeh why not?'

'Jessica, can you confirm where Harry is this afternoon, please?'

Bonny jumped in immediately saying, 'He is at Number One today – 9 to 5.30.'

'Do you know where everyone is at any time?'

'Yes, she does boss. She is an android.'

Bonny just shrugged. Tim shook his head saying, 'I'm going to walk over to talk to Harry. See what he says. I may see you later – bye for now.'

The girls waved him off.

When Tim reached the shop Harry had just closed and was pushing a broom around.

The two men exchanged pleasantries while Harry finished the task then Tim asked him, 'Can I buy you a drink Harry, a glass of something around the corner?'

'Yes, that would be nice. Can I ring, Sara?'

'Of course,' was the reply.

Shortly afterwards the two men were comfortably settled in the lounge bar of the Star and Garter with a large glass each of cabernet sauvignon in front of them.

'So Tim, what is it you want me to do?'

'Am I that easy to read, Harry?'

'Yes Tim. Your father and I were talking about it this week. We always know when you have job for us. What do you want me to do?'

'Harry, if I design the café, it will be an English one – it needs to be designed by an Italian who has spent most of his young life in Italian cafés, and that's you. What do you think?'

'I'm no designer, Tim.'

'Harry stop, shut your eyes – you're now in your favourite café back home in Italy. How much of it can you see?'

'Well, all of it of course. I grew up just around the corner – my friends and I were always in there.'

'Now, the outside, can you see the front door?'

'Yes.'

Tim pulled a piece of paper and a pencil from his pocket. 'Can you draw it for me?'

Harry drew it for Tim explaining as the drawing progressed. 'There was a large window set in the top half of the amber coloured wooden door. It had matching beading on all four sides with ornate scroll work in the corners. The name was on the glass here in gold paint,' he explained as he wrote Sophie's on the drawing.

'That Harry, is exactly what I wanted. Can you draw the rest of the interior, please? It does not have to be to scale. It is the feel of it we need. Thank you.' The discussion moved on to family matters for a while. Then Tim swallowed the last of his wine and standing said, 'I really do appreciate you doing this Harry. When you're ready we can put you together with Charlie the builder and he can start work. All the best Harry and say hallo to Sara for me.' Watching Tim leave the pub Harry thought, there goes a driven man.

✳

Later that evening at home on the Sea Maiden, Tim was sitting at the kitchen table after his evening meal jotting numbers down on the back of an old A4 envelope; after lots of jotting and pausing and scribbling out he sat back and said, 'If this venture falls on its face my biggest asset will be the houses, apart from that I'll be broke.'

Sophie abandoned the washing up for a moment, leaned over his shoulder and perused his figures. They were alone because it was Nanny's night off.

'With the income from the rental property and my money, we will still be comfortable by any standards.' She kissed him on the head and went back to her chores.

CHAPTER 36

Daisy was entering a café that was just one hundred yards from shop Number Two. Having a recent wage rise had meant that for the first time in her life she had a small surplus every week. For years she had envied the smart clever people who lunched; their laughter, their witty conversation. Most of all she envied their confidence, their sense of self. So now she could have lunch in the cafe, it was massive step forward. Also, nowadays she copied Sophie's dress sense of navy pencil skirt and cream blouse; she felt this helped her fit in. On this day, she noticed to her surprise, Mr Vieri was already ensconced at a table over in the corner wearing his standard black suit and white, Egyptian-cotton shirt. Seeing her he indicated he wanted her to join him. Unable to think of a polite way to refuse she made her way over. Standing up he pulled a chair out for her. She now felt extremely uncomfortable. He was an extremely overpowering individual; she had heard that all of his staff were frightened of him. He had been known to fire a staff member on a whim.

Taking his seat again he asked, 'What do you want to drink? This is on me,' he continued, 'so have whatever you like.'

'Sophie has been telling me how good you are and that they are considering asking you to become the training manager for the fresh staff.'

'Well, they ain't said nuffin' to me.' Now annoyed that her nerves had destroyed her diction she said, 'I mean, they've not said anything to me.'

Once not so long ago his smile would have rendered her speechless. Now a new-found ally came to her assistance, anger, she was a mouse no longer. She had begun to believe in herself. She had recently made a vow she would not be a human punchbag any more.

The waitress arrived with the dark fruit cake and coffee that she had chosen. Mr Vieri had his usual strong black coffee.

'I have already eaten,' he explained. 'The reason I am here today is to offer you a job.'

Daisy was so surprised she was rendered speechless. He made it sound as though Sophie had agreed. She would not sell her off, would she? WOULD SHE!!?

He was still talking – 'Initially you would be working under the current staff member who handles the training now.'

She missed the rest of what he said as she tracked back in her mind over the last few weeks. There was nothing that had gone wrong, wait, she was late one day, and Sophie had stood in for her. She did not seem angry when she explained that she had been helping Sara and had lost track of the time. What was he asking – how much did she earn a week?

'Why are you asking me that?' she queried her face set in a frown.

'So that I can tell you what I am prepared to offer you.'

'I'm sorry, I don't understand.'

I thought Sophia had said this girl was bright, he thought to himself. 'Let's make it simple. I will pay you 25 per cent more than you are getting now, that's a quarter more a week, and that may rise over time.'

He was clearly talking down to her. The rude b-------d thinks I'm stupid, she thought to herself. Scraping her chair back and standing up she said, 'Thank you for my lunch' – all of which lay untouched on the table. The anger in her voice clearly displayed what she thought of him. 'I'll work for Sophie for the rest of my days if she will have me. I will do it for nothing, if necessary. I am sorry I've wasted your time. Goodbye, sir.'

Leaving the restaurant, a little old lady, all bundled up in a big fawn coat and scarf with matching gloves and who had clearly overheard the conversation, clapped silently but visibly as Daisy walked out.

Mr Vieri settled back in his chair, raised his eyebrows and smiled. He finished his coffee and her cake before leaving.

Later that evening Sophie and Daisy were tidying up having closed the Number Two shop, when Daisy spilled it all out: the telling making her angry again.

'He talked to me as though I was stupid. I told 'im I wouldn't work for no one else except you for the rest of me days, if you'll have me.' Her face was a mixture of storm and rain.

'Daisy love,' said Sophie, 'you can work for us until the seas run dry if you want and we will be pleased to have you.'

Daisy was wiping the tears away with the palms of her hands. Once again she had forgotten her hankie; she had never owned one until recently when Angela had given her a small selection. She thought they were much too good to use. She had been deeply ashamed of the fact that she had not known it was not proper to use your sleeve.

'Daisy can I ask you a favour? Please do not say anything to Tim, if he finds out he will be kicking doors down. It will be World War Two all over again. I promise my father will get the tongue lashing he deserves from me, but if Tim finds out I do not know what will happen.'

Sophie remembered the first time Tim and her father had met at her families home. The two men had lost their tempers and had almost come to blows. Her father had accused Tim of being only interested in Sophie's considerable inheritance. He offered Tim a thousand pounds to go away. Her husband was one of the few men to face her father down as they stood toe to toe. He told her father to keep his money and he suggested that he disinherit his daughter, he went on to say that he would marry Sophie whatever.

Mr Vieri changed his mind about Tim when he discovered Tim had sat beside his daughter's hospital bed for three days and nights while she was in a coma after being knocked down in a road accident.

CHAPTER 37

Sophie and Daisy were sitting in the company office awaiting the arrival of the first applicant for the job as a shorthand typist.

Daisy was watching the sunlight on the young pale-green leaves on the tree in the front garden as they fluttered in the gentle spring breeze. Her mind had fled back to her own interview which had changed her life so dramatically.

'Daisy, Daisy,' called Sophie, realising the young woman was lost in a daydream.

'Sorry, did you say something?'

'No, but I noticed you were miles away. I was wondering what you were thinking about?'

'I was reminded of me own interview – what a poor scruffy little thing I was. I'm still right gobsmacked that you gave me the job.'

'Sara and I recognised your potential.'

'I'll never be able to repay you. My whole life has changed because of you.'

'You repay us daily Daisy – you always give 110 per cent.'

'One thing I know for sure is the memory of always being hungry which is a blooming good reason to work hard and keep your job,' replied Daisy. 'Sometimes me stomach was growling so loud people would turn to stare at me.'

Sophie recognised the enormous amount of effort that the girl had put into the changes in her appearance and her speech. All a product of Daisy's determination to improve herself. Smiling to herself, Sophie recognised that Daisy copied her fashion choices, the navy pencil skirts, matching sensible shoes with a low heal. The blouses the same, white or cream, the only difference being Sophie had the top button undone, while Daisy wore hers fastened to the neck, determined not to give any man any encouragement. This was confirmed by the severe hairstyle: short and purely functional. Sophie assumed that this was because of her father's attempted rape and the fact that he was a disgusting individual.

Sophie had only seen him once at a distance. He was revolting: overweight, unshaven and obviously drunk. Daisy had told her that he stank and was often too drunk to walk home, and he hit her mum. It was no wonder Daisy had no time for men.

Daisy interrupted her boss's thought process by asking, 'Aren't I supposed to be working with the new bloke, Oliver, today? I'm right pleased I'm working with you. I was told he's a bit posh?'

'He rang me last night,' Sophie informed her. 'He has the flu. He was dreadfully embarrassed – he said he never gets ill.'

'Will it be you and him doing the whatsits – the interviews in future?' asked Daisy.

'No, it will be you and him, Daisy. And before you get in a panic' –Daisy began to tense up. A faint sweat appeared on her forehead; her breathing had shortened. Sophie had noticed Daisy's growing alarm – 'you need to understand you are the expert. Nobody knows more than you about the shop floor. We are still trying to learn how you know so much about your customers and their preferences. He will be working hard to keep up with you. He knows the legal stuff. That is no longer our concern any more. You should not worry.'

The two women were brought back to the present by the doorbell ringing. This was their first applicant for the job.

'What is her name?' asked Sophie standing by the office door glancing at her watch. 'She is late.'

'Margaret Wilson,' replied Daisy.

Listening to what was happening in the hall she heard the front door open, then instead of a woman's voice there was a rich, Irish, male voice saying, 'Sure, I know I'm early, but I was sitting there waiting for the clock to go round and then I could wait no longer. I thought I might wait as easily here as at home, if that is all right with you.'

Sophie working hard to control a smile, said, 'That is fine, please come in.' She ushered him into the office indicating he should sit down. He was wearing a pair of brown trousers with a sharp crease, a green shirt and black trainers.

Daisy sensed Sophie was having problems recalling his name, so said enquiringly, 'Mr O' Connor?'

'That's me name,' he replied. 'Declan to me friends.'

Sophie introduced the two of them. 'Have you done shop work before, Mr O' Connor?' she asked.

'I'm more comfortable with Declan if you don't mind, and yes I have. In my father's shop in Galway Ireland. A tiny wee place, just a few houses, the pub and the post office beside a large blue lake. I wanted to see the bright lights of London – so here I am.'

'Do you have family over here?' asked Daisy.

'Indeed I do,' said Declan. 'I'm lodging with me mother's sister, she's by way of being my aunt. They have a huge rambling house full of the wee ones. But that's no problem I love them all, so I do. I think there's no better sound than children's laughter. I have a room at the top of the house so I can escape them if I needs to.'

The normal questions were asked and answered well; although he used ten words when two or three would have been sufficient.

'Do you have any questions?' asked Sophie.

'Not really, most of the detail was in the paper. Except, what shop will I be working in?'

'Number Two', said Sophie. 'The one on Fish Hill.' Declan was shaking his head. 'Do not worry we will give you all the information you require,' she continued.

Finally, Sophie raised her eyes at Daisy who nodded, 'We would like to offer you the job, Declan, if you want to take it?'

'I do indeed, that's truly kind of you both. I am absolutely delighted so I am.'

'Declan, you will be working with Daisy who is our training manager. She will show you the ins and outs of the job – ask her if you are unsure of anything.'

'Now how about that – am I not the luckiest man in all the world? Just off the Ferry I have a job and here I am working for one of the prettiest girls in all creation.' All this said with him smiling at Daisy. Declan agreed to start the following morning and left.

Daisy had been taken completely by surprise. There had been no discussion about her new role. She turned to Sophie saying, 'I can't be a training manager. I ain't got a clue where to start. I am right surprised you sprung it on me. You will 'ave to tell 'im in the morning.'

'Daisy, all we want you to do is show Declan how you do the job, nothing more. Just walk him through the tasks he will face. That is all.' Sophie was aware that Daisy always performed over and above what was expected of her. She also understood that Daisy loved the job and had an enormous pride in her work and viewed the second shop as her own.

Afterwards both women were aware they had conducted the whole interview with smiles on their faces. Sophie said. 'What a lovely man, I have never held an interview where there was so much laughter, he will keep us all amused.'

Sophie and Daisy were leaving the office five minutes later when they met a young woman about to knock on the door. She was dressed in a pair of old blue jeans and stained yellow T-shirt.

'Hallo,' said Sophie. 'Can I help you?'

'I've come about the job.'

'I am sorry,' said Sophie, 'we have just hired someone. I should remind you that your appointment was for half an hour ago.'

Longer than that thought Daisy.

'So, I don't get an interview because of being a little late.'

'No,' said Sophie. 'Goodbye.'

'Oh, lardy bloody da,' the girl called out as she walked away.

Initially Daisy was quite worried about the new job but then she reckoned she could do it. She would not have been given the job if her bosses had not been sure of her. As she walked towards shop Number Two, on the first day of her new job, she shouted out loud, 'You can do this girl.'

A woman who had just passed her going the other way wearing a bright red coat turned and stared at Daisy's retreating figure. After a pause, the woman straightened her red coat and her posture and called out, 'Thank you' – she strode away with a new confidence in her step.

CHAPTER 38

The following morning, Declan was standing waiting for Daisy outside shop Number Two. She walked him through all the basics, where things were and how the scales and the till worked. He settled in well during the morning, although there were a few false starts when he could not find something, but she decided that for his first morning he was doing well. It was obvious that he had done it all before. His rapport with the customers was good.

She did not feel able to relax and be herself, her nerves made her sound reserved and unfriendly.

In the early afternoon, she was on the telephone, and had been for a while, discussing an issue with a cheese supplier. John Pettigrew, a nice man but was beginning to struggle to provide the quantities of his products the shops were now selling. Declan had been hovering by her side for a couple of minutes with a query for a customer who was now looking at his watch and was clearly close to leaving the shop. Trying to gain her attention he put his hand on her arm, she jumped as though he had struck her.

'Don't touch me,' she barked at him, taking a rapid step away from him as she said it. 'What do you want?' she demanded holding the phone against her body to smother their conversation.

'I'm sorry, I won't do it again.' He had noticed his customer had seen the incident and was already leaving, the door held open for him by an elderly gentleman who was entering the shop.

As Declan walked away, he was totally confused. Daisy seemed to be a completely different person to the one he had met yesterday. Perhaps she was just nice and polite when one of the big bosses was there.

Funnily enough when he had got back to his aunt's the night before, she had said, 'That all seems a little too easy to me, it may not be all it seems. You just tread carefully.'

Ah well he thought, I can always find another job on my days off, it's not the end of the world. If she continues to be unpleasant, I can shrug it off. He was quietly polite for the rest of the day. There were no more eruptions.

Daisy was rattled by the incident, she thought she should apologise but realised that may make her appear weak, so she said nothing. Declan had been polite enough towards her since the incident, so she decided to leave well alone.

Reaching home that night his aunt hugged Declan as he reached the kitchen. 'How did it go today?'

'Not too bad.' His tone of voice indicating the contrary.

'That well,' responded his aunt.

Declan explained what had happened.

'Well, I had a feeling about this wonderful job, so … I have had a word with Mr Beresford, the greengrocer at the end of the street. He had a card in the window advertising a job in his shop. He's getting old he said and is needing some help. The money's not as good as what you're receiving now but you won't get growled at every day, and its local which will save your bus fare. You could pop along there now and see him – he might still be open.'

'No, I'll go in the morning and give me notice in – do it right. Find out if she wants me to work me notice or not. One thing I am sure of I certainly did misread her. She obviously has one face for the bosses and one for the peasants.'

His aunt, as she placed his dinner in front of him said, 'It might be, my darling boy, that she just doesn't like the Irish. She wouldn't be alone.'

Declan lay awake a long time that night. He was puzzled. He could not understand how he had misread Daisy so badly; she had seemed so nice. He had to admit to more than a casual interest in her. Now clearly nothing was going to come of that. Also, from what he had glimpsed there was a well-ordered organisation behind the shops. He had hoped there may be a chance for promotion, certainly more than there would be in the high street selling potatoes. He finally fell into a troubled sleep.

A few miles away, Daisy was tossing and turning in her bed recognising what a dog's breakfast she had made of her first day as a manager. She could see no way forward. Fighting back the tears she decided to creep downstairs and make a cup of tea. She tiptoed around the kitchen filling the kettle and carefully removing a mug from the cupboard. Waiting for the kettle to boil she sat on a stool unknowingly picking at the hem of her pink nighty and lost in thought.

She didn't hear the kitchen door open until Sara whispered, 'Are you all right, Daisy love?'

Startled she could no longer hold back the tears that flooded her cheeks.

Sara wrapped her arms around her and held her close, saying, 'Whatever is wrong?'

The kettle's whistle separated them. Harry woke and joined them minutes later just as Daisy gained enough control to explain why she was so upset.

She concluded her account by saying, 'I was really 'orrible to 'im. I've never been that rude to nobody in my life before. I don't know why. I really growled at him.'

Sara handed round the mugs of tea.

Harry said, 'You know why really, Daisy, don't you?'

She said, 'No.'

'This is your father's fault,' Harry continued. 'His attack on you has given you a fear of men, especially men you don't know and that's sad.'

Daisy thought for a while and then said, 'How can I face him in the morning? I'll be so embarrassed.'

'Daisy love,' said Harry, 'you will have to apologise.'

Shaking her head, she replied, 'I can't tell him what my father tried to do to me, I can't.'

'You don't have to love. Explain that something happened when you were a child, and it has made you a bit jumpy around men you don't know.'

'I am sure he will understand,' added Sara.

'Apologising will make you stronger Daisy, and he will think far more of you,' said Harry.

Soon after they all went back to bed and Daisy found some sleep.

The following morning Declan was already at the shop when she arrived. They exchanged good mornings. He stood back to let her in first, once inside he began to speak, 'There is something I need to say—'

'Sorry to interrupt but I want's to say somethin' first.'

Declan dipped his head in acknowledgement.

Taking a deep breath, she said, 'I needs to apologise for me 'avin a go at yur yesterday and I wants to tell yur why I behaved so badly. When I was young, a man attacked me and now, I gets very frightened around men I don't know if they touches me. So, I am right sorry. I hope we can put it behind us. What did you want to say?' She had a fairly good idea what he was going to say, but then he surprised her with what he said next.

'I'm really sorry that happened to you lass. I think you are extremely brave. We can forget all about it. I can feel in my bones we are going to get along right royally, so we shall, and if any man causes you a problem in the future, he will answer to Declan O' Connor. I promise you that.'

Much to her surprise she found herself blushing. She recognised that although she had known him for such a short time, she was aware of feeling the first flicker of attraction for the man, not something she had experienced before. There were butterflies in her tummy.

CHAPTER 39

Sara approached Tim one morning with a sheaf of papers in her hand. Always very polite she said, 'Good morning Tim, do you have a minute?'

Glancing at his watch he said, 'Is it important? I need to be on my way any minute.'

'I understand Tim. I am sorry I bothered you.'

Watching her walk away he could tell from her body language that she was disappointed. It registered that she was on occasion still nervous talking to him so for her to approach him it would be important to her. 'Sara, I'm sorry that was rude of me. I assume you have something to show me?'

'No, please it is nothing. Perhaps another time when you are not so busy.' All this said as she was backing away.

She always looked nice but today he sensed she had made a special effort. The soft pale-pink dress was one clue. 'Sara, now I feel really bad. Let me make a phone call then you will have my full attention.'

'No please, it's not that important, Tim.'

'I rather think it is,' said Tim noticing the thickness of the file she was carrying.

Holding the phone to his ear he said, 'Hallo Donald, how are you and the family? Yes we are the same thanks. Don, I have had something come up here I can't put off, can we reschedule our meeting please? Sorry to do this to you. Tomorrow morning, what day is that? Saturday, yes I can do that, can we make it early? Eight is good, sorry again … and you, bye for now.'

'I am sorry Tim, it could have waited,' said Sara.

'Oh no. I suspect that whatever this is it's a bit special. Come on we can go across the road. I will treat you to coffee and cake while you show me what you're holding.' Ten minutes later they were sitting in the steamy warmth of their local café exchanging banter with the owner and his wife who Tim had known for years. Sara chose carrot cake and Tim copied her. A few minutes later the table was covered with photos of plates of food, and a pile of their accompanying recipes set to one side.

'Sara, I am blown away,' said Tim. 'These are amazing. Who took the pictures?'

'I did,' she replied, going a little pink.

'Sara, this work is absolutely … well, I don't know what to say … how long has it taken you?'

'About two years.'

Tim sat entranced as he was going through them. 'This is making me hungry, Sara. Are you going to have it published?'

'Oh no, I don't want to be doing all that. I hoped the company would agree to do it. Also if it comes out in my name no one will buy it – if it has the company name on the cover it will get more recognition.'

Tim sat and thought for a while. 'It should be in your name, Sara,' he said.

'Tim if it is down to me on my own, it will never get published. I find the whole idea terrifying. I could not do it. I don't want to do it.'

'What does Harry say?'

'He thinks I have wasted my time. He says only chefs with Michelin stars have their books published, not some housewife from London.'

'Right Sara,' said Tim with a determined look in his eyes, 'we are going to show Harry and any other doubting Thomas that they're wrong. The company will publish it, but you will be the one credited with the work. How does that sound? Have you got copies of all this?' Sara shook her head.

'With your permission, we will ask Bonny to copy all of the pictures so you can have the originals back. Then we need to find a publisher – they may want to talk to you, is that acceptable?'

'Oh no, I don't want to do any of that. Can you do it?'

Tim was about to volunteer when he realised he had no time to do anything else. He suddenly had a brain wave. 'How about I ask Harry to help you? The publishers talk to Harry, he talks to you.'

'Harry won't do it – he thinks I'm being daft.'

'Will he think I'm daft?'

'No,' she said.

'So, do you think it might work with Harry helping?' Tim asked. 'I tell you I believe it is a wonderful piece of work – a first-class Italian cook revealing the secrets of her Italian cuisine.'

Sara's eyes were sparkling. 'Do you believe that Tim?'

'I do. If we can't get this published, I'll eat my hat. I'll talk to Harry later, OK?'

The following day, Tim asked Harry if they could have a quick chat.

'Has Sara mentioned that I have seen her work for the cookbook?'

'No she hasn't. I'm sorry she has bothered you with it – she's no world-class author. I told her not to be so silly.'

'Well Harry, it might surprise you, but I think it is an amazing piece of work. The photography is first class, the text is clear and concise. I think this is a goer, Harry. The company is going to get it published and sell it through the shops and the local bookstores.'

Harry was staring at him as though he had gone mad.

'Furthermore, Harry, I would like you to work with Sara and the publisher. I would do it myself, but I don't have the time and it will be easier for you two to do it as husband and wife. What do you say? It would really help me out, Harry.'

Harry was completely confused. Neither he nor Sara knew anything about publishing a book. Tim must be taking pity on his wife. He was trapped, if he said no, he would upset both of them. It won't last long anyway, he thought, we can get a few no thanks and that will be the end of that.

Harry did as he was asked sending some pictures and some text to several publishers who specialised in nonfiction. Shortly afterwards, in the same post, two polite refusals arrived. I knew this was a waste of time, he thought to himself. He was concerned because his wife was so upset. He would have a word with Tim next time he saw him. A week later it was Sara who opened the post; Harry was still in bed. Opening the only letter addressed to her, she noticed the address of a local publisher at the top of the page.

The first line of the letter said, *Dear Sara, we have great pleasure informing you that we would love to publish your book. If you could call the number above, we can arrange a meeting.* She found herself shouting: 'Harry, Harry come down.'

Harry, very alarmed, came running downstairs pulling a cream dressing gown on over his blue pyjamas. His progress down the stairs was considerably faster than usual and was bordering on dangerous he was calling out, 'Whatever's wrong.' He was extremely concerned for his wife thinking someone must have died. Her face was all sunshine and showers. Her cheeks were running with tears and were creased in a huge smile.

'Are you all right?' he asked.

Saying nothing she handed him the letter. He read the first line.

Suddenly he was unable to stand and sunk down on the first step of the stairs to read the letter aloud. Sara came and sat beside him. Harry was extremely embarrassed, he had been so scathing, but now he was married to an author, a writer. He was overcome with pride.

'I told you it was good, didn't I?' He burst into laughter as he said it.

Sara punched him hard on the shoulder. She left him rubbing the painful limb.

Standing at the sink later she thought, I could write about the desserts … the washing up did itself as Sara began to plan her next book.

CHAPTER 40

The sky was overcast but dry, there was not a breath of wind. It was, Tim thought, as though the world was holding its breath to see what would happen when the food hall opened this morning. He had been there since six am, making sure it was as good as he could make it.

The previous weeks had been frantic, and the staff training had taken a long time. Tim believed in role play as a training tool; some of the new people were uncomfortable initially but his persistence had paid off. Some of the scenarios he put forward where plainly ridiculous and people were in fits of laughter unable to continue at times. Now, however, they all knew what the company rules were given any difficult situation.

He was also able to watch new friendships being forged within the team with support being given. After two weeks, he could see those who may become leaders, those who were a little timid. Some he could not read, such as the quiet ones; he could sense their intelligence, but they were not ready to commit yet.

Daisy had been extremely useful explaining how her system of information gathering worked when collecting customers' names, their food preferences and family details. Tim stood watching as she explained her methods of gaining a customer's confidence. As the morning progressed he had watched the questions growing as the staff recognised her expertise.

Their respect for her skills grew evermore evident. As a result, Daisy's confidence grew rapidly. When Tim called a halt and announced lunch, a number of the team were still questioning her as they walked to the café.

Tim had taken her to one side and said, 'Well?' He realised she was extremely excited.

'Tim, I can do this. That was amazing.'

'I knew you could do it. Well done, that was excellent.'

As he walked away thinking of her growing confidence, her dedication and her skills, he wondered if she was ready for a bigger job. Sophie would know.

✳

At 8.30 am he started his walk round, making sure that everyone and everything was as ready as they could make it. He wished everyone good luck and assured them they were going to be fine.

The advert in the paper had promised some price reductions and one or two small freebies, a selection of unusual foods.

When he opened the doors at eight Fifty-five am there was a reasonable queue. Tim welcomed them in. As the morning progressed the numbers slowly grew. He watched his staff as they began to relax into their roles and most of them were clearly enjoying themselves.

Mid-morning, his father called in to see how things were going. His first words were, 'Well I am surprised. I honestly thought I would find everybody twiddling their thumbs.'

'This is all down to Bonny and her advertising ideas – the high-street posters, the local radio, the newspapers. We may have an additional role for her. She certainly knows what she is doing regarding the advertising.'

'She does. I voted against it – I was wrong,' said his father. Both men were silent for a few minutes then his father said, 'Listen to that noise, Tim.'

'What noise?' asked Tim.

'The hubbub lad, that's the noise of this enterprise starting to make money. Your idea is going to work.' Mr Cooper clapped his son on the back.

'Thanks Dad. You can stop hitting me now.'

'Well done once again, lad. I may see you later.'

At lunchtime Tim was pleased to see that some of the tables in the café were occupied by customers ordering food.

Harry for all his reticence had come up trumps with the design. Working with Charlie the builder, the two of them had designed a facia that was truly Italian. There was wooden varnished scroll work around the door and Sophie's writ large on the window in an attractive flowing gold script. The gathering of tables and chairs sheltering under blue-and-white-striped umbrellas set in front of the café was perfect; through half-closed eyes it did look and feel as though you were in a square somewhere in Italy.

He could see the customers admiring the barrows, lots of pictures were taken. Later he spotted the local newspaper reporter walking towards him, they shook hands.

'You have done it again, Tim. It's great, it even smells Italian. It must have cost a fortune.'

'I am quite sure I will get my money back, Robert. As long as I survive into my eighties – don't quote me on that.' Both men laughed. The relationship between the two of them had improved over time.

Several of his suppliers came in during the day to see how their produce was moving off the shelves. They all seemed reasonably pleased.

*

In the early afternoon, Tim was approached by a stranger who introduced himself as John Armstrong. He was of medium height, dark-haired, thin with an intelligent look about him. He was wearing a black Barbour jacket and black trousers. To offset the rather dour appearance of the rest of his clothing, he sported a multi-coloured Pringle scarf. As he shook Tim's hand he said, 'Can I buy you a cup of coffee, Mr Cooper? I have an idea to put to you.'

'Call me Tim, please.'

'Will do. I'm John.'

Tim led the way to an empty table.

'What do you want to drink, Tim?'

Both men agreed on a latte, when the pretty young Italian waitress arrived to collect their order. Tim had trained all the staff members to say, 'Hallo my name is ------. How can I help you?'

Tim jumped in saying, 'Don't tell me your name, it's'...' With his eyes closed he was racking his brain; finally he looked up at her and said, 'Maria. Am I right?'

Smiling she said, 'Yes, Tim.'

He had insisted throughout the training they call him Tim; now most of them were more comfortable with it.

Tim sipped his latte. He leaned back in his chair, holding his cup in both hands just short of his mouth and said, 'What's on your mind?'

'Firstly, I think what you have done here is superb,' John replied. 'I only came here today to have a walk round to be honest, but the café and the whole indoor-outdoor thing that was mentioned in the paper has given me an idea. I am a vintner – supposing I wanted to rent some space and open a wine shop, in a building like the café. To continue the indoor-outdoor theme. I don't know how this will work financially or otherwise but I am really taken with the idea, what do you think?'

Tim was quiet for some time taking bigger mouthfuls of his now cooling coffee.

One thing he was sure of was that if he did go ahead the shop building had to be owned by Sophie's.

Finally, he said, 'We could investigate it, there are obviously precedents for it. I have no idea how we might set it up John, but I am not against the idea. One or two early thoughts, Sophie's would have to own the building and we would not have any liability for your business.'

'That's a job for the solicitors if we get that far but I am extremely keen to go ahead Tim.'

Tim recognised that this could be a way of offsetting the running costs of the building. The two men swapped business cards and agreed to meet again once both had done some research.

CHAPTER 41

1981

Sophie was working with Jessica and Bonny in the company office. She had arrived only minutes earlier. Jessica commented on her apparently new blue maternity dress that Jessica had not seen before. Sophie did a little twirl.

With a frown on her face she said, 'Oh, I need the loo. I will be right back.' Sophie reached the top of the stairs and stepped into the bathroom as her waters broke. She had experienced mild discomfort since waking, but nothing meaningful, now a proper contraction hit making her grunt. She was sure her boy had decided now was as good a time as any. She called to the two women downstairs, 'My waters have broken, can you call an ambulance, please?'

Jessica bounded up the stairs, calling, 'Hallo, where are you?'

'I am in the bathroom. Be careful when you come in.'

'How are you doing?' asked Jessica, poking her head around the door.

'I get the distinct impression that this boy is in a hurry,' she gasped as another contraction gripped her. She tightened her grip on the towel rail. 'I am glad you are here Jessica, at least you know what is going on.'

Bonny called up the stairs, 'I told them your waters have broken – the ambulance is on its way.'

'Well done, Bonny,' said Jessica. 'Stay down there please. You can let the paramedics in when they get here.'

'Will do.'

'Are these the first signs you have had?'

'There were small pains this morning but nothing of any note.' As she said this her face screwed into a grimace and she grunted as the next contraction gripped her.

Jessica was now concentrating on her watch. 'You are right, I think this baby is on its way. Whatever you do Sophie, do not push. I have no maternity qualifications.' Both women laughed.

'Sophie, can I suggest we get you on to a bed just in case.'

'The spare room has a single bed – we can put some towels down.'

'Why do you keep calling the baby a boy?'

'When I was carrying Charley, a midwife told me she was a girl because boys are carried in front. This pregnancy has been completely different to the first one, and I am carrying in front.'

'Sophie I think that is a load of toffee – sorry to be rude.'

'To be honest Jessica as long as the baby is fit and well, I do not care what it is.' Minutes later the bed was covered by some towels and a sheet; Jessica helped Sophie on to it.

The contractions were coming regularly now, and more strongly. Jessica rubbed the back of Sophie's hand. The two of them were beginning to believe this was going to be a do-it-yourself job when the doorbell rang.

'I hope this is the cavalry,' said Sophie through gritted teeth.

Bonny shouted up the stairs, 'They're here.' There was muted conversation in the hall then the sound of footsteps on the stairs. Two paramedics entered the room and began asking questions.

'Right,' the older woman said. 'I am going to examine you and then we will know where we are.' Turning to Jessica she said, 'You can leave us to it now, thanks.'

'I will be outside if you want me,' said Jessica.

Minutes later the same woman reappeared. 'This baby is on its way. We will deliver it here. We would not get to the hospital in time. I need some stuff from the ambulance.'

Bonny who had been standing at the foot of the stairs had the door held open by the time the paramedic reached her.

✳

An hour later Jessica and Bonny were sitting at the kitchen table drinking tea when there was a crescendo of shouting then silence. Neither women said anything; then the noise of a lusty infant's first cry could be heard. The two of them hugged each other; both had radiant smiles on their faces.

A voice called down from upstairs, 'Hallo down there. Mum wants a cup of tea, so do we.'

Bonny scurried up into the room to check on who wanted milk or sugar. Jessica put the kettle on. Later as Martyn was getting his first feed all the women were standing round sipping tea. 'When we are all sorted, we will take you into the maternity unit and run the checks, but I have to say he looks fine to me,' said the senior paramedic.

'Why cannot the baby and I stay here?' asked Sophie.

'Normally if this had not happened – crash, bang, wallop – you would have had a range of checks before the birth started. Now this young man seems perfect to me, but I suggest we do the tests retrospectively.'

'I will shower before I go to hospital,' announced Sophie.

'See how you feel when you stand up,' said the nurse.

'I feel fine thank you. I cannot go to hospital like this – all mucky.' She moved to the edge of the bed and stood up.

'All right, but I will come with you. We don't want you passing out and knocking yourself around – I would be filling in paperwork for days.'

'Jessica, can you find some clothing for me please. You will find some in the drawers at the foot of the wardrobe. You know what to choose? I always leave some dresses and trousers here.'

'Will do,' she replied,

Bonny had played only a minor role in this drama but one thing she was now sure of, she wanted babies of her own.

*

The ambulance came to a halt at the entrance to the hospital. Sophie was told to sit still while a wheelchair was fetched. She said nothing, taking notice of the unspoken warning on the face of the paramedic. As the doors came open, Tim was standing there.

'How did you know where I was, Tim?' she asked her face lighting up.

'Bonny rang the shop.'

'Well done, Bonny,' said Sophie.

The wheelchair arrived and Sophie was manoeuvred into it and baby Martyn placed in her arms. Sophie noticed Tim was, as usual, getting emotional. He leaned in and kissed her.

'Well done, Mum,' he whispered. He cleared his throat then in a normal voice asked, 'Are we all ok?'

The senior nurse said, 'Everyone's good thanks Dad. We are going to do some checks on Mum and baby and then we will see how we go. You may as well go and get a cup of tea. I can recommend the lemon drizzle cake. Come through to the maternity unit when you're done.'

'How long will my wife be in hospital?' Tim asked.

'Twenty-four hours if everything goes well. I think that's the most likely. Mum and baby appear fit and well. See you in a bit, bye now.'

An hour later mother and baby were installed in the ward. Martyn was sound asleep now and Tim could see his wife's eyes fluttering closed while he spoke to her.

'Shall I let you sleep?' he asked.

'Yes, please Tim. I am absolutely shattered, sorry. Will you come and see me this evening? Nanny will have taken Charley to school.'

'No problem. I'll sort it.'

*

Later, after school Charley was sitting on Tim's lap, meanwhile Nanny was getting the child's afternoon tea. His daughter had adopted her dad's love of hot milk and spam sandwiches spread with Branston pickle. Tim had believed initially that it would be too strong for her and that she only asked for it because her Daddy liked it, but this was not the case, she really liked it. When she had eaten it, she would run her finger around the plate to get the last of the flavour, something Sophie thoroughly disapproved of. Tim never did admit that his daughter was copying him.

'When does baby Martyn come home, Daddy?' asked Charley.

'If everything goes to plan, Mummy and Martyn come home tomorrow.'

'Where do babies come from, Daddy?'

'Out of mummies' tummies. It will all be explained when you are old enough.'

'Why can't you tell me now?'

'Because you are too young to understand. You will be told when you are grown up.'

'But Daddy I am nearly grown up now.'

Picking the child off his lap and placing her on the floor he said, 'Enough now. Your food is ready, sit up at the table and I will sit with you. Are you going to join us, Nanny? Will you be all right with the new workload, the baby I mean?' he asked as Nanny sat down.

'Oh, sure I will. I'm really looking forward to it, so I am. Don't you worry about me.' Ruffling Charley's hair she said, 'You'll help me won't you lass?'

Charley nodded, unable to speak because her mouth was full of food.

Later that evening Mr Graham deposited Tim and Charley outside the maternity wing of the hospital. Nanny had cried off saying, 'You two carry on, this is a family thing. I will see the baby tomorrow.'

Charley was stomping along beside Tim as they walked down the brightly lighted hospital corridor towards the maternity unit.

Tim whispered to his daughter, 'This is where you were born.'

'Why was Martyn born at home, Daddy?'

'Because he was in a rush to become a member of our family and to meet you.'

Charley smiled up at him. 'Can I help look after him please, Daddy?'

'You certainly can.'

Tim held the ward door open; Charley stepped through and spotted her mother in a bed halfway down the ward. Shaking her hand loose from her father's grip she flew to the bedside.

When Tim arrived seconds later his wife was introducing the sleeping Martyn to her daughter. Charley was wide-eyed, confusion plain on her face. She was clearly aware that her world had changed, her innate confidence had been shaken.

'Tim, if you have the baby, Charley can come up here for a cuddle with her mummy.'

He nodded, indicating his awareness behind what his wife was saying.

As Charley was climbing the bedside to be with Sophie, Tim was around the other side taking charge of his son who still had not woken. Making himself comfortable in the armchair beside the bed, he introduced himself saying, quite loudly, 'Hallo, I'm your father. Now, you will have a lot to do, you have to carry the family name forward, continue building the empire your mother and I are constructing, and you have to be kind to your sister.'

Sophie broke off from talking to her daughter and gave Tim the hard stare. He watched as Sophie hugged her daughter to her saying, 'I love you, tuppence.'

'I love you Mummy,' was the muffled response from the child who had her face buried in her mother's dressing gown.

'And we all love Mummy, don't we team?' He addressed his statement to the still sleeping baby on his lap.

'Will you stop trying to wake him up please. I am the one who will have to get him back to sleep.'

'Well, I want my son to look at me,' said Tim, standing on his dignity. 'I am his father,' he said in a deep commanding voice.

Tim had to apologise and explain to Sophie that he had misspelt his son's name when he had registered it earlier. He had spelt it with a y instead of an I. Sophie could not be cross, firstly it made her boy somewhat unique, secondly, she knew it was a good example of Tim's appalling shortened lack of education. His mother's premature death and his father's subsequent prolonged mental ill health had robbed Tim of years of schooling. Tim was told months later that spelling his sons name with a y was Welsh and noble.

After some general chit chat about Charley's day, Tim saying when asked that it had been a very ordinary day; Sophie asked Charley, 'Do you think your father is a silly man?'

'No, he is not silly Mummy,' the child said vehemently, shaking her head.

Sophie rolled her eyes and asked her daughter, 'Would you like to hold Martyn?'

There was a long pause then the little girl said, 'Yes please, Mummy.' Sophie arranged the baby in her daughter's arms. The disturbance woke Martyn who smiled up into the young girl's face. Both parents could see the wonder that was shining from Charley's eyes; she then leaned down and kissed the baby very gently on the end of his nose. There was no visible evidence but, in that instant, a lifelong bond was formed between the two children.

Charley asked lots of questions: Why did he not have any hair? Why were his eyebrows black? Would he grow some teeth later?

Martyn began to cry Tim jumped in and said, 'I'll have him.' He lifted his son from Charley's arms. He walked away humming a Celine Dion song almost inaudibly. As he moved down the ward some of the mums smiled at him; one asked, 'Can I see him?' Tim walked to her bedside and held his boy so that the woman and her husband could see his face.

'He's going to be the perfect likeness to you,' said the man.

'Thank you,' Tim replied. There was no baby visible and Tim was too afraid to ask. Martyn rescued him by starting to cry. 'Nice to meet you,' he said as he moved away and started humming again. The couple smiled at his retreating back.

When he got back to the bed Charley was sound asleep and his wife was obviously tired as they swapped children.

'I am going to take this one home,' Tim said as he lifted Charley from her mother's arms. His daughter hardly stirred as she made herself comfortable on his shoulder.

∗

The following morning Tim was woken by his daughter climbing into bed with him and shaking his shoulder saying, 'Daddy, it's time to wake up. Nanny's here – I've let her in.'

Nanny knocked on the cabin door saying, 'Good morning, are you decent?' This an obvious reminder of the past when she had caught him stark naked.

'You can come in, Nanny.'

'You look tired, Tim. Are you ok?'

'I am tired. What with the food hall opening and the baby, it's been a bit full on.'

'Come on Charley, let's get you and Daddy some breakfast.'

'I'll be out in a moment Nanny – toast and marmalade please.'

Tim threw on his dressing gown and made his way into the bathroom. He joined Nanny and Charley in the front cabin.

'Did you watch Charles and Diana's wedding last night?' asked Nanny.

'No, I forgot it was on. We had a mug of cocoa each when we got back from the hospital, and we went to bed.'

'Daddy was snoring, Nanny.'

'I will watch the repeats this evening,' said Tim. 'I think she is stunning.' Tim had a lot of respect for the royal family and their sense of duty, unlike his mother who would have made them all resign and get a job.

'She made a lovely bride,' observed Nanny.

'Nanny, I am still concerned about how much more you will have to do when Martyn comes home. Will you be able to cope?' he asked.

Placing her hand on his daughter's head, she said, 'Tim I am never happier than when I am here with this one and the rest of you.'

Tim recognised that living on her own might be extremely lonely. 'We will try and keep you busy, Nanny,' he replied.

'Thank you, Tim. That will be grand, so it will.'

Mid-morning the next day, the phone rang. 'Tim, I am ready to come home. I have had my last set of tests – they are all good. Can you come now?'

'Yes, I can,' he replied recognising the urgency in his wife's voice. 'Mr Graham said he is ready whenever. I will ring him. See you very soon, my love.'

When he dialled Mr Graham's number it only rang once before it was answered by Mrs Graham. 'He is walking out the door as we speak Timothy. Our congratulations. Are Mummy and baby ok?'

'Yes, thank you everyone is fine.'

'He has just driven away, Timothy. He will be with you very soon.'

Shrugging on his coat, he saw Nanny walk into the back cabin, reappearing with a soft, blue, wool blanket tucked under her arm. 'Leave it to the professional,' he said. Nanny smiled at him as she handed it over.

Minutes later, Charley, who was watching out of the galley window; she always corrected her mother when Sophie called the galley the kitchen. 'Mr Graham's here.' Now the child was jumping up and down laughing and clapping her hands and singing, 'Mummy's coming home, Mummy's coming home, hooray, hooray.'

The two adults exchanged quizzical glances surprised by the girl's excitement, she was normally rather demure.

Kneeling to talk to Charley he said, 'I will not be long. You be good for Nanny – Mummy will be home soon.'

'I will Daddy,' He kissed her goodbye.

∗

Sophie was sitting in reception in a wheelchair holding Martyn who was swaddled in an attractive white crocheted blanket when Tim arrived. She was clearly pleased to see him.

'Where is the car?' she asked.

'Right outside,' he replied.

A nurse came over saying, 'I have to see you off the premises.' With no more ado she began to wheel the chair towards the exit.

The nurse led the three of them out of the hospital; she was going to ask which car, but Tim pointed to the Bentley. Mr Graham was standing by the door ready to open it.

Waiting until Sophie was in the car then the nurse handed her Martyn. Smiling at the Bentley she said, 'You are giving him a good start, anyway.' Tim and Sophie thanked the young nurse as they climbed aboard. It was only a few minutes to the Sea Maiden. A fine rain had started. Arriving at

The Sea Maiden Sophie passed the baby to Tim before alighting. Once she was upright he handed Martyn back.

Tim grasped Sophie's upper arm; he was worried that the boarding ramp may be slippery because of the rain.

The door opened to reveal Nanny and Charley standing there flanked by Angela. When she caught sight of Martyn, Charley began bouncing up and down.

Nanny's soft voice said, 'Steady lass, we don't want to frighten him.'

Sophie said quietly into Angela's ear, 'Will you hold Martyn for me, please? It is important that I make a fuss of Charley.'

Angela, a little surprised said, 'Yes.' She suspected that Sophie recognised that she had no role here. Holding the baby gave her one, it was also the reason that Charley was being given tasks to do. This way everyone was included. Martyn smiled up into her eyes. Angela was blown away; she felt a deep longing building within her. Now she was experiencing a heartfelt regret that she was childless. The front cabin was busy with everybody doing what needed to be done. Using this to hide her emotions she said, 'I will take Martyn out of the way.'

Sophie nodded at her before once again instructing Charley in the next task.

Angela stepped into the back cabin: the main bedroom. Martyn was still examining her face. The woman in her ached for what she could now never have.

She remembered back to the war years when her new husband, a fighter pilot, had sat her down and said if anything happens to me you must find someone else. Now seated on the end of the bed she was staring out of the cabin window, not seeing the activity on the river. Instead, she was sitting in a rented, scruffy, first-floor flat watching the activity on the airfield over the top of the perimeter wire fence.

An officer had called earlier to tell her that her husband was missing presumed dead. One of the other pilots had seen his plane go down. She was so young; she made a vow that day that whatever happened to her she would never tarnish his memory by taking another man into her life.

Now sitting in the cabin, she deeply regretted that decision. She loved Charley but the child had not stirred this intense visceral reaction in her that Martyn was doing now. She found herself mourning all the children she might have had. Now she was angry with herself. 'Pull yourself together,' she said out loud.

Martyn began to cry, sensing her mood. Moments later Sophie stuck her head round the door to check if everything was alright. Angela had put a brave face on and said, as she handed him back, 'Might he be hungry?'

'Possibly, I will try and see. Can you fetch his bag in, please?'

CHAPTER 42

'Tim, how do you feel about a holiday?' Sophie asked one evening shortly after he had come in from work.

'What's brought this on?' he asked.

Sophie was quiet for a while working out how she was going to phrase her answer.

'Tim if I stay here, I will have to go back to work. I love my children but having them 24 hours a day, here on board, is slowly driving me crazy. I do not know if that makes me a rotten mother but that's the truth.'

'Are you well enough to go away? What does the Doctor say?'

'I and the children have had a check-up and we are all extremely healthy. He sees no reason why we cannot go. The school holidays have just started so now is a good time.'

'Will you be all right on your own? Obviously I can't go, there would be no one at the helm.'

'Tim, no one is irreplaceable. Between them, your father and Harry have forgotten more than we will ever know about the retail trade – Jessica and Bonny are red hot with the admin. They will hardly notice we have gone.'

Tim would never admit it but since the two women had taken over the admin there was now a certain extra polish to that side of things. 'So where are you thinking of going?' he asked.

'Italy – to the house, to Puglia. We will be made so welcome by the locals, half of whom are distantly related to mother. The children will get spoiled. Charley can run in the fields in the sunshine. We can go to the beach. Angela spent all her summer holidays there when she was young – if you ask her, she will tell you she would go back tomorrow.'

'You seem very set on this – are you sure it will work?'

'I see no reason why not; the children will love it. Nanny will get a working holiday and it will not do us any harm.'

Tim was quiet for a while; Sophie let him ponder on it.

He thought, if necessary, I could be back in a few hours if something blew up. 'Ok then let's do it. When shall we go?'

'I think we can be ready in about a week. I hope Nanny has a passport.'

'She does. She used to go away with her family until she started working for us after they moved away. They went on walking holidays abroad.'

'There has to be one rule Tim, if we have to work over there, we only work mornings.'

'Is there a pool? Of course there is,' said Tim, answering his own question. 'It's your father's.'

'No, it is not actually. It belongs to mother.'

'Oh, that's interesting.'

'She and Angela used to spend summers there when my aunt was young.'

✻

Tim was surprised when the staff appeared so relaxed about their departure. He admitted to himself he expected them to put all kinds of problems in his way. There were none.

His father summed it up pretty well – 'Tim, Harry and I have been doing this since the last ice age, and you will be on the end of a phone. Jessica and

Bonny have a first-class grip on the admin, and you are not going to the moon. Don't worry lad – enjoy yourselves.'

∗

A week later the family Cooper found themselves in a queue ready to board the aeroplane at London airport. At the gate, an official pre-checked their tickets and guided them from economy class towards first class.

Immediately Sophie said, 'Tim, he has made a mistake, we do not have first-class tickets.' She was just about to call the man back when Tim restrained her and said, 'We do have first-class tickets.'

'We cannot afford them' – seeing his smile she continued – 'of course we can.' As a couple they never talked about their personal finances. She had forgotten how extremely wealthy Tim was now since his inheritance from his great aunt.

Pulling her to him he whispered in her ear, 'You need to get used to it, this is the future. This is why we work so damn hard. From now on my darling, I intend it to be first class for all of us all the way.'

The queue was much shorter for first class; while she waited, she mused on how much her husband had changed since she met him that day on the train. Then he was little more than a boy, working all hours to try to clear the large debt that had accrued after his mother had died. Now he was a wealthy young man. Yes, he had been lucky but a lot of it was a result of his almost insane work ethic. He really believed that extremely hard work was the answer to almost any problem. He had once been accused of being lucky and his response was, 'You're right, the harder I work the luckier I get.'

Sophie had flown first class before with her father, but Tim never had. They all enjoyed the space and the service; the crew were lovely with the children.

Tim enjoyed flying even when he had been bundled in with all the people in economy; the enormous power of the jet engines that thrust this huge aircraft aloft was a great thrill. He loved the increasing acceleration down the runway, the shaking around as they gathered speed, then the angle of the aircraft as the nose wheel lifted off the runway; then the banging and bumping stopped as the plane left the ground and climbed away into the blue sky.

Tim dozed during the short flight and was woken by the captain announcing their imminent arrival in Brindisi.

*

The Vieri property had once been a large working farmhouse with many rooms. The whole place was nicely decorated but not ostentatiously so.

'Sophie, I expected it to be very grand,' said Tim. I assumed your mother as the owner would want all the latest fashions.'

'Father would not have it, they had a heck of a row apparently, he and mother. Father insisted it had to be comfortable. Not a cold palace designed to impress mother's snooty friends.'

Sophie continued saying, 'Father wanted it to be a home from home – somewhere that welcomes you in, where you can relax, where people feel comfortable.'

'He has achieved that,' observed Tim, ' there is a warmth to the place. I love that here and there the wood has been polished smooth by years of use; the stone steps are worn from the passage of a thousand footsteps. The terracotta bricks and pantiles trap the sun's heat. We could retire here.'

Sophie was laughing. 'Tim, you will never retire. What will you do all day?'

'I will get up late, take my rickety old bike out of the shed and cycle into the village – sit outside the bistro sipping my glass of wine and eating tapas and watching the pretty girls go by.'

Sophie rolled her eyes and went downstairs. Tim moved outside on to the bedroom's balcony. He settled into a comfy but elderly armchair and watched the world go by. The traffic on the road at the front of the house just beyond the wall was sparse but those locals who noticed him sitting there called and waved. He was unsure what they were saying but he smiled and waved back.

He was shaken awake by Charley saying, 'Daddy wake up. Mummy has been calling you for lunch.'

Arriving downstairs, he met the two women from the village who ran the house, a cook and a cleaner; they told him one of their daughters arrived mid-morning to make the beds and so on. They were both dressed in red poppy -patterned, lightweight frocks and plain buff pinafores. The language was a mixture of Italian, English, and happy laughter. The meal laid out on the table was a wonderful range of Italian food: olives, sun-dried tomatoes, cured meats, warm bread and freshly churned butter. Something Tim had not eaten before was a cold farfalle salad with peppers, sweet cherry tomatoes, diced cucumber and tuna. With a tasty dressing. All washed down with a large cold glass of white wine.

As his eyes roamed around the table, he watched his wife and children interacting with the Italian women and he recognised that he was genuinely happy.. Everyone was relaxed and enjoying the moment.

'Tim we have been invited to a meal in the village – there will be food, music and dancing.'

Tim said, 'Nanny can look after the children.'

'No' – was Sophie's response, chastising him – 'we have all been invited. I am sure you would like to dance, Nanny.'

'I would,' she replied, glancing at Tim

'Sorry Nanny, that was thoughtless of me.'

'And I want to dance, Daddy,' declared Charley holding the hem of her dress out between her fingers.

Tim loved to dance, his mind sped back to the reception after their wedding when he had surprised Sophie with a waltz for the first dance and later in the evening they had jived.

Sophie laughing said, 'I know what you are thinking about, our wedding. We will dance again tonight.'

*

The family were made so welcome in the village: a bonfire roared in the middle of the square; strings of coloured lights were strung between the street lamps. A huge full moon shone down on the festivities; away from the lights a multitude of stars were visible. Tables laden with food were placed in a double row, each table had candles in glasses illuminating the multitude of dishes. A trio of musicians were playing on a low stage away from the fire. Couples were dancing, children were flying around creating impromptu dance patterns. The wine was flowing.

Tim did not think he had ever seen such a display of carefree happiness. Young and old alike were enjoying themselves. He, Sophie, and the children spent the first half hour being guided around the groups of people. The locals made sure the family were introduced to all Sophie's relatives however distant, especially the *Nonos*, the grandmothers. On one occasion an argument broke out in a small group of elderly women as to who was the closest relative to Sophie. Tim put his hand in the middle of Sophie's back and eased her onwards.

Nanny was worried for a moment because she could not see Charley. Tim noticed her growing concern, She was standing on tiptoe stretching up to see over the groups of people, her head snapping from one direction to another. Tapping her on the shoulder he pointed to where his daughter was learning the steps that a small group of girls were doing.

Nanny turned to him and said, 'Thank you, Tim.'

He would never admit his concern, but he made sure he knew where Charley was all the time. She was a gregarious and trusting child and would be easily led away.

The days fled by. Nanny proved she was still a strong swimmer both in the pool and the sea. The water was wonderfully warm.

Martyn was the only one who seemed not to like the water, even though Sophie held him firmly in her grasp. It may have been due to that one wave which had broken a yard away and thrown spray all over them.

Charley loved the water and had to be ordered to leave it.

One afternoon the family were strolling through the small town saying hallo to everyone, shaking hands and chatting. The locals were extremely friendly and spent some time explaining what their relationship was to her mother and therefore Sophie and the children.

There was only one dark moment when a man stepped up to Tim snarled: *'Turista'* – and spat at Tim's feet. Immediately the men they had been talking to angrily pushed the man away, berating him in Italian; two of them continued to encourage him to leave, jabbing at him with straight fingers, driving him away.

There were lots of apologies which Tim and Sophie waved aside saying, 'No problem, no problem.'

On the last day of their holiday, the house was full of people, mostly Sophie's relatives and their close friends.

Tim sat enveloped in the happy throng and realised for the first time that he would like to stay amongst the chat and the laughter. He vowed to himself that he and his family would spend more time here. He was also very aware how barren and lonely his own childhood had been.

CHAPTER 43

One evening, back at home, Sammy and Tom were sitting watching a film on the telly, both of them swathed in their dressing gowns. When it ended sadly, Tom said, 'That poor little boy. Life is cruel sometimes isn't it?'

'There's folks a lot worse off than I am the boy replied. What about all the kids what don't 'ave no homes? Livin' on the streets, beggin', and stealing' just to stay alive. Pushed around by the rozzers, chased by a lot of nasty beggars.'

'Did all this happen to you lad?'

'Yeah, that an' worse. I ain't gunna talk about it.'

'Sammy, why were you down on the south coast?'

'I ain't gunna tell you Mr, cause if I tells you, you'll send me back and I ain't never going back there.'

'Now listen lad, I'm not going to send you anywhere. You can stay here if you like. I enjoy your company. You and the dog have made the place come alive again. I didn't realise how lonely I had become.'

Bess lifted her head and gave a solitary switch of her tail.

There was a long silence, then Sammy said, 'I can't stay here anyways, there ain't nowhere fer me to sleep.'

'Ah, now I have been giving that some thought, lad. There is a lot of room up on the landing opposite the bathroom. I think we could put a bed there for now while we come up with an alternative. What do you think?'

'Do yur mean a proper bed?'

'Yes, of course.'

'It'll be better than sleeping under the bridge, I s'pose.'

Tom was going to admonish the child for his lack of gratitude, but he stopped himself. He realised that the boy had no decent role models; he had been living like a wild animal. It made him stop and think: Did he want to take on this poor waif? Who knew what terrible events had warped his mind? Did he have any moral code?

'I'd like to sleep here iffen I could, through the winter anyways Mr. Then I could move on in the spring.'

*

One evening some weeks later, Sammy didn't return until well after dark. He stood wet and cold and shivering in front of the living room fire.

'Have you been busy, lad?'

'No, one of the dockers told me he'd seen me mum. I've been up and down the river.'

'What's the name of her boat, Sammy?'

'She moors up over the other side, but I couldn't see 'er. Now it's too dark?'

Clearly the boy was not about to divulge any information that could identify him.

'Would you like some hot soup and some bread and while that's warming up what say I make a cuppa?'

'Could I have some of that hot chocolate? That warms me up right proper.'

Tom nodded as he made his way to the kitchen.

Later that evening man and boy were both dozing, toasting their toes in front of the fire. Full of cottage pie.

'How come your mum left you behind? She must have noticed you weren't onboard?'

'She made sure I wasn't on board.'

'Surely that's not true, Sammy.'

'Yeah, it is. She gets a bloke on board for a while until she's got their money then she turns them off. She'll becoming for me when she ain't broke no more.'

'Are you saying your mum's a ...?' He could not bring himself to say the word.

'Yeah, she's a prossie.'

'Sammy!!' exclaimed Tom. 'You shouldn't say that about your mother.'

'Its true Mr, she's been on the game for years.'

'Has she ever been arrested?'

'Yeah, quite recently. That's why they sent me to that children's 'ome.

'I'm not going to ask where it was Sammy, but can you tell me what it was like?'

'It was 'orrible, it were run by the nuns. When I got there two of 'em stripped me naked in the bathroom and started shaving me 'ead. I asked 'em why they were doing it, they said it were because I was a vagrant and would 'ave fleas and all sorts. Then they stood me in a big white bowl full of nearly cold water and started scrubbing me with stiff brushes and strong soap what stung me eyes. My skin was red and sore for days after.'

Sounds like carbolic thought Tom, poor little beggar. 'Then what?' he asked, thinking this was the most words the boy had strung together since they had met.

'I was put in a bedroom wiv loads of other boys. I got bullied bad. I used to get punished by the nuns for breaking the rules. I told 'em I didn't know what the rules were – they said I'd soon learn. 'I was often smacked on the hand wiv the nun's stick.' Sammy was holding his hands about two feet apart to indicate the length of the stick.

'The big boys would 'old me over the bannisters at the top of the stairs and say they was gunna drop me – it were a long way down. Sometimes they'd race downstairs holding one of my arms each, lifting me off the ground and telling me they was gunna let me go. All the boys called me a gypo. The big boys used to steal me food when the nuns weren't lookin'.'

That would explain why you're so thin, thought Tom.

'How did you get out, lad?'

'The bathroom upstairs had a big black metal pipe runnin' down the wall outside by the window. I'd had a right larruping that day because I'd left me workbook in my cupboard in the bedroom. I hung about until the dinner bell sounded – it's always a right palaver wiv 'em all trying to get in the dinner hall together. I snuck upstairs, threw me bag over mi shoulder and slid under the open window – it were one of them sash ones – then I climbed down the pipe. Halfway down a nun came to a window beside the pipe. I squeezed meself against the wall, shut me eyes and prayed she wouldn't see me. I walked all night.'

'How did you know which way to go?'

'I followed the norf star. Mum had a sailor on board one time for a week or so, he told me all about it. Later, I followed them signposts. I can't read much but I knows the signs what say London and some others. I lay low during the day and walked at night until I was far enough away so they wouldn't be lookin' for me. Then I hitched some lifts – one old couple took me in a café and fed me bless 'em. They told me they would take me to the police station, so I could get some help.'

'What did you do?'

'I told 'em I needed the loo and slipped out the back door. I hid for a bit then I walked all night again.'

'You certainly are determined lad. I can assure you that here you can come and go as you please. If you are going to move on, please let me know though.'

'Ok, Mr.'

CHAPTER 44

Angela arrived at the art gallery and pulled on the long, vertical, brass handle. Nothing happened, she tried pushing, the same result. The heavy, varnished, dark wood door was stuck. Looking inside she could see that there were people in there.

She was about to turn away when a man's arm reached around her and grasping the handle asked, 'May I assist you? I have told the owner he would do more business if it were not a trial of strength to get in,' he said in a wonderful French accent.

Stepping through the now open door she turned to see the gallant Frenchman. He was heart-stoppingly attractive. Of medium height with curly, dark-brown hair swept back at the sides and with curls sitting on the collar of his cream shirt. The white chinos and bare feet with sandals finished the ensemble. She was most taken with his eyes that twinkled with all sorts of promises.

'Have you been here before?' he asked.

'Once, years ago,' she replied.

'May I show you round?' he asked. 'Although first I have to give this to the owner.' Proffering the thin, square, parcel packed in brown paper.

'You are obviously busy, you carry on. I will find my own way.'

'No, I would love to show you around, please.'

He was holding another door open; his fingers were bunched around the tip of her elbow with just enough gentle pressure to add a physical pleading to his spoken one.

Angela was pleased she had overcome her original intention of coming out in old jeans and a scruffy tan jumper. The pretty pink dress with a similarly coloured jacket thrown over her shoulders was more fitting in the situation she now found herself in.

'Here is the owner now. Hallo, Mr Palmer.'

The man in question was short, about five foot two she guessed; he gave off an air of great confidence and ability. He was dressed in a mid-brown suit and a red bow tie.

'Hallo Alain, better late than never, eh. What have we got here?' he asked as he stripped off the paper and held the painting up.

Angela burst out laughing, then tried to stop, afraid it was the wrong reaction. Looking at the Frenchman she was delighted it was clearly the correct reaction.

Mr Palmer was staring at them both as they doubled up with laughter. Angela with her hand to her mouth trying to smother her amusement.

'It is amazing,' she said still laughing. 'Sunflowers and a sticky plaster over your ear and it is beautifully painted. You are incredibly skilled – that is a perfect self-portrait. You are so clever, although I think you are better looking than Van Gogh ever was.'

Mr Palmer, shaking his head and still unsure said, 'Alain, is it serious art? This gallery has a reputation to uphold. I'm, I'm not sure,' he continued, clearly confused.

'I will buy it,' said Angela. 'How much is it?'

'I will give it to you,' the young man responded.

'No, you will not,' she declared. 'What is the proper price, Mr Palmer?'

He told her how much it was. 'Alain is becoming more popular.'

'Will a cheque do?'

'Certainly.'

Afterwards Alain showed her around the rest of the gallery; he had gently pulled her arm through his. She had not objected. This extremely attractive and gifted young man was awakening feelings in her that had been dormant for years. His accent alone was captivating. She was a girl again. She loved his manners, his care of her, his concentration on her opinion when he asked for her thoughts, even the way he smelt – his cologne was attractively masculine. Guessing at his age she thought about thirty; it later transpired he was twenty years her junior.

'Can I buy you dinner? I don't know what is happening, but I do not want this evening to end,' he begged, all this in his attractive French accent.

He was so earnest, how could she refuse him; it had been many years since she had experienced this turmoil inside her – the shortness of breath, the raised heartbeat.

✳

They walked from the restaurant to Angela's house, laughing as they went. It was obviously a night for love: numerous young couples strolling arm in arm like Angela and Alain, who smiled and said hallo; like the other couples they moved from one puddle of light from a street lamp to the next.

She rested her head on his shoulder. As they had exited the restaurant, he had been so confident he had slid his arm round her waist and kissed her. It was the softest of kisses. It was her that increased the pressure as she leaned into him.

I shall wake up in a bit she thought, and all this will have been a dream. She knew what she wanted this night, and it was not for him to walk away.

When they got to her front gate he said, 'I know this is fast of me, but may I stay with you tonight?'

Thank God for that, she thought, if he had said goodnight and walked away, I would not have been able to ask him to stay. I seem to have become a scarlet woman, she mused.

✳

The two glasses of wine sat unfinished on the coffee table in the lounge, various articles of hastily shed clothing on the floor marked the route to the bedroom.

She never expected such joy, such an abundance of pleasure; he knew her body better than she. There were places where his kisses or his tongue hardly touched but still sent rockets of pleasure through her. Another time his finger sliding over her skin, as soft as a feather, triggered a line of delicious shivers in their wake.

As they climaxed, she used all her bodily strength to hold him to her, not wanting to break the bond; eyes tight shut she imagined they were floating in a vast white marble hall between rows of tall ornate columns.

As she returned to the world she was crying, Alain was gently thumbing the tears from her eyes, obviously concerned.

'I am sorry, I am sorry,' he was repeating. 'I did not mean to hurt you.'

'You did not hurt me, you were wonderful. I have not been with a man for many years.' Before you were born, she thought to herself. 'I had forgotten what an amazing experience it could be.' In truth she had never felt like that with her husband: his visits were brief, he was always so tired, and both were virgins when they met. It was obvious Alain was no virgin.

'What is the time?' she asked.

'Two am.'

She felt herself drifting off to sleep. Thank God, I had decent underwear on, she thought. Her mother had told her she must always be well dressed when she went out in case she got knocked down. She gave a low laugh; she had been properly knocked down tonight.

Unknowingly she had not drawn the curtains, the first rays of the sun roused her a few hours later. Alain, still sound asleep, was lying on his side facing away from her. Sliding from the bed she tiptoed to the bathroom. Once she had returned to the bed, she lay awake thinking, What would her neighbours say? What would Olivia and her friends say? With a mental shrug of dismissal she decided she would enjoy her time with this young man even if it was a one-night stand. There is no time like the present, she thought. She rolled towards him, placing her arm round him her hand slid downwards. This time it was slower and gentler. She went back to sleep afterwards.

About mid-morning she was woken by the smells and sound of cooking. Rolling over she saw him standing over her with a tray of bacon, eggs, mushrooms, and hot coffee and her dressing gown draped over his arm.

'Oh, thank you,' she said smiling at him as he handed her the gown to hide her nudity. Retrieving his tray from the table he came and sat beside her. There was a lot of laughter over breakfast. Initially she was a little shy, this boy had seen every inch of her. *Well, it is too late now to worry about that.*

When every scrap had been eaten, he removed her tray and placed it on the dining table. Picking up a sketch pad he said, 'I have a present for you.'

Carefully tearing a page from the pad, he handed it to her. The pencil drawing was of an attractive naked woman lying on her bed on her side, ; her top knee drawn up a little, her arm bent at the elbow, the palm of her hand cradling her face on the pillow, her breasts half buried in the sheet.

Angela, shocked said, 'Why on earth are you showing me a picture of a naked woman?'

'It is not a naked woman – it is a naked you. I drew you this morning while you slept – you are an incredibly beautiful lady. You were sleeping on top of the covers.'

'I do not look like that.'

'Oh yes you do,' he said smiling. 'If I had photographed you instead you would have looked exactly like that, I promise you. I have changed nothing.'

She sat staring at the drawing experiencing mixed emotions; never in her life had she been given such a personal present. She would never be able to show anyone – well maybe Sophie and perhaps Olivia if she wanted to give her sister a heart attack. The thought made her laugh out loud.

'What is funny?' asked a disembodied voice from the kitchen.

Ignoring his question she asked, 'What are you doing?'

'Washing up. I am nearly done.'

Appearing from the kitchen drying his hands on a towel he asked, 'What are you doing today? I have to show some of my regular clients round and talk them through the work. Would you like to come with me? I will take you to dinner afterwards.'

'Yes, I will thank you, that sounds nice.' It would give her more time with him. Once again, she had serious doubts about what she was doing but after a moments reflection she pushed them to the back of her mind. She decided to live for the day; this was the most alive she had felt for decades. If she was careful nobody should come to any harm.

*

Later that evening over dinner in a quiet smart restaurant, Alain reached across the table and held her hand. 'May I ask you something?'

'It depends on what you are going to ask me,' she replied, smiling at him.

'I would like to paint you, full size.'

'Not nude,' she whispered at him.

'No,' he replied. 'I have already done that with the drawing,' he said laughing. 'I see you in a beautiful high-backed chair in a long, blood-red velvet robe with just enough naked you to hint at the beauty beneath.'

She did not answer; deep in thought she realised that this was so far outside her normal experience she was lost. His magnetism and charisma could make her agree to anything. Feeling the need to put the brakes on a little she said, 'I am not saying no.' She saw his face brighten. 'I am not saying yes either – let me think about it.'

'I will wait,' was his response. They enjoyed a wonderful day together; some filled rolls provided lunch. They ate on a bench by the Thames, watching the traffic moving up and down the river. In the afternoon, she accompanied him while he showed people around the paintings in the gallery. One lady bought one, an atmospheric picture of a part of London Angela did not know. A riverside view of a backwater with old derelict red-brick factory buildings standing in the water slowly crumbling into the river. There were gaping holes in the walls where once windows stood, the glass had been smashed decades ago, blinding the building, even the frames had mostly disappeared. Purple Buddleia was rooted in the gaps in the sagging mortarless brickwork. Angela shivered; although beautifully seen by Alain's artistic eye she saw it as a metaphor, a picture of the decay of the human body.

They had dinner in the same place as the night before. As they were finishing the meal he said, 'Regrettably I have to be away for a few days to finish a piece of work. If you give me your phone number, I will ring you when I am done.'

Her heart fell, it was over already. Determined not to let him see how devastated it made her feel she smiled; she had hoped it might have gone on for a few more days.

Sounding bright she put a brave face on it and said, 'Do not work too hard.'

The waiter had called a taxi for him, she declined the lift. The last she saw was his hand waving out of the window. He had not even kissed her goodbye. Her walk home had no comparison to the night before when all kinds of deliriously happy futures lay in front of her. Now she was just lonely old Angela who had been unceremoniously dumped. She was determined not to cry, dabbing the first few tears away from her face with her handkerchief.

When Angela got home, she came close to tearing up the drawing but changed her mind and put it out of sight.

Switching the television on, out of habit, she saw it was a report on the Falkland's war, she was just in time to hear Brian Hanrahan saying, 'I counted them all out and I counted them all back.' He was referring to the British jet fighters going to attack the Argentinians. Turning it off she said to herself, 'I am miserable enough, I do not need to watch that.'

CHAPTER 45

Mrs Vieri paused in her conversation, now completely unable to remember what she was going to say next. Becoming very embarrassed she started to cry. In a small, frightened voice she said, 'Mother will be very cross with me.'

'YOUR MOTHER IS DEAD!!' shouted Mr Vieri.' Now Olivia was crying hard. 'This had to happen on the nurse's night off,' growled, her husband. 'They will have to supply a stand in. I will get Martha to come and put her to bed.'

Sophie exchanged a grimace with Angela knowing how wrong it was for her father to be so aggressive.

Tim could see the emotional pain Olivia Vieri was in, he sensed her loneliness, her fear. Without any forethought he rose from his chair and went and knelt in front of her taking her hand as he did so.

She tried to snatch it away, but he held onto it saying, 'I promise you, your mother will never be cross with you again.'

The terribly distraught woman stared into his eyes. 'Are you sure?' she asked in a small sad voice, her face bathed in her tears.

'I'm certain,' he replied.

Tim knew from what Angela had told him about her mother that she was a cold, hard, bitter woman who controlled her two girls with ridicule and verbal abuse. In truth, much as Olivia had been stern with Sophie she was never as brutal as her mother.

Martha the housekeeper walked in followed by Mr Vieri. Stopping in front of the distraught woman she asked, 'Shall I take you to your bedroom and help you get ready for bed?'

'No,' was the abrupt rejoinder. At the same time she reached out with her free hand so that she now had Tim's hand clasped in both of hers.

Speaking softly Tim asked, 'Shall I walk you to your bedroom, then Martha can help you into bed?'

'Yes please,' was the whispered reply.

Walking hand in hand the two of them left the room and moved towards her bedroom.

'This is my room,' she said quietly. She offered him an unexpected strange little smile or was it a grimace. She gave his hand a gentle squeeze before releasing it. 'Thank you Timothy, goodnight.'

✳

The journey home in the Bentley for Angela, Sophie and Tim was taken in silence. Tim was not sure what had just happened. He walked Angela to her front door, once there she held him close, kissed his cheek and said, 'You are a remarkable man, Mr Cooper.' Tim shook his head.

Once home and Nanny Bridget seen safely on her way, the children sound asleep, the tea brewing, and slippers on, Sophie sat on his lap and said, 'What …' She was clearly struggling for words. The puzzled look on her face, the tone of her voice indicating her dismay and lack of understanding.

Tim shaking his head did not reply immediately. Eventually he said, 'I thought I hated the woman, but I could sense her pain and embarrassment – I could feel it. I remembered when I saw you lying in the hospital bed unconscious after the motorcyclist had knocked you down. There was a writhing in my stomach, a real discomfort, a physical thing. The same thing happened tonight. Next thing I knew I was kneeling holding her hand.'

*

The old woman and the young man became firm friends. The two of them would go for drives in the Bentley. Soon after the jaunts began, Mrs Vieri asked, 'Will you call me Olivia please, Timothy?'

He recognised that this woman had been so desperately lonely all her life. Without any forethought he reached for her gloved hand, her fingers closed around his. He turned to look at her and saw a young women in her eyes smiling back at him. He had to exercise some fierce self-control to stop his emotions becoming all too visible. From then on as soon as she had arranged herself and her bag to her satisfaction, she held his hand. This became the norm.

Mr Graham would take them to quiet cafés where he knew Mrs Vieri would be comfortable. There were lengthy discussions about the cakes available, the final choice being dictated by the weather and Mrs Vieri. It would be her who made the final decision saying, 'No, no, Timothy, it is too warm for fruit cake, it needs to be a light sponge.' Occasionally there was a departure from the usual list and then perhaps a cheese scone would carry the day. An extremely rare customer was the hot, buttered crumpet. This was only allowed on days when ice and snow were present outdoors. Tim never argued but he was always a little sad when the crumpet was vetoed.

At family functions she insisted they sat together. To everyone's surprise there were occasions when her laughter could be heard. Tim alone saw the gentle side of her. She trusted him, and only him enough to lift the shield and reveal the woman she would have been were it not for the cruelty inflicted by her harridan of a mother.

CHAPTER 46

Declan and Daisy had been working together for almost six months, when Declan asked, 'Would you like to come with me to an Irish pub one evening for the music and the craic, just as friends?' He saw she was starting to shake her head when he continued, 'Now there'll be no funny business. It's no more than a wee walk so it is. There are rules – on the way there you will walk on one side of the road, and I will walk on the other, and there is to be no holding hands or any of that nonsense. Do you hear me?' Now he had her giggling. 'It'll be the same on the way home, you will have your side of the road and I will have mine. We could not be more respectable than if we were in church. So, what do you think?'

She had been laughing at his silly merriment most of the way through, but now her fear returned, she found herself shaking her head. 'No. I'm sorry, I can't do that.'

'Have a word with Harry and Sara, see what they say. I tell you what, they could come with us, am I not the cleverest Irishman you have ever met?'

'I don't think I could talk about going out with you with them.'

'I will do that for you. I will blind 'em with me Irish charm so I will.'

'No, you mustn't do that I would die of embarrassment.' A customer entered the shop and stopped the conversation.

Daisy stepped up immediately. 'Hallo Mrs Higgins, have you brought a friend?'

'This is my sister, Mrs Watts, who has come to visit. I have told her of the well and the light, may I show her?'

'Help yourself. I'm sorry it is a little overcast today, but the well is on. Call me if you need anything.'

Daisy watched as Mrs Watts was led to the glass-covered well, and she smiled when she saw her grab her sister's arm. Many customers did this when they saw how deep it was; the depth was emphasised by the internal lighting.

Out of the corner of her eye she noticed the light was growing on the stairway. The two women were about to get the whole show as the sun began to blaze down through the roof light.

Mrs Higgins turned her sister around. Mrs Watts put both hands to her face and walked into the light. Daisy saw the tears were spilling down the woman's face as she lifted it up into the sunshine. Daisy was unable to explain why a number of customers exhibited this reaction.

The two women spent a while wandering around the shop. Mrs Watts stood reading the menus on the walls. Having read one through she turned to Declan. 'Have you a pen and paper, please? I would like to write this one down.'

'I can do better than that to be sure – we have them already printed over here.' Walking to his left he finished up standing by the display of Sara's Italian recipe book.

Daisy was busy for a while, but she did notice that both women left having purchased a copy of the book.

CHAPTER 47

Declan had done as he promised: a week earlier he had called around to invite Sara and Harry for a night out at the Irish pub down the road. Both gave an enthusiastic, yes.

'Have you asked Daisy?' queried Harry.

'She said no. She would be too embarrassed,' he replied.'

'Hang on a moment, I'll call her. She is doing the washing up. Daisy come in her a moment, please love.'

'Harry,' said Sara, 'don't do this, she will be mortified.'

'She will be fine,' he replied.

Daisy entered the room bright red in the face. She had overheard the conversation. Looking at Declan she asked, 'What are you doing here?'

'He has invited Sara and me to that Irish pub down the road for a pie and a pint next week,' said Harry. 'I wondered if you would like to come?'

'I've already told him I don't want to go. He's tricked you and me into this. I won't go.' Turning on her heel she walked back to the kitchen, speaking over her shoulder she said, 'I shall see you in the morning at work Mr O' Connor.' She shut the kitchen door firmly behind her.

'I will have a word with her,' said Sara rising and walking towards the kitchen, 'and Harry, I will talk to you later.'

Declan looking deadly serious for once, said, 'What am I going to do,

Harry? They say don't they that you always know when you have met the one. I know Daisy is that person. I think of nothing else. When I saw her at the interview, I thought good God that's the wife, and now I have really upset her.'

'I'm not the person to ask Declan, I'm sorry to say.'

'I'll say goodnight.'

Harry watched the young man walk away down the empty road, a picture of dejection with only the glow of the street lights marking his passage.

Arriving at his aunt's she noticed his long face and asked, 'Are you all right? You have a face like slapped haddock.'

He explained what had happened. 'Sure and that's easily fixed – a large bunch of red roses and a card, not garage flowers, a florist and a card, and they have to be delivered by the florist. That will always fix it.'

Declan was unsure whether it would work but he had to give it try, blow the expense.

The following morning Daisy had barely said two words to him. At midday, a florist walked into the shop and handed Daisy a large bunch of red roses wrapped in pink paper with butterflies on. The card apologised for embarrassing her.

*

Daisy, Harry and Sara were walking to the pub, arm in arm. Declan was walking abreast of them on the opposite side of the road very straight-faced. Sara was trying not to laugh; Harry was laughing out loud. Daisy was bright pink and not sure whether to laugh or cry.

The weekly visits to the Irish pub became something all four of them looked forward to. Daisy had put a stop to the silly business of Declan walking on the other side of the street; started initially to make Daisy laugh and agree to going for a drink. Sara saw the young man's growing affection for the girl and worried. During this period, the two women had long conversations about a wide range of subjects from food to politics. Almost inevitably the younger woman's conversation touched on her upbringing and her father's behaviour; often Daisy while saying nothing would shudder and then change the topic.

*

One evening Harry was down the local pub with one of his friends, leaving Sara and Daisy alone in the house. The two of them sat in armchairs pulled forward towards the roaring fire. The weather had become bitterly cold; Daisy was wiggling her toes in her slippers that were pointed towards the warmth. She had her fluffy dressing gown on over her normal clothing The shop had been chilly all day with the door opening and closing. There were icicles hanging off the gutters.

The two of them had been quiet for a while, the younger woman broke the companionable silence first, 'May I tell you something?'

Sara nodding said, 'Of course.'

There was a long pause, then Daisy said, 'Declan has asked me out on a date.'

'And?' asked Sara.

'I got angry and told him I wasn't that kind of girl, and I didn't go out with boys. He looked really hurt. I know I gets scared when men sees me like that, but all that men and women stuff makes me feel right sick. I always sees me father's face when he tried to … you know what.'

'There are people who can help you to talk it through, help you to come to terms with it.'

'No, I ain't never doing that. I'm happy as I am, ta. I've got me job and this lovely 'ome you've let me live in.'

'First off, we are not letting you live here, this is your home for as long as you live if you want it.'

In fact, the older couple had been discussing leaving the house to Daisy in their wills very recently.

'Declan is a lovely gentle man, and you would have to be blind not to see how fond of you he is.'

'I can't help it. He'll 'ave to find someone else is all. Now he's done that there's a right nasty atmosphere at work. Do yur mind if I goes up? I'll try and get some sleep,' said Daisy as she rose from the chair and made her way towards the stairs. They exchanged their good nights.

Sara sat there for a while mulling over the problem. Harry and Declan may have to switch shops. She would sound out Harry when he got in.

*

The following morning Declan was surprised to see Harry waiting under a shop awning a hundred yards from the store, stamping his feet with his arms around his chest. His breath a cloud of steam in the freezing air.

Coming level with him, Declan, definitely not his normal ebullient self said, 'Morning Harry, I can guess why you're here. Have I lost my job?'

'No lad of course not. It's just a misunderstanding that will over time sort itself out, but for now we think it would be better if you and I swapped jobs. Is that, ok?'

Declan stepped to his right. He could not see the cars or the people, instead he was looking down all the years he would not be with Daisy, the woman he loved with every fibre of his being.

'I'll go to the other shop. Will you tell her goodbye for me, please?' His loss crashed over him like a fierce cold wave. He began to walk back the way he had come, scrubbing at his eyes with the back of his hand.

Harry stood motionless for some time, watching the young man walk away. Finally, he made his way to the second shop.

Hearing the bell, Daisy spun round then frowned seeing Harry instead of Declan.

'I thought that was Declan,' she said.

'No lass, he doesn't work here anymore.'

'Has he left?'

'No, he and I have swapped jobs. He now works at Number One. He said to say goodbye.'

'Oh, OK thank you.'

Harry could not tell whether she was upset or not.

Daisy regretted his going; she was going to miss his laughter and the way he always put her first. But she knew he would not be able to just have a platonic relationship. She could not agree to the sex, just thinking about it made her feel sick.

A week later she saw him in the street on the other side of the road, out of politeness she waved, he nodded and walked away.

Daisy stopped and stared after him – *God that stung.* She thought he was being rude, in fact Declan was so upset he knew he could not talk to her without breaking down. Since her ultimatum he had slept little and eaten less. He was seriously considering going back to Ireland. His father would be pleased.

*

Two weeks later Harry handed Daisy a letter as she reached the foot of the stairs.

'One for you lass,' he said. Daisy, frowning was surprised, she only received letters from her mum and those were few. When she recognised the handwriting, she experienced a riot of emotions. It was Declan's, he wrote with lots of flourishes to the letters. Turning on her heel she started back upstairs saying, 'Thank you Harry.'

Back in her bedroom she plonked herself on the bed and opened the letter. It was short and as she read it the tears began to flow. This couldn't be, she must have misunderstood; starting at the beginning she began to read again.

My dear Daisy

I have decided to return to my home in Ireland. You have finally convinced me that there is no hope of our relationship being anything other than friends. Daisy, I will always love you with all my heart and soul. I have to leave. Every time I see you it is so painful, knowing you will never be mine. I cannot go on like this. I have told my aunt not to give you my address, there is no point. I am leaving to make a fresh start. I will never forget you. I hope you will find happiness.

All my love always,

Declan.

PS. By the time you receive this letter I will be gone.

Daisy rocked forward, drawing her legs up she wrapped her arms around them. She was overcome by a terrible sense of loss, something inside was being torn from her, a cold loneliness was engulfing her, a low keening sound was being forced from her as the tears flooded her face.

Sara walked in through the front door returning from a trip to the shops. As she passed the foot of the stairs on the way to the kitchen, she could hear this awful pain-filled moaning.

Harry appeared and said, 'Hallo.'

Sara held up her hand to silence him. 'Can you hear that noise?' Harry shook his head. 'That's Daisy,' said Sara, as she bolted up the stairs. 'Daisy I'm coming.'

Opening the girl's bedroom door, Sara could see Daisy's distress etched on her face. As Sara reached the bed Daisy flung her arms round her.

'He's gone Sara. I've driven him away. What am I going to do?' Her crying intensified. The letter was proffered.

Sara reading it was reminded of a pop song's lyrics: "You don't know what you've got till it's gone."

Harry tapped on the door asking if it was all right to come in. 'I've made some tea,' he said.

'Will you leave it outside please love, thank you.'

The young woman declined dinner and said she was going to bed.

Often during that long night, Sara could hear the half-smothered cries emanating from the other bedroom.

The couple did not know what to expect the following morning, when they heard the shower running; shortly afterwards the girl appeared dressed for work.

'I can cope if you would like some time off,' said Harry.

'I'm fine thank you. I will go as soon as I have had a cuppa. Thank you anyway.'

There was little to see of any damage after last night's trauma; although the most obvious was that her hair was scrapped back from her head, less visible was the return of the closed guarded face that she had worn when she first came to them. Her responses were polite but issued in a flat monotone.

Harry collected up the crockery and made for the kitchen using it as an excuse to gather himself. When will life stop kicking this child in the teeth? He was so angry although he knew not what at.

CHAPTER 48

Late one evening, long after the shop had closed, Daisy was tidying the shelves ready for the morning. This was a common occurrence, as she always thought of the shop as hers.

The banging on the back door made her jump; moving close to it Daisy made sure the door was locked.

'We're closed, go away or I'll call the police.'

'It's your father, let me in or I'll kick the bloody door down.' She could tell he was extremely drunk. With that he began kicking the door, making it rattle in its frame.

Fearing that he would break the door down she shouted: 'If I opens the door you've got to behave.'

'Just open the bloody door yur silly cow.'

'I'm opening it now.'

Once he heard the key turn, he kicked it open, knocking Daisy across the room. She was struggling to remain upright as she teetered backward but gravity won, and she measured her length on the floor again.

When she sat up it was to find her father robbing the till as he had done before. Regaining her feet, she ran to the till and tried to pull him away; he swung a wild blow that she ducked. A display of tinned tomatoes flew all over the shop. In desperation, she seized the only tin left on the counter and hit him hard. He doubled over with both of his hands holding the back of his head. Daisy hit him again and this time he flinched away from the blow. This ensured she missed her target with the tin striking his shoulder hard. Now he was cowering on the floor. All her hate and fear and the memory of the years of hers and her mother's abuse gripped her. Lifting the tin as high above her head as possible., there was now no thought of outcomes, she was consumed by a terrible rage, a need to put a stop to this menace for the last time. Before she could deliver the fatal blow that was intended to have killed him her arm was gripped from behind.

A shape behind her said, 'It's OK Daisy, I can manage this from here.' She recognised the local bobby's voice. She was squeezing past the policeman with her back to her father, when she heard breaking glass. Turning around she saw her father falling to the floor; he lay there unconscious wrapped in his dark soiled overcoat. The policeman was holding his truncheon, and she noticed blood on the policeman's face. Reaching under the counter she grabbed a clean cloth and handed it to him. The cut was long, deep and bleeding profusely. He held the cloth to his cheek and said, 'Ring the station Daisy, and give them this address – tell them I'm cut. He bottled me the bastard.'

This explained the scattering of broken glass on the floor.

'Sorry Daisy love. I shouldn't be swearing but he is a … You had better ring, Tim while you're at it.'

Sitting waiting for the ambulance and police cars to arrive Daisy said, 'I wish you'd let me 'it him as I wanted to.'

'You might have killed him, Daisy.'

'I wish I 'ad. I wish you hadn't come in when you did. I'd 'ave finished the job.'

'Daisy this conversation never happened. All right lass?'

After a short silence Daisy asked, 'How were you suddenly 'ere?'

'I saw you struggling with him and then spotted the back door open, so I ran round. I didn't see where the bottle came from.'

'He always carried an empty bottle. His words – "just in case" I can remember him tapping his pocket with a nasty smile on his face.'

'You don't need to worry this time love. He's going away for quite a while. Judges don't approve of people injuring police officers. Oh, here's Harry, Tim, and Sara. You'll be all right now girl. I will need stitches put in this cut. Will you be all right?'

She nodded. 'Thank you for saving me,' she said.

I reckon I saved your father, he thought to himself as he left. He was quite sure she meant to finish the job.

*

Daisy was checked out by the ambulance man and found to be OK. Her father was lying on the floor holding his head and groaning.

'Please, can you tell me what will happen to me dad?' she asked a sergeant.

'He will be held overnight at the police station, and we will sort it all out in the morning. You will need to come in and make a statement tomorrow.'

'I'll run you in to the police station tomorrow, Daisy. You need to take a few days off to get over all this,' said Harry who was standing beside her.

'NO, NO NO!!! I have to work,' she shouted, stabbing her finger at her father, now standing handcuffed to a large police officer. 'I'll not let that scum affect me life any more. Never again, never!!'All this shouted through the tears that were flooding her face.

'Don't you talk to me like that you stupid cow.'

Daisy, now once more overtaken by the fury she had experienced earlier stepped forward and spat full in his face. 'You're going to prison. I will pray every day that you die there you, you …' Daisy choked back the word she was going to use.

Her father proving the fact that he was coward and a bully shied away from his daughter, clearly frightened of her and her barely controlled rage. The big police officer hauled him backwards, out of range. Harry drove her home.

Later at home that night with Harry and Sara having finished dinner, Harry asked, 'How do you feel, love?'

Daisy was silent for a while – eventually she said, 'My first thought, I'm afraid to admit, is that at least he won't be around to knock me and Mum about no more. Then I'm angry that he is still messing up my life. People will say that Daisy is not to be trusted, she's a Green you know. Her old fella's doing time, that's what they'll say right enough.'

Harry and Sara immediately both vehemently disagreed with her. Harry said, 'There is a shop full of customers who will defend you.'

Sara was nodding her agreement. 'You are extremely well thought of locally Daisy love.'

The following morning Daisy, accompanied by Harry, were both at the police station early, he had insisted on supporting her today. When she argued he said, 'As we used to say in the army, you have to do as I say, I outrank you.' Squeezing his arm she smiled up at him.

A plain clothes officer placed her in a small office, gave her pen and paper and asked her to write whatever she could remember. One thing she was adamant about was she would only tell what she saw, she hadn't seen her father attack the PC, she had her back to him. When she had written everything she could think of, she pressed a bell. Moments later a plain clothes policeman entered the room and introduced himself then read the page and said, 'That's fine. I have one or two questions.'

Daisy answered them as well as she could. She was now experiencing a peculiar detachment, as though her father was a total stranger.

'I expect you have questions for me, Daisy?'

'Yes, I do. Can you tell me what 'appens next, please?'

'Right, Mr Green has been charged with GBH, grievous bodily harm, plus other things we know about, his attack on you for instance and theft. There is quite a list. In the next day or two he will appear in the magistrates court. Because of the severity of his crimes they will hear his plea – I cannot believe he will do anything other than plead guilty. Then sometime in the near future he will appear at a crown court for sentencing.'

'How long will he get?' she asked.

'It's not for me to say, but at a guess he will get life, fifteen years.'

'Is our local bobby ok?'

'You mean Robo, PC Atkins? He's fine. I'll tell him you asked after him, he's on sick leave at the moment. It's not too serious, but it is quite deep, it punctured his cheek, and he had to have internal stitches.'

Daisy winced and pulled a face. 'Oh poor man, can you tell him I'm sorry. Wherever my father goes he causes trouble for others.' Standing up ready to leave she said, 'Prison is the best place for him.'

The detective watched her, and Harry walk away, he sensed that there was a lot of pain behind those few words.

*

When she arrived at the shop, to her complete surprise there were three photographers outside who started taking pictures as soon as they saw her. Then they began firing questions at her: 'Was she injured? Could she confirm that the assailant was her father? What's your full name love? Is it true he has a criminal record? How old are you, Miss? Do you live with your father? Is the policeman seriously injured?'

They were all speaking at once.

Harry asked, 'Would you like me to manage this Daisy?'

'Yes please,' she said as she entered the shop.

CHAPTER 49

Charley was doing what she always did when she visited shop Number Two: kneeling down, her hands on the floor peering over the edge of the brightly lit, glass-covered well. Tim was standing beside her talking to a customer. If Daisy failed to spot the child's entry sometimes a regular would call out, 'Charley's here.'

Both Tim and Sophie had reassured Daisy that it was not a problem, it made no difference. She always got the broom out and swept where Charley knelt, so her lilac-coloured dress was not sullied.

Charley was far too scared to stand on the glass herself. If Tim or anybody stood on the glass while holding her, she would scream her head off. Tim would sometimes step on to it to tease her until Sophie said, 'Stop doing that, it smacks of child abuse.'

The little girl was staring as always at who knew what in the depths of the well. The lighting and the moisture in the well had encouraged a few small plants, ferns mostly, to grow in the walls.

A small boy squatted down beside her, he was still in his school uniform: black shoes, grey socks and short trousers, a blue check shirt, and an obviously home-knitted, green jumper. The body of the woolly was a good fit, but the arms were bunched up indicating they were too long. Tim could imagine the knitter being reassured that the child would grow into them.

The boy asked, 'What can you see?'

Tim heard his daughter whisper, 'Fairies, but if I show you, you must promise not to tell anyone.' The boy nodded his agreement. Charley moved her head down nearer the well and stared intently into the depths.

Tim became immersed in conversation and heard no more, but minutes later he heard Charley in an excited voice say, 'See there on the wall.'

The boy, now with his nose almost on the glass said, 'Where? I can't see anything.'

'Over there, on the frond of that little green fern,' she said pointing down the well.

'I still can't see nothing,' he insisted, becoming disenchanted with the whole thing, and now believing the girl was making it all up. Then he saw it. 'Oh wow!!' he exclaimed. 'That's amazing.'

The two children high-fived each other. 'We have frightened them away she said but never mind, at least you saw them.'

The noise in the shop increased in volume as a crowd of young people entered laughing. Tim was unable to hear anything more, but he could tell the two children were deep in conversation with them both pointing at things.

A little later the boy's mother reappeared, smiled at Tim saying, 'Thank you for keeping him amused.'

'No problem,' he replied.

As the woman and child walked away, his mother asked, 'What were you two talking about?'

'The girl was showing me the fairies,' was his response.

The mother left with a puzzled expression on her face. Amused, Tim wondered what influence the previous fifteen minutes would have on the boy's life.

Then everything changed, when Tim's father came downstairs. The instant Charley saw him she leapt to her feet and weaving through the customers hurled herself into his arms. Her parents had both noticed she had become clingier to those she knew and loved since the death of Mr Woodman, obviously worried they may disappear like he had.

'Names, Grandad, names.' Tim's father was teaching her the names of all the merchandise, and she was learning very quickly. The old man and the child spent the next half hour roaming the counters upstairs. Charley it appeared was genuinely interested and remembered what she had been told. This was born out by the questions she often fired at her parents.

※

Late that night Sophie was feeding Martyn. The boat was being rocked by the small waves the strengthening wind had generated. Tim said, 'I love this.'

'Love what?' queried his wife.

'When the Sea Maiden comes alive.'

'Yes, I was thinking the other day, I remember when we first came aboard to live, we both had to hold onto things when she did this.' Tim nodded in agreement.

'Have you noticed? Charley does not have to hold on.'

'Yes, I have. She seems to know that if the boat rolls one way it will roll in a certain way next, so she is ready for it. I don't think it's a conscious thing, it's instinctive.'

'Cocoa?' asked Sophie, rising, and handing Martyn to her husband.

'Yes please,' was the reply.

CHAPTER 50

Daisy was mortified. The following morning her face was staring back at her from the front pages of the local paper. Thanks to Harry most of what had been written about the event was accurate, although they had misspelt her name. Somehow, they had uncovered quite a bit about her father and his various wrongdoings, things she had not known herself.

Daisy was extremely upset. 'Everyone's gunna be gawping at me ain't they?' Her diction had slipped again.

'Daisy,' said Harry, 'it will be a five-minute wonder. Something else will happen and your story will be wrapped around a bag of fish and chips.'

'Harry's right Daisy love. I promise you, in a few days it will all blow over,' said Sara.

The following day they had just finished their evening meal. It had been a busy Sunday, mass in the morning, Daisy went regularly now with Sara, Harry had a lie in. In the afternoon Sara and Daisy made the confectionary for the shops. The younger woman, in awe of Sara's skills; she watched her take just a few seconds to fashion another incredible example of her art.

Harry was drifting off, having consumed a generous amount of Merlot, when the front doorbell rang.

Daisy said, 'I'll get it.' She walked out of the room closing the door behind her.

'I don't know who that can be,' said Harry as he shifted in the chair to make himself more comfortable before closing his eyes again.

Daisy opened the front door and her world moved on its axis, everything changed. Declan was standing facing her holding a suitcase. He was wearing blue jeans and matching denim coat with an uncertain smile on his face.

Daisy burst into tears and threw herself into his arms; her head buried in his chest. Looking up at him she said, 'Thank God you've come back. Why are you here? Have you come back or ...' She did not complete the sentence, terrified of the answer ...

'I'm back if you want me to be.'

'Oh yes please. I was stupid sending you away. I have missed you ever since.' To confirm what she was saying she kissed him hard on the mouth.

The kiss was cut short by Sara coming to see who had called. Daisy was red in the face. Declan was laughing. 'Sure and haven't we been caught in the act. Hallo Sara, how are you?'

'I am very well thanking you and better for seeing you. This girl has not been herself ever since you left.' She noticed Daisy was still holding his hand.

'Harry will be pleased to see you, come in. Harry wake up, look who is here.'

'Well I'm blessed, it's great to see you lad.' Harry had become very fond of Declan, with his Irish wit, his charm and good manners. He was always good company and of course, like himself, Declan enjoyed a drink, even if it was only beer. 'Why are you here, lad?'

'My aunt saw you in the paper Daisy and rang to tell me. She said you appeared lost. So I packed my bag, got on a train and here I am.'

Daisy now holding his hand with both hers said, 'Thank you.'

'Have you eaten, Declan?' queried Sara.

'Not since breakfast.'

'Do you want to wait for something hot or I can do soup and lamb sandwiches?'

'Soup and sandwiches sounds great, thank you.'

'Have a seat you two, I will put the kettle on,' said Harry. Leaving the young couple alone in the lounge, Harry and Sara moved to the kitchen.

Sara said, 'The change in her is amazing. He has triggered some kind of light inside her.'

'I think it's called lurve,' he replied.

'You men are horrible,' said Sara. 'I can remember a young man who ran two miles to see if I was OK, when the factory I worked in blew up. You just held me and kept telling me how much you loved me.'

Harry now deadly serious said, 'I was so scared that day. I thought I was going to lose you like I lost my brother.'

'Well you didn't. I'm still here you old silly,' she said giving him a hug.

Balancing a tray of food in her hands she whispered, 'Should I knock or cough?'

Harry solved the problem by saying, loudly, 'Put her down Declan, your food is ready.'

Sara's response was a whispered, 'Harry' – accompanied by a frown of disapproval.

Entering the room she saw Declan was laughing; Daisy was red in the face and her hair was all over the place.

The four sat around the table with Daisy sitting close to Declan. She made up her mind that evening to do whatever it would take to keep this man sitting by her side including the Mr and Mrs thing as she called it. She hated the S word; it reminded her of her father and what he had tried to do to her.

Harry had put Declan's mind at rest by saying, 'The job is still open if you want it lad. We haven't advertised it yet. You can take tomorrow off if you like.'

'No, I'll start tomorrow if that's OK. Which shop do you want me in?' he asked.

'Two,' said Daisy, now blushing because she realised it was not up to her.

'Well that's sorted that out,' laughed Harry.

'You are clearly starting out as you mean to carry on Daisy, well done you,' said Sara, her face wreathed in a broad smile.

Turning to Declan, Daisy mouthed a silent, 'I'm sorry.'

'Sure there is nothing to apologise for, it would be my choice for certain. Do you want to talk about your father?'

'No, not tonight, tonight is about us.' She was amazed at her own brazen behaviour; she felt different, she was no longer alone. He must love her to just drop everything and come to her side. The major change was the fear that had been with her all of her life had gone.

'Where are you going to sleep?' asked Harry. 'It's getting late, I don't want to throw you out but ...'

'I can walk down to my aunt's – she never goes to bed early.'

'There is always the couch,' said Sara glancing at Harry for agreement.

'That's fine by me. Do you need to contact your aunt?'

'I could let her know where I am.'

'The phone is in the hall. I am going up,' said Harry. 'Don't talk all night, sleep well.'

'I will get some blankets,' said Daisy following Harry and Sara upstairs.

Declan was still on the phone when she returned. In his absence she sat down and spread the red blanket along the seat and pulled it over her lap.

Returning from the hallway he asked, 'Aren't you tired?'

Shaking her head in denial, she lifted the end of the blanket to allow him entry. Once he was seated, she arranged the covering around them, so they were warm. Lifting an arm she cupped his cheek with her hand.

'Are you ok?' he asked in a soft voice.

'Yes, I need to confirm you are really here. I missed you so badly.' He could see tears forming. 'Will you stay with me?' she asked.

'I am here forever if you want me to be.'

'Yes please,' she said as she moved in to kiss him.

Sara lay awake a long time that night. She could hear the murmuring but not the content of the exchanges, and there was occasional subdued laughter. As she started to drift off to sleep, she thought to herself, finally Daisy, you stand a chance of happiness.

*

Harry was first up as usual. As he entered the lounge he found the young couple tangled in the blankets and each other. He noticed they were both fully clothed. That's a blessing he thought. Entering the kitchen he started banging the kettle and crockery around.

Declan called from the other room, 'We're awake Harry.' The older man could hear the laughter in Declan's voice, then came the sound of Daisy scampering upstairs.

Daisy and Sara came face to face at the top of the stairs. Obviously embarrassed Daisy said, 'We fell asleep.'

Sara kissed her cheek. 'It doesn't matter. I am just so happy that you are happy.'

*

Tim called into the shop early that morning, to find Declan bringing in large boxes of tins from the storeroom, he could hear Daisy singing quietly upstairs.

'Hallo Declan. Welcome, we're pleased to have you back on board,' said Tim, offering his hand.

Declan shook hands saying, 'I'm delighted to be here so I am.'

'Daisy doesn't sound too upset about it,' said Tim with a smile on his face.

Declan smiled and nodded. 'I thought I'd lost her forever.'

'She deserves to be happy – tell her I said hallo.'

Tim waved as he left the shop.

The following evening the four of them met up at Harry's intending to go to the pub for a meal and the music.

Harry was last in. 'Sorry I was late, the police called to tell me about your father.' Declan felt Daisy slide her hand into his.

'He has appeared at the magistrates court and has been charged with grievous bodily harm and has pleaded guilty. He has been remanded to be sentenced at the crown court,' explained Harry.

'I've been thinking about him, today. He was never my father, not ever. I know that sounds odd but it's how I feel.'

'Do you still want me to field the stuff from the police for you, Daisy?' asked Harry.

'Yes, please.'

'Right, that's no problem. Let's go I'm starving,' he said opening the front door and stepping into the street.

*

A fortnight later Daisy was told her father had appeared at the crown court for sentencing and had been remanded for fifteen years.

Daisy was surprised by her own reaction. She had been carrying a heavy sense of guilt, feeling that she was responsible for his arrest. Now she was experiencing an enormous sense of relief. A great weight had been lifted from her shoulders; no longer would she have to be forever watchful, listening for his heavy tread or his drunken growl.

Soon after she had moved in with Sara, Daisy had placed a truncheon under her bed. She had told Sara, 'He will never catch me unawares again. Next time I will kill him.'

Sara had hugged Daisy to her. 'Hush lass,' she had said, 'you have nothing to fear here. Harry would get to him first. He has hinted to me about some of the things he had to do in the war – your father would not stand a hope in hell, and anyway nothing like that will happen, I promise.'

She would now be far more relaxed in the future. However, the one thing that would persist was her concern when people were walking close behind her, she still stepped aside and let them by.

Talking to her mother on the phone, she was surprised when she confirmed she felt safer as well. Her mother said, 'Never again Daisy will I feels frightened when I thinks I hears his growling and his shufflin' feet.'

Daisy decided that in future she would tell strangers her father was dead.

*

Over the coming months Declan and Daisy saw a lot of each other. It was very apparent that she was more light-hearted and laughed more often.

She was surprised that Declan, apart from the kissing, had not tried any further intimacy. Daisy had been perusing Sara's women's magazines searching for guidance. She found some articles. She was certain that what was described in one magazine was definitely a no, no. One suggestion that seemed OK was to sit on the man's lap to start with; it was recommended because the woman could stand up and move away if things got out of hand. One of the things that more than one writer had insisted on was the couple had to keep talking to each other. It is clear she thought, I am going to have to orchestrate the progress. Anger flared through her, all because of her 'B' of a so-called father. She made a vow that night she was not going to live a half-life because of him. Then she giggled, *Declan was going to get a heck of a shock.*

Lying in bed that night she understood that her father's imprisonment had changed her: the perpetual fear had gone, she was stronger, braver, more able to stand up for herself. Declan had helped work the transformation; her certainty that he loved her had helped to empower her.

The next Friday in the Irish pub her normal single glass of Pinot Blanc was replaced by two. On the way home she was a little wobbly.

They were walking behind Harry and Sara when she half-missed her step again. 'Are you drunk?' Declan asked her quietly.

'A little,' she admitted giggling.

'You'd better hang on to me,' he said.

'I'm definitely gunna do that,' she replied moving closer. Declan said nothing, his raised eyebrow indicated his confusion.

Daisy had, during the day, told Sara what her hang-ups were and what she had read and what had been recommended, all the time bright red in the face.

Sara had hugged her and said, 'I will get Harry to have an early night – you and Declan can talk.'

When they reached home Sara said, 'I am making a pot of coffee if anyone wants one. Harry and I are having an early night so you young people can have some privacy.'

Harry never said anything, he just seemed confused and shrugged his shoulders. The older couple balancing their coffee cups disappeared upstairs.

Declan was sitting in an armchair reading the newspaper when Daisy came to stand in front of him and said, 'We need to talk.' Tapping his knee she said, 'Move your leg, I want to sit on your lap.' She sat crosswise on his lap so she could see his face, he wrapped his arms around her as she wiggled her bottom to get comfortable.

Getting redder in the face, if that were possible, she said, 'You know me father's attack on me, and watching me mother getting beaten gave me a fear of men and the Mr and Mrs thing. I hate the S word.'

'Can we call it making love?' suggested Declan. He could see her trying the phrase out in her mind. Then she nodded.

'I've done some reading – it seems that my problem can be overcome but you'll have to be very patient. It'll be one small step at a time, and sometimes we may not make much progress for a while. Are you able to do this? If you need any encouragement I do like ordinary kissing, we can do a lot of that.'

'OK where do we start?' he asked.

Bright red in the face she described they just had to cuddle, with their eyes shut.

Her eyes were still firmly shut, he leaned in and kissed her, she kissed him back. It was, he thought, all very proper, but it was a move in the right direction however small.

She did discover how pleasant it was to have her feet massaged, especially when she bought some perfumed oils and had Declan do the massage.

Progress was slow but progress it was; little by little she was learning to trust him, to enjoy his touch, the smell of his aftershave and deodorant, and to her surprise the maleness of him.

She began to allow herself to dream of children, a home of their own and a long life together. She made up her mind that however difficult it would be she was going to overcome her fear and build the kind of family she knew others had, based on love and care. She wanted babies, lots of babies. For a moment she was imagining feeding her first born cradled in her arm. She wanted a man who was kind and loving. Surely that should be possible.

Declan knew they were finally making some headway when one evening, standing on Harry's doorstep saying goodnight, she didn't move away as she had always done when she sensed his growing excitement, this time she leaned in further and slid her arms around his neck. Their kissing became more urgent, more needy, their bodies locked together.

The spell was broken when Harry opened the front door to put the milk bottles out. 'Oops,' said Harry, 'pretend I'm not here.'

Daisy moved away a little, now searching Declan's eyes, confused, unsure what had happened to her; her body still felt as though it was giving off sparks. Declan would be shocked if he knew what she wanted to do to him … never mind him, she was shocked that she could imagine even doing it.

'Are you OK?' he asked.

She nodded, both of them were breathing hard. They kissed goodnight; this was a pale version of what had happened moments ago.

Walking back to his digs at his aunt's, he realised Daisy and he could not carry on like this; they weren't silly teenagers, they were both young adults. Lots of his friends were living with their girlfriends and fiancés. If he and Daisy got engaged, she may agree that they live together. Where to live? They couldn't live at Harry's, or his aunt's come to that, they needed some privacy.

Lying in bed that night he decided the next move was to buy a ring.

*

A week later Declan overheard Tim talking to his father in the shop. 'I don't think we should leave Mr Woodman's flat empty; Tim. Places tend to get grotty without someone living in them.'

'Your right, Dad, but it needs someone we can trust.'

'Aye lad you're right.' Scratching his head Tom said, 'I don't know anyone who fits that bill.'

I do, thought Declan as he sorted the customer's change. He noticed Tim had walked out the door and was striding away down the street.

Declan said, 'I won't be a minute.' Then left the shop and raced after Tim, calling his name as he ran.

'Hallo Declan, is there a problem?'

'No … I hope you're not cross, but I could not help overhearing your conversation with your father about the flat. I am not one for the earwigging, as I hope you know but …'

'Declan,' said Tim checking the time, 'I'm already late, sorry to be rude, but I must move on, walk with me. What are you driving at?'

'I have told no one this but I am going to ask Daisy to marry me. I'm hoping she will agree for us to live together while we save for the wedding. I wondered if she and I would be trustworthy enough to rent the flat?'

'You daft devil, you would not be working with us if we were worried about you. Tell me when you have asked Daisy, then I will talk to the board. I can see no problem but who knows.'

CHAPTER 51

Tim was on the way to The Boat pub; most of his family now considered it their local, it wasn't posh, it was old. The smoke from the large open stone-built fireplace had darkened the interior. Tim loved its antiquity. Apparently its history reached back centuries. Minutes later he was sitting next to his father gazing out over the river that was as busy as always with both commercial and private craft ploughing up and down.

Tim recognised that there was something different about his father. For a moment he couldn't work out what it was, then he realised he had taken care of his appearance, his white shirt was ironed and there was a crease in his tan trousers. All of this Tim understood was a sign of his father's climb out of the terrible depression that had crippled him for years as the result of his wife's, Tim's mother's, premature death from the flu.

His father was chatting to Chick Evans, the landlord, who turning to Tim asked, 'You and the family are all well, Tim?'

'Yeah, we're good thanks, and you?'

'I'm fine, all the usual problems with the wife of course,' this said with a big smile on his face, knowing full well Molly could hear him from behind the bar.

A damp teacloth flicked out and caught his ear. 'Ouch!' yelped Chick, and then said, 'I may call you two as witnesses when I sue for divorce.'

'Sure you could divorce me – you'd be creeping back when you got hungry, you useless lump.'

All three men were laughing. Chick left them in peace. After an appreciative swallow of their beers Tim said, 'Why did you want to see me, Dad?'

'I'm considering having a small extension built on the back of the house, a downstairs toilet. The stairs are getting steeper, and I have to haul myself up hand over hand some days. I have discovered you have to make more visits as you get older. I'm not asking you to pay for it. Just to oversee it for me, you know what I'm like with paperwork.'

'Your bedroom is up there as well,' said Tim thinking out loud. 'There is a fair bit of room behind the house isn't there? Let me think about this for a minute, do you want another beer?'

'Yes, please lad.'

Standing at the bar waiting for Chick to pull the pints, he was thinking hard. Tim paid for the drinks and made his way back to the table. 'A downstairs toilet is only half the answer – how would you feel about a bedroom and an en suite downstairs?'

'I don't want to spend that sort of money lad. I can't know what kind of expense I might meet in the future.'

Tim was silent, staring out the window at the river. He knew that his great aunt had left his father a considerable lump of money; however, if he didn't want to spend it that was his decision. Tim's elbows were on the table, his chin resting on his hands.

His father sat quietly. Knowing his son so well he recognised Tim was working something out.

Eventually he said, 'Why don't I pay for it? If all the facilities are downstairs, you can stay in your own home for a lot longer.'

'No son, I'm not comfortable with that. I will settle for a toilet downstairs if you can sort the paperwork for me.'

'Where will you sleep when you can no longer climb the stairs?'

There was no reply.

Tim said nothing for some time, then placing his arms on the table and leaning towards his father he said in a voice just above a whisper, 'Dad I have thousands and thousands of pounds in my savings and investments as you well know – you know the amount my aunt left me. Should I decide to build a whole new house, or a row of houses it would make little difference to the amount in my bank. All I am offering is to make it easier for you to stay in your own home in comfort for as many years as possible.'

'That's extremely kind of you lad. Can I think about it?'

Tim drew a long breath in and then said, as he scratched his head obviously frustrated, 'Of course you can. Let me know soon – shall we say a week? I am sorry to put you under pressure but otherwise it will drag on.'

Tom Cooper rang Tim a few days later and said, 'Tim, I would like to go ahead with the bedroom and en suite extension please. It was, I realise, just my silly pride getting in the way. It will all come to you anyway when I shuffle off this mortal coil.'

'You sound like Mum with your quotations, Dad.'

'You're right lad. I am happy to do all the practical stuff, and obviously I will keep you up to date. Are we using Charlie as usual?'

'Yes Dad. I see no reason to change, better the devil we know. Can you give him a ring please and can you find some bathroom furniture? Don't scrimp, make it nice for yourself. Is Sammy still at yours?'

'Yes, he says he will move on in the summer. I hope he doesn't, it's dangerous out there.'

'He could have your bedroom once you move downstairs,' said Tim knowing full well that this was one of the reasons his dad wanted the second bedroom. 'I think it's a good idea anyway. I don't know what we would do if you took a tumble down the stairs. So bath or shower, Dad?'

'I've thought about this. I'd prefer a bath, but I would be a bit jiggered if I got stuck in it.'

'You need an alarm button, just in case.'

'So Dad, good quality furniture, no nasty cheap stuff. We won't want designer gear though, will we?'

'No son. I will run it all past you before we go ahead. I'll ring Charlie in the morning first thing. You happy to let him sort out the other tradesmen as usual, Tim? We will need an architect unless you know one.'

'No I don't. Charlie will. Are you OK to start the ball rolling?'

'This is very generous of you, Tim,' said his father knowing full well that his son would simply add the house to his portfolio of investments after his demise.

Over the next few weeks drawings were completed, planning permission was sought and gained, and the digging began. Much to Tom's surprise Sammy stepped in and offered his services. He made tea for Charlie and his son Tommy, he helped shovel soil into the wheelbarrow. He was not strong enough to push the barrow up the plank and into the skip. Tom felt sure the lad would get bored after a while, but he didn't, it was the reverse; as his understanding of what was going on increased he became ever more useful as he was able to anticipate what was coming next. He was working extremely hard, he had started his job at the docks again, doing small errands for the dockers, running to buy their cigarettes and sandwiches. More than once he had fallen asleep after dinner, too tired to watch television.

Charlie was not too amused when Tim arrived one morning to take a peek at how things were going. 'Morning Charlie, are you digging a well?' Charlie was shoulder deep in a trench. Tim could see the sweat running off him, his shirt was soaked.

'Oh ha, ha, no I'm not. The building inspector called yesterday and insisted the foundations have got to go down a nuvver two feet.'

'Why is that?' asked Tim.

'He reckons it's made-up ground. I dunno. Anyways I'm almost there now. I should be able to start laying the foundations tomorrow.'

As Tim was about to leave, a man walked into the house ignoring him.

'Hallo,' Tim called, 'can I help you?'

Without turning round the inspector shouted: 'I'm the building inspector, you cannot deny me entry' – with that he walked on.

'Rude pig,' said Tim under his breath. 'Bye Charlie,' he called out as he left the building.

'Bye Tim,' was the response.

The next time he called a few days later he was surprised at the progress that had been made, the brick work was completed, the roof was finished, the windows and doors were installed. Larry the electrician was connecting sockets and switches to the wires hanging out of the walls.

'Morning Larry, this is coming together very quickly.'

'Morning Tim, it's only a little job. We will soon be done. Have a squint at the en suite.'

Tim walked into the bathroom; it was, he recognised, a wet room with a black marble floor, white tiled wall and a smart wash basin and toilet.

Larry walked in behind him. 'What do you think, Tim?'

'It's very smart. If Sophie sees this she will want to come ashore to live. Will the floor be slippery when it's wet?'

'No, Tim they're nonslip – especially designed for bathrooms.'

Tim nodding said, 'It's very smart, nice work you guys.'

'When will we start on the restaurant, Tim?'

'It will be a while yet. I hadn't understood what a complex beast it is. The kitchen's like something out of *Star Trek*, then you have to work out how guests and staff will use the space. Where to put the toilets and so on. Lots of problems to solve but we will get there. I must be off, goodbye Larry. Well done – tell the lads I think it's great.'

'Thanks Tim.' I don't think that man ever stops, he thought to himself.

CHAPTER 52

Sophie, Charley, Martyn and Nanny Bridget were putting the last things they needed for an afternoon out into a large, colourful, striped canvas bag. Martyn was well-wrapped up in the pushchair. Tim had half an eye on proceedings. The table was covered with piles of paper. Sophie had reminded him earlier that he was breaking the 'No work on a Sunday' rule. Finally they were ready to go, Sophie kissed him, he kissed Charley and waved goodbye to them all. A very colourful caravan left the house with all the females in their bright summer dresses.

Left on his own he surveyed the paper-strewn table, sitting back and watching out of the window he saw it was a beautiful day, he'd had his nose to the grindstone since breakfast.

'I'm going rowing,' he said out loud pushing the paperwork into his briefcase rather haphazardly.

Grabbing his trunks, T-shirt and a towel and locking the door he raced after his family. They were all pleased to see him; Charley as always wanted to abandon Sophie's arms for his.

Sophie said, 'Nanny and I spend hours looking after this wretched child but as soon as her father turns up, we are less than nothing.'

Tim, now with armfuls of Charley, said to his daughter, 'They don't get it. I've tried to explain that it's a father and daughter thing, but they don't understand.'

'Right,' said the child's mother, 'the next time she needs attention at one am it is all down to you.'

'Oops now see what you've done,' said Tim smiling at his daughter. Charley was nodding.

＊

The greeting on their arrival had been friendly even though it was the first time for Tim since the original visit, Sophie had been a few times.

Sophie was soon changed and sitting in a skiff ready to go. 'I may be some time, is that all right?'

'Of course no problem, have a nice time,' Tim responded.

'Wave at Mummy,' said Nanny. All three of them waved as Sophie pulled away.

Gordon came up and said, 'I could watch her all day Tim, she makes it look effortless. I will not be able to row that well even if I train until I am an old man.'

Tim was aware that a number of club members had watched her pull away. A group of three were discussing her technique, accompanied by lots of hand movements being used to illustrate their observations.

＊

Tim placed his first foot into the skiff; as he moved to put the second foot in, he overbalanced and in he went on the far side of the craft. There was a lot of laughing as he swam around the stern and hauled himself out of the water.

Gordon explained, 'You have to make sure your weight is always in the centre of the boat.'

Tim's only comment was to complain about the cold. The second attempt was no better, in he went again. At least this time he got both feet in inboard.

The third attempt began successfully, he was in and sitting down but was rocking from side to side as he struggled to maintain his balance. Instead of sitting tight until he had control he pushed off away from the bank. He was now fifteen feet away from the side, remembering his instructions to gather the blades together so that they were across the craft with the backs of them resting on the water. Still jiggling about he achieved the first part of the manoeuvre, but the blades had to be turned over. Halfway through this he lost his balance again. This time he found he was trapped under the boat. Some part of the skiff had given him an extremely heavy blow on the head just above his eye that was now closing because of the blood running into it. His face was above the water breathing the air trapped in the upturned hull. He didn't know it but the air around him would last a long time.

His consciousness was coming and going, and he was unable to remember any of the safety instructions he had been given. He could sense that the strong current was sweeping him rapidly downstream. He began to feel claustrophobic. As a child he had suffered quite badly when the school bully had shut him in a small cupboard in the library, locked the door and left him in the dark. It was an hour later before someone had heard him shouting and let him out.

Gordon's head popped up alongside him asking, 'Are you ok?'

Tim made no response.

'Tim, can you hear me?' asked Gordon, shouting now.

'Er yes,' he replied.

Gordon recognised Tim was not with it. 'Tim, you are completely safe in here, there's lots of air and your life jacket is keeping you afloat. I am going outside to start pushing us towards the bank. Do you understand?'

'Erm, yes.'

Gordon's legs were visible as he kicked the craft towards the shore, twice he ducked under to check on Tim's well-being. They quickly reached the river bank. Tim took a lungful of air then crawled out from under the boat and stood up, he staggered a couple of steps then fell down.

Gordon was by his side saying, 'You're not quite the thing are you Tim. That crack on the head may be a little more serious than it looks.'

Three club members were waiting for them: Gordon's wife, Sam, and two men he didn't know.

Gordon assisted Tim as he climbed up the bank. He was feeling better by the moment.

Sam tilted Tim's head up and said, 'We need to clean that cut up. Let's get you back to the club.'

Tim went to touch his forehead. Sam slapped his hand away. 'Don't do that Tim, look at your hands, they are filthy from when you scrambled up the muddy bank, there's bird muck and goodness knows what on them. You can catch some nasty diseases from river water. Come on we'll get you back to the club house and clean you up.'

'I've brought the car,' said the stranger. 'It's over here. My name's, David.'

'I'm Terry,' said the other man. 'I'll row the boat back to the club house.' Both men were in shorts and T shirts, neither were wearing life jackets.

Back at the club, Sam, having cleaned his head said, 'This may sting a little.' She anointed what was a nasty cut.

As the damp lint touched his head, Tim reared back and shouted: 'Ouch! That's not a little.'

'You big baby, stay still. I will be done any second.' She held his head while she finished the job.

Sam was wiping the last of the blood from his face as Nanny returned pushing the pram with Martyn sound asleep inside. Charley running ahead as usual scrambled up on to her father's knee. Seeing the bandage she poked it, hard asking, 'What's that Daddy?'

Once again Tim shied away, shouting: 'Ow!'

Charley, now frightened, began to cry and swivelling round held her arms out to Nanny Bridget.

Scooping Charley up into her arms she said, 'Did naughty Daddy frighten you? You're all right now my little treasure, Nanny's got you. Are you all right, Tim?' she asked as she rocked Charley into silence.

'Yes, I'm fine, thanks.'

'Good. I'm going to walk her and Martyn around a bit.'

'OK,' he replied.

Gordon lowered himself into a chair beside him saying, 'Sorry that didn't work out Tim.'

'Not your fault, it's obvious my balance is poor.'

'You would get used to it.'

'I'm sure you're right but I suffer with claustrophobia, so I'm not good if I get trapped in small places.'

'There is a sailing dinghy you could use. That may be fun. Have you sailed before?'

'No,' he replied.

'I would be happy to teach you. To be honest, I prefer sailing as I get older, not such hard work. What do you think? We made the dingy here – the local Co-op store donated all the wood to the club when they refurbished all the counters. That saved us a lot of money, but the boat is mostly thick mahogany, so it weighs a ton, however, that does make it very stable.'

In truth Gordon had some self-interest in keeping Tim as a member. Should he leave the club Sophie may go as well. He had been advertising her arrival at the club and trumpeting her history as a former member of the Oxford women's Eight. This had resulted in a few new members.

'I can lend you a book on how to do it if you like – see what you think. One thing though I must have the book back.'

'Yes, I'll have a read if I may, thank you.'

Sophie returned and was alarmed when she saw the bandage. 'Are you ok?'

'I'm fine. I fell in and banged my head. Sam has sorted it out for me.'

'He will be fine,' said Sam as she approached. 'I have cleaned it well and it has stopped bleeding.'

'Thank you,' said Sophie as Sam moved away.

'Are you sure you are ok, Tim?' asked his wife, speaking quietly.

'Really, I'm good, there is no need to worry. Do you want to go out again?'

'No I am done for today. I will get changed and then we can go. Where are Nanny and the children?'

'Over there, feeding the swans,' said Tim pointing.

*

He decided he would have a go at learning to sail. One thing he would do if something like that happened again was to remember to stay calm and sort things out. It was his claustrophobia that had tripped him up, he was usually clear thinking under stress. Tim sat absorbed in the how-to-sail book. It became obvious as he read that it was mostly physics: a subject he had enjoyed at school, the little bit he had done.

He would always regret his lack of education. He knew that it was this that was driving him onward with the Longstaff trust. Nowadays his interaction with the work of the trust was at arm's length. His and Sophie's workload was punishing. His only contact with the trust was his monthly briefing from Jessica and Bonny.

The trust now had seven children in the scheme from five schools. The schools themselves were supportive of the trust and each school had nominated a teacher or a pastoral support worker to work with Jessica and Bonny. The two of them appeared to thoroughly enjoy this part of their job. Tim realised that as the workload got greater he may have to make it a separate department. He was unsure about how to do that; the last thing he wanted to do was to upset them by taking away from their interaction with these clever, gifted children, but he could not spare them from the main task of running the admin department of Sophie's. Perhaps he could find a part-timer to do the basics in the annual busy period when the students were choosing whether to stay on at school or not.

CHAPTER 53

Declan and Daisy were sharing a box of chocolates that Declan had bought her earlier. Harry and Sara were out. The young couple were sitting on the sofa in the lounge. He went to take one when Daisy shouted: 'No, you can't have that it's my favourite.'

Declan laughing popped it into his mouth; her face was a picture of complete surprise. She slapped his arm and several chocolates jumped from the box on to the floor – he knelt down to pick them up while Daisy berated him.

When they were all back in the box he said, 'Daisy there are two layers, but while I am down here there is something I have to ask you.' While he was talking, he was striving to remove the small box containing the engagement ring from his pocket. Daisy was now wearing a silent frown wondering what on earth he was doing. Finally, his pocket released whatever Declan was struggling with. He now had it hidden in his fist. Looking up into her eyes, he said, 'I love you more than you anything or anyone. I am asking you to marry me, please?'

As he finished speaking, he revealed what had been in his hand: it was a small box covered in red velvet. He popped it open to reveal a diamond engagement ring.

Daisy was totally overcome; the tears were flooding down her face and she was shaking her head as if in denial. This was not really happening. No man would want her, she was damaged goods. Her father's face filled her thoughts again like some grotesque phantom.

Declan, really worried now, rose from the floor and sat back down beside her. Putting both arms around her he held her close. 'Daisy please, if I don't marry you, I shan't marry anyone. Please say yes, we can overcome any problem if we love each other.'

'Declan you know 'ow mixed up I am. I'd love to be normal, but I don't think I ever will be.'

'We can work on that. In fact if you do my washing, the cooking, and the cleaning, I'll be fine so I will.'

Daisy was laughing through the tears. 'So all you want is a skivvy?'

'You have got it in one lass. Seriously though, my darling, I want you for my wife, so what do you say?'

Leaning forward she placed her hands on each side of his face and kissed him. When the kiss ended with their lips still touching, she said, 'Yes please.'

Declan placed the ring on her finger. She sat looking down at the diamond. As it caught the light it threw off a countless number of bright reflections. She moved her hand to make it sparkle.

A little while later she said, 'I love you, too.' Standing up she rearranged his limbs and sat on his lap so he could cuddle her properly. 'Where will we live? We can't live 'ere.'

'I may have the answer to that. I've mentioned it to Tim, and he's agreed to ask the board if we can live at Number One above the shop.'

'We will 'ave to pay rent.'

'He has not mentioned money Daisy. I don't suppose he's bothered.'

'That's not what I mean – we 'ave to pay our way. I'll never be beholden to no one never again. Whatever we achieve it'll be because we earnt it. It would be right lovely living there. Mr Woodman was always kind to me.' She was quiet for some time; Declan became more concerned as the silence continued.

Eventually Daisy said, 'There's one thing Declan – I'll live with yur, but I ain't gunna marry yur, not yet.'

Declan unsure of what was happening asked, 'Why not, I don't understand?'

'I won't tie yur down, if I can't be a proper wife to yur, in the bedroom and out of it. I won't marry yur. I knows yur want children, so do I but unless I can become a proper woman, I'm not gunna marry yur.'

Declan went to say something more, but Daisy said, 'Let me think.'

Declan, now worried, felt the answer he wanted with all of his being was slipping away.

Daisy was again quiet for some while, obviously deep in thought again. After a while she said, 'I don't think me mum will mind, she just wants me to be happy. It's Sara and Harry I'm worried about. If it's going to upset them I can't do it, sorry Declan. They have been so good to me.'

Declan was not hopeful, it was not Sara he was worried about it was Harry, he lived by an extremely strict code.

As though by prearrangement they heard the key in the lock.

Harry held the door open for Sara, they were deep in conversation, but spotting the young couple Harry looked at his watch and said, 'You're up late.'

'We have something to tell you,' said Declan.

'I can see what it is,' said Sara suddenly excited and becoming emotional. She was moving rapidly across the room to take hold of Daisy's hand. 'Harry, they are engaged.'

Declan stood up, ready to receive Harry's outstretched hand. The older man congratulated him pounding Declan's back with his free hand then kissing Daisy's cheek. Sara kissed and hugged them both, wiping the tears of joy away as she did so. The wine was poured, the cheese and biscuits offered and accepted.

Sara sitting next to Daisy was examining the ring once more, looking up at Daisy she asked, 'Have you set a date? I suppose it is a little early for all that.'

There was a long silence then Daisy said, 'We won't be setting a date yet.'

'Why ever not?' asked Harry, frowning, and obviously confused.

'Can I speak to you in the kitchen please, Sara?' asked Daisy.

After the two women had left the room and closed the door behind them, Harry asked, 'What is all this about then, Declan?'

'It's women's stuff Harry. I would stay well out of it if I were you.'

Harry now with two hands in the air, palms facing Declan he said, 'You don't need to tell me twice, I stay away from all that sort of thing. Whatever happens I hope you will both be happy.'

Declan asked, 'What was the film like?'

Harry, welcoming the change of subject enthused about the plot and the acting. The conversation was starting to run out of steam when the two women returned from the kitchen.

Daisy resumed her seat next to Declan and grasped his hand, Sara said, 'I think you two have made a very sensible decision, Declan.'

She went to continue but Declan said, 'I'm sorry to interrupt, I need to say this was Daisy's decision. Sure, I would marry her whatever, but if that's what she wants I'll agree.'

Harry, now getting cross said, 'Why don't I understand what's happening? There is something going on here that you don't want me to know about.'

'I'll tell you later Harry,' said Sara.

'No, you won't, you'll tell me now!'

'Harry, please don't lose your temper. Daisy and Declan are going to live together for a while before getting married.'

All of them could see Harry's face changing colour and his body stiffen. Now he was shouting: 'What, live in sin? Not in this house you're not. I know a lot of the younger generation have no morals, but we do – how will we face the neighbours? They will say you are a tart and worse, you won't be able to show your face in church ever again. You obviously have no regard for me and Sara after we have taken you in and treated you like one of our own.'

'Harry, Harry, stop it,' said Sara, 'you don't know what you're saying.'

'I don't know what I'm ... it's not me who has agreed to allow them to shack up together. What happens when he gets her pregnant?' Now standing and wagging his finger at Daisy he was shouting even louder. 'You needn't think you can come creeping back here afterwards madam.'

Declan jumped to his feet and said, 'It's not like that.'

'What is it like then?' shouted Harry. 'I thought more of you Declan.'

'I'll tell you what it's like Harry.' Daisy was now standing beside Declan, tears running down her face. She had obviously lost control; her hands were bunched into fists at her side. Shouting back at him she said, 'It's twenty years of watching mi father come home so drunk he could 'ardly stand and then treat me mum like a punch bag. Sometimes I had to 'elp her get up off the floor. When I was fourteen, he tried to rape me. He would 'ave done too if my mother hadn't woken up and 'it him with a fire iron. Until Declan came along, I couldn't even let a man touch me let alone make love to me, and we haven't by the way. I won't tie Declan down until I knows I can be a proper wife to him. Can your aunt put me up Declan until we sorts out some better accommodation?'

'Yes, I'm sure she can,' he replied.

Harry was standing, shocked, looking like a man who'd had the ceiling fall on him. He went to say something.

Before he could speak Sara growled at him, 'Keep quiet Harry, you've said too much already, go to bed, we will talk about it in the morning.'

Resembling a whipped dog Harry crept from the room.

Sara hugged Daisy asking, 'Are you sure you want to do this my love?'

'Yes,' she replied. 'Now's as good a time as any. I'm going to pack a bag. I won't be five minutes, Declan,' said Daisy wiping the tears away.

'I am so, so sad to see you go, but I do understand. I will help you pack – you can borrow one of my suitcases.' It was apparent that Sara was fighting back the tears.

Daisy remembered back to when she arrived at this house with all her possessions in a black plastic sack. Now she had a little more to pack, although not a lot. Ten minutes later the two women arrived back downstairs with Daisy carrying a small tan suitcase and her coat slung over her shoulders. Both of the women were tearful. Sara hugged Daisy hard saying, 'We will see each other at the shop.'

Daisy replied, 'You'll be able to come to us soon, won't she, Declan?'

'Of course,' he replied. Earlier on in this drama he had decided that to say as little as possible was his best option.

Sara kissed them both at the front door and stood waving as they walked away. She stayed staring down the street for some time afterwards, long after they had disappeared from sight, hoping for she knew not what. All she did know was that her baby had left home, never again would she come home from work keen to discuss the people she had met and who had said what to whom. She pulled a blanket around herself. She was experiencing real pain; she had never understood what heartache was. Now she knew. She sat on the couch, her arms locked around her chest rocking backwards and forwards, her head dropping further towards her knees, tears falling from her eyes. All she could think was my baby's gone, my baby's gone. She held a pillow over her face to mask the cries of anguish that were being forced from her.

Harry tiptoed downstairs in the early hours to find his wife curled up on the couch cuddling a pillow. She came to as he entered the room.

'Would you like a cup of tea?' he whispered.

'Just go away, you've driven my baby out of the house you stupid, stupid man. All because of your silly pride and your bad temper. Go away and leave me alone.'

Harry went to the kitchen to make a cup of tea. Sara could hear him trying not to make too much noise. The progress of his endeavours were indicated by the differing sounds. The flow from the tap, the kettle's whistle, quickly silenced, the sounds of the teapot being filled and stirred, after a long silence, the clink of the tea strainer, the sound of the cups being filled, the china being placed on the tray.

Entering the room he said, 'I made you a cup anyway. I am so sorry. I don't know what more I can say other than I am dreadfully sorry for hurting you so badly.'

Sara's only response was to pull the blanket over her head.

Harry placed a cup on the floor near her and walked away to go back upstairs to a long, lonely night. He could not remember the last time he had slept on his own. He knew that he may have done irreconcilable damage to their relationship.

✳

A similar scenario was occurring at Declan's aunt's house, the young couple and his aunt were sitting around the kitchen table drinking tea. His aunty Megan had heard Daisy's voice when they had arrived, and it had drawn her downstairs. The two of them had just finished explaining what had transpired earlier. Declan's aunt was thrilled for them over the engagement. Daisy had been very forthcoming over the reason for not setting a wedding date and why she wanted Declan and her to live together first.

Megan was quiet for some time afterwards, then she said, 'I understand your decision, Daisy. I think it's very brave – you could find yourself alone again if things don't work out for you.'

'I knows that, but I'll not ask this man to live like a – a monk if … well if I can't be a proper wife to him.'

There was another silence while the trio sipped their tea and thought over the events of the evening.

Eventually Megan asked, 'You think you have somewhere to live permanently Declan, don't you?'

'I hope so,' he replied.

'I have a suggestion for you two youngsters,' said his aunt. 'I don't want to move one of the children this late. Daisy there is a bed and a couch in Declan's room. Daisy you can sleep in Declan's bed and Declan you sleep on the couch. I know I can trust you to behave.'

Daisy felt her face flame. If she was going to share a bed it may as well be here as anywhere, she thought.

Later upstairs Declan asked, 'Do you want to go first in the bathroom or shall I?'

'You go first,' said Daisy, desperately embarrassed.

'Right oh,' he pulled his pyjamas from under the pillow and left the room. Daisy noticed they were white with a fine red check.

All too soon for Daisy he was back again. 'Your turn, the bathroom is to the left, first door on this side.' He was sitting on the end of the bed flicking idly through a magazine, after a few minutes he became engrossed. It was only sometime later he became aware that Daisy had not returned. He tiptoed down the hall and tapped on the bathroom door. 'Are you all right in there?' he whispered.

He heard the bolt slide back, then nothing. 'Can I come in?' Again there was no reply. Opening the door very slowly he discovered Daisy sitting on the loo with the lid down, crying silently into a sodden hanky. She was wearing a thick, pink, cotton nightdress that reached to her toes.

'Come with me – you can sleep on the bed, I will sleep downstairs,' he said, offering her his hand. Taking it, she allowed him to lead her down the hallway and into the bedroom. Her clothing bundled in the other arm.

Daisy sat on the bed in the same place that she had sat earlier. Declan pulled a pillow onto the floor and dragged his sleeping bag from the wall cupboard preparing to move downstairs.

Daisy was becoming cross with herself. 'I'm falling at the first hurdle,' she muttered. 'Declan, I want to sleep in the bed with you. If I can't even do that there ain't no hope for us. I might as well leave right now.'

Daisy changed her mind about which side of the large bed to sleep on and climbed in to lie against the wall.

'Would you not rather sleep on the outside?' he asked.

'No thank you. You have to protect me from the wild animals,' she said smiling at him.

'Oh, I see, so they eat me instead of you?' Daisy nodded. 'Light on or off?' he asked as he reached for the table lamp.

'Off please. Can you hold my hand?' Declan obliged as he plunged the room into darkness.

Daisy felt herself drifting off to sleep quite soon after.

*

Harry's sleep was fitful, he was cold, he shivered when he could not find Sara's warmth, then memory returned, and he was forced to relive the terrible things he had said.

*

Declan was jerked awake by someone hitting him and crying out. He was struggling to make sense of what was happening as he surfaced from a deep sleep. It was Daisy, his turning on the lamp and flooding the room with light brought her to her senses. Struggling to draw breath she said, 'Summat touched my arm.'

'It must have been me moving around in my sleep. I'm sorry.'

'I was so scared. Will you hold me please?' Much to his surprise she rolled up against him and pulled his arm around her. There was almost full body contact, not something she had allowed before.

'This is nice,' he said softly in her ear. He was sure she had no idea how much self-control he was exercising; the wonderful smell of her hair, the armfuls of soft curves.

'Mmm, I feels very safe thank you,' she said as she snuggled closer still.

It was a long time before he fell asleep.

The following morning, Declan surfaced with a smiling Daisy laughing into his eyes from two inches away. 'Good morning – thank you – it were my best sleep ever. I'm sorry about the silly nonsense in the night. Funnily enough it was better once you was holdin' me.'

She kissed him and he kissed her back then he noticed the time on the wall clock. 'Daisy we will be late for work.'

'Let's stay here and never get up again,' she responded.

'Well, I'm blowed. Is this that well-known workaholic talking?'

Before Daisy left for work, she made the bed and placed their night clothes on the relevant pillows. Declan noticed but said nothing, he recognised it as a declaration of intent. Declan's aunt never commented.

*

When the two of them arrived, it was to find Sara standing outside waiting for them.

'Can we talk please? Harry and I had a terrible row last night after you left. I slept on the couch. I was horribly rude to him. We have never had a row like that.' Now she was becoming ever more distressed. The tears were running freely down her face. 'He has asked if you could come tonight so he can apologise and explain why he was so disturbed by what you intend to do?'

Daisy stepped forward and hugged Sara, seeing her pain she could do nothing else. 'I'm right sorry to 'ave upset you like this.' Now facing Declan with a questioning look.

'Sure,' he said.

'Thank you both,' she said as she went to leave. 'I told him I would not be surprised if you never wanted to see him again.'

Later that night the young couple were standing on Harry and Sara's doorstep holding hands. Declan rang the doorbell. Both of them were nervous, wondering what the evening held.

Sara answered the door; she hugged them both and ushered them in without saying a word. As they entered the lounge Harry was standing in the middle of the room. Daisy could see the pain in his face. When he saw her, he marched across the room and swept her into a bear hug.

'I'm so sorry I caused you such hurt, please forgive me – I'm just a silly old man. I'm living in the past. Can you forgive me, please? Sara has explained a little of what your father did to you and your mum. He is better off in prison. Whatever you and Declan decide is all right by me, and if anyone else says anything out of line they will regret it.'

Sara interrupted and said, 'We will have a cup of tea, then Harry can explain why he behaved so badly. Can you help me in the kitchen please, Daisy?' The two women left the room. Daisy shared with Sara that she and Declan had shared a bed, just cuddling, she assured her. 'There was one funny bit as Declan turned over in his sleep he touched me arm, I panicked and started hitting him – I think he's forgiven me.'

'I don't expect he thought it was funny,' responded Sara.

Harry said, 'Sara was so upset last night Declan she called me some awful names. I now know I was wrong. Is Daisy ok? Sara and I think of her as our daughter. She has filled a big void in our lives,' Harry's Italian accent was now growing stronger as he became yet more emotional.

The two women came back into the room carrying tea and biscuits.

After a period of general chat Sara said, 'Ok Harry tell us about your cousin and why you got so upset last night.'

Harry spent some time staring into the distance, when he rejoined them he said, 'This happened before the last war in a very Catholic Italy. One of my girl cousins came home one night and told her parents she was pregnant – she was, I think, about sixteen. There was a ferocious row. It became known that she had a one-night stand with a sailor who had gone back to sea. My uncle was so upset his wife thought he was going to have a heart attack. He was going to throw her out that night, but my aunt persuaded him to allow her to stay the night and leave for good in the morning.'

Harry paused as he was drawn back again to an era that no longer existed. 'As far as I know she never set eyes on her parents again. A year or so later my aunt and uncle moved away. He couldn't shake off the belief that people were talking about them.'

'They may well have been talked about Harry, when people took against you in those days, you were shunned, it was a strict code of behaviour,' said Sara.

'I was frightened that the same would happen to you and us. Sara pointed out when she could bring herself to talk to me that this was a different land and a different time. I am so sorry. Will you forgive me?'

Daisy rose from her seat and went and hugged Harry saying, 'Of course I forgives you, you silly old man.' Harry's smile said it all.

The following day, Tim informed Declan that the board were comfortable with him and Daisy living in Mr Woodman's flat above shop Number One.

'You can move in whenever you like,' said Tim.

'How much will we pay in rent, Tim? Daisy will insist we pay a proper amount.'

'Harry has already warned me she won't take charity. Can you pay ...?' Tim was thinking, eventually he mentioned a figure. '... that's per month?'

'Yes, we can, and I knows you're being really generous, so you are. Thank you.'

'I hope you will be happy there. I'm glad someone will live in it.'

A few days later Declan noticed at breakfast that Daisy had the top button of her blouse undone, such a small thing in itself but of enormous significance in reality, a clear signal of her progress.

CHAPTER 54

Tim was sitting at a small, plain, wooden table in a large empty space on the first floor above the food hall that would one day be his first restaurant. Sitting opposite him was an older gentleman with a young man sat beside him. A bottle of red wine and three glasses stood on the table, a corkscrew and cork lay to one side.

Tim had met both men at his and Sophie's wedding. They were some of the large tribe of Italians that were her extended family. He supposed they were therefore his relatives-in-law as well – he was unsure.

Giorgio, the large, heavily bearded senior of the two men leaned forward and in a warm Italian accent asked, 'Shall I pour? This will be easier with the wine to smooth the conversation.' He was conservatively dressed, white shirt, black trousers and black shoes.

'Yes, by all means. Victor tells me we are related?'

'We are, but only the *Nono*s, the grandmothers, really know.' He drank a mouthful of the wine, as he swallowed he lifted the bottle and saw it was from a vineyard in Puglia. He realised Tim took pains to get things right. He smiled and nodded at him. Tim smiled back. 'Can I introduce my nephew, Lorenzo?'

Tim leaned across the table and shook the young man's hand saying, 'Welcome, Lorenzo.' There was a silence while Tim looked at the youngster who was wearing a wild-patterned shirt and blue jeans.

Then he said, 'I need to get one thing out of the way, Lorenzo. To me you seem too young. To be honest you would not be here if Victor Vieri had not sung your praises. What can you say that will change my mind?'

'Will you call me Enzo, please? Everyone does. I have been working for my uncle for years, it was the only place I wanted to be. I came in from school and went to the restaurant.'

'I had him sweeping up at first,' said Giorgio, 'then he stood on a box and washed up, then as he got older, I noticed he was watching me work. Now he can do anything I can.'

'How old are you, Enzo?' Asked Tim.

'Twenty-one next birthday, Mr Cooper.'

'It's Tim, Enzo. Can I explain what I am striving for with my restaurant? I am not interested in getting people in and out as fast as possible. I want them to come and spend time, enjoy the atmosphere, the food, and the wine, as I have seen them do in Italy. I want a seven pm curfew for children. I love children, but I know some Brits don't want to pay a lot of money for a meal to have it spoiled by ill-behaved kids. I want the staff to be attentive, polite, well-trained, and friendly – the wearing of a smile is obligatory. The customer is always right. I want our customers to be comfortable. I want them to bring their friends. Anyone who is uncomfortable with what I have just said is in the wrong job. Over to you, what do you bring to the table?'

Enzo spent a moment gathering his thoughts then said, 'I will cook the food I grew up with in Italy, preserving the original flavours but improving the presentation. I agree with you, the atmosphere needs to be cosy, relaxed. I want people to be able to take off their jacket without being frowned at by the head waiter. I will train the staff to briefly explain what is involved in their meal.'

Tim jumped in saying, 'I agree with you in principle but if it is overdone it can become tiresome. We need to ask them if they want to know, some won't. Sorry, carry on.'

'There will be no problem with ingredients Tim because you know where to get them from. By the way I met your father, Tom Cooper, some years ago in Italy, I was just a boy. You and I will plan the menus. Obviously, I will keep you informed but you will be taking me on for my skills and I must be able to use them. I will run it as my restaurant, if at the end of the year it is not in profit, sack me. I believe Puglia is the cradle of culinary excellence. That is what I will bring to our customers.'

'That sounds like a good start. How will you staff it?'

'I will prefer to employ Italians. We bring a feel of Italy, it is the music of the language. I don't believe you can fake that so I would like to advertise for Italian speakers. Will I be allowed to do so?'

'I don't see why not. Where do we go from here?'

Giorgio asked, 'Have you contacted a designer?'

Tim reached into his case and drew out a thick maroon folder and placed it on the table. 'I have to admit to you I am at the stage where I don't know what I don't know. I'm extremely pleased that I'm dealing with family, otherwise I'm quite sure I would get ripped off.' All three men were aware that Tim was making a statement that because of his ignorance he did not expect to be taken advantage of. 'How long are you over here for and where are you staying?'

'Victor has insisted we stay with him. I can stay a week or so,' said Giorgio, 'but I am happy to fly back and forth if needed, at your expense of course.'

'What will you cost me?'

'Nothing apart from the air fare and out of pocket expense, meals and so on. My intention here is to get this young man set up properly with a good start.'

'I assume you will start work straight away, Enzo?'

'Yes Tim, there is much to do, long days and short nights. I am really excited by it – this has been my dream since I am a child.'

The three of them discussed Enzo's salary and finally arrived at a figure.

Enzo said, with a smile on his face, 'When we are turning them away Tim, I will want a lot more money.'

'If we get to that stage, I will be pleased to talk to you.'

'How does this kitchen company work?' asked Giorgio, pulling the shiny folder towards him, he began muttering quietly to himself, it was apparent that he was reading it word for word.

Enzo and Tim were walking around the space with the youngster talking through the way it may look.

When they rejoined Giorgio, he said, 'It is important that you read this and understand it as much as you can,' he said looking at Tim. 'We are allotted our own project manager who arrives on day one – it starts as a design brief and then we work together as it slowly becomes more specific. Once the design is finally agreed we get a document with all the details then we get the chance to choose the parts. There are site visits throughout, then there is a problem-solving process followed by testing and commissioning. They provide a full set of operating and maintenance manuals. Air conditioning and fire systems are built in. Tim you could pay a lot less, but you will not get a more comprehensive deal.'

'My usual rules will apply, gentlemen. Three quotes for all the large stuff. I am not concerned about having the prettiest kitchen, I want the best kitchen at the right price.'

The two Italians nodded in agreement.

'Enzo, if you need me ring me, I will always be available.'

This was to be the first of many meetings as they chose the kitchen equipment, then the décor. There were some arguments over this, Giorgio wanted the usual dark décor that was popular in some Italian restaurants. Tim and Enzo disagreed: the tall windows let in lots of light it was a shame to squander it.

Working together, Tim and Enzo came up with a design for the interior.

All the woodwork was pale honey, varnished oak. The tables were small, suitable for two guests sitting opposite each other. The chairs were high-backed with scrolls at each corner at the top. Removable mid-blue-grey cushions were secured to the seats and the backs of the chairs. They were unable to agree on the table settings: Tim preferred the large, white damask tablecloths hanging down all round, Enzo favoured small individual white damask place settings with Sophies in small red lettering in the top right corner.

'Tim, if we serve say fifty customers in an evening, that could be twenty-five tablecloths, think of the laundry bill – it's an unnecessary expense.'

Tim thought for a moment, there were numerous reasons why Enzo was right, the initial cost for a start. He was very aware that the expenditure was running away with itself.

One thing they did agree on was the wall covering and the lighting. The walls were to be white with an almost undetectable hint of soft pink, the wall lighting was to be set behind flat translucent wall-coloured shades encouraging the warm white light to fan out from behind them. Tim wanted lots of pictures of Italy in wooden frames: the backstreets, the little cafés.

'Tim,' said Giorgio, 'one expense we have not discussed is the cleaning. Everywhere must shine, from the toilets to the seating areas and the kitchen. As one restaurateur explained to me the place has to be as clean on Friday night as it was last Saturday. Should people think the place is dirty they won't come back.'

Tim had to admit to himself that this was not something he had given much thought to.

'Tim, can we have modern white porcelain for the china, please?' asked Enzo.

'Any decoration?' asked Tim.

'No, it is all about the food,' responded Enzo, 'and Tim I would like to have these floorboards sanded back and sealed, there is so much character in them it would be a crime to hide it.'

Tim pondered on it; they could always change it in the future if it did not work. In the years ahead he was to be pleased he had agreed.

∗

Early one Monday morning in the restaurant space above the store a short, bearded man walked towards Tim calling out, 'Mr Tim Cooper, I believe.'

Shaking the man's hand Tim said, 'That sounds like a Cornish accent?'

'You're spot-on Mr Cooper. I'm Jago Pengelly your project manager. I am here to guide you through this project every step of the way, every time you turn round, I will be here.'

Tim was aware Jago was a bit of a showman, slightly larger than life, his dark-green trousers and red shirt were a clue.

'Call me Tim, Mr Pengelly. I feel better about everything already. Have you been doing this long?'

'Next year is my twentieth year in the business, and please call me Jago.'

Tim said, 'Let me introduce Giorgio and Enzo. Giorgio has his own restaurant at home in Italy, and this young man is his nephew, who is our new chef. Giorgio has assured me he has taught Enzo everything he knows. We are apparently all related.'

The two chefs did most of the talking. Tim said, 'Jago you are not making any notes.'

'I have been blessed with a good memory, as Giorgio and Enzo were saying what they envisaged, where things would be I can see it in place, so no notes. Have you read the brochure?' They all nodded. 'You remember at the end of the design stage you will be given a series of drawings, showing how, why, where and when?' The men agreed. 'Tim, this is your venture, what are your thoughts?'

'I have discussed this with these guys, and we agree. It has to be relaxed, somewhere people come for the evening, superb food. It must have atmosphere. I have been in some restaurants that are dead, cold, bleak places. It has to be happy, there must be laughter and banter. We will cosset our patrons – my intention is they will all feel like family – we will know their names, their likes, and dislikes, who is having a baby and when. I want to have Italian staff, as Enzo said, "It is the music of the language." I want it to smell like Italy, and obviously taste like it.'

'You are there with the smell already. It's wonderful and Tim what you have done downstairs is extra special … outdoors indoors …'

Quite often over the next few weeks, Tim did not understand a word the other three men were saying. As far as Tim was concerned, his only task was to sign another cheque – he said to Enzo, 'How many years will it be before I make my money back?'

'Not that long, people will be flocking to eat here. Don't forget Tim, downstairs is a tremendous draw with the barrows and the streetlights, and the café where you can choose to eat in or out. I think there needs to be more seating down there around the walls under the lights, and perhaps music in the evenings. We could serve drinks from a small bar.'

'Whoa Enzo,' said Tim, 'let's learn to walk before we start running.'

'Tim, I believe if we get it right this restaurant will become one of *the* places to eat in London.'

'That is extremely ambitious, Enzo,' said Tim appearing sceptical.

'Let us aim for the stars and see what happens, Tim.' As always when the young man became emotional his Italian accent thickened.

CHAPTER 55

It was late evening; Angela was in her cream, silk, nightdress and blood-red velvet robe. Fresh from the shower, she had drawn all the curtains, turned off all the lights, her cocoa was sitting on an occasional table beside her armchair, ready to be transported upstairs to her bedroom.

The knock on the door surprised her, then frightened her a little, opening the door just far enough to see who it was she peered out through the narrow opening; whoever it was pushed the door further open making her totter backwards. The intruder stepped inside dropped a valise on the floor then pulled her too him and kissed her firmly on the mouth. He stank of alcohol. Angela was terrified. Her struggles were to no avail; he was going to rape her. When he released her, she stepped back and slapped him with all her might, it was no gentle pat, years of Sunday afternoon tennis had put muscles on her arms. The blow was given further impetus by the fear that had gripped her. The smack to his face knocked him sideways against the wall. The sound of his head hitting the wall was surprisingly loud. Finding the switch she flooded the hallway with light. She recognised her intruder. It was Alain – concern for his well-being replaced her fear, she knelt down and cradled his head.

'I am so sorry,' she said. 'I did not know who it was.'

He was mumbling something she could not hear, moving her face closer now she could hear him muttering, '*Je t'aime, Je t'aime.* I love you' – then he kissed her again.

Angela could not have been more confused; what did he mean *Je t'aime*, I love you? Pulling away from him she was now worried that the blow had caused this rambling nonsense.

'I think you should go to hospital. I am so sorry I hit you so hard.'

'No, no,' he said, shaking his head, this was clearly the wrong thing to do because he moaned and put his hand on his forehead. 'I am … very tired, I need to sleep.'

Angela half carried him to the back bedroom, throwing off his pale gabardine he lay down on the bed and began pulling the blankets over himself. She removed his shoes, clicked the bedside lamp on and asked, 'Are you ok?'

'Yes,' he replied as sleep swept over him.

She sat with him for some while listening to his breathing. When the clock in the hall chimed one am she decided he was ok and went upstairs.

It was still dark many hours later when she became aware that he was climbing into her bed, and she discovered he was naked; turning over and rolling towards him about to tell him off, he kissed her and moved into an embrace, cupping a buttock he eased her into full body contact – she was very aware of his arousal. All her memories of their earlier coupling surged through her head; she knew she should push him away but the memory of the joy of their last encounter was so strong. The kiss continued, to her complete surprise her body began to react in spite of herself, she found herself leaning into him, their tongues touched; she realised she was making little mewing noises. His hands were drifting over her body, pressing her hips against him she gave him unspoken permission to continue.

Wherever he touched or kissed her a small fire was lit – how did he know how to caress her like this? Now her breasts were receiving his full attention, triggering loud sharp intakes of her breath as his lips found her nipples. His kisses travelled down her body. She spread herself for him saying, 'Oh that's nice.' Her arm slid down her body, found his head, tangled her fingers in his hair to hold him there. Minutes later her world exploded. She rolled away from him. Angela was no longer aware of time or place, she was lost. She did not know that she had cried out.

Alain surfaced and lay beside her not touching. After a while, her curiosity got the better of her and she rolled on to her side to see what he was doing, thinking he was asleep. To her complete surprise he was wide awake, both eyes open and smiling. Now he was lifting himself over her and gently moving her legs apart with his knee.

As he entered her, she said, 'Alain, I do not think I can do this.'

It started slowly then shortly after she was rocking her hips to meet his thrusts, their world fell away, they were suspended in space. They climaxed together; they were gripping tightly on to each other with arms and legs and hands, trying to remain in that magical place. Angela was incapable of coherent thought, there were fireworks going off in her brain. Her whole body was thrumming; this a legacy of the amazing experience she had just undergone.

When they had both returned to the here and now, Angela became aware Alain was talking to her in French, too fast for her poor sixth-form grasp of the language. His face registered complete surprise, his eyes wide open, his mouth in a half smile. He was still talking French.

'I do not understand,' said Angela.

Reverting to English, he said, 'With all the women I have been with it has never been like that, never.'

As her passion cooled a deep-seated anger began to replace it, slowly becoming a forest fire. She recognised she had been used again.

Almost spitting with fury, she said, 'You bastard, you have used me again. When are you leaving? Tomorrow, or will you stay three days this time then break my heart all over again? What's all this

Je t'aime, you love me nonsense?'

Alain remained silent.

'Well say something for God's sake.'

He didn't move towards her as he wanted too; the slap in the face still stung, but eventually he said, 'I love you. I admit I have been with other women since we parted—'

'We did not part, you used me and left, without even a kiss goodbye.'

He acknowledged that with a nod and then continued saying, 'The problem was they were all a disappointment these other women. Why? Because they were not you. I would wake up in the morning with your name on my lips and it was not you, it was a stranger. I have spent months trying to forget you, denying that I love you. I know you have no reason to believe me, but it is true. I love you. I will always love you. I want you to be my wife, I want to spend the rest of my days with you.'

Angela snorted but was otherwise silent, she felt certain that he would hurt her again. A storm of different thoughts swirled in her head. He had lit up her life. She could return to her solitary, drab existence, or she could take a chance and allow him to stay; perhaps marriage would slow him down, or at least living with him would give her a better idea what he was up to from day to day. She wondered what her friends would say, or more importantly her family. Staring into his eyes she could see no guile there.

'I am too tired to think any more tonight, we will talk more in the morning.' Turning on to her side she faced away from him. Sometime later she felt him move close to cuddle her and put his arm around her waist. That was so good, to be cuddled to sleep rather than her normal lonely nights. She was sure he knew exactly what he was doing but for tonight that was fine, she was unaware of the smile that wreathed her face as she slept.

The following morning, he was up first – she could smell mushrooms frying. Shortly after Alain came back into the bedroom carrying a tray loaded with a cheese, mushroom and diced olive omelette, toast, and a pot of coffee.

'I will sit over there,' she said, pointing at a small, round, slim-legged Queen Anne table with two chairs of the same pedigree. She did not trust herself to let him back in bed with her. Pulling on her robe she joined him at the table

The discussion over breakfast was of no real substance: the heat wave, etcetera. Angela understood they were tiptoeing around the critical issues; the truth was she knew she could not trust him any further than she could throw him, and she was angry. Her fury had abated a little in the night, but she still had a powerful desire to hit him again.

'Have you had any more thoughts about my proposal?' he asked.

'No, the only thing I have thought about is that I wished I had hit you harder – I may do that yet.' Alain moved his chair a little further away.

'Angela my proposal was, is, genuine – I love you. Whatever you decide it will not alter, I am prepared to wait as long as you need to be sure that I mean what I say. May I live here? I am able to pay my way. When I go away, I would like you to come with me. I can now afford good hotels. I will need a local studio.'

Still, she was silent. She made no reply. How could she decide? She was not sure if the emotional wounds his disappearance had caused her last time had healed yet.

Alain set off on his second trip to collect the rest of his paintings from his old studio; he had been unable to get them all in his little van last night.

The paintings from the first run were on the floor, propped against the hall wall. She was sitting on the carpet going through them. It was a series of women in various poses mostly nude, it began to dawn on her that these women resembled her. On the fifth painting, she saw she recognised a painting derived from the drawing he had made of her on his last visit when she had been asleep: naked, face down on her bed; then she realised that the studies of women were all of her. She continued to go through the paintings, there were some that were not of her, two were of a large house with a family standing outside. Many of the rest were her, naked, half-dressed, undressed; she realised he must have a photographic memory. No one seeing them could doubt who the sitter was. Her favourite was her naked standing with her nightdress a pool of cream silk around her feet, holding a bouquet of red roses. She had to admit he was a very skilled artist – in many ways, she thought wryly.

He had made her beautiful; did she honestly look like that? She found herself becoming emotional; the hundreds of hours he must have spent painting her. She was still browsing through them, holding a hankey to her face to stem the tears when he returned.

He walked in and placed more paintings further down the hall, then came and sat down beside her and placed an arm round her and kissed her cheek.

She now understood that he did love her; this body of work was a silent testimony to how he felt about her.

He rose from the floor and began to search through the rest of the paintings she had not seen yet, drawing one from the rest he sat down beside her again and placed it in her lap saying, 'This is a gift of love.'

It was the painting he had asked her if she would sit for the first time he was here. She was sitting in a beautiful high-backed, dark wood chair in her blood-red velvet robe showing just enough flesh so that the viewer knew she was naked underneath it, but she remained decent, unlike most of the other paintings of her. She wondered what her family would make of Alain. Her sister Olivia was too far gone these days, lost in the confusion that was Alzheimer's disease. Her sister's husband, Victor? He was unpredictable, the arrival of his granddaughter and grandson had softened him, but he could still become very dictatorial on occasion. Sophie described it as the Italian in him.

She wondered what Tim would think; she went a little pink realising he would see the pictures of her naked. She had once said to her sister that were she younger she would have given Sophie a run for her money with Tim; Olivia had accused her of being common. Angela had long ago admitted to herself that if Sophie stepped aside for any reason, she would be in there like a shot, blow the age difference, she loved the way he smelt. He had no idea of how attractive he was to women. Angela understood it was difficult to define, it was a combination of things: his self-confidence, his masculinity; the fact that he really cared for those he loved, it was all these and more.

She realised that Alain would have to show his work in the hope of selling it.

Concerned because of her silence he asked, 'Are you OK with this?'

'Do you mean the paintings of me naked? Yes, I am, you have made me beautiful. How soon will you be able to get Mr Palmer's gallery to exhibit them?'

'Oh, I am not showing them here, I will hold it in France. That way it will not embarrass you.'

'No, you will not, you will hold it here.'

'Really, are you sure? Some people will be really shocked you know. You will be in for some criticism – they will call you all sorts of rude names.'

'Listen my darling boy, all I have ever been called is Silly Angela – whatever they call me will be a step up from that.'

'Am I now your darling boy?'

'Yes, it is official, from now on you are my darling boy.' While she had been speaking she had moved on to her knees and was pushing him onto his back so she could lay on top of him. The kissing became more intense, his hand was holding her bottom.

He ended the kiss to say, 'The van is unlocked, and the front door is open.'

No sooner had he warned her than the local postman's head peered around the door saying, 'Hallo – oh, sorry, this needs signing for.'

Angela, rising from the floor said, 'I hope we did not embarrass you? I have just said yes to my boyfriend's marriage proposal.'

'No, a cuddle is nothing, some of the things postmen see would make your hair stand on end. I'm going to write the book when I retire. Congratulations to you both.'

Alain had joined Angela at the door; he joined in the thanks.

Pushing the door shut he gathered her into his arms, 'Was that a yes?'

'It was my darling boy. I would have to be blind not to see the love that pours out of those paintings.'

Releasing her he said, 'I must lock the van door. We are going out to celebrate. You cannot overdress for where we are going.'

*

Early the following morning Angela shook Alain awake. 'Wake up, wake up,' she demanded.

'Whatever is wrong? What is the time? Good God it is only six o'clock,' he said squinting at his watch.

'I have had an idea for your studio.'

'Angela, there is something you need to understand, we artists never rise before lunch, for us six o'clock does not exist.'

'Put some clothes on.' He was an attractive man, but she was not as comfortable with his nudity as he was.

'I have something to show you.' Watching his smile spread across his face, she raised her hand saying, 'Behave yourself – put some clothes on and follow me.'

Minutes later he was following her towards the back of the house, grumbling in French. Opening a door at the end of the corridor a set of steep narrow stairs were revealed, stepping aside Angela indicated he should go first. She was a little embarrassed because she had not been through this door in years and the stairs had become dusty and were strung with spider's webs.

Waving his arms around to clear a path, he quickly ascended the wooden stairs that complained as he stood on them. When she joined him upstairs, he was standing in the middle of the space. It was an attic room that stretched from side to side and front to back of the house. Large windows at each end revealed a panorama of the roofs and chimneys of the surrounding buildings with London's famous architecture beyond. A gathering of pigeons lifted off from a window sill clapping their wings as they left.

Alain was jubilant: turning around and emitting a stream of excited French that was completely unintelligible to her. She remembered her French teacher's comments in her end-of-year report that said, Angela strives hard to master the language but regrettably fails to achieve any success whatsoever. All of this was written in French; she had to ask her best friend at school, Elizabeth Manning, to translate it for her. Her friend had called the French teacher a very rude name when she saw how upset Angela was.

Alain was now speaking English. 'See,' he said pointing to the windows at the far end, 'there the light is perfect' – striding towards the window in question and throwing his arms wide. 'Here I will make great art, and here will be my couch' – pointing to a small alcove. 'It will be nice to have some heat and water, with your permission this we can fix, and some mains electrics.'

Turning around and hugging her he said, 'You are the most wonderful woman I have ever met. Thank you so much.'

CHAPTER 56

Sophie had just laid the baby down to rest when she heard Tim's chair scrape back followed by a deep sigh, then nothing. He had been up early working through the pile of paper he had brought home from the office the day before. This was the second Sunday that work had got in the way of their early morning '... cuddles.' Ensuring Martyn was safe, she made her way to the kitchen table. She was surprised to see Tim still in his pyjamas, his chair at an angle, his chin resting on his hand, his elbows on the table, the paperwork brushed into a disordered heap, gazing out of the window. She sensed he was struggling.

Sophie went to sit on his lap; he made more room for her. 'Do you want to talk about it?' she asked.

Tim gave a giant sigh – '... it's all such bloody hard work.'

Sophie knew the only thing she could bring him at the moment was comfort, slipping her arms around him she brought his head to rest against her breast and placed her lips in his hair. She was aware that women had been doing this for millennia: offering solace to their menfolk and children. Not her mother though, she had no understanding of offering comfort; her normal response was to rebuke her, assuming it was her that was in the wrong, and then offering suggestions of what Sophie should do. Thank God her father was Italian, She had realised when she was quite young that in many cases the English reserve hampered the middle classes from giving love and comfort to their suffering children. When she cried her father had gathered her up and held her while she sobbed. It was usually all she needed. She recognised her mother's mother was far worse. She had heard her grandmother once say that children were unavoidable and should be sent off to boarding school as soon as possible.

Tim was silent for some time … eventually, taking a deep breath he said, 'Sometimes it all gets too much.'

'What gets too much,' she asked.

'All of it, the job – it's all got too heavy.'

'Go on,' she said.

He sighed again. 'It was good fun when we only had two shops. I knew everybody, the workload was manageable. The other day in the food hall there was a man working, clearly a member of staff – I didn't have a clue who he was. I went up and asked his name and apologised because I should have known – he was good about it. I was extremely embarrassed – that was the first time it has happened, not knowing a member of staff I mean.'

'Is there anything here that has to be ready for tomorrow?' Sophie asked.

'Erm, no.'

Standing up and taking his hand she said, 'Come on, get dressed. It is a beautiful day. We will go for a walk by the river. That will help. I will put the baby in the pram.'

'What is Nanny doing today?'

'She is out with her friends – tonight its bingo then down the pub for fish and chips.'

'She deserves a break,' said Tim. 'When are we expected at Angela's for dinner?' Charley had spent the night at Angela's where she was thoroughly spoiled.

'7 for 7.30,' she replied.

*

Tim walked and talked, using Sophie as a sounding board. One thing they had both agreed on was that there was going to be some major changes to the structure of the company.

The river as always worked its magic, strolling under the trees with his wife and baby and watching the craft on the water restored his equilibrium.

CHAPTER 57

Tim, Sophie, and Angela were enjoying a pleasant evening at Mr Vieri's; his wife was no longer comfortable in company. Angela had explained Alain's absence , he had received a commission to paint somebodies wife.

Sally was there to take notes if needed; this was the current euphemism in place to account for her presence. The meal had been superb.

The family were laughing at something Sally had said, when she was rendered inaudible by the shouting and smashing of glass and crockery and the foul language coming from the kitchen. Martha rushed into the room extremely alarmed. 'Mr Vieri your wife she is going crazy in the kitchen. She is smashing things and saying terrible words.' All this said in a strong Italian accent.

Mr Vieri leapt from his chair and started towards the source of the mayhem. They all sat in silence, frozen in their seats, then they heard Mr Vieri shout, saying, 'STOP THIS NOW YOU STUPID WOMAN BEFORE YOU HURT YOURSELF OR SOMEONE ELSE!!'

This apparently failed to quell the distraught woman's panic, she was now screaming obscenities at the top of her voice. Another heavy piece of crockery was heard to smash to pieces.

'Tim, can you do anything? She seems better with you,' asked Angela.

Sophie went to say something but changed her mind. She gave Angela a hard stare; she was clearly annoyed that her aunt would suggest her husband should get involved. From the corner of her eye Sophie saw Tim was about to stand up. Her hand darted out and grabbed his arm to try and hold him in place.

'There is a trained carer out there and Martha and my father – I am sure they will manage.' No sooner had she stopped speaking than the screaming resumed, more things smashed against the wall.

'I need to try and sort this. She usually listens to me.' Tim stood up and made his way from the room.

The kitchen was a battleground, broken glass and crockery littered the floor; the carer had a nasty cut on her cheek. Martha was fending off the missiles with the top of the laundry basket, and Mr Vieri was swatting the thrown objects away with a towel-wrapped arm.

Mrs Vieri, now hysterical, lost in her panic, pain and rage, her feet bleeding from the glass shards scattered around her. She resembled a mad woman from some Greek tragedy. Now, Tim thought, she is insane, at this moment in time she has no idea what she is doing. It was then he noticed the carving knife in her left hand.

'Olivia it's me, Tim. I've come to help you.'

'No one can help me,' she screamed. The noise gained in volume as she stepped forward onto more shards of glass. Now she sounded like a tortured animal, beyond all reason.

Tim could have cried for her. Picking up a glass jar that had somehow remained intact he threw it against the wall behind her and to her left. She spun around to see where it had gone. Tim made two quick strides towards her, seized her knife hand with his left and captured her other hand with his right, this to stop her hitting him with the saucepan she was holding. Now she was trying to bite his chest, the heavy woollen jumper he was wearing foiling her attempts.

Mrs Vieri's hand had started to slip through his grasp; he felt the blade cut into his little finger. She pulled her hand again and the pain increased. The sharp edge slid slowly across the bones of his fingers as she continued to pull.

This level of pain was now intolerable, and it triggered an automatic response; without any forethought he let go of her other hand stepped back half a pace and slapped her around the face.

Dropping the knife and the saucepan she collapsed against him. He had his arms round her waist and was holding her upright. The silence was loud in his ears.

In a quiet calm voice Tim asked the carer – he didn't know her name – 'Can you arrange a hot water bottle please? Martha can you a fetch a broom? Victor will you ring the Doctor?' Sophie had appeared in the doorway. 'You can't come in, but can you find a chair with wheels?' he said in a gentle voice.

'There is one in my office,' called Mr Vieri from the hall. Martha was methodically brushing the glass into a corner. Sophie returned with a secretary's chair and her mother's woollen dressing gown. Tim sat the wrecked woman in the chair and wrapped her gown around her. Mrs Vieri was silent now, head bowed and shivering. Tim checked the hot water bottle was not going to burn her, while Martha offered a clean towel to wrap it in and then placed it in the silent woman's lap. Mrs Vieri reached for his damaged hand; Tim gave her the other one to hold and she lifted it to her lips and kissed it.

Sophie saw he was bleeding. 'Tim, let me see your hand. Oh my God. Tim, I can see the bone on both fingers.'

Tim was now kneeling down holding Mrs Vieri's hand in his.

'I am sorry I got cross,' she whispered, 'can I go to bed now, I am very tired?'

Tim heard the doorbell ring. He said, 'That will be the Doctor. He is going to give you a quick check-up and then it's bedtime.'

'Am I still allowed to have my hot chocolate?'

'Yes,' said Martha.

The Doctor appeared in the kitchen doorway; Victor said, 'You were quick Doctor.' The medic nodded as he opened his bag.

Tim started to get up to give the Doctor room.

'No, no, you stay,' Mrs Vieri insisted.

'I will stay until you go to bed, is that ok?' asked Tim.

'Yes,' she said, nodding.

Angela appeared at the kitchen doorway holding a large handkerchief to her face to mop up the tears. 'I am sorry,' she said. 'I am always frightened when people go mad.'

The Doctor was some time removing the pieces of glass from Mrs Vieri's feet and applying ointment and plasters then he gave her something to help her sleep. 'Do you know what triggered this outburst?'

'She was going to boil some water in a plastic bowl, Doctor. I tried to stop her, then she went crazy,' said Martha.

'Tim, show me your fingers.' The Doctor had spotted the blood. After a brief examination he said, 'Hospital for you Tim, I am afraid.'

The Doctor treated the carer's cut before he left.

∗

Tim and Sophie sat in A and E she holding his right hand. They had not exchanged a dozen words since they had arrived. Tim was going through possible other actions that he could have taken rather than slapping her, but he couldn't think of any. The knife she had in her hand had been long and sharp.

'What are thinking about, Tim?'

'I wish I hadn't hit her. I have never hit a woman before, and I never will again.'

'Tim my love, I do not see what else you could have done. She was insane, she could easily have stabbed you.'

'Well, she didn't so let's not worry about it.'

The triage nurse came to ask them some questions. She became steadily more concerned as they told her what had happened. '… and then I slapped her,' said Tim.

He could see the nurse was struggling to appear non-judgemental.

'What was the name of the Doctor who attended your mother, Mrs Cooper?'

'Jacobs, Dr Jacobs – he is the family Doctor.'

'Will you excuse me a minute?' asked the nurse, moving away towards the reception desk. She began an animated conversation with someone on the other end of the line.

When she returned to the couple she said,' Your Doctor has put my mind at rest. He said I was to congratulate you on how well you managed the problem.'

'Please do not tell him that,' said Sophie, 'he already has an ego the size of a house.' The two women laughed.

Tim whose mind was elsewhere said, almost to himself, 'She forgave me straight away and apologised. I shall never hit a woman again whatever the circumstances.'

Aware that Tim was upset the nurse said, 'Let me find a cubicle that's free.'

Moments later Sophie was sitting on Tim's lap holding him. He was shaking his head as he repeated, 'She apologised to me.'

Sophie did not understand why he was so upset, then it became clear. 'Mum told me that hitting a woman was the lowest a man could stoop – there is never an excuse for it.'

'Tim, this may be one of the few times it was necessary. My mother was beyond reason. I am quite certain that had you released the hand holding the knife she would have stabbed you.'

The surgeon drew back the screen. 'Mr and Mrs Cooper?' They both nodded. 'Mrs Cooper will you take a seat in reception, this may take some time. Mr Cooper, please follow me.'

*

Tim was lying on his back on an operating table with an extension to the table stuck out at right angles. His left arm was laid upon it and the surgeon was sitting by his left hand.

A pretty, petite, young nurse came into the room. Tim guessed she was Japanese; she was tiny like a lot of Asian girls. Her distinctive pretty eyes and her lustrous shining black hair helped to endorse his belief, Tim was told her name, he forgot it immediately, he wasn't quite with it he realised. He was taking long deep breaths, trying to control his fear.

'Now Tim, this going to hurt. I need to find the nerves that have been severed so I can't give you any pain relief. When I find them, you will not need to tell me, I will know.'

He lay there for what seemed ages, every so often the pain shot up his arm and he gritted his teeth to stop himself crying out. He could not control the low, deep, growl that the agony generated; when this happened there was only the back of his head and his heels on the table. His torso was bent upwards in a rigid arch. Through all of this his hand lay perfectly still, the young nurse her face inscrutable, her tiny cool hands gently holding his arm in place. When it was over, and his hand had been dressed the surgeon explained that Tim would not be able to use his hand for a while. it was encased in a large white dressing.

Tim asked, 'Why is the dressing so large when it is only a couple of my fingers that are damaged?'

'The padding is there to prevent you knocking the fingers themselves. You would find that extremely painful.'

'Don't get it wet if it gets hot or smells come back in. You will receive a letter telling you when to come back to have the stitches removed.'

As Tim sat on the corner of the operating table he asked, 'Why was the nurse so tiny? I could have hurt her.'

'If I had put a big man on there you would have wrestled him all over the room. Most men try to protect the nurse.'

Tim went to stand up and the room spun around him, the Doctor grabbed him. 'Sit back down Tim I will get a chair.'

The nurse came back in with a wheelchair. He was going to say he didn't need it, but he knew that wasn't true.

Sophie was shocked when she saw him in the wheelchair, his face was haggard and as white as a sheet.

'Stay here, Tim', said the Doctor. I will write a prescription which you must collect tonight – your hand is going to be extremely painful.'

Tim had taken to his bed on arrival back at the Sea Maiden. Later when Sophie was talking to him, he heard Nanny and the children. Nothing was making much sense to him. Realising she was wasting her breath, she kissed his forehead and said, 'Do not worry I will sort it out.'

Tim remembered little about that night. His sleep was interrupted every time the pain came back; Sophie had been adamant that she would not allow him any more tablets until the four hours had elapsed as per the prescription.

*

Tim stared down at the face of his dead wife, he was desperately tired, he had been awake for forty-eight hours ever since the Doctor had diagnosed Sophie's problem. He couldn't remember exactly what the condition was called, some kind of sudden death syndrome. The pain of his loss had rendered him helpless.

Now he was in the bathroom gazing into the mirror holding the sides of the washbasin for support, completely unable to stem the floods of tears and the animal cries.

Every bone, muscle and sinew ached as a result of her death. Though not religious he had prayed in the hours before her demise – 'God if you are there take me, not her, take me.'

His love for her was greater than anything he felt for anybody.

His loss was now unendurable, his body was shaking, his very soul was crying out – he jammed the hand towel into his mouth trying to smother the terrible sounds that the grief was tearing from him. He was worried that he would wake the children. He had seen that any display of his grief caused them fresh pain.

Something strange was happening; somebody was calling his name. Whoever it was they were a long way off, but they sounded as though they were getting closer; now the hand towel was being eased away from him – a face was swimming in front of his eyes, a woman's face, Sophie's face, she was pulling the towel away.

'Tim I am going to turn the light on.' Now he could see that the towel he was holding was in fact a corner of his blanket. For a moment he was unsure where he was.

'Where am I?' he asked

'You are at home with me Tim, on the Sea Maiden. I think you have had a nightmare. I expect it is all the painkillers you are taking that are to blame.'

He could hear both of the children crying.

His throat was sore, his eyes red-rimmed; he gathered Sophie to him and held her close. I haven't been that scared in years, he thought. Later that night the ghost of the nightmare disturbed him again.

In the early morning Sophie felt him leave the bed, she assumed he was going to the toilet; she was drifting back to sleep when she realised he had not returned. The first light from a grey dawn was driving away the darkness. When she reached the front cabin, she found her husband sitting holding their little girl. The pair of them were covered by a soft yellow throw. She thought they were both asleep but as she approached them, he lifted his head and smiled at her. He seemed healthier than last night.

'How are you?' she whispered.

'I'm feeling better, ta,' he said. 'Cuddling this one seems to help.'

'Cup of tea?' Tim nodded. Charley yawned and stretched like a cat then rearranged her limbs all without waking.

Martyn must have heard the kettle, his cries slowly gathered volume. Now they were all awake.

CHAPTER 58

Tom and Sammy had just watched a comedy that they had both laughed at. Tom handed the lad the newspaper, Sammy handed it back saying, 'No thanks Mr, I reckon I'll go on up ta.'

'Sammy now hold on, you said you trusted me, right?' The lad nodded tentatively.

'Listen lad, a nod is not good enough. Before we go any further you need to know I will never put you down or make fun of you. Do you understand?'

The boy said, 'Yes Mr.'

'Now what I am going to propose will be our secret, ok? I want to teach you to read and spell and later on some other stuff.'

'I can sign me name Mr. Me mum told me I didn't need no nuffin' else.'

'Listen Sammy you're a clever lad. You sort out all the money for the dockers don't you? Who taught you to do that?'

'I taught meself, wiv the dockers help.'

'That's clever lad. I've watched you, you're quick to work things out, but Sammy, without the reading and writing you will always be a labourer. You can be so much more than that. We will start tonight – sit here beside me.'

Tom wrote out the alphabet then three simple words: cat, sat, mat. He got Sammy to copy the sounds he was making, both the letters and the words.

'I ain't never gunna get this Mr, it's too 'ard.'

Tom had already recognised this might fail at the first hurdle, so he had an incentive, reaching into his pocket he pulled out a coin and hid it under his hand.

'I reckon you might want to lad.' Tom lifted his hand. 'Learn this, the fifty pence is yours.' Tom noticed a change come over the boy's face. There was now a flame of determination alight in his eyes.

'Show me agin then, Mr.'

The man and boy sat bent over the paper in the pool of light from the small table lamp. The fire threw flickering golden shapes on the walls and ceiling. Beth was asleep under the table, her chin on Sammy's foot. The coin sat on the mantelpiece for a few days then one evening it was Sammy's.

Over the ensuing months, Tom gave him the gift of literacy and numeracy. Sammy could work out a percentage faster than anyone Tom knew. The boy grew steadily more confident. He developed a love of reading. Tom drew enormous pleasure watching the boy flourish.

One of his proudest moments was when he met a docker who said, 'Your Sammy's dad ain't yur, Tom Cooper?'

'I'm not his dad – he does live at mine though.'

'Well, when the boy talks about yur, he always says he lives wiv his dad Tom Cooper.'

Those few words warmed Tom for the rest of his life.

CHAPTER 59

The Number One Shop phone rang, Harry answered it. Tim heard him say, 'Hallo Sophie, how are you and those babies? Good, good – you want Tim, I will get him for you. All the best love. Tim, it's Sophie.'

Taking the phone off him, Tim said, 'Thank you, Harry. Hallo my love, how are you all?'

'We are fine,' she replied. 'I have had to go into work for a couple of hours. That's not why I rang you. Angela and Victor have had a real falling out. I thought I would warn you in case you bump into them. I will explain when you get home, bye now.' Tim put the phone down and wandered away, completely unable to come up with anything Angela and Victor might have a row about.

He was a little late getting back to the houseboat: one of their suppliers needed a chat. Dinner was on the table as he walked onboard. 'Sorry I'm late, a last-minute problem. Are we all well at this end?'

Charley nodded; Sophie laughed.

'Well go on then – I have been trying to come up with a scenario where the two people in question would fall out.'

Sophie was laughing hard now. '… Angela's Frenchman has returned, and they are now engaged to be married.'

Tim shaking his head with a frown creasing his face said, 'I don't understand.'

'No, that's not the reason for the fireworks. Alain has asked Mr Palmer at the gallery to put on a showing of his latest work.'

Tim was by now completely confused. 'So?' he said.

'The work is all Angela, nude, semi-nude, dressed, undressed. Apparently, he has been painting her from memory all these months he has been away.'

Tim was in fits of laughter; his mouth was wide open as were his eyes, his face was registering total disbelief.

'You do mean our Angela?' asked Tim now joining Sophie in fits of giggles. 'He must have a good memory this Frenchman.'

'Do not be rude, please Tim.'

'If he has painted her nude, he must have seen—'

'Tim!' admonished Sophie forcefully, stopping him from completing the sentence. 'Now you are being crude.'

'No, I'm not,' he said still laughing. 'How did Victor find out?'

'Apparently Mr Palmer, the gallery owner, rang my father to gain his opinion. He is one of Mr Palmer's better customers and, over the years he has recommended a good number of his friends to the gallery.'

'What does nude mean Mummy,' asked Charley.

Thinking quickly Sophie said, 'It means someone without enough clothes on. It is rather rude'

'So, what's happening now?' enquired Tim. His words interrupted by his bouts of laughter.

'Stop it, Timothy. Angela says she is going ahead anyway. Victor will never allow it. I cannot see any way out of this, Angela can be as stubborn as him if she wants to be.' Sophie was working hard to smother her own amusement.

＊

There was an intense argument going on in Angela's house. She was insisting the pictures were displayed in Mr Palmer's gallery. Alain was determined they would not be.

'It makes no sense to upset your family from the beginning of our relationship. We will hold the showing in France where it will meet with a better reception. We French are more comfortable with nudity. We see the beauty – you English, you are ashamed of the human body. You see pictures of a naked woman as pornography. This is a great shame, the human body, male or female in its finest form is one of the most stunning sights you will ever see. Michelangelo's David in the Accademia Gallery in Florence is proof that it does not have to be a female nude.'

Angela was quiet for some time, usually she would fight her corner; however, she was aware there were good reasons for not pursuing this. Firstly, their romance was, because of the short time they had been together, quite fragile, they did not know each other that well yet. She was not about to risk her new-found happiness just to win an argument.

'OK, you win this time,' she told him, the smile on her face indicated that this would not always be the case. The truth was, on reflection, she was keen on the trip to France and possibly to gain a little notoriety. This was a lot better than being called 'Silly Angela.'

CHAPTER 60

On Sunday afternoon it was decided that they would all go to the rowing club. Tim, Sophie, Charley, Martyn, and Nanny set off after lunch.

Tim said, 'It's like a military manoeuvre.' Martyn was in the pram; Tim was carrying Charley – his daughter had insisted that he carry her. He suspected that Sophie had put her up to it. Tim was soon puffing, it was high summer, and the sun was blazing down. To make it hotter still the heat was reflecting back from the pavement.

Sophie and Nanny Bridget were walking and talking. With the military theme still in mind as they arrived at a busy road they had to cross Tim said, 'Squad halt.'

Sophie reprimanded him saying, 'Tim, that is a little thoughtless.'

Nanny said, 'If you're telling him off on my account please don't worry, it was all a long time ago. This reminds me more of the Bedouin caravans crossing the desert.'

'Yes, and I'm the camel,' quipped Tim.

'Yes Daddy,' said Charley not sure what she was saying. Everyone laughed.

Soon the child began struggling in his arms saying, 'I am too hot Daddy, I want to get down.'

'Remember the rules, you must hold my hand,' said Tim as he lowered his daughter to the ground. Charley was nodding.

Arriving at the clubhouse they were made welcome by three members who descended on Sophie as soon as she arrived asking if she could explain some technical issue.

As they walked away toward the boats, Tim, shaking his head caught Nanny's eye.

'I didn't understand either Tim,' she said. 'Now we,' she continued, talking to the children, 'are going to make ourselves comfy over there on the grass in the shade of the trees out of the sun where we can see what is going on.' A number of the mums came to make a fuss of the children, this included Sam, Gordon's wife, who was carrying a tiny life jacket.

'Tim there is a club rule that a child of Charley's age has to wear a life jacket on site. You can borrow this one today.'

'Say thank you Charley.' The child did so. 'That makes sense Sam, thank you. Where do you buy all the gear?'

'I will jot it down for you, I'll find a pen.'

Tim watched his daughter comparing herself to the other members, then she tucked the long cord around her waist and out of the way as the others had.

Taking her hands in his he said, 'You must not go near the water, do you understand.'

'Yes Daddy, Mummy has already told me.'

Tim decided his daughter already looked the part: life jacket, red T-shirt and white shorts; her appearance closely matched the other club members.

'Now when I have got used to the sailing dinghy, I will take you out with me. Would you like that?'

Charley was nodding then saying, 'Yes please, Daddy.'

Gordon arrived beside them saying, 'Hallo do you want to sail today?'

'Yes please,' said Tim, 'and by the way, I have brought your book back – it's fascinating.'

'You can hang onto it for a while longer,' offered Gordon.

'No, you're fine thank you. I've ordered a copy.'

'Well done, 'said Gordon thinking, this is a good sign – if I can get him hooked on the sailing Sophie may stay.

The dinghy had a cherry-red hull and cream interior with varnished wooden seats and a matching transom at the stern. The sails were a well-used off-white.

Tim received a short lecture on the major parts of the dinghy while it was still on the trailer on dry land. 'You live on a boat, don't you? So you know about the bow and the stern.'

Tim said, 'Yes but I would prefer it if you assumed I know nothing, please.'

'Fair enough,' was the response. Walking around the craft Tim's tutor was tapping parts of the dinghy and saying the names. 'Rudder, tiller, centre board, main sail, jib' – the list was a long one. 'You will learn as we go, I will always give the name and then explain what I am referring too. Minutes later the trailer was pushed down the slipway and into the water. Tim had been given the mooring rope and told to hang onto it.

'Otherwise, Tim, you will be swimming after the dinghy' a bystander cracked.

'Can you swim, Tim?' asked Gordon.

'Yes,' he replied. The two men had previously donned life jackets. Tim hauled the dinghy back to the bank once the trailer had been removed. He was surprised how strong the current was. There was considerable pressure on the rope. Without being asked he made it fast to a bollard. I know that much, he thought. He remembered Tabby the Boatyard owner showing him how to safely secure the Sea Maiden.

'There is only one thing you must remember – when I say, ready about, you are going to move smoothly from one side to the other, the boom will swing over like so.' Gordon was now pushing the mainsail across the boat holding onto a beam of wood that the bottom of the sail was secured to.

'If you forget once you will never forget it again if you survive it that is.' All of this said by the joker who had put in his twopence worth earlier.

'Mike,' said Gordon, clearly irritated, 'can you go away, please?' Mike left muttering to himself. Ten minutes later the small dinghy with the two men on board was sailing away from the clubhouse, almost silently apart from the chuckle of water under the bow as the dinghy eased her way through the water.

'We are going about. When I call, I want you to move across to the other side ducking your head as you go, letting go of the rope you are holding. Mind your head, ready about.'

Tim started to do as he had been instructed; as he moved the boom came across and tapped the top of his head. Lesson learnt, he thought as he hauled on the jib sheet on the other side.

Gordon called out, 'We had better return Tim, people will worry.' The time had flown by all too soon. When he checked his watch he estimated that they must have been on the water for over half an hour.

'We will get back quicker Tim; the wind will be blowing us home most of the way. We won't need to do all that side-to-side stuff like the tacking.'

The trip back to the club was accomplished much faster than the journey out. Sophie was still out; she had spent some while helping others. Tim assisted Gordon with putting the dinghy to bed, as he had described the process, and was now sitting beside his tutor at a large wooden table in the clubhouse, both of them silent.

'What do you think, Tim?' said Gordon.

Tim was quiet for a while. 'That was amazing, it's almost silent and it's free, there's no pollution. Mankind has been travelling like that for how long? Centuries, I guess.'

'It is special Tim, I love it. There are costs – you need your own boat and there are fees to pay, but it is well worth it.'

*

Back on the Sea Maiden that evening the meal had been prepared and eaten, the children were sound asleep, a result of their time in the fresh air. Sophie and Tim were watching a film on the telly.

'Did you enjoy the sailing?' she asked him.

'I did, it's …' Tim paused searching for the words, '… somehow timeless,' he continued. 'I said to Gordon, mankind has been moving across the waters of the world since we stood upright, countless centuries, thousands and thousands of years. Just using the wind. I read somewhere that Polynesians sailed across oceans using all sorts of old techniques, one of which was tasting the changes in the salinity of the sea water, so they knew when to make a course correction. What's that poem? "I need to go down to the sea again, to the lonely sea and the sky, and all I ask is a tall ship and a star to steer her by." I don't remember any more, Mum knew it. I guess our fascination with the sea is because we are an island race. We must have salt water in our veins,'

'You have really enjoyed today I can tell,' observed Sophie.

'You're right. I've always been comfortable on the water. When Mum was alive we used to holiday near Hastings, and we would go on a trip around the bay. I remember the rougher it got the more Mum and I enjoyed it. One day it got really rough, the speedboat was bouncing up and down.' Tim was now chuckling. 'The water was flying over the side, the spray looked like showers of diamonds with the sun shining through it. Mum and I were hugging each other and laughing our heads off. We didn't realise poor old Dad behind us was throwing up. I never felt seasick, nor did Mum.'

Sophie recognised that this was the first time he had ever talked about his mum and laughed. She decided not to mention it, the fact that it had happened was good enough.

'Will you go sailing with Gordon again?' she asked.

'Yes' – was the enthusiastic response – 'he has agreed to give me an hour's tuition any week if I can make it. I have said I will contribute to the club funds. If I become proficient at this sailing malarkey we could all go out.'

I will need some proof of this proficiency before I risk my family on the water, thought Sophie.

CHAPTER 61

Daisy and Declan had spent the day wandering by the river. He had been very attentive all day, walking arm in arm or holding hands. Declan had admired her new dress. It was blue cotton and made more of her figure than anything else she owned. On one occasion he had placed the palm of his hand on her bottom to gently move her ahead of him through a gap in the crowd. Historically a man's hand on her bottom would have triggered a panicked and terrified flight response.

This time it generated a completely different reaction. It signified an intimacy that she had believed she would never experience; her woman's smile was the only external visible indicator of the warmth suffusing her whole body and the powerful need she had of him. Other people were walking and talking the same as them, enjoying the sunshine, the scenery and in her case, she was enjoying the company of the man beside her.

Slipping her arm around his waist she pulled him towards her so that their hips touched. Declan responded by copying her with his arm around her waist then kissing the top of her head. He loved the way her soft wavy hair held her perfume.

This was the first time in ages they had spent a whole day together. They had both recently volunteered to do evening shifts in the food hall, the only problem with that was they were not always rostered together. Still, they had both agreed they needed the money and redecorating the flat over the shop was proving expensive. Tim had been so good about it. When Declan had first suggested it, Tim had been unsure about changing it, then he had come back to them and said yes as long as there were no structural changes. He admitted Mr Woodman would not want Tim to turn it into a memorial for his godfather; however, the furniture would remain.

Doing the washing up later that evening while Daisy was busy, hands immersed in warm soapy water, she reflected back on the day they had shared. She was smiling again, she seemed to do a lot of that lately: it was Declan and his obvious love for her. For the first time in her life, she realised that she was unafraid because she knew Declan would always protect her.

Declan put down the book he had been reading and stood up to put a shovelful of coal on the fire. Noticing Daisy in the kitchen he was very moved. The picture of domesticity she created was very appealing. Now standing behind her he wrapped her in his arms and bent his head to kiss her neck.

Daisy, her body already tingling because of her day-long proximity to him, experienced her emotions catching fire. She was aware that her body was shouting at her. Her heart was racing, she wanted this man now. Undoing the buttons on her blouse she held his right hand and placed it inside her clothing. His hand was still for a moment then his hand travelled up her back and released her bra. His thumb began to play with her nipple. He was breathing in quick short breaths; she felt his growing excitement and pushed her bottom into a firmer contact with him.

Turning her around their lips meshed, he was still fondling her, after some time she freed herself and stepped back.

'That's a shame that was lovely,' said Declan.

Daisy silenced him, putting a finger to his lips, now with her face bright pink she whispered, 'Take me to bed.'

Declan was extremely surprised, 'the petting' as Daisy chose to call it had become more intimate, but it had always ceased before intercourse.

Reaching the bedroom she said, 'Shut yur eyes, I ain't that brave yet.' She was going to leave her knickers on but then decided that was daft. Declan was in bed first and then started opening and shutting the drawers in the bedside cabinet.

Pulling the bedclothes up round her neck she asked, 'What are you doing?'

'I'm searching for some condoms,' he said, sounding extremely embarrassed.

'We don't need them. I'll be delighted if you get me pregnant.'

Turning to look at her he said, 'Are you sure?' He was obviously surprised.

'Yes, I am, now for God's sake shut up and get on with it.' As she was saying this, she was pulling him on top of her.

Initially there was some pain, then her body demanded she continue. They rode the experience together, the range of sensations she was experiencing were indescribable. The pleasure was so intense, the pressure built and built, then her senses exploded. It rendered her almost semi-conscious for a short while, she had no grasp on reality.

As they both returned to the world Declan said, 'Wow!' In between his struggles to breathe.

Daisy thought, I was so close to never experiencing this.

Declan asked, 'Are you ok?'

'Yes, I'm more than ok ta, that was bloomin' amazing. Why are you askin'?'

'There was a whole lot of shouting at the end there, so there was.'

'Sorry I didn't know I was doing that, do yur mind?'

'No not at all. It is I suppose a kind of noisy complement.'

'Oh, it was that all right, thank God I found you. You funny little Irish person.'

'Will you marry me now?' he asked, in a serious quiet voice, his Irish brogue to the fore, unsure of her answer. He was more nervous now than he had ever been before.

Without hesitation she said, 'Yes I will.'

Declan kissed her and said, 'Thank you,' then held her close.

By common consent they wrapped themselves in each other and let sleep wash over them.

Hours later Daisy was struggling to untangle the knot of clothes and legs. Declan came awake and checked the time. 'Daisy we're going to be late, we are late, almost. I will jump into some clothes and run there.' He was struggling into his underwear, when he noticed her, she was bright red and trying to smother her laughter.

'Well, that's got that out of the way,' she said.

Declan rolled his eyes. 'It's all right for you, I've got to get past Tom downstairs, he will know exactly what has been going on.' As he was speaking, he was jamming his feet into his work shoes. Then kissing Daisy he said, 'Thank you, last night was amazing.' He made for the stairs.

Daisy heard Tom Cooper ask, 'Did you sleep well, Declan?'

'I slept very well thank you Mr Cooper, did you?'

'Like a top lad, like a top.'

Declan was obviously extremely embarrassed, he never called Tom, Mr Cooper.

She made herself a cup of tea, Declan could cope on his own for a while. Staring into the distance and dwelling on last night she recognised that from this day on her life had changed, now she could have all those things she thought were denied her. She loved how gentle he had been with her. Now she had a man who loved her, she had overcome her own fears and banished her demon. With a wave of euphoria washing over her she said out loud, 'And I can have my babies.'

As she was shrugging into her coat, she half remembered something she had read years ago that applied to her today. She struggled to remember, then again out loud she recited, 'I went to bed last night a girl and arose this morning a woman.' Straightening her shoulders and standing tall she marched down the stairs, ready now and able to face whatever life threw at her.

CHAPTER 62

Late one afternoon Tim was concerned about the level of noise the construction of the restaurant was causing. Downstairs in the food hall earlier he had seen some people grimace when the grinding noise had been at its worst.

This had prompted the discussion he was now having with Charlie, the builder. 'How long is this going to last, this noise?' Tim asked him, having to shout to make himself heard.

Charlie had a short conversation with the workman responsible for the din then came back to Tim. 'Mark says about an hour to an hour and a half, then it will all be much quieter.'

'Right, well I'm sorry, but it has to stop now, people are leaving the building. Can I ask you guys to go and get a meal in the café on me, then come back after closing and I will pay an hour and a half overtime? Is that acceptable?'

There was a lot enthusiastic nodding then they all trooped downstairs.

Later as arranged, the work started again. Charlie came and stood close beside Tim having to shout to make himself heard. 'I think you may get a nasty shock Tim when you get the bill for the food and the wine.'

'That's not a problem Charlie,' Tim shouted back. 'I am fairly sure it will not amount to as much as if lots of people had left the store earlier because of the terrible row the grinding was making.'

Over the next month Tim watched as the kitchen began to take shape. He found it fascinating, to his eye it appeared exactly like something from *Star Wars*. There were numerous bits he did recognise, the stoves, for instance, the vast deep sinks and the draining racks. A multitude of pipes of numerous sizes wound their way around under the ceiling.

Jago, the installer's project manager, was laughing and pulling Tim's leg saying, 'Tim all these questions, all you will ever need to do is to make sure your waitress gets your order right.'

Today Jago's clothing choice was even more flamboyant than usual: carrot orange trousers and a shirt with large squares of green and white.

'Thank you, Jago,' responded Tim. 'When I am spending this sort of money I do like to have some grasp of what is happening.'

'Ok,' continued Jago. 'This set of pipes are part of the fire control system. They are designed to snuff out any fire before its begun, well almost, this set over here are the hot water and cold main's supply.' Jago then went on to start explaining the intricacies of the wiring.

Tim put his hand on the Cornishman's arm saying, 'Yes, yes, you've made your point, I'll keep quiet.'

CHAPTER 63

Jessica's husband Gerald had returned that evening from a week-long conference in Brighton. His welcome for Jessica was lukewarm to say the least, it was a peck on the cheek and a gruff hallo as he walked away from her down the hall towards the lounge hanging his grey suit jacket on the newel post at the foot of the stairs.

Further proof, she thought to herself, that our relationship is in a hole at the moment.

'Are you ok?'

'Yes, only tired,' he said without turning round as he entered the lounge. Moments later she heard the football start on the telly. At least she didn't have to cook for him. He had phoned ahead and said he was eating in Brighton before he started home. Her and Polly had eaten earlier. Jessica carried the bag of dirty washing downstairs that she had just liberated from his suitcase. She was disappointed in his disinterest in her: she had showered, spent some time on her hair, shaved her legs and was wearing makeup, a new perfume and a rose-pink dress he had commented on some time back.

*

Upending the bag onto the laundry room floor she found herself standing there stunned, staring down at some woman's black lace underwear all mixed up with his. She knew it was not hers, she had nothing that fancy or that expensive. Now her anger was building. He could not be bothered to bed his wife; no he was too busy screwing someone else. 'Gerald,' she shouted, 'come down here.' Twice he ignored her.

The third time she called him he shouted back, 'I'm watching the bloody television woman.'

Picking up the offending clothing with the laundry tongs she marched upstairs and into the lounge, then stood in front of the television blocking his view, when his eyes met hers she dropped the underwear in his lap. Her temper was beyond control, spitting, she said, 'No wonder you are so tired, you have been screwing someone else in Brighton.'

'You what, it's yours you silly cow. Surely you can recognise your own clothing.'

'It is not mine – you are lying. I have never owned or bought, or more importantly had anything like that bought for me.' Now she was shouting at him with all the force she could muster. 'Did you meet her down there or did you take her with you? How long has it been going on? Weeks, months, years? I suspect it is a long time – you have shown a complete lack of enthusiasm in our bed for a long, long, time. I want you to leave – get out, get out now.'

'I will leave but only as far as the pub. I can watch the rest of the match there, and if you lock me out, I will kick the door in, you see if I won't. You need to pull yourself together.'

His talking down to her was the final straw. He saw the slap coming and caught her arm before it connected, squeezing her arm painfully, he slapped her back, hard, saying, 'You need to think on woman, you're married to your job, not me. This is not all my fault. We can talk later when you have calmed down a bit.' His fierce grip on her arm had stopped her being knocked backwards.

After he had slammed the front door shut behind him, Jessica crumpled to the floor and cried her eyes out.

Polly in floods of tears ran downstairs and threw herself into her mother's arms.

Jessica phoned Sophie at the houseboat and explained what had happened. 'Pack some clothes, Tim and I will come and get you. If Tim is there when he returns there will be no more slapping so you can take as long as you like. Oh, and pack the offending articles in a clean bag, try not to handle them. We will be there shortly.'

*

'Nanny will you be able to stay awhile?' queried Sophie. 'It appears Jessica is in trouble.'

'Yes of course, I will make myself comfy on the couch. I hope she is alright.'

'Mr Graham will drive you home when we have sorted everything out.'

'Thank you.'

'I will ring Mr Graham,' said Tim

'Tim, he will be settled in for the night, let's call a taxi.'

'Sophie darling, as your father once said about his driver, they do very well out of us. Free accommodation and wages on top, and anyway if we call a taxi Mr Graham seems to take it as a slight. He has assured me that this is what he is there for, and it is only 7.30.'

Reaching for the phone Tim sought and received Mr Graham's confirmation that he was on his way.

*

The various orchestrated manoeuvres in the dark, as Tim called it, had the Bentley arriving outside Jessica's house with Sophie and Tim sitting in the back. Jessica appeared holding a white cloth to her eye with Polly holding her other hand crying hard.

The last of the four cases had been swallowed by the cavernous boot in the big car and Sophie, Polly and Jessica were ensconced on the back seat. Tim was sitting in the front with Mr Graham.

'How is your eye?' asked Sophie.

'It is sore, but it is not too bad,' was Jessica's reply.

Polly turned to Sophie and said, 'This is a very posh car, isn't it?'

'It is a lovely car. It used to belong to a beautiful person called Mrs Longstaff, now it belongs to Tim.'

'Who was the beautiful person?' Polly asked.

'Tim's aunt, a very grand old lady who loved Tim very much and when she died left Tim this car amongst lots of other things. She looked after Tim when his mummy died.'

'I expect he was sad when she died but he is so happy now that he has you. My mummy and Daddy are not happy – they argue a lot.'

Jessica heard what her daughter said and turned to stare out of the window.

Sophie took Jessica's hand and held it.

Jessica and Polly were soon made comfortable in the rooms above the company office. Jessica was so grateful for Tim and Sophie's help and care.

Reaching home and tip toeing on board the couple found Nanny and Charley cuddling on the couch both sound asleep. Sophie putting her head around the nursery door discovered Martyn was also in the land of nod.

Charley barely stirred as she was transferred to her own bed. Mr Graham whisked a sleepy Nanny home.

*

The following morning Sophie called early at the office to see how Jessica was. Mrs Graham answered the door when she rang the bell, the woman was clearly concerned. 'Oh Mrs Cooper, I'm ever so worried.'

Jessica marching down the hallway interrupting the older woman said, 'There is no need to worry, I can see out of it ok. I will admit it is fairly painful, but I am sure it will soon clear up.'

'Show me,' commanded Sophie.

Horrified, Sophie exclaimed, 'Oh my goodness, that is horrible, hospital for you lady!' Jessica began to remonstrate with her. 'Listen your eye is damaged, it appears to be filled with blood, and it is nearly closed by the swelling.' The inflammation around the eye was an obvious dark blue. 'There is a nasty cut below the eye as well,' continued Sophie. 'Mrs Graham can you go and explain to your husband what is happening and tell him we are going to A and E, and we need to drop Polly off at school. Thank you.'

As the elderly woman was opening the door, Bonny was arriving. Everyone said hallo, then she was informed about Jessica's eye.

'Oh, you poor thing,' said Bonny, screwing up her face and wincing when she saw it, 'that must hurt like blazes.'

'Yes, it does,' admitted Jessica, finally.

'Can you hold the fort, Bonny?' asked Sophie.

'Yes, no problem, there's a fair bit to do but we sorted it into an order yesterday. I will get it done before closing.'

'Well done,' said Sophie. 'I may see you later.'

'Bye, bye, Grace,' said Mrs Graham as they all trooped out of the door.

'Why does she call Polly, Grace?' whispered Sophie as they made their way towards the car.

'Apparently she does not like nicknames, so ever since I told her Polly's christened name was Grace that's what she calls her. Even Polly has tried to correct her, but she will not have it.'

'Why did you call her Grace?'

'It is his mother's name,' was the cold clipped response.

Sophie noted that she did not refer to her husband by name.

After arriving at A and E Jessica was called through promptly. She was gone some time, but eventually she returned to the reception area, wearing a black patch over the damaged eye.

'Was that painful?' asked Sophie, screwing up her face like Bonny had earlier.

'It was and still is,' observed Jessica. 'I have been prescribed painkillers and I must do nothing for a week. I have to visit the Doctor's in a few days. I have a letter for her.'

'I will drop that in for you on my way to work.' Sophie noticed that Jessica was shedding silent tears; taking a step forward Sophie wrapped her friend into a careful embrace.

'Everything has fallen apart, I have no home, no husband, I have only my income. I am completely alone,' she mumbled into Sophie's shoulder.

People were walking around them in the reception area. Jessica seemed completely unaware. Sophie decided that it did not matter, the staff in this department must see more than their share of distress and grief.

'We will talk in the car. Are you ready to leave?'

A whispered, 'Yes,' was the response.

As the two women approached the Bentley, Mr Graham stepped from the car and held the passenger door open for them. Once in the car he turned in his seat to talk to Jessica. 'I hope you don't mind – my wife has prepared a light lunch for you Jessica. She will understand if you can't manage it.'

'That is exceedingly kind of her, please thank her for me.'

'On the same tack, Jessica,' said Sophie, 'Tim and I discussed your situation last night. We are both agreed you can live at the office for now, there will be no rent to pay. There are three bedrooms there so you can make yourselves reasonably comfortable and you will have use of the kitchen etcetera. You can use my father's solicitor when needed, the company will pay for that.'

Jessica was crying again. 'I cannot accept all this – I have to pay for things. I am not even family.' All this said through the sobs.

'Jessica, Tim has been keeping an eye on the extra hours you must be doing at home – you could not achieve what you have in a normal working day. We owe you hundreds and hundreds of pounds. That will pay the rent for quite some time, so please do not worry about it, and as regards your being family, since uni I have always considered that you are the closest thing to a sister that I will ever have. Now we are taking you back to the house and you are to put your feet up and let Mrs Graham spoil you both.'

'She will do that for sure,' affirmed Mr Graham smiling at them in the rear-view mirror.

Jessica napped most of that day away. Early the following morning, someone tapping on her bedroom door roused her from a deep sleep. Mrs Graham's head appeared holding a tray with her breakfast on it. Jessica's watch told her she had overslept, almost certainly as a result of the painkillers she had taken in the night to overcome the agony that had assailed her.

'Polly will be late for school. I must get up. Sorry, I have no time for food,' she said as she was rolling back the bedclothes.

Mrs Graham putting the tray down on a side table placed a hand on Jessica's arm and restrained her attempts to leave the bed.

'Jessica my love, everything is under control. Grace is fed and watered and dressed ready for school. Mr Graham will take her in if you agree for him to do that.'

Makes my daughter sound like a horse, she thought. 'I need to write the school a note, Mrs Graham.'

'That's all done, my dear. Bonny came in early this morning and has typed the letter. If it's correct, you can sign it and Mr Graham will give it to the headmistress when he delivers the little one. It's here on the tray.' She handed the letter to Jessica.

As usual Bonny had been super-efficient, there was the change of address, the list of people that Jessica was happy to have deliver and collect Polly, and the office phone number. Bonny had excluded Jessica's husband by name.

'That is fine Mrs Graham. Say thank you to Bonny for me, please.'

'There's no need to do that Mrs Graham I'm on my way up.' As Bonny came through the door she said, '... and you don't need to thank me boss it's the least I can do.'

Jessica smiled at her and mouthed, 'Thank you.'

Then the girl spotted how much further the bruising had spread over night and was overcome, putting her arms around Jessica and with her head on the other side to the injury she hugged her gently.

'I'm going to come up behind him one night with a piece of four by two.'

'What is a four by two?' queried Jessica.

'It's a heavy length of wood,' replied Bonny, 'four inches by two inches thick that you bash people with. It's one of my father's expressions.'

Mrs Graham, uncomfortable with the way the conversation was going, said, 'I'm going to make sure Grace is ready. I'll send her up to kiss you goodbye.'

'Thank you Mrs Graham. Bonny, will you stay please?'

Bonny went to speak, but Jessica put her finger up to her lips to silence the girl and waited till she could hear the older woman talking to Polly downstairs.

'I know what you are going to say,' said Bonny. 'Mrs Cooper told me she'd fire me if I let you work.'

Jessica said, 'She will not do that, it was her way of telling me that she knew I would work anyway, and that she disapproves. I am lying here with my life in ruins, work will distract me. Today I will stay in bed, it hurts when I walk about any way. Tomorrow I will stage a remarkable recovery and get up. Do you mind if we work in here today? You will have to tell me the details, my vision is a little wonky. I am assured that it will improve. Are you all right with that?'

'Yes, no problem, but can I hug you again?'

'Yes please,' was the response. Jessica was aware that she had not experienced such genuine concern for her well-being from anyone in years until now.

'Will you be able to see to sign?' asked Bonny as she stepped back.

'Yes, that will be OK. I will have my breakfast then we will start.'

The two of them worked hard all day; as she suspected the work helped her take her mind off her ghastly predicament.

CHAPTER 64

The following Sunday afternoon, Tim and Jessica arrived outside her house in the Bentley to collect some clothing and other things she needed.

'Can you take your eye patch off when I say?' asked Tim. Gerald's car was on the drive, so they knew he was home.

'Why do you want me to do that, Tim?'

'If you go along with what I am going to say, we'll scare the bastard to death.'

Jessica went to ring the doorbell, Tim stopped her. 'Do you still have your door key?'

'Yes,' she replied, obviously frightened.

'You are going to let us in then put your key away again out of sight.' She did as he instructed. Tim stepped through the door as Gerald came out of the lounge. The front of his shirt was stained with food.

The way he swayed as he walked towards them, it was clear he was drunk.

'Get out of my house you—'

He never did get to finish the sentence as Tim stepped forward and started jabbing him in the chest hard with straight fingers saying between each jab, 'You - can - shut - up.'

Gerald retreated with each jab. Tim knew he was a bully and a coward. 'You are lucky my friend you are not in a cell.'

Turning to Jessica he said, 'Show your husband your eye, please.'

She was now in tears as she removed the eye patch and revealed the full extent of her injuries. Her eyeball was red not white, the surrounding flesh was mottled black and yellow, and badly swollen almost closing the eye itself. The stitches in her face were very apparent.

'Sod off, I didn't do that,' mumbled the drunkard.

'Jessica, would you go upstairs please and collect what you need?'

Gerald went to say something, Tim stepped close and shouted in his face: 'Your task this evening, sir, is to shut up and pay attention. I was here just minutes after you assaulted you wife. I have photos to confirm it. Also, my wife and Mr Graham were witnesses that evening. We have been trying to get her to contact the police, but she won't. The Doctor and the hospital have records of the injury she was carrying that evening. I am arranging for the company solicitor to represent her when she divorces you.'

'She won't divorce me mate,' he sneered. 'Where's she gunna live? What's she gunna live on? She'll soon be back. She knows which side her bread's buttered.'

'Listen you fool,' Tim was now shouting at him even louder, 'I've arranged accommodation for her rent free, the company owes her a lot of money for all the work she did on a recent project. It's clear that she doesn't need you anymore. Now listen hard, if you cause her any more grief, I will do everything in my power to see you in prison. I'm having trouble keeping my hands off you now, only the lowest of the low hit women.' Tim's nose was now only two inches away from the frightened man's face. Tim still shouting said, 'Am I making myself clear?'

'Yes,' he muttered.

'Now go into the other room and keep out of the way until we have gone.'

Minutes later Jessica appeared at the top of the stairs with two full suitcases. Tim sprinted up the stairs to assist her. 'Have you got your jewellery and anything that means a lot to you.'

'Oh, I need Polly's dolls. I will not be a moment.' She quickly reappeared with who knew what in a clean white sheet boasting a large knot holding it closed.

Mr Graham whisked them away.

Jessica looked back and saw a pale lonely face watching her leave from an upstairs window. For a moment she was tempted to tell Mr Graham to stop the car and run back to him, but the discovery of the black lace underwear and his attack on her had removed what small vestige of affection that had once existed. She fixed her gaze forward through the windscreen towards her new future.

CHAPTER 65

Tim sat at a table on the slightly raised section of the restaurant watching his guests laughing, chatting, and enjoying the food. The waiters and waitresses were smiling and talking to the diners, Enzo was walking around checking people were enjoying their meals. He soon disappeared back into the kitchen.

Tim was honest enough to know that his first instinct, which had been to decide the young man was not experienced enough had been wrong; Enzo he realised had a gift that had been polished by the young man's determination to excel and Giorgio's guidance and training. The food was superb.

He was pleased with the décor: he was sure that the decision he had made, and that Enzo had endorsed to keep the dining area bright was correct. The lighting could be adjusted to provide a little more intimacy and privacy later in the evening. Just as importantly the place had atmosphere, there was a welcoming warmth, it smelt and tasted like Italy. He, Enzo and his uncle had discussed whether the staff should speak Italian to each other in front of the diners or English.

Enzo had been adamant saying, 'If this is supposed to be a little piece of Italy, the staff need to speak to each other in Italian and to the diners in English as they do at home, otherwise this is a sham. Let's not spoil what we have created, and Tim as I have said before, it is the music of the language.'

Tim and Sophie were watching Charley their daughter standing talking animatedly to the Italian members of the family, on the other side of the restaurant. She was pointing down into the food hall explaining how it all came to be.

'You know what's a little scary, Tim?'

'No,' he said.

'She knows what she is talking about. Thanks to Tom's instruction.'

'She will be running all this in the future,' he replied smiling.

Tim, thinking he had said it in jest recognised that it may be true. He knew that his daughter although young, was a force of nature, a real amalgam of his own and her mother's personalities.

He sat quietly sipping his wine and reminiscing over all roads he and his loved ones had travelled to arrive at this moment in time.

Sophie, who had been chatting to her father and Sally with Martyn on her lap leaned against Tim and said, 'A penny for them?'

'I was thinking how hard we all had to work to arrive at this place in our lives. There was once or twice you know when I would have given it away to anyone who would take it.' Tim was now speaking softly into Sophie's ear. 'I could not have done it without you picking me off the floor and giving me the strength to continue.' He kissed her cheek.

'I never doubted you would do it. I have never known you fail when you set out to do something. Shall we just say that there were a few holes in the road I helped you cross.'

'It was more than that my darling. I'm going to say a few words.' Tim stood up and tapped the side of his wine glass.

'Good evening, ladies and gentlemen, I am going to speak for about an hour.' This was met by laughter and a few deep groans. 'Seriously though, there are people I need to thank. Firstly, my wife, Sophia, who has supported me throughout, especially those days when I would have sold it to anyone who would buy it for a tenner.' There was more laughter and some adamant nodding of heads.

'I need to thank my father who started this whole thing on a market stall and travelled across Europe to find the produce. When my father handed over the reins of the stall to me, Harry here helped me enormously, and I need to mention Sara, his wife, our world-class confectioner, and the staff, some of you, like Daisy and Jessica who have been here since the early days.

'I noticed when you did the extra hour or two, but you never mentioned it, or you arrived here in the dawn's early light without any thought of reward, just a desire to get the work done as well as possible. Everyone here tonight has contributed.'

Turning to his right he said, 'I need to thank my father-in-law, Victor, who is always prepared to listen when I have a problem and Sally who often assists Jessica and Sophia, thank you to all three of you. The same to, Declan, Bonny, the list goes on, to all the new men and women who have joined us, some from foreign lands – welcome to our family. Sitting over on my right is George Wainwright, our estate agent, who found this beautiful building for us – I am sorry we make him work on a Sunday, Mrs Wainwright.'

The lady in question had the good grace to smile. Tim knew George was often in the doghouse for a day or two afterwards. George had confided in Tim that the enormous bouquet of roses she had received this time had helped.

'I want to thank Giorgio, Enzo's uncle who gave of his time freely and is responsible for us gaining a chef, Enzo, who is a child prodigy.' Thankfully both men laughed.

'As the kitchen was installed, I believed we were building a set for *Star Wars*. Enzo is it all right if people want to see round it afterwards?'

'Of course.'

'The team who did a lot of the building work are sitting over there. This job set a new record for the gallonage of paint that went on the walls both upstairs and down – thank you, Charlie and co.'

'Mr and Mrs Murdoch, our relationship has improved – he no longer laughs when I tell him my latest idea.'

'I do still laugh Tim, but only after you have left the bank.'

This generated a round of laughter and applause.

'I need to say a few words about my great aunt, Mrs Longstaff, who cared for me after my mother died. Her generosity in settling her estate on me is what has made all this possible.' He waived his hand around – 'and it has provided us all with a job.'

'I want to say a huge thank you to everybody. We could not have done it without the teamwork. To anyone I have forgotten, please accept my apology.'

Tim was now standing quietly, waiting; people began to wonder what was going on – he continued to stand there.

Finally he said, 'There is one man who isn't here tonight. Without his generosity, his unfailing support of my ideas … his guidance both personal and commercial, neither you nor I would be here now. Will you fill your glasses, please? I would ask you to stand to drink a toast?' Tim waited while people got to their feet and had filled their glasses. He saw his father turn to Harry. Both men knew who it was going to be.

'The toast ladies and gentlemen is … Mr Woodman.' The gathering responded, the new staff said it without understanding, all of those who knew him said it quietly with profound respect. Because of the newspaper they had learnt of his war service, being torpedoed twice and his medals, and the injuries he had sustained and the months he had spent in hospitals. It was said that his wife had died of a broken heart, thinking he had perished. All who had known him shared a great respect for a special human being. Everyone was quiet for a moment longer, then Tim said, 'Please everyone have a drink – enjoy the evening.'

Returning to his seat Sophie captured his hand, squeezed it, and said, 'Well done.'

THE END

I hope you have enjoyed my second book.

If you would like to continue to follow the lives of my characters you can get my books from my website www.billcarmen.com or on billcarmen@btinternet.com or contact me on 0770 380 9619.

Love in Store, Book One, the paperback, is now only available from me at any of the above.

The rest of my books, including e-books are available from all the major outlets.

Join my readers' group and get your FREE short story, Daisy The Early Years from my website.

This is a further look at her courageous climb out of her deprived and turbulent childhood.

Those of you who join my readers' group will be the first to learn of gifts and giveaways.

Bill Carmen was born on a houseboat on the River Thames in post-war Surrey. This gave him his lifelong love of all things water-based. He now lives in Worcestershire with his second wife. He has two daughters and two grandsons. Now retired he spends his time writing and growing orchids. *TIM'S PROGRESS*, the middle years is the second book in the LOVE IN STORE SAGA.